Driftwood Orphans

PAUL KRUEGER

This edition first published in Great Britain in 2023 by Gollancz
First published in Great Britain in 2022 by Gollancz
an imprint of The Orion Publishing Group Ltd
Carmelite House, 50 Victoria Embankment
London EC4Y 0DZ

An Hachette UK company

1 3 5 7 9 10 8 6 4 2

A CIP catalogue record for this book
is available from the British Library.

ISBN (Mass Market Paperback) 978 1 473 22906 8
ISBN (eBook) 978 1 473 22907 5

Typeset by Deltatype Ltd, Birkenhead, Merseyside

Printed in Great Britain by Clays Ltd, Elcograf S.p.A.

www.gollancz.co.uk

To everyone who stayed,

and convinced me not to leave

Contents

Four years ago

Age 26

You are Cheza Tenlonghari, blood-daughter of Daning Tenlonghari. Heart-daughter of Benilda Lacanilao. Sister of Diwata and Dalisa Lacanilao. Chosen heir to the greatest criminal empire Driftwood City has ever seen.

You are the Red Rose, fearsome vigilante, protector of the downtrodden, warrior without peer. With your comrades, the Thorn Orphans, you patrol my streets, beating down gangsters and protecting workers on the picket lines.

You are my shaman. Blessed by me with incredible powers, and charged to use those powers in the service of one mission: protecting your ailing city and the thousands who call me home.

You are Tenny.

And you're about to die.

Anyone with a map will insist that there's no such place as Driftwood City. Challenge those people to get out their best globe or chart, and they'll gladly oblige you. Smugly, they'll jab a finger at the spot in the Porcelain Sea, tracing a line beneath the inked characters that label it *Meyongphirin*. You would likely label these people *assholes*.

Not for nothing did I anoint you my champion, Tenny.

But as it happens, these assholes have a point, or at least part of one. Meyongphirin is the name that appears on the sliding oak doors of my city hall. It's splashed on the hood of every police car in my four boroughs. It's the name on the arching front gate of the Unified Utilities Plant, where the people get all the power and water and food it takes to make me a city, and not a glorified shipwreck. It's printed on my blue paper money, and stamped on my shiny zinc coins. On none of these things will you find the name Driftwood City.

But asking a map—or a building, or a piece of valuable paper—is not the same thing as asking a city.

In the eight years you've fought for me, you've bled all over me. You've taken bullets. Knife blades. One time, you didn't give a gull a piece of your kelp roll and it pecked the shit out of your hand. At some point or another, all four of my boroughs have tasted your blood. But only the borough of Birchbarrel has ever gotten to drink this much of it.

Beneath the spot where your prone, chewed-up body has just fallen, my wooden floor runs red. More blood flecks the cracked lenses of your glasses, or runs in streams down your sweaty forehead. A trail of it leads to you, with more of your blood outside your body than in it. If someone were to follow that trail back far enough, they would see still more of it sprayed all over the walls. And at the very start of that trail, they would find the place where your blood mingles with the pool around Pham Binh Cong's lifeless body.

Binh is dead.

Through all your pain, that thought is like a dog on the wrong side of a door, clawing to be let in.

Binh is dead.

There was a time when you would've been paralyzed by the thought of him lying there, bloodied and ruined.

Binh is dead.

But right now, you have to focus on other things.

Like the fact that you, courtesy of your closest friends and comrades, are heartbeats away from joining him.

Depending on who you ask, I am either four boroughs, or two. Always, there is the Rock: a sea-born mountain with beautiful manors and estates bolted on to its craggy face. And below it all, there's a collar of streets that extends miles out into the sea, every floating inch of it constructed from sturdy, weathered wood. For those who like maps, these are the other three boroughs of Meyongphirin: Oakyard, the Shoots, and Birchbarrel, each named for the wood from which they are built.

But for those who actually live in Driftwood City, these are all a single borough: the Slats.

I begin as a group of sailors who blunder into the Rock when it's just that: a rock in the middle of the ocean. I don't live there yet. The barest idea of me doesn't even live there yet. I am a city, and a city is nothing without its people.

It's only by luck those sailors find sapphires in its crags, enough to justify building a mine. There's no real shoreline, so the crews sleep on the ships that have brought them there. In time, they build gangways from one deck to another. In more time, those ships drop anchor, and the gangways become bridges, then decks in their own right. By the time the last mine runs dry, wooden streets spill out a solid mile into the chop in every direction. But dry mines aren't enough to stop what those sailors started.

They keep building, out and out and out. The Porcelain Sea is a big, empty place, and suddenly here is somewhere for ships to

3

stop on the long crossing. The crews make good money trading. The people on the Slats make good money serving the crews. And the bastards up on the Rock get rich off all of them.

In time, industries are born: tourism; fishing; even water. At some point along the way, those buildings and industries and people melt together into something new: Meyongphirin. A city.

Me.

You scream for me to save you.

Normally, I move through you like a song you were born humming. With my walking bass, you can reshape streets. With my trilling horns, you can open any door. In the dancing of spectral fingers across my keys, you can hear every secret the Slats keep. But now, you listen to that song as if it's coming to you on a tinny radio with a bad signal. Teeth of static bite through every measure and phrase. You can feel me trying to reach for you, too, but there isn't enough of you left for me to grab on to.

Something else catches hold of you as five shadows fall over your body like the fingers of a dark, grasping hand. And when they do, your connection to me goes off the air for good. With what little power you have left in your muscles, you roll over to face my other shaman. If this is it, you figure, you want to go out looking your death in its familiar face.

With the exception of one, they all wear the uniform of the Thorn Orphans: black longcoats, black flatcaps, black carpenter's masks, and roses in their lapels. But your tired eyes find the details within their familiar silhouettes. Roulette Wu's wide-brimmed cattleman hat and glowing cigarillo, his hands clutching gleaming revolvers with handles of yellow bamboo. The clanking form of Anjali-the Armored, wrapped in a new cocoon of gleaming blue steel. The elegant composure

4

of Knife-Edge Ngo, lit by a pair of glowing pink crystal blades. The inky sprawl of black tattoos spread across the muscular, shirtless frame of Mhap the Monster. You wonder when Cole gave them those new toys. Is that how he bought their service?

But as you reflect on how efficiently they've set to killing you, you wonder if he needed to buy them at all.

You want to hate him for it, Tenny. But even lying in your own lifeblood, you can't hate him for buying their service with power. After all, as a hard and mercenary part of you knows, I bought your service the same way.

Flanked by two on each side is Cole himself: short, skinny, and stiffer than a starched shirt. Even in the scant light, the slick, silvery blaze of his hair is unmistakable when he takes off his flatcap. In the lapel of his long black coat, he's pinned his signature white rose. Your bloody teeth grit at the sight of the thing. Wearing it to your execution is the final insult ... at least until the next one.

As he strides to you, the heels of his boots click against the boathouse floor. Each step brands itself into your memory.

"Tenny," he sighs. *Click, click, click.* Whether it's real or not, the sadness in his voice is fresh salt on your countless wounds. "I admit, even with my powers of foresight ... I never saw us ending like this. But I suppose I've always respected and admired your bottomless ability to surprise me."

You hock up a bloody glob of spit. It sprays ugly across the floor between you. It's all you have for him now. He's taken your city. Your powers. Your love. Your friends. And when you are gone, the flower you gave him will become his, too. He's truly left you with nothing.

He regards the bloody spit, unimpressed.

"That," he says, "wasn't a surprise."

"Cole," you rasp. Your throat is still raw from a few minutes ago, when Mhap punched it. A thousand threats leap to your

5

mind, each more exquisitely foul than the last, and each an emptier promise. But your mangled lips can't form any of them. So instead, all you have is his name. You hope you've made it sound like a curse.

"What do you want us to do with her?" rumbles Mhap, no doubt hoping to play with his food.

"I'll make it quick," says Anjali. Armor plates clank as she raises one of her arms. It's cold comfort, knowing at least one of your betrayers wants to be nice about it.

"No," Cole says. Has his voice always sounded this cold, you wonder? Is it something he's putting on for the occasion, or just something you've never let yourself notice before? "This business is mine to conclude. The most regrettable board to lay in the foundations of our new Driftwood City."

You can't even find it in you to feel despair anymore. You already know nothing you could say would make him change his mind. Apparently, it was made up a long time ago. But you glare up at him all the same. You have so many questions: how is he suppressing your powers? Why did he murder your boyfriend? Why is he doing this to his own best friend?

Were you ever really his friend at all?

Sorrow flickers through his deep brown eyes. His whole body draws up even stiffer, as if you've pulled a knife on him. But the moment passes, and his stare burns into you like a low, patient flame.

"Tenny," he says again, but you can tell he isn't talking to you anymore. He speaks up, like he does whenever he gives his big, grand speeches as a fiery crusader, as the White Rose. "What we do to you today brings none of us any pleasure or satisfaction. Driftwood City gave you powers so you could serve it. It was my regrettable duty to take them away. You've demonstrated that when forced to choose between the city's welfare and your own, you chose yourself."

6

Your addled brains whirr like out-of-control machinery as you try to parse what he's saying. How have you failed me? How can your own best friend be so sure? And how did all that lead to them dropping you and Binh like this?

You reach for me one last time, but you can't even hear the bass of my music anymore, no matter how loudly I play it for you. He really has taken it from you, somehow, even though this isn't a power you ever knew I'd given you. It never would have even occurred to you to try. And you can't puzzle out the how, not with fresh fear clawing at you from the inside. Ah, Tenny, you've grown so used to having my power that you've forgotten what it means to be without it.

Lying there, you realize your last moments in this world will be quiet and cold.

He gestures grandly, and beneath you the floorboards begin to pry themselves up out of place. Their slats curve up around you, as if you're falling into the ribcage of some huge beast. You would've called their bending unnatural, but you've seen similar feats for years now. *Done* them for years now. Wood isn't meant to bend this way, but that's never stopped you and Cole before.

"You've incurred a sizeable debt at the expense of the people of Driftwood City," he declares. "And with your life ... I consider it paid."

He clenches his hand into a fist.

The slats wrap tighter around you. Darkness closes in as those bending boards slowly form your coffin.

"Cole ..." Your mind isn't all there anymore. It feels like a balloon tied to your body, straining against its string to fly away. "What are ... you doing ...?"

Through the groaning of the wood, you hear him speak again. His words slip through the shrinking gaps like a knife between ribs, and just as sharp and cold.

"Everything."

You catch one last glimpse of the five Thorn Orphans: your comrades. Your partners. Your friends.

And you promise that if you survive this ...

The steamship mortally wounds me. The airship finishes the job.

Just like that, the world doesn't need places between places anymore. There's the start and the end. Everything in the middle is just time to kill. But when the tourist and tariff money dry up and trade routes shift, the folks on the Rock find other ways to keep themselves above the rest. Things get more expensive. Wages stay the same. People turn to bootleggers just to get some drinkable water, because the stuff coming out of their faucets is too pricey.

I cling to life, my grip eroding more with each passing year. But no matter how bad things get, every year there are still people who live on my Slats and call me home. People whose faith in me changed me from some place into *somewhere*.

And for those people, I have one pair of dice left to throw.

You don't get to finish your promise. The driftwood coffin plunges itself straight through my lowest deck and drops you into the huge, dark ocean.

You are lost beneath the waves.

And above you, your city moves on.

Part One

The First Revenge!
The Fortune of the Yellow Rose

1
Now

Age 30

Hey, Cole. Wanna hear something I've never told anyone?

I hate sharing a birthday with you.

It's been four years since you killed me, and in that time I finally managed to get myself to a point where my thoughts wouldn't automatically drift back to you, and the Thorn Orphans, and the bloody full stop you put on our story. But on my own Bird-given birthday, what choice did I have except to think of you?

However you celebrated your thirtieth, I knew I was gonna read all about it in tomorrow's papers. Even though you were a foreign head of state, the press over here in Biranba couldn't get enough of you. You were young, you were magnetic, and you were making big moves in a town the whole world had written off. And your story was irresistible: high society's wayward son, who single-handedly burned it all down so he could give the city back to its people. That kind of thing gets someone a lot of column inches.

I don't know what was more frustrating about seeing that

11

version of you: how often I had to put up with it, or all the ways it was almost true.

It curdled my stomach to think of you living it up at some gala, dressed your best and throwing back champagne, while I sweated to death in a greasy diner kitchen. Surrounded by the friends that'd been mine in another life, while I was surrounded by strangers in matching aprons. Dancing through life to the sweet music our city played to us, while I got to listen to Chef's bellowing. It shouldn't have mattered so much to me that your lives all didn't freeze in the moment you did for me in that boathouse.

And yet.

It was a hot night, even for a sweat-trap town like Malañong. Folks crowded into the diner so they could park themselves under our collection of poor, overworked ceiling fans for an hour or two. The work had been non-stop since I'd hopped on the line that afternoon, and it'd only ramped up as the sun went down. Now we were at the height of dinner rush, and it seemed like every three seconds that damn order bell was ringing. Knives flashed, pots roiled, and Chef barked orders like she'd missed her calling as someone's scary, shitty dog.

I, on the other hand, had ducked into the walk-in ice closet.

Officially, it was to grab another sack of rice so I could get back to washing. But by now, Chef had to have noticed that I ducked into that walk-in every chance I got. I savored the cold, rare in a steamy country like Biranba. I savored the quiet, rare in the vibrant capital of Malañong. But I left the door open, because when I found myself in the dark my mind had a funny way of sketching in details I didn't want it to.

Standing in that chilly gloom, I didn't look like the Tenny you remember. I'd grown my hair back out, and tied it up in a tight black braid. That swaggering brawn that'd made me so good in a fight? Long gone. In just four years, I'd wasted away to a broom handle with legs. I still wore glasses, but the eyes behind them had dulled from topaz to dishwater. And instead of my slick Thorn Orphans blacks, I wore a dingy, sauce-stained apron, currently folded at my waist so that my carved birchwood necklace could dangle free.

I'd snagged a lumpia from the frying tray a few minutes back. It was only the one, a far cry from the huge platters Benilda had made me every birthday. But I'd take it. It was long cold from its stay in my apron pocket, but at least the shell was still a little crispy as I took my first bite. I'd gotten good about tamping down my hunger while I was on the line, but the moment I tasted that room-temp pork and cabbage, my whole body screamed out for more.

"Happy birthday to me," I muttered.

You've seen me demolish a feast in five minutes, Cole, so you'd have been impressed by my restraint. I savored each bite, as if letting it linger on my tongue long enough would turn it into a genuine Driftwood City kelp roll. And if I focused hard enough, I could almost dredge up the taste, and pretend I was—

"Cheza! Hoy!" Chef roared from outside.

The lumpia tumbled from my fingers. Before I could stop it, it rolled right into a puddle of ... well, it didn't matter what. When it comes to the backs of restaurants, there's no such thing as a good puddle. I hung my head, kicked the lumpia under a shelf, and shrugged my apron back on over my necklace. Then I shouldered a fresh sack of rice—the fragrant Samnati kind, with an elephant stamped on the bag.

"The fuck are you doing in there?" Chef snapped the moment I emerged. She was a small, meaty woman who I'd once watched cleave a whole hog down to its chops in three minutes flat. Intimidating enough, unless you'd grown up in Nanay Benilda's house. "I don't pay you to kick your feet up!"

13

"Wasn't kicking my feet up, Chef," I said. My Biranese had gotten better over four years, the language sanding off the hard edges of my natural Driftwood City accent. Between memories of the lessons I'd had as a kid and what I'd picked up since washing ashore here, I now sounded like a grown-up and not just a smart kid. But no one with an ear for Biranese would mistake me for a local. "I was just getting more rice."

"It takes two seconds to get a new bag of rice, and you don't have to let the cold out while you do it!" Chef said. "Now get your ass on the line and back to work!"

In my last life, I'd sent entire gangs to their deaths with a wave of my hand. I had made the powerful sink to their knees as they felt true fear for the first time in their lives. I'd grown up in the house of the Slats' most feared criminal mastermind, learning everything she knew about how to command respect. Most people wouldn't have even wanted to talk to me this way. And the ones who might've, never would've dared.

But that was my last life. In this one, I was Cheza the line cook, and all Cheza the line cook could do was mutter, "Yes, Chef," into her collarbone and get back to work.

"Fucking right," Chef muttered, then turned from me to scream about someone's pancit plating.

I'd been washing rice for hours. My fingers were pruned and swollen, and they ached every time I so much as twitched. I could think of nothing I wanted to do less than wash more, least of all on my birthday. But it'd been hard enough for me to get this job in the first place. If I got tossed out, where was I supposed to go? Rent would be due soon enough, and I had to eat. I was an immigrant with no papers. The only thing I had going for me was that I looked like the locals, and that illusion went away the moment they heard me try to talk.

As I headed for the basin with a big old sack of rice over my shoulder, it was hard not to think about the other ways I stood out. The kitchen was balmy, but no one else was sweating as much as me. They'd all grown up here, where you practically needed gills to breathe in the summer. Me, I've always been the kind of person who would walk around the Slats on the chilliest night of the year with my coat open.

I know you know that already, Cole. I'm gonna end up telling you a lot of shit you already know before my story's done. Settle in. You just might like the way I tell it.

So I sweated more than them. I talked funny. And when we went for drinks after a hard shift ... I mean, sure, I was there with them. I sat at the same table, drinking the same beer they drank. But they'd spent a life in Biranese culture, and I just hadn't. It was like I was playing the same song they were, but in a different key, in a different time signature, while making up my own lyrics on the fly. And the few times they'd thrown me a bone and tried to let me play a solo, I could feel my notes hitting theirs at all the wrong angles. Eventually, I stopped piping up. And now, it'd been more than a year since they'd roped me into after-work beers.

Feeling bad for me, Cole? You have no idea.

When I washed up here, my first thought was to head straight for the underground fighting rings. After all, I'd gotten everywhere else in life by hitting the right people. My nasty little life had left me with only one real skill, but it'd also made me the best at it. I knew how to play in the crooked game, and the Great Bird knows I've always loved to scrap. Whatever future I had, I was gonna write it with my fists. I wouldn't change the world anymore, but I could at least do what I'd always loved, and do it for me.

Except, funny thing about my first and only time in the ring: instead of fighting, I froze. And instead of a sweltering auto garage, I just found myself back on the boathouse floor, blood fleeing my body as mercy fled your eyes.

15

I know you meant to kill me that day, Cole. And you did. But even though my heart's still beating, you have no idea how well you succeeded.

The water finally ran clear on the rice, so I set it aside and started prepping a new batch. Everyone else just left it running the whole time, but I made sure to shut the faucet off between washes. That was the other big tip-off to the rest of the staff that I wasn't from here: I didn't treat water like there'd always be more of it.

Suddenly, I was thinking of my twelfth birthday. Benilda had broken open her stores of bootleg fresh water for the whole neighborhood. All day long, a line of grateful folks stretched out the door as they stopped by to pick up their bottles and pay tribute to me and Benilda. Afterwards, I'd asked her why. Water was more valuable than gold on the Slats. Wasn't it bad business to give it away for free?

She'd clicked her tongue, like she always did, and adjusted her elaborate, flower-brimmed hat. "No investment returns better than loyalty."

That was all it took to buy loyalty back home: *water*.

And here, I'd pissed away gallons of it by myself just to wash some rice.

Other birthdays followed, dragged behind my twelfth like a chain of memories. Benilda's elaborate dinners. Whiskey with the other Thorn Orphans on a rooftop as we watched the sun come up over the Slats.

And of course, the eighteenth—our eighteenth—when you and I were reborn in fire and water.

Now instead of friends, I only had co-workers and neighbors. If I disappeared tomorrow, not a one of them would remember what my face looked like after a week. But better that, I figure, than let someone get close enough to my heart to put a knife in it. And besides, there was no point in celebrating a birthday alone. It was just a day where someone got older, and people did that every day.

So I washed rice on our thirtieth birthday, Cole. I weathered a dinner rush. I guzzled down a gallon of water at least, and sweated and pissed out half again as much. When the last guest left and the cooks started shutting down the line for the night, my clothes were ten pounds heavier from all that sweat. And I wasn't done; now, it fell to me to wash the dishes from service. More sweat from my pores. More water down the drain.

"Cheza."

I set the plate I was washing back into the basin. Killed the water. "Yes, Chef?"

She waddled up, jerking her thumb back toward the dining room. "Got a guest. Need you to take the order."

"What?" I said, forgetting myself for a moment. "I'm not a waiter."

"Kulima went home," Chef grunted. "You take the order."

With a wrinkly hand, I gestured at the gleaming pile of dishes I'd just torn through.

"You can rewash one," said Chef, ignoring the pots and pans I'd also have to scrub again, too. She pointed to the dining room again. "Go."

I made sure to face away from her before I let myself grumble. I took off my apron and did my best to smooth out my clothes. Pointless, especially this late in a shift, but I had to at least try. And once I was kind of presentable, I hurried to the dining room, muttering darkly to myself about what kind of soulless, worthless, good-for-nothing, entitled piece of shit would walk into a restaurant five minutes before close and demand full service.

The kitchen's dented metal doors swung open with their usual creak, and I stood in the humid dining room for the first time that night. The fans were still working at full speed, but

17

all they did on nights like this was push hot air from one place to another. The lights were down, but I could see across the floor to our sole guest.

He gave a small wave. "Howdy," he said in decent Biranese. A lit cigarillo bobbed in his lips when he spoke. "Thanks for seating me. It's a pain, I know, I know."

I froze.

I've been hit in the head a lot, Cole, and my vision's always been shit. But my memory ain't completely worthless, and I could still see across a dimly lit room.

And that's how I knew without a doubt that I was talking to Roulette Wu.

I know I looked like life had chewed me up good, but he hadn't aged a day since I last saw him in that boathouse. He was still dying his hair blond, his bangs a jagged diagonal line across his handsome face so that only one eye glinted at me. His limbs were still long and rangy, and he didn't sit at his table so much as lounge at it. He was only missing two of his trademarks: the revolvers that usually hung at his hips, and the yellow rose that had adorned his lapel for the years we'd fought together.

Roulette Wu.

The Yellow Rose.

Was here.

Fuck.

I hadn't moved since I'd spotted him. He didn't seem to have clued into why. "Sorry, sorry, my Biranese ain't the best," he said, even though it was almost as good as mine. "I say that wrong?"

This had to be a trap. Somehow, from that throne where you sat so comfortably across the Porcelain Sea, you'd gotten news of a down-on-her-luck prep cook stashed in the back of

18

a Malañong greasy spoon, and sent her a birthday present. There was no other logical explanation.

Except, a little voice in my head said.

Except back at the boathouse, you hadn't given any of the other Thorn Orphans the honor of killing me. You'd wanted to save me for yourself. If you knew I was here, you wouldn't have sent one of the others to do this for you. And if you did send one of them, you sure as hell wouldn't have sent a fast-and-loose player like Roulette Wu.

But then ... why was he here?

I'd stood still too long. I had to make a move now, or get closer and figure out more. The old Tenny wouldn't have even hesitated to make her choice.

Lucky for Roulette that I was Cheza these days.

"Sorry," I said, putting on my best Biranese accent. It wouldn't have fooled anyone in the back of the house, but I didn't need it to. I just needed to file off all the textures in my speech that could've marked my first language as Slatspeak. "End of a long shift. I'll be right there."

A pitcher of cold water stood on a little cart by the door, and I fetched up a glass and filled it. As I took my time pouring, I glanced at a nearby window. The reflection was imperfect, but from what I could see he wasn't making any moves toward me.

"That's some kinda thing to see," Roulette said, chatty as ever. "You know, growing up where I come from, a glass of clean water was harder to come by than a six-suit hand in pektong. You ever been out Driftwood City way, darlin'?"

"No," I said carefully.

"You ever get more'n a day off at a time, you should take the flight," he said. "Hell of a town, hell of a town."

I gripped his glass hard as I brought it over. "You don't talk like the people I've met from there."

"Did some time fighting on the Tsunese coast," he replied.

"A couple years like that'll change a person. Hell, you'd know."

I froze. "What?"

"I talked to two cabbies, eight street vendors, a shoeshiner, and one idiot who went and tried to pick my pocket on my way here." He stretched out lazily, but I searched for any sign of tension in his muscles. Roulette only moved at two speeds: slow, and too fast. "You don't sound like a one of 'em."

I found myself slumping more as I neared him. I couldn't help how tall I was. But he was used to seeing a straight-backed warrior, not a shambling garbage pile in a blotchy uniform. Maybe he really was just luring me in. But if he hadn't figured out who I was yet, I wasn't gonna make it easy for him.

"You have a good ear, sir." My smile was bland and submissive: alien on Tenny's face, right at home on Cheza's. "I'm from the outer islands. Here to make a new life." I set his water down next to his hat, which he'd placed upside down to air it out. Sweat daubed its liner; clearly he was having the same trouble here that I did. "Have you looked at our menu?"

"Nah," he drawled. "Don't need one, don't need one. I like to trust in my luck, me, so I'll roll the dice on a plate of your very finest kare-kare. Oh, and one other thing ..."

He reached into his coat.

My fingers wrapped hard around the pen I was using to take his order. Quickly, I did the math. I figured about half a second for him to clear his shoulder holster and fire on me. Could I jam my pen into his neck before he got the shot off? Or was a mutual kill the best I could hope for?

But instead of a gun, he produced a book of matches. "You got an ashtray?"

My grip on my pen eased.

"Of course." I grabbed one from a nearby table and plunked it down right next to his water.

"Much obliged, much obliged." He sparked a match, and the air around us filled with heavy, sweet smoke. The fans overhead swirled it around us like evening mist. He glanced up at me, curious. "I doing something wrong? There some kind of special tense I oughta be using?" Another drag. "You're looking a mite jumpy there, friend."

I blinked hard and fell back into the moment. For just a second there, I'd been remembering the last time I'd smelled that tobacco.

"Sorry," I said again. I had to stay on top of things, or he'd start looking at me more closely. "Just tired. I'll be right back with your kare-kare." I turned and headed for the kitchen.

"I understand," he said sagely at my back, like he knew what I was talking about. "I understand. Always held the working person in high regard, me." I heard him sigh a mouthful of smoke. "'A society's only as rich as its poorest,' ain't that right?"

I froze again. You know why I did that time.

We both know it wasn't Roulette Wu who came up with those words.

"Yes," I said carefully. At my side, my aching hand clenched into a fist. "It is."

With each step back to the kitchen, I braced for a bullet to slam between my shoulder blades. And then I was through the swinging metal doors, still not daring to breathe.

Chef pounced on me the moment I came through. "What's he want?"

"Kare-kare." Through the window in the kitchen's swinging doors, I studied him. He was slouched low in his seat, blowing smoke rings at the ceiling. Guy wasn't even looking my way.

"Of course," Chef snorted. "Right after I put it away." She jerked her thumb to the ice closet. "Get it out. It should still be warm. And you better serve it to him with a damn smile on

21

your face, you got that? I saw you being surly. I won't stand for it, Cheza. If a restaurant is not its best, Malañong will eat it alive. Now hurry up. I'll be in the office."

Shutting herself up back there was probably the best thing I could hope for. She'd be looking at the books, because Chef knew how to keep a place in business. But it also meant she'd be opening up the rum she kept in her bottom desk drawer, and she didn't like to be interrupted when she did that. Usually, that meant she wouldn't hear me when I took off a few minutes early. Today, it meant she wouldn't hear me when something went down in the front of the house.

I actually took the time to portion some kare-kare out with some rice, and heated them both up. I even heated the bowl, so the guy would get the proper experience. As far as last meals went, you couldn't do much better than Chef's kare-kare on some white rice. Its sweet peanut aroma was almost strong enough to unknot the balloon animal my stomach had tied itself into. I would've said it was better than Nanay Benilda's, if I wasn't so sure that'd get my ass haunted.

As I headed back to the door, I lingered at Chef's station. There on the bamboo countertop, she'd left her knife roll. That's probably lost on you, Cole, what with you not being Biranese, but it spoke to how safe she felt in her own restaurant. To the Biranese, a knife is more than just a knife. Leaving yours out is like leaving your soul exposed.

I glanced toward the front of the house, then back at the countertop. And then with the practiced, nimble fingers of a thief, I plucked her paring knife from its place.

Ain't gonna win me any gunfights, I thought as I slipped it into the pocket of my apron. And it sure wouldn't have helped me against an actual blade fighter like Knife-Edge Ngo. But while it was a bad idea to bring a knife to a gunfight, it still beat showing up empty-handed.

22

Roulette's chair was tipped up on its back legs. He waved again at me as I appeared tableside.

"Now that right there looks like some proper kare-kare," he said as I set it down in front of him. He took a deep sniff, then leaned back even farther in his seat to savor it. "You know in Driftwood City, we don't make it with cow? Ain't any places to run a cow, and ain't enough water to keep no grass, so we have to do our kare-kare with fish or gulls. Only fancy folk ever got to eat stuff that had hooves. But I'm told that this here is the way it's supposed to be."

I know, I thought. *I told you*.

His chair's front legs hit the floor with a *thump*, and he messily dug in. I still don't know how such a narrow, angular face could open its mouth python-wide, but he did it anyway. He savored the bite with a satisfied smile, and took his sweet time swallowing it. I watched as the ball of his throat bobbed once with syrupy slowness.

"That," he said eventually, "was worth the four-day flight alone."

I slapped on a food service smile. "The chef will be happy to hear that." In my front pocket, the paring knife felt heavy. Casually, I slipped my notepad in next to it, so my hand could brush against its polished ebony handle.

"I bet, I bet," said Roulette, with a smack of his lips. "There's a kind of appetite you only build up from being on the road a long spell, and your chef's kare-kare is just the thing to break it. You might want to turn away, missy. I'm about to get mighty uncivilized with this here plate." And he slopped a big spoonful of saucy rice and beef into his mouth.

As the kare-kare disappeared from his plate, I busied myself putting up every chair on the tables. And as I worked my way through the dining room, I eventually found myself standing directly behind Roulette as he ate.

I considered my options. At this distance, I could have the blade in the back of his head before he could blink. One flash of steel and it'd be lights out, just like that. There were passers-by that'd see it happen through the diner's big, friendly windows, but I didn't have to worry about them. Malañong was a massive, sprawling city with wide streets and winding alleys. I could lose myself here. I'd done it before.

Quietly as I could, my fingers wrapped around the paring knife. I slid it from my apron pocket with a steady hand. Blood stirred in my veins like it hadn't in years. I wasn't even in the dining room anymore; I was back in the boathouse, watching gunfire light up my friend's grinning face as he let off a hail of bullets on me and Binh.

Binh.

My grip tightened on the knife. In my heart, an old familiar song began to play. If I couldn't kill Roulette for me, I could sure as shit do it for him.

The kitchen doors swung open and Chef came lumbering out. My muscle memory fired up, and I flipped the paring knife up along my palm and forearm so it was out of sight.

"Hoy," Chef said. "You seen my paring knife?"

"No, Chef," I said, as its point gently dug into my skin.

Roulette stood. "I hear that right? You're the chef of this here joint?"

"That's me," Chef said.

Roulette sauntered over to her, then took her callused hand and respectfully pressed his forehead to it. "Thanks for a mighty fine meal, ma'am, mighty fine. I was lucky to have it."

Chef beamed at him. "Always! We love visitors here in Malañong!" said the woman who paid me half what she paid the rest of her staff and didn't think I knew it. She nodded past him, straight at me. "Is Cheza bothering you? I can make

24

her wait to put up the chairs. She thinks she's special, just because it's her birthday."

My heart plunged right into my gut. Roulette had only met one Cheza in his entire life. He'd always called me Tenny, but he'd known that wasn't the name on my birth certificate. And he definitely knew when my birthday was.

I gripped the knife tighter.

"Nah, nah, that's all right," Roulette said, turning around and surveying me curiously. He sauntered back toward his table. "She's just doing her thing"—he took his seat—"while I'm doing mine."

Chef cast a suspicious eye my way, but grunted.

"You're gonna help me find that knife when you're done here," she said to me, before heading back to her open bottle.

I eyed Roulette very carefully as he took another bite of his rapidly disappearing kare-kare. I didn't feel like I could turn my back on him anymore.

He swallowed, then picked his cigarillo back up and gave it a good, hard drag.

"So." The word came out as a puff of smoke. "Cheza, huh?"

My stolen knife tickled my skin. "It is."

He nodded, as if he were considering it like a bite of food. "Common name round the other islands, I conjure?"

He knows, hissed the voice in my head.

"A lot of parents who all had the same idea," I said.

"And it's your birthday, too?"

I felt the knife tip starting to break skin. "Two parents who had the same idea."

A smoky laugh burst from him. "Reckon so." He stubbed his cigarillo out, though there was a solid half-inch of it left to smoke.

He knows! my instincts shouted again. *Do it! Kill him now!*

It would only take a flick of the wrist to get my grip back.

Another to end him. It would be a justice he'd spent four years dodging.

And Binh . . .

I made a show of fumbling with my apron, and slipped the knife back into the pocket. In my head I called myself every name I could think of, and I deserved them all.

"I gotta get back to work," I said, then turned and headed back to the kitchen at last.

"Appreciate the company . . . Cheza."

I turned at the doorway. He was dabbing at his sweaty forehead with that yellow handkerchief he always kept in his jacket pocket. I knew the one.

"Enjoy your meal," I said, and promptly disappeared inside.

Beyond the doors, I pressed myself up against the nearest wall and breathed deep. My heart fluttered, a bird caged in my ribs. When I exhaled, my vision swam. I'd held my memories at bay, but now they flooded through me like venom: me and Roulette side by side, sending gangsters and mercs and strike breakers to early graves. The wailing horn of my powers, grounded by the steady drumbeat of twin revolvers in the hands of the city's luckiest gunman.

Just like that, the battlefield had become the boathouse, and one of those bullets was in my back.

The wound had long since closed, but the spot throbbed as my muscles knotted and unknotted themselves.

I looked down at the pinpoint of blood on my forearm. The knife was still clutched in my hand. What was I doing? I'd had a clear shot to avenge Binh, and I hadn't taken it. The hell kind of a warrior was I?

No warrior at all, I reminded myself. *Tenny was a warrior, and they killed her. You're just Cheza now.*

I ground my teeth against one another. My chest ached, and I didn't know why. Had it just been the sight of one of my old

26

comrades? Or was it disgust at my own weakness, eating me hollow from the inside?

When my breath was finally steady again, I risked a peek out the window of the kitchen door.

All four chair legs were on the ground. A few bills lay folded on the table next to the empty bowl. Freshly exhaled smoke swirled in the air.

And Roulette was gone.

The bus commute home always made me miss the Driftwood City boatways. Sure, bus schedules didn't get affected by the tides, but the dense Malañong traffic more than made up the difference. Even past midnight, I always ended up standing shoulder to shoulder with commuters and revelers, bouncing against them with every bump in the road. They followed winding routes, which had once been cattle paths meant to take the local herds from one green to another. After four years of them, I yearned for the simple straight lines of the boatways, and their cool night air that smelled of salt.

I staggered off near the very end of the Red Line and limped the remaining seven blocks to my place. The sores on my feet were starting to blister; somehow, all these years on my feet had done nothing to toughen them up. But I barely even registered the pain tonight. I was playing that encounter in my head over and over again, like a reel from a motion picture on a loop. What'd made me stay my hand?

It's obvious, I told myself. *Tenny would've taken the shot. Cheza isn't that kind of woman, and Cheza's the one who's alive.* That was the story I'd told myself a lot these past four years.

But when I'd been standing behind Roulette, knife in hand and blood pounding in my ears, I'll tell you this much, Cole: I sure as hell hadn't felt like Cheza.

In a daze, I climbed the three sets of stairs to my grubby little

27

studio. Hell of a thing: it was way smaller than our Kelptown place. But at least it had its own bathroom. Another thing even the poorest person in Biranese life could just take for granted.

I came home to a mattress on the bare patchwork wooden floor, a single chair next to it, and little else. I didn't even have a kitchen in this thing; I just ate what I could take home from work. It was a far cry from Benilda's house, or even from our one bedroom. Hell, it was basically just a coffin with a door. But in all the lives I've lived, I've never been a woman who's needed much.

I kicked my shoes off. Didn't bother shrugging out of any of my other clothes before I collapsed onto the mattress. All my strength fled me. Normally, I would've gone right to sleep, and woken up with just enough juice for the diner to squeeze back out of me tomorrow. But tonight my mind raced like the roaches in the walls.

I sat up with a grunt, ready to get a glass of water, at least.

And underneath the crack of my door, I saw a shadow in the hallway.

Instantly, I was alive again. My hand flew to the necklace of polished birch I wore as I searched my meager apartment for a weapon. Didn't keep one on hand, and now I regretted that something fierce. I guessed I'd just have to take him on with my bare fists and hope I could get in close before he got a shot off.

Carefully, I stood. If he sensed I was getting close to him, odds were good he'd start shooting through the door. I was good, but I couldn't punch through my own door.

Well, not anymore.

Carefully, I crept barefoot across the floor until I was lurking right beside the door and safely away from any spot he was likely aiming his gun. I clenched one fist tight at my side, while the other slowly reached for the door handle. He was

28

probably waiting for me now, so I had to be even more ready when I finally slid it open.

I closed my fingers around the hot metal of the handle.

I glanced down at the shadow on the floor.

Just as it shrank out of sight.

I tore the door open and was in the hallway, just in time to see a man in a yellow hat sprinting away in the gloom.

With a growl, I took off after him.

I was tired. I was the most terrified I'd been in four years. I was getting splinters in my bare, aching feet. But I ran with everything I had. A second out of my sight was a second for Roulette to draw on me. So when he disappeared around a corner, I gave it a burst of speed and hurled myself on to him with a roar. We crashed to the floor, me on top to pin him in place. I cocked back a fist as his hat fell away, revealing—

—some guy I'd never seen before in my life.

Too late, I realized I'd been played.

Too late, I heard the *click* of a hammer behind me.

Too late, I smelled sweet tobacco smoke.

I closed my eyes in resignation.

"Let him go, Red Rose, let him go." Roulette had dispensed with the Biranese; now, he was talking in our native Slatspeak. "Guy's just someone I paid to smoke you out, and this here's between you and me. Do it slowly, now; I ain't gonna kill you just yet, but I got no qualms about laming you first."

I blinked back furious, frustrated tears. Once again, I'd been beaten. But I wasn't ready to finish dying yet.

Slowly, I rose with both of my hands clearly visible. The scared man crawled out from underneath me and practically fell over himself trying to flee.

And I had no choice but to stand perfectly still as Roulette Wu stepped past me, a bamboo-handled revolver pointed right at my head, so he could retrieve his fallen hat.

"So ..." He settled it back on his head. Looked me up and down. Sighed a lungful of smoke. "Reckon I owe you a happy birthday."

2

Twelve years ago

Age 18

"'Roulette,' huh?" There were a few of us at the table—you, me, the dealer, and the other players. But I was talking to the rangy guy across from me who was sitting behind a stack of what had recently been my money. "What's with that name? Gonna guess it ain't the name you got for your birthday."

I remember it was hot for Driftwood City, enough to make the Slats groan and twist like someone having a nightmare. Inside the smoky, raucous Seven Phoenix Hall of Chance, electrical fans kept players cool and the help brought drinks around: beer fresh from the mainland, and water fresh from the illegal still under the floorboards. But there was no escaping the heat.

It was four in the morning. I remember that, too. I've always liked me a good amount of sleep, so I was swaying where I sat. You were doing better than me, since you and sleep were polite acquaintances at best. But the young man in the wide-brimmed yellow cattleman across from us had been at the table for six hours, and showed no signs of slowing down.

At the question, a smile spread across his lips, slow as an egg cracked into a pan.

"You fixing to get to know me better now? 'Cause even if I end up liking you kids—and I do like you kids—I ain't gonna give you your money back."

Though we'd been watching Roulette play for six hours, we'd only been sitting with him for two. I didn't really see the point in spending so much time here; we could've just as easily spent the evening busting heads, then swooped in at the last second to ruin this guy's night. But you seemed to think we had to wait out the whole time, so I trusted you. And after four hours of waiting our turn to get to the table, we'd proceeded to lose one stack of kwae after another to him.

I was never one for gambling; when I liked to test myself, I kept luck as far out of the equation as I could manage. But even so, I liked winning. And each smirk Roulette shot me after I played another losing hand pricked like a little needle. You weren't nearly as bothered. I guess you didn't mind the money going his way; after all, we'd stolen it all from the Black Pockets yesterday.

Tiles clacked on the table as the dealer, well paid to stay out of the conversation, dealt out fresh hands. I peeked at my tiles and saw that once again, the deck had fucked me—two plums and a cat. That was the fifth bad hand in a row for me. I shot the dealer a look: *What the hell?*

The guy shrugged: *Your problem.*

"You don't gotta give my money back." I tried for nonchalance, and figured I got within spitting distance of it. "You're gonna lose it, same as anyone else."

"Not the way you've been playing." Roulette slid a few chips to the center of the table. A big bet. But that was how Roulette liked to do things, I'd noticed. Most players would start small and build their way up. But if the table was a still pool, Roulette liked to chuck a big rock into it and see where the ripples went. And I had to admit: so far, they'd all gone his way.

I tossed my ante in as a fistful, while you slid a neat little tower of chips to the center.

"My friend only asks because it's not every day you meet someone with such a colorful soubriquet," you said. "Is 'Roulette' a name you won, or chose?"

Roulette snorted like some mainland pack animal. It was strange, hearing such a rough-hewn noise come from such a delicately sculpted face. "Folks all choose their names out on the frontier." He slid a few more chips in—easy enough for him. He had so many now, he could as soon have built himself a house out of them as he could've used them to buy one. "Real question's who gets to live long enough to earn the one they chose."

"You gonna be cryptic all night while you take our money?" I said. "Or can we pretend your winnings there are payment for a straight answer?" I dropped in my stake, then raised it just a little. I could raise one more time, if he pushed me.

Roulette shrugged. It felt less like he'd been persuaded, and more like he'd stopped caring. "First month of my tour, a Ghost Spider chucked a grenade right into my lap. Should've blown my balls and brains to bits ... but the fuse didn't catch." He sighed, leaned back, and lit up another cigarillo. In a few minutes, its remnants would join the other six in the crystal ashtray in front of him. "Second tour—you gonna call, or what?"

You shook your head and slid your tiles back to the dealer. "This hand is just between you two."

And that was it. Our signal.

As we'd outlined our plan, I'd asked you why I had to be the one to do this. Why not you? You actually knew how to play pektong. I'd spent my whole childhood getting my ass kicked by my sisters any time when I played.

"Because he'll recognize that I know what I'm doing," you'd said. "If he sees me win, he'll think it's skill. If he sees you win, he'll think it's luck." When I frowned, you shrugged. "I'll bore him, and you won't."

It'd all sounded like overthinking to me. But you seemed sure of it, and I trusted you.

So as you folded, I finally opened my ears and let the city serenade me. I'd been keeping it at bay all evening so my losses would look authentic. But now all at once, scraps of knowledge began to flit through my mind: about the gambling house we sat in. About the dealer and his dreams of singing stardom. About all the people who had ever laid a finger on this particular set of pektong tiles we were playing with.

And of course, about Roulette Wu.

"Suit yourself, suit yourself," the man himself was saying. "Anyway, next month I took a bayonet in the gut, and damned if the thing didn't miss every major organ I got sloshing around in there. Doc said it was a one-in-a-million stab. I was Roulette after that. The wheel kept spinning, and it always came up my number. Of course," he added with a nod to the two shiny black revolvers at his hips, "these here helped." He slid in just enough chips to tap me out. "You've been fun and all, girl, but a game can't go on forever."

A smart player would've seen that confidence and folded. Even a stupid player probably would've. At least that way, they could still walk out with enough for boatway fare.

But even the smartest smart player would never be as good as an idiot who was also a shaman.

"So you got the name 'cause you were lucky, yeah?" I said, keeping my tone light.

"Looks that way for certain from where I'm sitting," Roulette said with a puff of blue-grey smoke. He reached into his pocket for a yellow bandana to dab his sweat-beaded forehead.

"So you were lucky enough to get out of the Shoots, and then lucky enough to survive the Tsunese coast." I dropped the last of my chips into the pot, calling his bluff. "What're you doing with that luck now? Just floating from one game to the next and spinning that wheel?"

His game face was good, but the spirit told me I'd pushed the right button. He looked at what I'd just done. Didn't peek at his tiles, though I saw his hand twitch to. The smile he gave me in reply was a limp, anemic thing, like a teenage boy's first mustache. "Things had to break your way at some point." He slid his tiles back to the dealer.

I nudged my glasses up my nose and scooped my winnings closer. "Guess so. Nice playing with you." I started to rise, but he held up a hand.

"How about you see how long your luck really holds out?"

I glanced at you, then back to him. "If you insist."

So it went for another solid hour of play. We'd built Roulette up patiently over two hours, and then in just a few hands we put him back in the poorhouse. He watched with fraying calm as the pile of chips in front of me grew bigger and bigger, while his dwindled. He played well, near as I understood pektong. He was wily with his bluffs, careful with his tells, cunning with his baits and traps. But the city was singing his secrets right into my ear. When he had a good hand, I folded. When he bluffed, I went big. And round after round, you watched patiently.

Come five in the morning, it had finally cooled down. A new dealer handled us now. And hers was the face I grinned up at as she pronounced me the final winner of the set.

She turned with professional politeness to Roulette. "Would you like the house to extend you credit, sir?"

For a moment, I saw the idea catch in his eye like a spark to tinder. But then he shook it out and produced another cigarillo. "Reckon I've done me enough losing for a night." He lurched to his feet and touched his hat to us. "Y'all have a good morning."

I glanced over at you, and you were smiling.

We let him get all the way out to the street before we stopped him again. I fell into step with him on his right. "You knew we were cheating back there. Why'd you play me anyway?"

Roulette glanced at me, more annoyed than anything else. "Only thing worse than a sore loser's a sore winner, kid," he growled. "It's only on account of your age that you get a warning, and not a warning shot." He jammed his hands in his pockets and walked on.

"It's because you trusted in your own luck," you said, appearing on his left. "To carry you, and to tell you when it was finally time to walk away."

At last, he noticed the coats we were wearing, and the roses tucked into each lapel. Slowly, he came to a stop. Recognition flickered in his eye. "Where'd you get them flowers?"

"Your luck got you this far, Roulette," I said. He was tall, so I got the sense he wasn't used to looking up at people, but he had to look up at me. "Got you back to your home, busted and broke as it is. And now that you're here, you can do something to help us fix it, instead of just handing your savings over to the bosses one game at a time."

"Why would I wanna do that?" He was scoffing, but he also wasn't going anywhere.

"Because," you replied in a delicate voice, "you want the bullets you fire to mean more than the holes they leave behind. You want to make your own luck, not trust in something that will always turn on you eventually."

He eyed us one at a time. "What're y'all really trying to

36

talk to me about here?" He produced his yellow handkerchief again and dabbed at his neck. He stopped when he saw me holding my hand out for it expectantly.

I gave him a look over the top rim of my glasses: *Just do it*.

He shot me a look as he handed it over: *Whatever, weirdo*.

Deftly, my fingers shaped his handkerchief into the familiar folds of flower petals.

"Let us buy you some tea," I said, offering him back a yellow rose. "And we'll show you."

3
Now

Age 30

I let him march me into my own apartment with a gun at my back. I would've tried to make a move, but he was too smart to fall for that. He kept a respectable distance and let me lead the way.

I heard him whistle long and low behind me as he took in my apartment for the first time. "This how you've been living?" he said with a chuckle of disbelief. "Reeking of dish soap and fry oil, then crawling back to this rat trap?"

"Never knew you to look down on folks who'd hit hard times," I said, switching to Slatspeak. When my tongue traced those familiar shapes of my native language, I felt more like myself than I had since the day I washed up here.

He shrugged. "Can't blame a guy for being surprised. I knew a very different woman than the one I'm chatting with now." With his boot, he nudged my door shut behind him, then sauntered over to my one chair and sat himself down in it. He took another drag of his cigarillo. Ashed right onto my floor too, the bastard.

But I was studying the piece in his hand. When we'd fought together, he'd always used a pair of simple black six-shooters. This one was different: bigger, with a gleaming silver barrel and a handle of polished yellow bamboo. I'd seen it once before in my life, when it was firing bullets at me and chewing up that lonely boathouse in Birchbarrel.

"When'd he give it to you?" I said, nodding to it.

"Just before." He didn't have to specify. "Told me it'd be the finest trigger I ever pulled, and he ain't been wrong so far." He tilted his wrist to show me its bright yellow wooden grip. "Genuine bamboo, harvested straight from the Shoots."

My mouth tightened. When did you get those commissioned? What, had you gone to night school for gunsmithing or something? Every answer was just giving me more questions.

I decided to change the subject. "And when'd you make me?"

"Got your boss to thank for that one, there." He sighed smoke. "Moment she let slip it was your birthday, it all fell into place." He grinned. "What're the odds, huh? Lucky me."

"So you've got me," I sneered. The colossal unfairness of it all stung me, but I shouldn't have been surprised. Roulette Wu had always led a semi-charmed kind of life. "Why haven't you pulled that trigger yet?"

"Not often a pal comes back from the dead," he said. "I reckon whatever a dead woman's got to say, it'd be something worth telling the wind. So I reckon we can catch up a bit before I put a stain and varnish on this whole affair." He studied his burning cigarillo. "I figure about five minutes."

"You sure about that?" I said. "You're a human chimney."

"I'll smoke slow." He exhaled. "So how's about we start this all off with you telling me how the fuck it is you're still alive?"

"I don't totally remember."

"You're full of shit."

"*You think I give a fuck if you believe me?*" I snapped. "I woke up in a fishing net as I was getting hauled aboard. Biggest catch that little tub had ever landed. They were out of Kolkalang, so they dropped me off there. After that, my choices were head back to Driftwood City, or ... don't."

"And you wound up here," said Roulette. "The homeland."

"Hoy!" I snapped at him again. "My home was Driftwood City, same as yours. I didn't owe this place a damn thing."

"Then why'd you wash up here in the end?"

"The fuck do you think, Roulette?" I said. "Where else was I supposed to go?"

"Anywhere," he said. "Big old world, if you haven't noticed. I've seen some real pretty parts of it."

"But you ended up here, same as me," I said. "How's that work out? Doesn't sound like you came here with my scent in your nose."

"I didn't, I didn't," Roulette agreed. He'd been holding the gun perfectly steady for several minutes now, and his hand hadn't wavered at all. That wasn't great for me. "Truth is, I'm here on a mission of public service."

"Of course," I sneered. "The Thorn Orphans are the new system now."

"Yeah, I'm damn near respectable these days," Roulette said. "Came here looking to buy up timber, and Biranba's got some fine trees on its shores. Today's trees will be tomorrow's schools and roads. No more rotting Slats, not on my watch."

"Your watch?" I said. "What are you now, the town sheriff?"

He grunted. "Nah, not me, not me. The Armored got that job. And if you ask me, she should have it. Ain't any real gangs left on the Slats now. You're talking to the head of the Meyongphirin Municipal Department of Transportation."

I wrinkled my nose. "Only assholes call it Meyongphirin."

"You think I don't know that?" Roulette said. "But that's

what it says in the fancy gold paint on my office door, so ..."

I glanced at his cigarillo. It was maybe half-burned now.

"So you made the world a better place. Roses every day, and all that." I couldn't keep the disgust out of my voice. "If you all did such a good job, why do you still wear those guns?"

He tipped the chair back onto two legs, keeping his revolver trained on me. "World don't stay perfect on its own. It'll always need folks like the Thorn Orphans."

"You're not *Thorn Orphans* anymore," I spat. "We were never supposed to be running the show! I don't know what the fuck you all are now, but you don't deserve to wear those roses."

Roulette shrugged. "I ain't gonna apologize for doing a job and doing it well."

"So," I snarled, "that mean you didn't come here looking to make things right with me?"

His smirk grew strained. "Look, it ain't like I don't have my own regrets about where things fell that day," he admitted. "But you didn't give us any kind of choice, Tenny."

"*You were trying to kill Binh!*" I roared. "*The fuck was I supposed to do?*"

"Easy there, now." He leveled his gun at me. "These floors and walls don't look all that thick. I don't wanna spend my bullets on anyone but you tonight, but if anyone comes looking, they're gonna catch one."

I wrestled my temper back under control. I hadn't meant to lose it like that. So many times, I'd rehearsed these conversations while I was washing rice. But I hadn't anticipated the effect of actually seeing one of my old pals. I had to keep it together.

"As for the question of what you were supposed to do when you saw us going after Binh? I reckon you could've tried remembering who the Thorn Orphans were." He took his last drag, then dropped his cigarillo to the floor. His chair rocked forward, and he ground his smoke out under the toe of his boot. "When we come for someone, it's 'cause they had it coming."

And just like that, I was out of time.

"That's it?" I said. My temper roiled like a stormy sea, and that was no good. I needed to be like you: low and steady and ever-burning, like a blue gas flame. "You don't want to know what my side of things looked like?"

"I ain't survived as long in this line as I have by stopping and asking questions like that," said Roulette. "You were a good friend, Tenny. We fought a lot of good fights together, and did a lot of good for folks who needed it. But you ain't the first good friend I've killed."

In my ears, phantom music swelled.

Roulette didn't hear it. "You will, however, be the first one I kill twice."

His trigger finger twitched.

And in the instant that it did, the entire wooden floor of my apartment came to life, springing up like the jaws of a trap.

Before he could get a single shot off, Roulette Wu found himself encased in unnaturally flexible, age-darkened birch. It wrapped around his wrists. His ankles.

His throat.

"What the——?" He struggled, but he wasn't strong enough to break boards. "Tenny, what the fuck? You ain't supposed to have powers!"

"Luck gets you far in life, Roulette," I said. "There are some doors that only luck will open. But you never did know what to do when you were up against someone who could make their own. You kept your eyes on me this entire time, and you never once looked at the floor you were walking on."

He still had his eyes on me. He was fighting to aim his weapon

42

my way, but I'd bound his gun hand to point directly at the nearest wall. His other one was pinned to his side, helpless.

"You see, Roulette," I said, "this ain't the first time you've walked on this floor. Don't you recognize it yet?"

He nearly dropped his gun as the math all added up. "The boathouse?" he breathed, as best he could with a birch noose around his neck.

"The one piece of home I had left," I said with grim satisfaction. The ethereal song swaggered through me, big and brassy, as I flexed my power for the first time in years. "You really should've just let me die there."

"Now, hang on, hang on," Roulette said, eyeing me with proper fear for the first time. "I know you got a lot to be pissed about, and I ain't trying to skip out on what I owe you for that. But you sure that killing me's the way to go here?"

"What case you gonna make that it ain't?" I said. "Do you have information for me? I'm gonna guess not. Cole never trusted you with any of the important stuff. And even if you did, what would I use it for? I ain't ever heading back there. You all took Driftwood City from me, and you can keep it. I've got all I need from it right here." I weighed what I was about to say, then decided to tell him just the same. "I spared your life tonight back at the diner. I could've put a knife right in the back of your head, and I didn't. I let you go. You're the one who went kicking a dead woman. And now you're surprised she kicked back."

"Tenny, *Tenny*," he said, his voice rising in pitch as I started to tighten my wooden grip around his neck. "I told you, I didn't come looking for you! This is just me and my luck, doing what me and my luck do!"

"You followed me to my apartment and set up an ambush," I said flatly.

"*So I could've played that better!*" Roulette said. "I didn't know if you were planning to get the drop on me, or what! I had to be sure!" His hair fell away, revealing his second eye, wide and desperate. "Look, I came here on business, and now I get a chance to make things right with someone I wronged! You've gotta see there's poetry in that!"

My fist unknotted itself, and the birch collar I'd wrapped around Roulette's throat loosened itself just a little.

"Thank you," he rasped.

"I loosened it so you could talk without sounding like the bad guy in a fucking puppet show," I growled. "Now, Roulette, why don't you tell me exactly how you think you can make things right with me?"

"The way I figure it is this," he said. "If you had it in you to use your powers even away from home, you probably could've come back to try to make things even for what we did to you. But this whole time, you ain't made your move. And betting man that I am, I'd wager it's 'cause you weren't sure you could win. But you remember what it was like to fight with me at your side, don't you?" he added with a hopeful grin.

"Come back with you and kill them all?" I said. "And all I have to do is trust you, the man who flips on his teammates the moment the going gets tough."

"Hey, I fought for my side as hard as I could," Roulette said. "You can't blame a guy for wanting to live. You take me back, and I'm yours."

"Until I start to lose."

"No, Tenny," he said soberly. "I ain't gonna bet against you twice."

I nodded slowly as I considered the offer. Certainly, there were tempting parts of it. "So you'll fight alongside me," I said eventually, "because you want to live?"

"Sure do," Roulette said. "Sure do."

It was the opening I'd been waiting for him to give me.

44

"Do you know who else wanted to live, Roulette?" My voice was quiet. Certain.

He turned as pale as his bleached hair. I felt a grim and furious pleasure as I saw him finally realize that he'd never stood a chance of changing my mind.

"Tenny," he said. "Killing me ain't gonna bring him back."

Furiously, I tightened my fist. The music swelled as that birchwood noose began to squeeze on his throat again.

A gunshot filled the room, drowning out my shaman song. A revolver barrel strobed, and wood splintered. It felt like a violin string snapping mid-bow.

My reflexes took over. The sharp splinter of driftwood around my neck ripped itself free of its leather cord. It flew across the room like a bullet and drilled itself right into Roulette Wu's throat.

Instantly, blood sprayed. I released my grip on him, and he collapsed to my floor, clawing pathetically at his neck. But it was already too late for him; even on pure reflex, my aim had been too good. One of his guns lay forgotten at his side; the other was still in its leather holster, which was smoking and burst open at the end. Immediately, I understood: he'd gotten a grip on it with the arm I'd pinned to his side. And while we'd been talking, he'd been lining up to try for a lucky shot from the hip.

"Well, Roulette," I said, "I guess I'll give you points for being consistent right up to the bitter end. But you were never easier to beat than the times when you thought you were winning. And since I don't want to leave you wondering as you drift off: I wouldn't have made it hurt this much if you hadn't brought him up."

His eyes were wide and despairing. With each passing second, the capillaries in them grew redder and brighter.

I paged through my memories, and my mental finger fell

on the right words. The only words one could really say to a dying Thorn Orphan.

"*Roses every day,*" I recited.

His hand fell away from his throat. The rise and fall of his thin chest became shallower with each breath he took.

I limped over to him, so he could look me in the eyes as he went. It was more of a send-off than the Thorn Orphans had ever given me.

As he lay there, for just a moment I remembered fighting back-to-back with him against the Silver Tide Tong. I remembered laughing at his jokes, and the hooting cackle he'd let out when I hit him with mine. I remembered the way his eyes lit up when he slammed down a winning hand, and how quick he'd always been to spread the wealth around. I remembered all the times this loud, sloppy, double-talking, gunslinging degenerate had made himself one of my favorite people in all of Driftwood City.

That was my final kindness to Roulette Wu, Cole. I remembered who he used to be.

I made a pulling motion at the air, and the splinter slipped itself out of Roulette's neck like a blade from a sheath. It floated in the air in front of me, dark and slick with fresh blood. I'd have to wash it later. Right now, though, I didn't have time. I had to get him out of here and clean up all this blood. Police didn't really care what happened in this neighborhood. Once they got word a visiting foreign dignitary had last been seen here, though, they wouldn't shy away from kicking down doors.

But as I considered how I could smuggle this corpse down to the harbor, something caught my eye: a small yellow thing peeking out of the lapel of Roulette's coat.

Back in the old days, he'd been the Yellow Rose. And he'd always favored the color anyway, for making him stand out.

But for whatever reason, this scrap of sunburst struck me as funny.

It was a yellow piece of paper, thick from all the times he'd folded it up. When I folded it back open and smoothed it out, I saw it was a bill of sale. And typed on that stationery was a transcript of a telegram sent from an office near the diner where I worked.

MALAÑONG
RED ROSE BLOOMS

I glared back down at his corpse. "Roulette, you absolute *motherfucker*."

The Great Bird hadn't even given me enough time to enjoy my victory before shitting on my head. With the time difference, odds were that you wouldn't read this message for a few more hours. But whether you read it now or with your morning edition of the *Meyongphirin Blue Star*, it didn't matter. Eventually, you would read it. And you wouldn't just shrug it off, either. I knew you too well. I had to believe that even with the shit you'd pulled, you still had some respect for me. When you saw that Roulette Wu had sent you this telegram, you would already mark him among the dead.

As I stood there in my glorified cell with his cooling corpse at my feet, I worked through my choices. The first: I could just stay here in Malañong. And in between shifts at the diner, I could wait around and get myself ready. Because sure as hell, you were going to come for me.

But I thought of the people down at the diner. The neighbors who'd barely lost a wink of sleep from Roulette's gunshot. Maybe Malañong hadn't treated me particularly well, but the people of this city didn't deserve to have a tornado blow through their lives like this.

Second choice: I could just fucking leave. I didn't have much, but living in this pisspot of an apartment had let me scrape together some savings. I could get myself on an airship easy enough, even if it meant sleeping with the luggage. I wasn't sure where I'd go, but Roulette had had a point: there was a wide world out there, and it was full of newer and deeper and darker corners for me to hide in.

But again, I knew you too well. First, you'd send people here. And once it became clear I'd tried to go to ground, you'd get them on my scent one way or another. I could flee Malañong, but I'd never be able to flee fast or far enough to outrun you forever. I could grow old on one of the cold islands to the far, far west, tending sheep on a rolling green hill, and I'd still lay good odds that I would wake up one morning to be met by someone with a rose in their lapel.

Third choice: I could do your job for you.

I'd entertained it more than once over the years. Even now, I couldn't tell you if my continued survival was proof of bravery or cowardice. But as I thought about the position you were leaving me in, I was starting to see no way out ... or at least, no happy one. Why prolong things, then? Why not just find a rooftop and be done with it? Every day of the past four years had been borrowed time, anyway. And all the people I might've ever hoped to mourn me? They were either dead already, or they would've volunteered to give me that last push.

The world would've undoubtedly been better off without me in it, my every breath poisoning its air. The more I thought about it, the more logical it started to sound. But something deeper inside me pushed it away. It wasn't a *never*, so much as a *not yet*, but it was strong enough to stop me from heading for my building's stairwell.

And that left me with only one real choice.

I'd sworn I would never go back to Driftwood City, Cole. I'd made peace with the idea of leaving it to you and the others. I didn't even like tugging at the faint tether I still had to the city's spirit. I was so certain that somewhere on the other end of that line, you would feel me and know me. After all, every thread we pull has another end.

But now, I promised myself, I was going to do what I should've done all along. I was going to make you answer for what you'd taken from me. What I could take back, I would. And what you could never give back to me . . .

I froze there for just a moment, feeling the phantom touch of big, callused hands resting gently on my shoulders. The memory of warm breath on my neck. The weight of him on a mattress next to me.

My fist clenched tighter around the bloody piece of driftwood in my palm.

We Thorn Orphans had grown our garden with an eye toward making the powerful feel fear. And somewhere along the way, Cole, you'd become powerful. So I was going to fulfill our mission—the original one we'd agreed on all those years ago. I was going to pluck the flowers from your garden, one by one. For the first time in years, I let my mind trace the familiar shapes of their names:

Roulette Wu, the Yellow Rose. Already picked.

Anjali the Armored, the Blue Rose.

Knife-Edge Ngo, the Pink Rose.

Mhap the Monster, the Black Rose.

One by one, I'd take them from you. When I was done, you would feel as isolated and alone as I had, drowning in that driftwood coffin. And once you knew what you had lost, and that I was the weed that had choked the life out of your garden . . . then and only then would I finally trim you at the stem, too.

I studied the crumpled-up yellow telegram again. I had

49

smeared blood all over it, but I didn't care. I was trying to remember something I hadn't done in a good long while.

Roulette hadn't been wearing his usual yellow rose tonight, and no flower store would be open at this hour. But when you and I had started out as the original two Thorn Orphans, we hadn't used real roses, had we?

Tonight, life had not given me a yellow rose to leave you. But it had given me a piece of paper, and that had always been enough for the Thorn Orphans.

Deftly, my fingers began to guide that bloody paper along familiar paths and folds. Bit by bit, petal by petal, a familiar flower took shape. And when I was done, I placed it gently on Roulette's unmoving chest, like a wax seal on an envelope.

It was the first message I'd sent you in four years, but I knew you would read it. Because soon enough, the police were going to find this body. When they found it, they'd learn who he was. When they learned who he was, they'd tell you how they'd found him.

And when they did, I wanted to be absolutely sure you knew who'd sent him to you.

4

Twenty-three years ago

Age 7

Hey, Cole. Wanna hear something I've never told anyone?

I don't remember my mom's face.

I remember the broad strokes of her, like how she was tall (I had to get it from somewhere). She had a long face, and a short, practical haircut that came down just to her ears. But any more than that, it gets vague. I obviously know she had eyes and a mouth and a nose. But I don't remember their shape. I don't remember how the light caught them when she was happy or tired or playful or thinking hard. And whenever I try to think about her, all I can ever summon up is Benilda's face.

I've been tempted to go back and look at her before. I don't know if I ever told you that. I know where our old house was in Birantown. I know who lives there now. I knew how our powers worked. If I'd really wanted to, I could've made my way into that kitchen and taken a fresh look at her, courtesy of the memories she left in the floorboards.

But I knew if I let myself do it even once, I'd probably spend the rest of my life going back to that kitchen and looking for her. And I know myself well enough to know that I don't want to gamble on the hope that I might prove myself wrong.

You'd probably say I don't trust myself enough, Cole. And maybe you'd be right. But I disagree. I think this is me trusting that I know exactly who I am.

So I haven't seen my mother's face in twenty-three years, and now I don't remember it.

But even if I can't remember her, I remember this.

I'd turned seven that morning, but now it was the afternoon and we were in our kitchen. I can't remember much about that place either, except that it always felt warm, even when it wasn't. I was at the counter, watching her make kelp rolls. Her fingers moved deftly, like a pianist's across keys. One after another, she took rice wrappers, stuffed them with chopped kelp, and rolled them up tighter than fine mainland cigars. Some of them, she stuffed with slices of fish, too, but most of them were just kelp and a bit of sauce. As I watched with big, curious eyes, the pile grew and grew.

"Do you know about these?" She held up the most recently rolled one.

I shook my head.

"Back before I came here, there was a time when people here didn't have enough to eat."

"A famine." I'd heard the word in school.

"Yes, a famine," my mom agreed, like we were both academic types and I'd just made an important discovery. "But people needed to eat. So they dove down into the ocean and pulled out all the seaweed." Her cold foot came to rest gently on mine.

I shrieked and pulled mine away, laughing. "Gross!"

"That's how seaweed feels on your feet when you swim somewhere shallow enough," my mom said mischievously.

"So the people brought all the seaweed up on to the Slats and tried to eat it, but they didn't like how it tasted."

I looked in the red wooden bowl where she had her kelp. It all looked like a pile of green worms.

"But the Biranese people thought to wrap it up in a shell like this and fry it like ... Do you know the name of the dish?"

My little face screwed up with thought. Then, I remembered: a tray of the things, stacked in a little pyramid, at the huge home of my mom's best friend where we'd been dinner guests once. "Lumpia?"

Pleased, she caressed my cheek with her thumb. "Look at you. A proper Biranese lady. Yes, we wrapped the kelp in rice wrappers and fried it like lumpia. People liked it so much, they started eating it all over the city. And they still do. Even the people that don't like us Biranese much can't stay away from kelp rolls."

That was definitely true; there were kelp roll shops all over the Slats. Some folks even wandered the boardwalks, selling them from little carts. "Do they eat kelp rolls in Biranba?"

"Oh no, not at all," my mom laughed. "They don't like kelp rolls over there. But do you know what, Cheza?"

I do remember her leaning down, as if she was about to tell me a secret. And I remember leaning in close, so I could hear her better. "What?"

"They're the ones who are missing out." She kissed me on my nose, and went back to rolling. For another minute, I just watched her, trying to memorize how her fingers magically transformed some rice dough and seaweed into perfect packages. (For the record, Cole: twenty-three years of practice, and I still ain't got the trick down.)

But eventually, I said, "Why did you leave Biranba?"

"Because your lola left Biranba, and I had to go with her," said my mom, not looking up from her work.

"But why did lola leave?" I pressed. "Can we ever go back?"

I know she smiled here. I wish I could remember what type of smile it was, instead of just subbing in my memories of Benilda's cunning grin.

"Do you see that street out there?" She pointed out our window.

"Yes."

"Would you rather sleep there, or in your nice warm bed?" said my mom.

"My bed," I said immediately.

"Your bed," my mom agreed. "Would you sleep on the street if there were spiders in your room?"

"No."

"If there were spooky noises coming from the floorboards?"

"There *are* noises coming from the floorboards, and they don't scare me," I insisted.

"If it was on fire?"

I thought about it this time.

"I'd sleep on the streets if my room was on fire," I conceded eventually.

"Of course you would," my mom agreed again. "But if your room wasn't on fire, you'd still sleep in it, even if it wasn't very nice?"

I nodded, confused. What did this have to do with Biranba?

"So how bad does it have to be before a person leaves their home?" my mom asked gently.

Ah. I looked up at my mom with dawning understanding ... at least, partly. "But you said they don't like us here either," I went on. "So isn't this a fire, too?"

I still can't remember her face, but I can remember how sad it felt when her hand gently ran itself through my short-cropped hair.

54

"You'll see for yourself when you're old enough, *anak*," she said. "The world is one big fire."

Eleven years later

Exactly eleven years later, as it happens. It was my eighteenth birthday, and her words resounded in my ears.

My world was ablaze.

Fire consumed the Unified Utilities Plant's entire work floor. Alarms wailed, my fellow salters screamed, and above it all the flames snarled and roared. The ferocious heat made the air ripple, and it twisted metal, and it made human meat sizzle and spark.

All of those notes collided in my ears and in my head, until they weren't even a song, just a dirge. Even through the other stenches, I smelled burning rubber, and yanked my boots off the steel floor. I had to keep moving, or the soles would melt right where I stood.

I took off at a run. I didn't know why; I didn't know where to run to. I could see masses of folk in grey coveralls pressed against the emergency exits. But the doors weren't open. The flames were spreading. Even now, I watched it jump to more equipment. More people. The smoke stung my eyes. Soon, I could barely see at all.

I felt small, Cole. So small, like I was seven again and in that warm kitchen. I was used to towering over almost everyone I met, and now I felt like an ant. All around me, titanic machinery burned. Huge crowds of people burned. And the heat made it look like even the ceiling beams were bowing down to us. All around me, I felt my phantom orchestra falling silent. Instrument by instrument, the music was getting smaller. But in its remaining notes, I felt an urge: *Do something*.

"What?" I roared over everything. A fleeing salter shoved past me, and I nearly tumbled to the searing floor. "What the fuck am I supposed to do?"

And the word that formed in my head, Cole, was *Anything*.

My heart pounded. My breaths were shallow. My vision was turning more and more tunneled by the second.

But within that melody inside me, I found a cadence. Started matching my breathing to it, and the falls of my feet. And inch by inch, I took back control of my body.

And then, I was in control of so much more.

I learned later that this is how being a shaman worked, at least for us. It was a power that had a way of teaching you how to use it. But in the moment, I didn't know that I was being taught anything. I just saw the fire, smelled the smoke, heard the screams, and knew in my heart that if anyone could do something right now ... it was me.

I don't know how I reached out, but it felt as natural as stretching out my arm. But instead of gripping something with my fingers, I was gripping it with ... not my heart. Not my spirit. Just *me*.

And in this case, that something was the huge reservoir of water beneath the Plant.

I hear some folks call it "the ocean."

It rose to me slowly, but gaining speed with every passing note and measure. And when it all crescendoed, a gigantic wave erupted straight up through the grated floors. It hissed as it touched the fire, and the steam warred with smoke. But the water kept coming, and in moments the fire was in full retreat. Survivors were staring in wonder as the last of the flames were snuffed right out. And then, the water wasn't coming up from the ocean anymore; it was raining back down: on the Plant, on me, and on everyone else who was lucky to still be alive.

BOOM!

I don't know how the water line next to me could have ruptured. But it did. Steam and shrapnel spat from it. I had enough time to see what was happening, not enough time to act—

—as a patch of wall ripped itself free and whipped into my path like a shield. The shrapnel embedded itself into it. The steam shot around me, and once again the air grew hot. My glasses fogged up, but at least my skin didn't scald off my skull.

I glanced around wildly. I didn't understand what I'd just done ... but I knew I hadn't done that.

And then I saw you: your fine black clothes covered in ash and soot. Your silver hair a mess. A fresh cut, bleeding on your eyebrow. And your hand extended toward the unnaturally twisted wall.

You looked as haunted as I felt.

I gaped. I knew the heir to the Plant when I saw him. And I'd already recognized you earlier that morning, as the asshole who'd stolen my birthday thunder with your own. But neither of us was celebrating now.

Urgently, you grabbed my arm. "I don't know what's happening to us," you said, "but we need to go."

I almost agreed, but over your shoulder I saw an orange flicker in the distance. Felt that new power surge through me ... and through you.

"We're not done here yet," I said.

I ran toward it, and you ran with me.

Part Two

Return!
The Red Rose Blooms Anew

5
Now

Age 30

Have you ever seen our city from the sky, Cole?

I know you've seen the same paintings I have, the same newsreels and motion pictures. And I know you grew up on a balcony on the Rock, overlooking the Slats with your nose in a book and a cup of oolong in your pale little hand. But all our power came from walking its streets, so I'm asking: were you ever brave enough to step away from it, to see exactly what it was you were fighting for?

I'd left Driftwood City in an underwater coffin, so the first time I saw it was when I finally came back. I'd scraped together a single outfit for my travels: a dark red longcoat, for the chill. A red bell-shaped hat, to hide my face. Sturdy black boots, for long walks and kicking teeth. Next to me was my driftwood, shaped into a big birch traveling trunk. We stood together on the observation deck of the airship *Cloudwhale* as it drifted gently into Driftwood City airspace.

And I've gotta tell you, Cole: even though the sight turned my stomach, it was worth the long flight.

When I'd last laid eyes on it, the Rock had still looked like a mountain, its face dotted with mansions and estates. A roost for the rich, so they had somewhere nice to stand while they pissed down on to the Slats. But in the four years I'd been gone, I guess you'd been busy. Thick rows of homes encrusted the bottom of the Rock, and even from up here I could see the skeletons of future homes creeping up its slopes like moss up a tree trunk. Dotted among them were towers and wires that marked out cable car stations and telephone lines. It was like you had thrown your hat over a fence. Where those stations were, homes and streets would follow.

And it wasn't just the Rock that was changing. The sun had sunk low, and the lights of the Slats had awoken to keep the dark at bay. Even from where I stood thousands of feet in the air, I saw a wooden expanse ablaze with headlights, stoplights, streetlights. When we'd been growing up, that had been an impossible strain on the city's aging power grid. Neighborhoods had been tiled: light, dark, light, dark. But now through the lenses of my old, scratched-up glasses, all of the lights bled together into a halo around the magnificent sight of Driftwood City.

A throbbing ache stirred in my chest, like I was being gently stabbed in the heart.

"It really is something," said a proud voice next to me.

There was a time I would've enjoyed a stranger talking to me, but now my skin prickled. I'd barely spoken to anyone for the four days we'd been in the air. I'd stayed in my cabin as much as possible, even taking my meals there. The only reason I'd come out now was because I'd felt us starting to descend at last.

The speaker was a little old woman. I mean, everyone's little when you're as tall as me, but she was like some kind of doll. She'd sidled up next to me and stood on her tiptoes to peer out the porthole. She had nut-brown skin, same as me. But even though we'd embarked from Biranba, I could tell right away that she wasn't Biranese. And even if the shape of her narrow eyes hadn't done it, her language would've; she was using good old Meyongphirin Standard. Or, as you call it if you're not a fucking asshole, Slatspeak.

I'd never met this old lady before, but there are some lessons about respecting elders you never really shake off, especially with an upbringing like mine. I laid down my trunk so she could stand on it. She offered me a cheerful bow of thanks, then stepped up.

"A wooden trunk?" she mused. "Is that birch?"

My grin was friendly, but guarded. "Good eye."

That seemed to satisfy her. "I grew up down there." She pointed out the window. "When I was a girl, everything was falling apart. You couldn't run down to the drugstore without getting a hundred splinters in your soles. Now, even from all the way up here you can see where they're refinishing it. They've promised to have all the Slats redone by the end of the year." Her wrinkly face pruned up further as she smiled down at the sight below.

The uneasy flutters in my stomach settled as I saw how she looked down at Driftwood City. We were looking out the same porthole, but we were seeing two different places down there.

I let the moment sit a while, filled by the big and steady hum of the airship's engines as they rattled through the metal decks.

"What were you doing in Biranba?" I asked at last.

"This was a business trip, I'm afraid," she said, like there'd been no pause at all. "Nothing worth telling the wind. Just run-of-the-mill supply matters. I run a fabric and dye shop, and your people are excellent at making both." Her expression clouded with thought. "I'm sorry. Not *your* people. You may

63

look Biranese, but you sound like you're from ..." She smiled as the answer came to her. "Oakyard?"

I cracked a reluctant grin. "Got that right," I sighed. "Same as you."

"Yes, I've been living in Akashi Heights my entire life. And yourself?"

My grin faded just as quickly as it'd appeared. "Birantown."

The old lady was already back to peering out the porthole. "Well, you sound like you're from Oakyard all right, but I can hear a bit of Malañong in that voice of yours. You must have been there for quite some time."

I turned to face the city as it grew in our porthole. I wondered if I was as easy to see through. "Four years," I admitted. "You got a sharp ear, you know that?"

"The places we live always leave a mark on us, one way or another."

A faint song stirred in the splinter on the end of my necklace. All at once, my old wounds began to throb.

Oblivious, she smiled at me. "I'm Pham Hoa."

My heart nearly stopped at the mention of her family name. I wanted to ask her if she was any relation, but I stopped myself. For one thing, Pham was a common last name. For another, she didn't have that particular Pham family's trademark thin nose. And besides all that, if fate was cruel enough that she actually was related to Binh ... what would I even say to her?

She didn't say anything when I failed to return her introduction with one of my own. Instead, she placed a knotted old hand on the porthole. "So you were away for a while, then. What brought you there?"

It was a hell of a personal question. But even though I still had it in me to kill someone while they looked me in the eyes and begged for their life, I guess didn't have it in me to say, *Fuck off, old lady.*

So instead, I said, "Had to go away for a bit. Figure some things out."

Fresh wrinkles appeared on her face as she beamed at me. "I'm glad you seem to have found whatever it is you're looking for. And what is it that brought you back home?"

Carefully, I considered my answer.

"Same as you," I said eventually. "Business."

Night had fallen by the time we landed. The shipyard was drenched in light, so I was able to watch as six people in black uniforms trotted across the boards with a pair of heavy metal winches. As they drilled them straight into the slats of the landing zone, the airship's crew let out long, thick cables of oily woven steel. In minutes, the ground crew was ratcheting us closer and closer to them, working levers that took three people apiece to operate.

I shook my head in wonder. The Rock had been dead set against establishing an airport in Driftwood City, convinced airships were a fad technology and nothing more. Now, we not only had an airport, but one staffed by crew who knew exactly what they were doing. When had you found the time to get that done, Cole? What else had you built while I was gone? And what did the city have to say about all this?

As I was herded across the shipyard with the other passengers, I found myself stuck on the question of what the city thought. When we were growing up, this space had all been tenement housing, an old development called Bark Gardens. The folks who lived here had always told the same joke: *No gardens, no bark.* I remembered that there'd been a bicycle shop three blocks from where I stood, where this old couple hand-wrought each one out of scrap iron and rubber. There'd been the boatway trench at Hoang Plaza, with the missing step everyone had to hop.

Now, though, there was ... nothing.

Well, not nothing. There was a big, flat expanse of boardwalk, and a blue-painted walkway that led to a small, broad building with a glittering, well-lit sign that read: MEYONGPHIRIN INTERNATIONAL AIRPORT.

Somehow, you'd managed to throw together a handsome little airport in the past four years. It was a place of clean, slanted lines that naturally drew the eye up and out, the walls painted in bold greens and blues with details of glittering silver. The ceiling overhead had a majestic, welcoming curve to it, where all those lines came together like the sun meeting a horizon. All the materials around me were hard and slick, and they gave every voice and footstep an echo. The longer I stood there, the more the echoes collided with one another, until every sound I heard was a fuzzy and loose-woven thing.

To someone like me, who knew Driftwood City, the building's design sent a message: *Welcome to the future.* And yet I frowned at the floor, with its interlocking octagonal tiles of black and white with thin lines of still more silver between them. It didn't sit right with me, to be on the Slats and standing on something other than wood.

I froze as I heard a snatch of song in my ear. A simple five-point melody I hadn't heard in four years. It was the song that the city always hummed to us when we communed with it. Its timbre and pitch and arrangement were always changing, depending on where I was and what I was talking to it about, but eventually the melody always came back to those five notes. My ears drank it in like it was cold, clean water.

I blinked back tears. I was home.

I was home, and the city was reaching out to its lost shaman at last.

But then the old lady from the airship strode right past me, humming it. And when I looked up, I saw loudspeakers dangling from the ceiling. I scowled up at them, fierce enough that I thought they might burst into flames. That had been *our* song, Cole. You were never supposed to share it with the whole damn world.

As the first taste of Driftwood City air hit me near the door, I came to a stop. My breath caught in my chest, sweat bloomed across my palms, and the thought hit me like a knife in the back: *this was insane*. What I was doing was absolutely insane. I'd gotten lucky with Roulette. The others were going to see me coming. There were quicker ways for me to kill myself.

"Hey, keep moving!" someone snarled at me as they jostled past. I watched them resettle their coat on their shoulders like a bird ruffling its feathers, and walk into the cold.

I took a deep breath. I stilled my shaking hands.

And I reminded myself that you couldn't kill someone who was already dead.

My breath puffed when I stepped out on to the wooden streets of Birchbarrel. There was no rain yet, but I could tell from the taste in the air that it'd only be a matter of time. And based on all the shuttered news stands and hustling people, I guessed we were looking at sooner rather than later.

But there was no ethereal song to greet me, either. I couldn't detect even the slightest strain of it in the traffic around me, nothing rising up from the twisted old grains of wood underfoot. I couldn't feel any power humming in the wires, or radiating off the people who passed me by. All I had was what I'd brought with me in my driftwood trunk, and it sounded like a single violin trying to fill a huge concert hall by itself.

I'd expected that. Prepared for it, even. But you and I both know that being prepared ain't the same thing as being ready.

You hadn't been able to completely change Driftwood City, it seemed, but you were doing your damnedest. The new buildings were of a piece with the airport, bright and looming and streamlined. Traditional Driftwood City design called for sharply slanted roofs, the better to shunt off snow and rain. But it looked like you and Roulette had developed a taste for curves: in the rooftops, in the façades, even in the shapes of the doors and windows. And everywhere I looked, silvery inlay glittered in the little details. I told myself it was no different than some idiot bravo flashing cash to impress. But fuck me, Cole, if I wasn't impressed anyway.

As I walked on, I looked closer at the front doors I passed. In old times, people would've put buckets on their stoops before a good, heavy rain. The Rock and the bootleggers had kept a pretty tight hold on the town's water supply, but even they couldn't control the skies. Rain was one of the only reliable ways to get your hands on free water, and the people of the Slats never missed a chance to collect some.

But apparently, in your Driftwood City, people didn't do buckets anymore.

Back in the day, buckets had gone away before. Your grandmother had given gangs of badges overtime pay to go through neighborhoods after a squall, kicking over every bucket, bottle, and bowl they could find. And Benilda hadn't allowed buckets in Birantown, convinced they would tell the outside world that she couldn't provide for her people. It got so bad sometimes, folks had taken to punching holes in their own rooftops just so they could get a little extra water to get by on. No city has a thousand problems; it's just got one problem that wears a thousand faces. And for Driftwood City, that problem's always been water.

All your fixes to the city had been so big and obvious, I could see them from the sky. But had you managed to finally sort out the city's water problem once and for all, too?

No, I told myself after a moment, storming onward. *No fucking way*. Working together in our peak and prime, we hadn't been able to crack it. The thought that you might've done it working on your own ...

Part of me wanted to stop and drink in the feeling of being home again, but my mind was stuck trying to work out my next move. You, I knew I had to save for last. That much was obvious. You were the most dangerous. There was a chance you already knew I was here. In a straight-up fight I could take you easy, but straight-up fights weren't exactly your deal. I had a tiny shred of power humming through my necklace and my wooden suitcase, but that was it. You, on the other hand, had the power of an entire city behind you. Even setting aside all the mind games I wanted to play with you, I wouldn't take that on until I absolutely had to.

So that left Knife-Edge Ngo, who would be clever, but not unbeatable. Anjali the Armored, who would maybe be the hardest one for me to face, after you. And Mhap the Monster who ... well. Whoever I went after first, it wouldn't be him.

Besides, the question of my next target wasn't the biggest problem facing me.

The first raindrop fell heavily as a glob of spit, staining the wood dark. Overhead, a rumble of thunder told me I had to get inside, and soon. I considered doubling back to the airport, but no, I'd come too far now. There were a few hiding places on the edges of the Slats where I could lie low, as long as I kept moving every few days. I'd burn through all of them in about two weeks, but surely I could have the four of you iced by then.

If not, though ...

That was as far as I let myself think before I shook it off. I'd taken this leap. I had to believe that sometime between now and when I hit the ground, I'd find a way to land on my feet.

See, this was the other tricky thing about the situation you'd left me in, Cole. If I'd tried to make my comeback right after you took me out, I might've had a chance. You were my best friend, but you hadn't been my only one. There were people I could've fallen back on, favors I could've called in. But four years is a long time to leave a relationship untended, even when they don't think you're dead.

I could try my luck turning up on someone's doorstep, but how was I supposed to trust they wouldn't turn right around and ring you up? Whatever goodwill I could promise, I bet it wouldn't rate next to the promise of the Governor's favor. Off the top of my tired, dented head, there were maybe two people I could think of in all of Driftwood City who wouldn't turn me in to you. One of them, I couldn't even imagine facing. And the other never would've let you kill me before she got a chance to do it herself.

A levee broke in the clouds above, and a faint drizzle began to fall. Muttering to myself, I found a nearby stair leading to a canal. The station would have an awning, so at least I'd have somewhere dry to wait for the next eastbound ferry. The street's lights reflected down on to the dark chop of the canal, their images rippled and warped by the falling rain as I took a seat.

I sighed. On days like this I'd felt most connected to the city. We'd always had a good relationship, the city and I, but it'd spoken to me the clearest when it spoke through water.

I reached for the wooden shard around my neck. In its splintered grains, I felt a faint pulse stir at my touch. Back in Malañong, I'd always wondered if you were sitting on the other end of that spiritual string, feeling the vibration every time I pulled on it. Now that I'd brought this driftwood back into the city proper, I found myself searching its grains for any hint of you. Had you felt me return? I didn't know how deeply its connection to you might still run.

But seeing how I was already here ...

70

I shut my eyes and ran through every meditation trick you'd ever taught me. I slowed my breathing. I stilled my thoughts. I took in all the city sounds around me and strained to find the symphony hidden in them. I dreamed of the city coursing through me like electricity. I remembered running and leaping across city rooftops with feet as light as raindrops. I remembered seeing a city that I could love.

But none of those memories were complete without you. And as you appeared in my mind's eye—all black clothes, tousled silver hair, embers of concern on your face—my eyes snapped open.

My glasses had slid down my nose, and I irritably nudged them back into place. That little spark of power I'd felt inside my necklace guttered and went out. I growled to myself. For just a moment there, I'd felt so close to something.

My lower jaw had started to develop a chatter. Safe in my small dry island, I shivered freely as I waited for the ferry. Had Driftwood City always been this cold, and I'd just forgotten? Or was this chill the city's way of welcoming me back? Had it changed, or had I?

I looked up just in time to see lightning bleach the sky and clouds above. I blinked as thunder shouted over the roiling sea. And in that second my eyes were closed, the air beneath the canopy somehow got heavier.

When I opened them, I wasn't alone.

In the gloom, Mhap the Monster's obsidian eyes glittered with triumph. "Hello, Red Rose."

I whipped my wooden suitcase up in time to block his first punch. My elbows buckled from the sheer strength of him. He'd already been fuckoff big and fuckoff strong, and it looked like he'd been hitting the gym while I was away. I was up on my feet, trying to get away, but he was right there with me. As I made for the stairs, he slid to block me, somehow fitting in a space no man his size should've. I didn't react fast enough, and his next punch caught me right under my chin.

I don't remember flying. I just remember the hit, and then I remember lying on the wet pier. He'd only hit my head, but every bit of me hurt. Groggily, I staggered back to my feet. As raindrops collected on my glasses and weighted down my hair, the Monster approached.

He'd updated his look, I saw. Instead of our old flatcaps, he wore a neat black bowler hat over his bald, tattooed scalp. And he'd ditched the carpenter's mask and black longcoat, instead wearing only a white dress shirt that the rain had turned all but transparent. Its sleeves were rolled up to reveal his muscular, equally tattooed forearms. As he neared me, he calmly tucked his black tie into the gap between two of his shirt buttons.

"It's good to see you again." Prick actually sounded like he meant it.

I slipped into a tired fighting stance. "How the hell did you—?"

"I know you, Red Rose. You've always been arrogant, standing on the shoulders of your patron spirit and thinking yourself tall ..."

"Where are your eyes, asshole?" I snapped. "I *am* tall."

He ignored my interruption. "And I knew that even in the absence of that favor, you would still be arrogant enough to slink back into our city through its front door."

When his next hit came for me, I blocked the blow with my suitcase and willed my power into its wood grains. The birch spread and flowed around Mhap's fist like liquid, before re-solidifying into a heavy wood gauntlet.

I flooded the wood with more of my will, and ghostly horns brayed in response as his fist's wooden prison slammed itself hard into the slick wet pier. Mhap tried to budge it, and I felt my hold strain against his sheer strength. That was unfathomable; no one could possibly be that strong without help. But fathoming was what you did best, Cole. I was just gonna hit him a whole lot.

I curled my hands into fists. "This," I snarled, "is for Binh."

I laid into him with everything I had. A long walk and a longer flight had made me stale, while he was fresh as spilled blood. But in the absence of fair odds or a good set of weapons, I knew four years of quietly simmering rage would serve.

As the downpour soaked us both, I rained blow after blow on to his face. Savage satisfaction flooded me with each strike. His head rocked with each impact, but only for a second before I sent him reeling the other way with my next punch.

At last, my fists fell to my sides, arms sagging and knuckles bloody. My hands, which just a night of dishwashing could turn achey, throbbed like my bones were on fire. I was breathing heavy, and glaring down at the Monster with as much hatred as I could muster.

And he looked back up at me with a feral, bloodstained grin.

Slowly, he rose to his feet. I flooded the driftwood around his fist with all the willpower I had, trying to draw it back down to the ground like one magnet to another. But no matter how hard I pushed, the Monster pulled harder. Inch by inch, he fought me. Inch by inch, he won, until he loomed over me again and I gaped up into his huge tattooed face. I'd hit him with all my best shots, and I hadn't even left a scratch. And suddenly my birchwood coffin looked less like a prison for his hand, and more like I'd given him a weapon.

My mind jumped to Roulette's revolvers. Knife-Edge's crystal blades. Anjali's new suit of armor. Obviously, I knew where they'd gotten their toys. But the Black Rose was a barefisted fighter like me. So what gift had you given him?

I didn't have time to wonder any further, as he swung his

73

wood-gauntleted fist at me like a hammer. I leapt back out of its reach, but already he was surging for me again. I managed to avoid two, three more swings, but I couldn't see an opening to turn the tables on him. I couldn't even gather the focus to take my driftwood off him.

And then, as I made to dodge another swing from the hammer-hand I'd accidentally armed him with, I saw his knee coming for me too late to block.

Once again, he sent me tumbling off my feet in a single hit. My whole side lit up with pain. I would've been amazed if something wasn't broken in there.

My will slipped from the driftwood around his arm, and it fell away like rotten bark from a tree, clattering to the wet pier. I tried to scrape together the will to bring it back into the fight, but I could barely even get up. Could barely even breathe.

"I've always found your combat skills lacking compared to mine, but I admit I expected more from the woman who killed Roulette Wu. Did death steal your edge, Red Rose?" He thought about it a moment, like I wasn't even there. "No," he decided, "it's time that's blunted your thorns."

"*The fuck ... are you talking about?*" I spat as I staggered to my feet. "*I'm the same ... I've always been!*"

The bastard almost sounded sad as he answered: "Precisely."

I wanted to think he was just trying to intimidate me. But I couldn't ignore that he kept hitting me, and then waiting patiently for me to get back up. That wasn't what you did to someone you thought could beat you.

"An enemy isn't the opposite of a friend," he rumbled. "I always understood that better than you."

He moved like oil, slick and dark and sinister. I threw a punch into his path, but it was pointless. He flowed around it, just like my driftwood had flowed around him, and then his

74

hand closed around my throat like an iron collar. I struggled against his grip, but he was unmoved.

Too strong for you, I whispered to myself as dots burst in my vision. *Just like last time*.

"He will want to see you one more time before he kills you," said the Monster. He sounded casual, like he was gardening and not tearing me apart one muscle fiber at a time. "He would want me to bring you to him. He's counting on that. He always entrusts his most important missions to me.

"But I'm not going to do that. You always distracted him from the important things, and he has more important things to do than ev—"

I didn't have time to listen to speeches, least of all from him. So while he was talking, I channeled my will into my driftwood necklace, which shot straight up and drove itself into his left eye.

Blood spurted from his socket and he dropped me, gasping, to the ground. He staggered back, and for the third time I found myself scrambling to my feet. But this time, I had a second to think. Mhap was on my list. Killing him would only make the world a better place. He'd more than earned a painful death, and there was no one better to give it to him than me.

But I'd barely handled him when he was calm and holding back. My four years of rage hadn't made a dent in him, but I had a feeling his would make plenty of dents in me. Even one-eyed, he still had the edge on me. It was time to go.

I plucked at a string of power, and as the note echoed my driftwood hurled itself into the water below. I leapt in after it, and my booted feet landed on solid birch. It bobbed low in the water, but only for a moment before I buoyed it with more of my willpower. And then I was zipping through the canal, crouched low and leaning into the breeze as needles of rain stung my face. The pier was shrinking into the distance behind me, and Mhap the Monster with it.

Since I wasn't consumed with the task of not dying anymore, my heart decided now was a good time to stage an escape attempt via my throat. The edges of my vision went dark, and the faint song in me was off-key and out of beat. My neck crawled where the Monster had laid hands on it. Over and over, I replayed the exact moment I realized my best hits had done nothing to him.

That just didn't fucking happen, Cole. My whole life, when I hit someone, they went down. But this time, I'd only got away because I'd left my necklace sticking out of the guy's fucking eye.

I actually considered heading right back to the airport and seeing where I could stow away. My instincts back there were right: I'd been fucked from the very beginning. This was suicide.

But even as I chewed on the idea, I realized exactly how likely it was that I'd get out of Driftwood City alive. Now that I was here, I was here. Only thing to be done was hope you couldn't find me before I'd had the chance to finish what I'd started with Roulette Wu back in Malañong.

I gritted my teeth. That was maybe the worst part of this whole thing: Roulette had been right. There was no way I could do this alone.

And that meant I needed to drop in on an old friend.

Which is a tough thing to need when you don't have any.

Carving a white wake through the boatway canal, I weighed which life I wanted to ruin tonight. One of them was east of here, and she'd definitely try to kill me the moment she saw me. The other was probably still to the north, and odds were good she would take me in without a question, feed me, and give me all the time I needed to get back on my feet.

But if I went there, I'd have to look her in the eye.

When I put it that way, the choice was easy.

East it was.

6

Twenty-three years ago

Age 7

My new sisters were playing in the greenhouse when my new mom took me to meet them.

The Benilda I hold closest in my memory is Benilda just before she died: squat and short, wrapped in bright flowered dresses. Her stubby fingers always sported a collection of rings, and it seemed like she had a different fancy hat for every day of the year. The Benilda who held my hand on that day was younger: a bit slimmer, with more black hair than grey, and only the faintest traces of wrinkles on her face. Most knew her for her ruthlessness; her cunning; her fierce way of conducting business.

I knew her as my mom's best friend.

And, according to Biranese kinship, the only family I had left in the world.

I started to drag my feet when the first wave of hot air hit me.

"Cheza," Benilda said calmly. Gracefully, she knelt so her eyes could meet mine. "What's wrong? You've played in this greenhouse before."

"I like the cold." Beyond my rapidly fogging glasses, my vision filled with swaying green leaves.

Benilda shrugged off my excuse. "The plants need the heat to live, anak. And I need the plants to live."

My eyes went wide with alarm. I'd already lost one mother. "Without them, you'll die?"

Kindness and concern crinkled the corners of her eyes. Even at my young age, I knew not many people got to see that. "I will not die, but there are things worse than death."

I looked away. I couldn't think of anything worse right then.

Tenderly, she ran a hand through my hair, and clicked her tongue at how short it was. "I have two hearts: the red one gifted to me by the Great Bird, and the green one that I grew myself. And now, anak," she said as she tugged me along, "it is your heart, too."

I remember how small my hand was in hers. In three years, I'd be shoulder height to her; in six, able to see over the top of any of her hats. But back then, with my mom freshly fed to the waves, Nanay Benilda looked downright huge, like she could step to anything else the world had to throw at me, and win every time.

The twins, I knew, weren't Benilda's daughters by birth; they'd belonged to her brother. I'd seen them once or twice since they'd come to live with their aunt, but my mom hadn't been taking me around the Lacanilao house recently.

I think it was Dalisa I saw first. She poked her head out from behind a rose bush, her thin face curious as a cat's. Diwata was next, loping out from behind that same bush like ... well, also like a cat. They both had the kind of long, braided hair that Benilda liked, and they wore identical dresses of green and gold, but I could tell them apart right away. There was no mistaking the way each twin held herself, or the way the light hit their eyes. Dalisa's stayed wide and polite; Diwata's narrowed the moment they fell on me.

"Dawa. Sasa." Benilda's voice was soft but firm. Even at age seven, I recognized that it belonged to someone who never heard the word "no." And with good reason; even at age seven, I'd also heard plenty of stories about what happened to people who said no to Nanay Benilda.

She didn't need to command them to come; they just came and stood dutifully in front of her. "Do you remember the day you came here?" she said to them. I noticed that for them, she didn't kneel.

The two of them didn't even look at each other for cues. They just nodded: perfect unison, exact same amount of time, exact same angle. "Yes, Tita Benilda," they chorused.

Benilda let go of my hand, then rested it on my shoulder. I could feel the weight of her many thick rings as she prodded me toward the twins. "This is Cheza," she said. "You might remember her. She has come here, too, and she'll be staying. Play with her."

This time, the twins were different again. Diwata crossed her arms. "You're Tita Daning's, then?" she said, even as Dalisa bowed once more and said, "Sorry for your loss."

I looked up beseechingly at Benilda. I knew a little about the twins, both from what I'd seen and what I'd heard: they were four years older than me. They kept to themselves and didn't like to play with the other kids in the neighborhood. And they loved confusing people about which one they were talking to. But right now it was so obvious to me that one of them might as well have been missing her nose.

"I don't want to play, Benilda," I said. "I wanna go with you."

"Hoy!" Diwata barked, an eleven-year-old drill sergeant. "You call her Tita Benilda, you got that?"

80

Benilda chuckled and patted me affectionately.

"She can call me that for now."

Dalisa absorbed this information with a nod; Diwata by standing very still and saying nothing.

The few wrinkles in Benilda's face smoothed as she knelt once more to talk to me.

"The things I do with my days are for women, not girls," she said gently. "You and your new sisters will look after each other when I can't be there to look after the three of you, understood? You—"

I heard the slide of the greenhouse door, then footsteps on the hardwood floor. I was the only one who turned to see Tatay Indawat approach. He was a neat man, his clothes subdued compared to his wife's bold floral print dresses and extravagant hats. My own mother had once told me that when the two of them were together, Nanay Benilda was a beautiful picture, and Indawat her simple and elegant frame.

"Hello, young Cheza," he said warmly to me, as if I were the most important person in the room. He bowed to the twins. "Girls." And then he turned to his wife, producing a polished wooden cigarette case as he did.

"I have told you not to smoke those disgusting things in here," Benilda warned him.

He held up his matches to show he hadn't lit up yet. "Loongon is here. He says he has an apology to make to you. The sort that must be delivered in person."

Benilda sighed and stood. "My kindness has made him lazy. Is he prepared to offer a finger?"

Indawat bowed respectfully. "He is prepared to accept whatever your judgment calls for, my love."

"Then he is not entirely useless, after all." She cast one last look back at us. "Play well until I return."

And then she swept from the room, Indawat trailing behind

her. He paused in the doorway to light his cigarette at last, and to wave warmly to me. Then the door slid shut.

The three of us stood there, surrounded by bright green leaves and thick, humid air.

"So." Diwata folded her arms again. "You're Cheza, huh?"

I shook my head. "Tenny."

"Tita Benilda called you Cheza, so that makes you Cheza." She jerked a thumb at herself. "And I'm your até now, so you've gotta do what I say, you hear?"

I folded my arms to match her posture, and glared up at her. "The kids at school call me Tenny."

"You're not going to that school anymore," Diwata sneered.

"You'll be attending Pakuanjang Academy with us," Dalisa said, a good deal more kindly.

Her gentleness didn't really do anything for me. I dug in. "My mom called me Tenny."

"That was when you were a Tenlonghari," Dalisa said. Despite how young she was, she had the pleasant patience of a first grade teacher. "You're a Lacanilao now."

"And besides," Diwata added, "your mom's dead."

There was no build-up. I just erupted toward her, a snarling cloud of short hair and sharp nails. But before I got close, strong arms held me in place no matter how hard I pushed. Dalisa stood in front of me, hands pinned to my shoulders, her deep brown eyes staring right into mine.

"We lost our father, too," she said firmly. "Hanging on to her won't bring her back. Trust me, Ch— *Tenny*. We've both been there."

I wasn't the most rational girl in the world, but her words managed to cut through the rage fog that was choking my head. I looked at her over the top rim of my glasses, and for the first time since we'd been introduced I saw a girl who was like me. Inch by inch, degree by degree, I relaxed. Dalisa gave me a small, grateful nod, and let her arms fall away.

And then Diwata said, "Yeah. You spend all your time crying over your mommy, you'll never make it here."

"*Dawa*," Dalisa snapped at her, but it was too late. I'd slipped past her with a roar and tackled her sister to the ground, dead set on biting off her fucking nose if I could.

Diwata and I were so wrapped up in fighting each other, and Dalisa so intent on separating us, that none of us noticed the familiar shadow of Benilda until it was too late.

Diwata and I leapt to our feet. Her dress was torn, my glasses askew, and both of us were breathing hard. Dalisa was better for the wear than either of us, and the first to sink in to a respectful bow. Diwata and I glared at each other over her arched back, then copied her.

"This was a test," Benilda said simply. "And you failed."

All three of us straightened up.

"Benilda," I said, "you didn't hear what she—"

"I tried to warn you," Diwata cut across me. "You started a fight. Now you failed the test."

"No, Dawa," Benilda said. "The one who failed the test is you."

Diwata sputtered like a wet cat. "*What?*" she shrieked. "Me? What did I do? She's the one who started it! She'll never fit in here!"

"She belongs with us," Benilda said, firmly and simply. "You are her até now. That makes you responsible for her." She gestured to the greenhouse around us, and to the mansion it was attached to. "We Biranese came here, to where people hated us, and built this from nothing. We did it because we had family. Someday, all of this may be gone. And when it is, the only thing you will have left to rely on—the only thing you can ever rely on—is family."

Dalisa sank into another respectful bow, but her sister wasn't getting the message.

"But she's a Tenlonghari!" She pointed at me, exasperated. "She's not a Lacanilao like Sasa and me! She's not *family*!"

Benilda's face softened as she took Diwata's hand in hers. The feeling of that gentle hand over mine was still fresh in my memory. But it couldn't have been farther from what I saw: Diwata squirming with pain as Benilda patiently squeezed her little hand tighter and tighter and tighter. When she finally cried out, Benilda let her arm drop, and Diwata cradled it to her body. She looked up at her aunt with wide, hurt eyes.

Benilda replied with a cold, firm stare. That, and a simple sentence.

"She is family now."

7

Now

Age 30

By the time I got to her doorstep, my legs had all but given out. I didn't really talk much to the Great Bird these days, but with every step I took, I caught myself reciting all the old prayers that'd been drilled into me in school. My tongue wandered down familiar paths, paved in verses and pleas I'd uttered a thousand times before. But my mind kept it simpler:

Great Bird, please let her still live here, 'cause I really don't wanna have to explain this shit to a stranger.

With one hand, I traced a final sign of the pinion on my forehead.

And with my other, I knocked on the door.

As I waited for an answer, I took in the place with tired eyes. The construction had all the hallmarks of a rush job: chipped floorboards and low, narrow hallways, to save on material. Shallow stairs had led me up here: good for short-term build crews, useless for day-to-day life. And the whole building itself was so spindly that the only thing stopping it from tipping over was the other tenements it was butted up against.

85

That, I knew, had actually been a design choice by the original developer. A boom of workers and immigrants at the turn of the century, all needing a place to live, and all desperate enough to overpay for it. Making the tenements lean against each other saved on material costs, and it kept the tenants good and dependent on the buildings' owner for occasional repairs.

Your family was a piece of work, Cole.

But it ain't like I could say different about mine.

I heard light, controlled footsteps. To the untrained ear, a dancer's. But I knew it was the gait of someone used to sneaking up behind folks and slitting a throat or two. I just had to hope I could get a word in edgewise before her old habits kicked in.

At last, the door slid open. The woman behind it was Biranese, like me. Not as tall, but a damn sight prettier than I was. Her bare arms were corded with lithe muscle, the way mine had been once, though she sported forearm tattoos of big, leaping fish. Honestly, she and I didn't look that much alike at all. But if you hung around the two of us long enough, you'd know right away from how we walked and the words we used: we were family.

I nodded at the smoldering cigarette in her mouth. "Smoking, até?" I felt my tongue getting clumsier as exhaustion took hold of me. "You'd break Benilda's heart."

It tumbled from her open lips.

"Put that out," I said, as it spat sparks across the floor. "And wait for me to wake up before you kill me."

And then I pitched forward like a rose snipped at the stem.

I'd have given my odds of waking up the next morning at 50/50, tops.

I'd have given the odds of waking up under a warm, heavy blanket a big fat zero.

86

And yet.

I sat up and clutched my midsection with a groan. I guessed whatever the Monster had done to my ribcage wasn't the kind of damage I could just sleep off. My arms felt like rice pudding after last night's scrap, and my hands hurt like I'd just come off a triple shift. All yesterday's travel had left my feet throbbing and aching. Worst of all, my back hurt like hell, too.

But near as I could tell, that was just from being thirty.

My glasses were on a low wooden table right next to me. When I put them on, I wrinkled my nose; they'd been parked right next to a half-full ashtray, and somehow managed to absorb a bit of the smell. But I guessed by now, I probably smelled like an ashtray, too.

I'd never known my sister to be much of a decorator, but her place was better than the dungeon I'd made this place into back when it'd been mine. It had only a single narrow window, but mirrors on the walls meant even the faint grey morning sun could light up the whole room. There was a comfortable-looking old couch with a sagging middle, and I was lying on a soft white rug that had been stained faintly yellow by years of cigarette smoke. My wooden trunk sat in the corner like an obedient dog.

Reflexively, my hand went to my chest. I was fully clothed, but when my fingers closed around the empty space where my necklace should've dangled, I suddenly felt naked.

On the low table next to me was a greasy brown paper bag. My heart began to beat faster. I recognized those grease stains. And sure enough, when I opened it there was a trio of kelp rolls, their crispy golden shells still oily and warm.

"You know how fucking long it's been since I had a real, honest-to-Bird kelp roll?" I rasped into the apartment.

A reply sailed to me from the kitchen at the far end of the place. "I really don't care."

You remember your first ever kelp roll, Cole? I remember you telling me you'd had them before, then describing to me some prissy little thing you'd eaten off an appetizers tray at someone's yard party once. I remember you frowning a little when the waiter had set ours down in front of us. And I remember the slow spread of rapture across your face after your first bite, muted and powerful like a bomb going off underwater. I think that's how I felt now, taking my first bite in my sister's sitting room.

They were at least twenty minutes old, but they were still good and crisp. And instead of the pork and scallions you got from Biranese lumpia, these had a chewy saltiness that was like nothing else in the world. I hadn't ever known it to catch on anywhere else in the world, so maybe it was a flavor you could only love if you'd grown up with it. But as far as I was concerned, after the night I'd just had, these kelp rolls were maybe the best fucking thing I'd ever eaten in my entire life.

My words navigated their way around my last mouthful. "You gonna come in here and talk to me, or are we just gonna shout at each other until I go away?"

"There's a lot of knives in here, Tenny."

"If you were gonna kill me, why the kelp rolls? Fattening me up to eat me? Times can't be that lean."

At last she appeared in the doorway, a scowl on her face. She'd done her hair up for the morning, and she sported a white medical patch on her bare brown shoulder. In one hand, she held a steaming cup of tea. In the other, a big and shiny knife. "They weren't, until the ocean spat you back up on my doorstep."

I eyed the knife carefully. I'd expected her to have one, but I was still wary. Every culture has knives, but they meant something extra if you were Biranese.

And more specifically, if you were Biranese and had a grudge to settle.

I decided my best way forward was to ignore it unless she tried to stick me with it. "What's with the shoulder? Cut yourself shaving?"

"New hormone treatment from the mainland," she breezed, sitting down on the couch opposite me and setting her tea where my glasses had been. "I only have to do it every other day."

"Guess it beats the pills," I ventured. I remembered her taking them every morning with breakfast, as much a morning ritual as me doing my hair.

Her expression clouded. "The pills were a lot easier to get my hands on when I didn't want to leave a trail. The patch, you need to sign all kinds of papers, which is really something when you're supposed to be dead. Which, speaking of, why the fuck are you alive, Tenny?"

"I'll get to that in a sec. Thanks for the tea." On the Slats, offering someone the precious water that went into making tea was a sign of welcome. The fact that she'd come out with one cup instead of two sent me a pretty clear message, but I reached for it anyway. I was parched enough to risk the rudeness.

Fast as a striking snake, she stabbed for my hand. I yanked it back just in time and the knife quivered upright in the table. She left it there, waiting until it was completely still before she repeated, "Why the fuck are you alive, Tenny?"

I leaned back and tried to play it casual, then immediately regretted it. Turns out when you lean, you use a whole lot of muscles along your ribs. Who knew?

"I ain't," I tried. "I'm just a branch snapping back after it's been bent too far."

"The story I heard was a whole lot less poetic." Her voice was tight and small, like a watch spring.

89

"Oh yeah?" I said. "And what *was* the official story on where I went? I'm still piecing shit together, you see."

She laughed. Not in a nice way. "You won't like it."

"You think I like anything about all this?" I snapped.

"After he took over, our new governor called a big press conference. Laid the whole story out for the entire city to hear." She reached for her smokes.

"Could you please not?" I asked, with a rub of my temples.

She ignored me and dropped the lit match into the ashtray. I turned my nose from her, but the stink found me anyway.

"He told us," she went on, "that his former partner, the vigilante known as the Red Rose, had been brought to justice and executed ..." She took a long drag, but I could tell she was hesitating. But she couldn't keep it up forever, so at last she had to finish: "For murdering labor activist Pham Binh Cong."

I was beyond shocked. My rage was trying to spark to life, but it was like striking matches on a windy day. By the fucking Bird, Cole, I'd thought you were a bastard among bastards before. But now you'd given me license to make our reckoning messy.

At the thought of what I'd do to make you pay for this, my fury finally started to take shape. But before I could let any of it out, my sister brought her hand to rest on the handle of her knife.

"You've got a more colorful temper than most, Tenny," she said. "You express it in any way that could endanger my security deposit, I'll simplify this situation real fast." Apparently I didn't wipe my anger off my face fast enough, because she tightened her grip ever so slightly. "I didn't make up that story. Your old friend the Governor did. So don't make this my problem, because you won't like how I solve it."

I forced myself to shake off the vivid image of how it would

90

feel to break your bones one by one, starting with your finger-tips and working my way up your arm.

An ugly feeling wormed its way up my throat, childish and afraid. It forced itself out of me as a question that made my voice tremble when I asked it. "Do you believe it?"

"I watched you kill your own sister, Tenny. What the hell do you think?"

I flinched at the invocation. Like the knife, I'd known it was coming. And like the knife, knowing it was coming hadn't made confronting it any easier.

"That," I rasped, "was diff—"

"But even if you never gave a shit about family," she went on, "I can trust that you've always given a shit about yourself. So no, Tenny, I never bought that story."

It was hard to feel any gratitude, even though I knew I owed it. I was being eaten alive by my sheer hatred for you. And the odor of her cigarettes made my temples throb. But I stopped myself from saying anything nasty, which was a big step for me.

"That said"—she stabbed out her cigarette in the ash-tray—"I do want to know what happened that day."

There was a short list of folks I felt like hashing out that day with, and she wasn't one of them. "Nothing worth telling the wind."

She sighed. "You don't seem to appreciate the position you're in here. You spilled the blood of my blood. Honor de-mands I spill enough of yours to make us even. Or have you forgotten pahingán?"

"'Course not," I muttered. My eyes traced her knife's edge. Was that a speck of dried blood I saw, or just a trick of the light?

"And even with all your scary powers, I bet I could prob-ably do it with the shape you're in. So if you wanna keep your secrets, that's fine. You can take them to your grave. But if you want my help, which you clearly do ..."

No one cuts through you like family does, Cole.

"Why didn't *you* ever kill Binh?" I asked at last.

"Oh, I drew up a whole load of plans for it," she said airily.

Fresh fury gripped me.

Unfazed, she pulled out another cigarette. "You're really that surprised? He ran a union. We were strike breakers. Of course we thought about having him killed. It was always Benilda who held us back. Said she didn't know what you'd do to us if he turned up with a knife in his brain." She took a long, slow sip of tea. "She wasn't wrong."

"No, she wasn't." I was starting to wonder if being here was a mistake. Being around her, hearing her casually invoke Benilda's name ... it was all making me realize I hadn't buried my baggage half as deep as I'd thought. "Point is, he calls me out of the blue one day and says he needs help. When I show up to rescue him, my whole crew's there. They killed him. And when I ... had something to say about that, they killed me."

There was more to it than that. She knew it, I know it, and you sure as hell know it. But I wasn't in a mood to share any more than that.

She absorbed all this over another long sip of tea. Settled her mug back down on the table. "... Well, shit."

"Yeah."

"So let me guess, then: now that you've had some time to catch your breath under some sky the Bird's never flown, you've come back to kick-start your roaring rampage of revenge." She placed her mug next to her knife and gave me a look so stern, for a moment I could've sworn it was Benilda staring back at me. "And you've decided to make it my problem."

92

I blinked. "Well, if you wanna be an asshole about it ..."

"I do," she said. "Whose blood did I wash off you last night? I know it wasn't all yours."

"A mix," I muttered. "Most of it mine. But some of it came out of Mhap the—"

I didn't even have a chance to finish his name before she was up on her feet. "What the actual *fuck* were you thinking, leading that animal to my home?"

"Easy," I said. "He couldn't have followed me last night, not after I took the bastard's eye. He'll at least need a day to put some ice on it."

Her eyes narrowed, unamused. "I've spent the past ten years doing my best to live under a fucking rock—"

"It's Driftwood City," I said, with a bitter jab at the mountain silhouetted out her tiny window. "Living under a rock is all we do."

"—and once you put my scent in the Thorn Orphans' nostrils, all you feel like doing is telling jokes?"

"I gave him the slip."

"How can you *possibly* know that?"

"Because if I hadn't," I said quietly, "neither of us would still be breathing by now, and you know it."

She considered that, then at last sat back down. She drained her cup of tea in one steady go before continuing. Slowed her breathing, but I saw her hand trembling as she laid it in her lap.

"How did he even get the drop on you, anyway?" She gestured to the air around her head, which I guess was supposed to mean *shaman*. "I thought with your ... you know, your thing, no one could sneak up on you?"

The question caught me so off guard, I almost told her the truth.

"I think Cole found a way to block me from seeing them

93

all coming." The lie came as easy as the breath that carried it. "The only reason they managed to kill me last time was because he'd figured out a way to cut off my access. I'm still getting on my feet, after being gone for so long. By the time I take them on, I'll be back to all my old tricks."

It felt weird, to be talking about my shaman powers with her. Fighting on opposite sides of a union war, the Lacanilaos had figured out pretty fast that you and I could do some pretty wild stuff, but it wasn't like we'd ever sat down over dinner and chatted about it. Letting her ask about it now felt like exposing my bare throat.

I guess I was lucky she didn't know enough about shamans to call me on my shit. "Well, you'll still be facing the five of them," she said. "Plus, they have a whole army on their side. Every badge in the city's working for them. Not a bent one left. Your old pal with the metal pants has seen to that."

I frowned at the mention of Jali. She'd always been a fighter I respected, even tougher than the armor she wore. My show-down with her would've been tough enough one-on-one. But me versus her, plus a legion of badges at her back ...

I shook it off. There'd be time to reckon with her.

"What about the gangs? There has to be someone in the crooked game who's not happy with how the Governor's running things. Every thread you pull has another end."

She raised an eyebrow in recognition, but didn't comment on it. "There are a few players left, but none worth mentioning."

I gaped. "Not one?" You and I had spent eight years fighting gangs, and anytime we'd taken one down there had always been others ready to replace them.

"You think the glorious governor let them survive once he took over? He killed every gang who didn't surrender to him."

"What about the ones who did?"

"Who do you think wears the uniforms and badges these days?"

I hung my head. Great.

"Well," I sighed, "at least I already picked one rose. Only four to go."

She shot me a sharp look. "What?"

"Had a run-in with Roulette Wu in my other life, over in Malañong," I said. "Only one of us made it back here."

I wasn't sure what I expected her to say to that. I think I wanted her to be proud of me for killing Roulette, or at least impressed. But she looked at me with an expression that reminded me of a closed door.

"You went to Biranba?" Her voice had taken on an edge of awe. She carefully folded her hands into her lap, and I recognized it right away as the listening posture that Benilda had trained into all three of us growing up. "Did it measure up to all of Tito Indawat's stories? What was it like?"

I shrugged. "Hot. Like if Benilda's greenhouse was a whole country." I chuckled, even though it wasn't funny. I tried for a smile, but I was surprised by her expression. She wasn't annoyed or impatient; she looked disappointed. The silence between us hung, heavy and empty.

"Everything was a lot older over there," I said eventually. Lazily, I swept an arm to indicate the apartment around us. "All the stuff on this block goes back a hundred years, tops. Most of it less. The Slats we're living on? They got laid down three hundred years ago. Over in Biranba, though ... shit. There are *doorknobs* older than this entire town. It gave those places ... I dunno. Weight."

Her expression grew distant as I talked. For the first time since I'd woken up, the corner of her mouth crept up into the ghost of a smile. I got it. Only Driftwood City had ever been home, but it was hard not to develop an attachment to this mythical motherland the grown-ups always went on about. It didn't even feel like a real place, from the way Benilda and Indawat had talked to us about it. Biranba had felt like a land in a storybook.

I gave her a second to sit with that feeling before I pressed on. "Why didn't you ever go there?"

Her smile melted away, the last ice in a drink. "To Biranba?"

"Or anywhere, I don't know," I said. "The mainland's a big place." I tried to shift positions, and every part of my body told me to consider doing something else. That's how you know Mhap's a persuasive guy: he makes decisions for you even when he's not in the room. "The only reason you managed to last this long on the Slats was because I kept everyone off your back. Once you heard I was dead, why'd you stay?"

Her laugh was joyless and dry. "Tenny, the Slats are my home." She laughed again, bitter as over-steeped tea. "Where else would I go?"

I didn't have an answer for that. Driftwood City had only made sense when the world was a bigger place. But even though there had never been much for the people of the Slats as long as I'd been alive, they had hung around anyway for the exact same reason.

"How is he?" I asked eventually. "As governor, I mean."

"Well, the boatway runs on time now," she said, finally reaching for another smoke. "Can't fault him for that." She thought a moment, then added: "Everything runs on time now."

"Why's that sound like a bad thing when you say it?"

"I guess it's not ..." She took a thoughtful drag. "People don't have to collect rainwater anymore."

"I saw."

"But they don't get to stay out after ten, either."

I thought back. It was true; I hadn't seen anyone else waiting for the ferry last night.

"They don't have to worry about where their next bowl of rice is coming from, but they can't build anything that's not in the Governor's plan. And good luck trying to get the *Blue Star* to print anything that isn't a glowing write-up about what City Hall's done for us this week." She indicated her shoulder patch. "There's a group of folks like me that I see around town. A lot of them are all for the Governor, because he made the deals with Tsuna that got these stocked in our hospitals. And I won't lie: it beats the pills. For some of my friends, that's as far as it goes. Me . . . I don't know."

"You don't know?" I said. "Sounds pretty clear-cut to me. What's not to know?"

She blew a contemptuous mouthful of smoke right in my face. "I like being able to get what I need. I don't like relying on one guy to give it to me. Especially since I know how fast he can turn on someone."

A petty part of me was thrilled to hear there was something to be unhappy about. On the surface, the things she'd been talking about were everything you and I had ever fought for. And from what little I'd seen of Driftwood City since I'd been back, it looked like you'd gotten it all: water for everyone. Dignity for the worker. The end of crime. The death of the rich.

Roses every day.

But what I was hearing, Cole, was that as powerful as you were, you weren't a god.

"You know what I'm here to do. And you know what might happen if I succeed."

She nodded once. "I'd gotten there, yeah."

I studied her a long moment. "And . . .?"

"And what, Tenny?" she snarled at me with sudden impatience. "For one thing, I don't think you can pull it off. And even if you did, I don't think you could actually change things

97

by yourself. We've got all kinds of motion pictures and books and radio plays that tell us one person can make a difference, but not really. A person can kill another person by themselves. You specifically could kill five, maybe. But one person can't kill a system."

I hadn't said a thing about making changes. But I didn't feel like correcting her. So instead I laughed, doing my best to ignore the line of pain that carved itself up and down my ribcage when I did. "You can when the person and the system are the same thing."

"Well, it's not just any system, Ten. You're talking about killing a system that *works*." She gestured to the white patch on her arm once again. "That was how you always told yourself you were better than the family, right? 'Cause of what you were fighting for? This is it, right here. You're sitting in it. And if you were always willing to sacrifice yourself to make it happen, like you always said, how's it any different than the way things ended up shaking out for you?"

I narrowed my eyes. "You can't sacrifice what ain't yours," I said. "And Cole has never owned me."

I was satisfied when she didn't have an answer to that. Instead she said, "All that for a dead guy, huh?"

I didn't rise to the bait. "Of course for him," I said. "I've never been worth avenging. But Binh never asked for any of this shit. Least I can do is make that right."

"And for help, you came to someone who's honor-bound to spill your blood."

"You think you were my first choice?" I snapped. "I know you're bound by pahingán. I'm asking you for your word that until I take care of things, you won't take up that knife there and balance your scales. Once I've killed Cole, if you still really want to make your move ... I won't stop you."

Another sarcastic laugh from her. "And I'm supposed to

trust that if I decide yes, you'll sit there and let it happen? You, with all those powers of yours?"

I shrugged. "My song ended four years ago. You'd just be playing the coda."

"And then," she went on, "I'm supposed to believe that you'll actually trust me to make good on this promise if I make it to you?"

"No," I said. "I don't trust you. But I trust your honor. No matter how bad things got between us, até, I never doubted that."

That gave her some pause.

"You know," she said eventually, "I keep waiting for you to throw it in my face, that you're the reason I'm still kicking in the first place ... Why haven't you?"

"Because I didn't do it for you," I said, and meant it.

I could feel her probing for any hint of a lie. And I knew what she was thinking: she'd grown up in a house with me. If there was anyone left alive in the world who'd be able to tell when I was full of it, it'd be her.

She growled in frustration, then ground the heels of her palms into her eyes. "Tita Benilda," she muttered. "I wouldn't even be thinking about this if I didn't have Tita Benilda's voice in my ear right now."

"'*The only thing you can ever rely on is family*,'" I recited. Benilda had had a hard accent to pin down; a mishmash of Biranba and Driftwood City, the kind that you only ever heard from someone who'd truly let their heart belong to more than one place. Four years ago, I wouldn't have been able to do it. But the past four years had made me capable of a lot.

She let her arms drop and stared at me in grudging, impressed disbelief. "All the rest of us are dead, but you still really think you're a Lacanilao, don't you?"

I shrugged. "There are worse things to be."

"The girl I met in that greenhouse didn't think so. She would've died before she stopped being a Tenlonghari."

"And then she did," I snapped. "I'm just what's left. And if you help me, you can be the one to finish me off. For our sister."

If I'd invoked her too soon, she might've just gone for my throat and been done with it. But I wanted her to see I was serious about my offer. I'd already been waiting to die for four years. Killing you was the first time in a long time I'd felt any kind of direction. And once I'd done it ... well, what good would it really be to keep me around?

At long last, she withdrew her knife from the table. I readied myself in case she felt like throwing it, but instead she gently laid it down in front of her. "Put blood on it," she said. "Your life for my help. The way I see it," she added grimly, "you got your own blood oath to fulfill before I can get to mine. And if I kill you before it's done, I'll have to take it up for you." She heaved a tired, ragged sigh. "Our ancestors really should've thought of this shit when they were writing the rules for pahingán."

Without hesitation, I picked up the blade and ran my thumb across it. A bright red bead slid on to its surface and hung there like a jewel set in silver. It was a promise from one Biranese to another: a guarantee that the blood within you ran as true as the words without.

She inspected it, then nodded for me to put the knife down.

"So," she said, "this mad plan of yours. You've already done for Roulette. Who's next on your list?"

I ran through the options. "Anjali the Armored," I said, my voice quiet and firm as a footstep in a dark alley. "She's next."

Diwata inhaled hard through her nose, then let it go as a sigh. "I guess I should've known that when we're up against a go master with a blade fetish, a guy who likes to pretend he's a ghost, and an all-knowing, all-powerful city wizard—"

"Not a wizard," I said.

"—there would be no easy choices. But did you have to start with the one who carries enough hardware to storm a beach by herself?"

"Not just by herself," I said. "She's head of the police now, isn't she?"

Diwata hung her head. "Someday when I'm dead, I'm gonna give our ancestors an earful about these pahingán rules."

For just a moment, I eyed the knife on the table. Was Diwata having second thoughts? How quickly could I shape my driftwood trunk into a weapon or a shield? Just in case, I started to hone in on the faint musical aura living in the birch, readying myself to sing for my life.

"Well," she said eventually, "if you're gonna do that, you'll need info. What do you need me to do? Light some candles? Burn some herbs? Make you a salad and dress it with gull's blood? What?" she asked defensively when she caught my look. "I'm not the expert on how you wizards—"

"—not a wizard—"

"—do this stuff. What do you need from me so you can go into one of your trances and find out what you need?"

"For someone who doesn't seem to know the word 'shaman,' you sure seem to understand how it works."

She shrugged. "I've been to the motion pictures. What do you need?"

I shifted my weight and tried to channel some of that serious tone you always took when you were talking about mystical stuff. "I can't just rub my hands together and make a vision appear in a poof of smoke, you got it? This whole city is made up of threads—threads of life, threads of history, threads of time, threads of feelings that were felt deep enough to leave a mark. Every time I use my powers, I tug on one of those threads. And he's at the other end of every thread I tug. It's been interfering with my visions."

She stared unblinkingly at me as she crushed out her second smoke in the ashtray. "Really."

"I can't rely on anything I see in them. It could be him leading me into a trap. So I'm gonna need to get my information another way," I plowed on. "I need to do what Benilda did: listen to the wind."

Diwata raised an eyebrow. "You think a zephyr would talk to you? A Thorn Orphan? Hell, you think there are even any zephyrs left?"

I folded my arms. "I know there are, Dawa. Driftwood City isn't itself without zephyrs. Now, do you know any, or not?"

Diwata considered it. "All right, yeah, I know someone," she said. "One of the only ones left in the city these days, thanks to you all. But if I take you to them, you know they only give info for trade. So what're you going to trade to them?"

Sheepishly, I coughed.

My sister slumped in her seat and reached for another cigarette.

8

Fourteen years ago

Age 16

The first time I crossed paths with him, I was working on the line.

I was fresh out of Benilda's house. I hadn't told her I was planning to go, so I was sure she still had folks tearing the Slats apart to look for me. I hadn't really figured out what I was gonna do about that yet, but I did know that I needed money. And if I wasn't gonna play the crooked game to get some, that meant finding work. And the easiest place to catch a job in Driftwood City was at the Plant.

The Unified Utilities Plant was made of three departments. Its west wing was Farming: a stack of hanging fields where basically all the city's food grew. Its east wing was Power: a whole mess of turbines and generators that turned water into electricity. And the central wing, the most important one of all, was Water, where we inhaled the sea below us and exhaled it out into the city as its crystal-clear lifeblood. No matter what department they worked in, the thousands of folks who crewed the line were called salters. And as of two days ago, I was one of them.

The day I met him, my grey coveralls were still so new that they barely had any white salt spots on them. I'd made sure to get a job working Water; most of the Biranese salters were over in Farming, and they were sure to recognize me. I knew for a fact Benilda was tearing apart Birantown looking for me. Last thing I needed was for word to get back now, just when it felt like I was starting to make things happen for myself.

So I'd cut off my braid and tossed it in a gutter. Made sure to keep my flatcap tugged low, to shade my eyes. I did my best not to get noticed. And I'd thought I was doing a pretty good job, right up until I heard someone behind me call out, "Hey! You!"

I pretended like I didn't hear. I'd been assigned to give these bolts a good wrenching, and by the fucking Bird I was gonna wrench the shit out of them. And besides, why bother? He was probably talking to someone else anyway.

"Tall Biranese girl with the glasses and short hair!" he persisted.

He could mean anyone, I told myself.

"The one pretending that I'm not talking to her!"

That didn't leave me with much wiggle room.

I stopped with the wrenching and turned around. The man standing there was a few years older than me. Handsome, in a rough-hewn way, with sideswept black hair and tattoos of lotuses and lilies up and down his muscular forearms and a slender nose that looked like it'd been broken a few times. His beat-up coveralls were so flecked with salt that they were more white than grey. "When's the last time you stopped for some water?"

I glowered at him and stopped myself from automatically

104

wiping away some sweat. "None of your fucking business," I snarled, and turned back to my wrenching.

"You're new here," he told my back. "You don't know how much you're sweating out. Can't have you passing out when you're on the line." As he'd spoken, I'd heard him getting closer to me. Now, he came up alongside me and prodded a dented metal canteen under my nose. "Drink."

In the years after, we joked about it. I know now that he was trying to look out for his comrades. Especially the new one who seemed dead set on working herself to the bone. But just then, fresh from Benilda's house as I was, I'd had just about enough of people trying to look out for me.

I met his eye. "You're saying if I lose any more water, I could be in danger?"

He nodded.

Holding his gaze, I hocked a glob of spit right on to the floor.

Later, when I came to after passing out from dehydration, he wasn't around to gloat. Instead a younger woman, maybe about my age, perched at my side. Unlike Binh, she was slight and birdlike. But her slender nose looked just like his, minus a few punches to the face.

"What?" I fought to corral my thoughts against my pounding headache. "I don't rate a personal visit from the big guy? He sends his, what, cousin?"

"Sister." She dropped a canteen on my chest. "Whatever you were trying to prove, new girl, you proved something else." And then she left me there.

I never skipped a hydration break again, right up until the day my career as a salter came to its fiery end.

I saw Binh and his siblings around after that, but we never talked much. I kept away from the salter drink-ups, since the last thing I needed were the Biranese ones snitching me out to Benilda. Binh tried to be friends with all his comrades, but I wanted to be invisible. One of us had to win, and that time it was me.

The first time I met him—*really* met Pham Binh Cong—I was with you.

Two years after that

Two years before we met in the blaze of the Unified Utilities fire, a shipment of bootleg water hadn't yet been stolen out from under the noses of the Silver Tide Tong. And those bottles certainly hadn't reappeared mysteriously in Kelptown the next day, to the astonishment of everyone beneath the neighborhood's green-shingled roofs.

Two years before we realized we shared a rare gift, Benilda Lacanilao hadn't yet begun to observe a steady decline of her criminal operations in the borough of Oakyard.

Two years before we answered our city's call, your fathers were still sitting at the top of the Rock, pushing their workers as hard as they could because they didn't yet know what it looked like when the people pushed back.

Two years before we transformed from citizens into shamans, the powers that lurked in the shadows of Driftwood City on either side of the law had not yet raised their voices in an outraged chorus to ask: *Who the fuck are the Thorn Orphans?*

But you know as well as I do, Cole: a whole lot can happen in two years.

That particular evening was foggy. The darkening sky teased us with the promise of rain, and folks were leaving their buckets out anywhere they could. As we walked past one rickety wooden stoop, I saw a child putting out a whole collection of clay teacups next to their family's tin buckets. There was something growing in the air, like a fruit about to ripen. I smelled it in the wind and heard it in the city's song. Something big, it promised us, was coming.

"I never feel worse than when I see this," you sighed as we walked past stoop after stoop crowded with buckets and pots. "The thought that my family's driven an entire city to beg the sky for scraps ..."

"Ah, I don't know about that," I said with a big old grin. We'd been friends and roommates for six months now, and I'd gotten a good feel for your moods. It was fun to smile when you got like this. "I mean, don't get me wrong. Your dads are pieces of work, no question about that. But ... I don't know, Cole. Before Benilda took me in, I liked bucket parties."

You shot me a surprised look. "You ... did?"

"Sure." I pointed up the block, where another group of kids were chasing each other with buckets. "For long pours, you had to be out here, constantly switching out buckets so you could dump full ones in your basin. So you and your neighbors would have contests to see who could bring in the most water. You'd race each other through the streets, trying to see how fast you could go without spilling a drop."

You gaped up at me.

"... I feel like I'm not conveying the fun here," I deadpanned.

"You all had to make a *game* out of *survival*!" you squawked. "That makes me feel even *worse*!"

I chuckled and decided now was a good time to stop you from disappearing up your own ass.

"Yeah." Casually, I slipped my hands into my coat pockets. "We made a game out of survival. And even though that's kind of fucked up, it doesn't mean the game ain't fun."

You considered that, then coughed a little awkwardly. "It occurs to me," you said, "that maybe some things are ... not about me?"

"Don't worry." I cuffed you fondly on the shoulder. "Only some things, I promise."

You brooded. And for a solid block, I let you get away with it. Sometimes, you just needed to burn your embers down a bit. But as we crossed the narrow commuter bridge that stretched over a boatway canal, it became clear you fully intended to do more brooding, and I just didn't have that kind of time.

"We didn't become shamans so you could feel sorry for yourself," I said.

"No." You sighed again. "We became shamans so I could feel sorry for myself while being incredibly, incalculably powerful." Your turn to smile, and you did, in a pained sort of way. "I just want to tell these people that there's a better way, and it's coming soon. Right now, they just think of the Thorn Orphans as a particularly friendly gang."

"If they've even heard of us," I muttered.

"They don't know how much more we're capable of." You gestured, and I felt a tugging at the strings of power around us. Overhead, the gutters of the next four houses all gently bent themselves downward. Right away, I saw why: now the water they caught would flow more directly into the waiting buckets below.

"Why," I said, "do you always have the best ideas?" I picked up the game: subtle bends and twists in the gutters and eaves to channel the rainwater. The whole way we walked, we left a trail of secret waterworks. I caught your smile growing less cautious as we worked.

"So, " I said, "any idea what it wants us to see out here? I'd kind of been hoping to spend tonight in with a cup of tea."

"I'm only a shaman, the same as you are. Just because I speak for the city doesn't mean I know what it's saying. But I figure it has to be at least somewhat important, because—"

Without discussing it, we turned a corner, led by the city's

108

song. And when we did, we nearly walked straight into a column of marching people in salt-flecked grey coveralls.

We halted at the same time. Exchanged looks.

"Did you know?" I hissed.

"How would *I* know?" you said. "I'm a shaman, not a fortune-teller."

It was the first time I'd been around so many salters at once since the day of the fire. And for a second, I smelled smoke. Heard screams. As I saw those grey bodies pressed together, my breathing turned short and—

A hand laid itself on my arm. You looked up at me with calm, caring brown eyes. "*You're here*," you said softly. "*The place you went to is a memory, and one that you survived. Let me guide you back to where you are, and make sure you don't lose your way.*"

Moment by moment, my breathing slowed. And once I was able to take another breath, I managed to say, "Thank you."

"Of course." Your hand withdrew. "I remember what it was like, too."

I eyed you carefully. "And you're all right, seeing them like this?"

"No," you admitted after a moment. Your patrician face was a study in calculated calm, but for just a moment I saw your eyes glint with something else. "I remember it all, too."

In front of us, the salters marched: not like soldiers, in perfect little rows with their boots falling like sticks on a drum. But I heard a syncopated beat in their steps anyway. And when they raised their voices, they raised them as one.

"*No blood for salt!*" they chanted. "*No blood for salt!*"

You and I were far from the only ones standing there and watching them pass. Folks were coming out of their shops, or else glaring out from behind their windows. Kids put their buckets down and stared: in confusion. In fear.

In awe.

"What do you think all this is?" I said.

"Something we were supposed to see." Excitement danced in your eyes like flame. "Come on."

We trailed the column to Suchapratnam Park, where it linked up with another salters' march. You and I lingered at the park's weathered wooden archway as line after line of folks in grey coveralls paraded past us. And though there was no way they could have possibly heard it, I noticed that their footsteps fell perfectly in time with the city's song.

"How the hell did this sneak up on us?" I asked you, still in awe. "Ain't the point of being shamans that we're supposed to know everything?"

"We know what the city wants us to know ... and when it wants us to know it." A smile was creeping on to your face, spreading bigger with every second. If your mind was a machine, I would've heard its wheels spinning and motors roaring. "Let's see what else it wants us to know."

We definitely drew looks from the salters around us as we ducked our way through the crowd. Or at least, you ducked through. I was the kind of tall that meant folks just sort of moved out of my way. When I caught glances lingering on me, I turned up the collar of my long black overcoat and tugged my dark flatcap down lower. But that feeling of anticipation I'd felt in the air? It'd only grown stronger the further we dove into the crowd, like a quickening pulse.

And then, I came to a hard stop. You bumped right into my back.

"What is it?" you asked.

"I see it," I said, my voice quiet with surprise. "I see him."

"Well," you grumbled down by my shoulder, "that sounds wonderful for you."

"Should've eaten your vegetables, rich boy."

110

But my jab was half-hearted. A hush was falling over the crowd around us, and I found I wasn't immune.

Binh stood atop an upturned wooden crate, upon which someone had stamped the word MUSHROOMS. Even from this distance, I clocked new ink on his forearms, and his black hair was combed forward instead of swept back. But there was no mistaking him. Two salters flanked him, holding up a banner that fluttered in the pre-storm breeze. In the script of four different languages, it screamed: BRETHREN OF SALT.

You and I exchanged a glance as the city's song faded away. It was like we'd arrived right in time for the overture to end and the curtain to rise.

"Some of you know me, and some of you don't," Binh began. "Some of you were born here in Driftwood City, and some of you washed up here because life's cruel that way. Some of you work in Power, bringing light to our streets. Some of you work in Farming, putting food in our bellies. And some of you work with me in Water, pumping blood into the veins of our home. But no matter what division you're in ... *we are all of us salters*."

Cheers erupted.

"There was a time when the Rock knew that we salters were the lifeblood of Driftwood City." He pointed to the distant silhouette of our city's other borough. Only half of it was visible through the gloom. The rest of it had been swallowed up by fog. "There was a time when they treated us like workers. But they've forgotten, and now they only see us as another mine to pick dry!"

The assembled salters exchanged cheers for jeers. Though the city was quiet in my ear, I felt it stir as if it were laying a bow across its strings.

"Think of the wood on which we stand!" he boomed. "All of it, harvested and brought hundreds of leagues across the ocean to build the Slats! But you can't just cut down trees; you have to plant them, too!"

The crowd started to make more noise, but this time he gestured for them to be quiet. I've never known a rowdy pack of salters to take a cue. But their voices lowered when he raised his hand.

"Conditions at the Plant have deteriorated," Binh said soberly. "These days, if a salter gets their hand stuck in a machine, they're shown the door without a coin of severance or care. They charge a fortune for food and water, and don't pay any of us enough to buy it. Now, if we want water to drink, water to cook with, water to wash with, we've got two choices: pay too much to the bloodsuckers who think it's theirs—"

You shifted uncomfortably.

"—or pay too much to the gangsters who prey on us in our time of need!"

And then it was my turn to copy you.

"They have made it so we can't live, because we're all too busy surviving!" he shouted over the rising cheers and chants of *No blood for salt*. "And as of six months ago, we can't even do that anymore! Malfunctioning equipment! Locked exits! *And management that would light us all on fire just to keep themselves warm!*"

The crowd wasn't cheering anymore; they roared. The anger I felt in their voices could have seared my cheeks.

You looked around uneasily. "He's going to start a riot."

I shook my head, unable to take my eyes off him. "Watch this."

As loud as it was, Binh's voice cut effortlessly through all the noise, clear and strong.

"We've soldiered on in our fight for dignity and equality without the raised voices and strong hands of three hundred and fifty-two of our brethren, but I promise you this—*we will*

112

not lose a single soul more to their negligence and greed! Standing before you now, I officially declare that the Brethren of Salt are walking away from the Plant, and we will not come back"—he pointed up at the huge, dark shape of the mountain above us all—"*until the Rock moves!*"

When I looked down at my hands, I saw that they'd practically started applauding on their own.

"Suriwong Pakuanjangnambhar has forgotten an important and unavoidable truth: that a society is only as rich as its poorest. But starting tonight, my Brethren ... *We! Remind! Him!*"

And right on fucking cue, the rainclouds burst open.

Raucous cheering erupted all over the crowded park. Everywhere we looked, salters were pumping their fists into the air. Stamping their feet. When he leapt down from the crate of mushrooms, it was into a sea of callused hands, all reaching out to pat him on the back and lift him up. They marched, and now the falling rain was their drummer.

"Who is that man?" you breathed. You stared at him in wonder.

Wonder stirred in my chest, too ... among other things.

"Binh," I said. "His name's Binh."

"Incredible." Your breath instantly fogged on the cold, rain-spattered glass of our sitting room window.

"Why're you acting like you've never heard of him before?" I said. I sat at the lopsided little dining table beneath our big round window, chowing down on a bag of kelp rolls we'd grabbed on the way home. "Guy's been a troublemaker since long before this. You telling me your fathers don't keep a list of guys like him in a drawer somewhere, to take care of down the line?"

"Of course they do. But it was only ever a list. They believed that those employees could talk as loud as they wanted,

113

because economic pressure would be more than enough to keep everyone else in line." You turned from the window, shame on your face. "And I'm embarrassed to admit that I believed it, too."

I rolled my eyes. "Again with the guilt thing," I sighed. "How many times we gotta do this, Cole? You were a kid. You couldn't have made a difference. You only just came of age now, and look at you!" I gestured to our meager apartment, with its mismatched furniture and scuffed floors and the permanently indented sofa where you slept every night. "You threw in with the right side, didn't you? First chance you got. We both did."

I expected another embarrassed admission that I was right. I mean, I was.

But instead, you frowned a little and then took your usual seat opposite me. "Have I ever told you what happened to me when I got my powers?"

"Uh, yeah," I said. "I was there, remember? Big fire, lots of death?"

You shook your head, and a lock of your silver hair fell loose down your forehead. You smoothed it back into place, and delicately helped yourself to a kelp roll. "I was at home when it first happened. Sitting in my room, getting ready for the day, when I was swallowed by a vision."

I cocked my head. You'd never told me this before. "What did the spirit show you?"

You swallowed a mouthful of kelp roll before answering. "A machine, Tenny. A big, clanking nightmare that belched black smoke into the sky. Politics and police and media all interlocking like gears, their teeth greased with blood. And when those gears turned, I felt the pain of every single person who'd ever been crushed between them. I heard every. Single. Scream." You bored into me with haunted eyes. "And after only a minute of hearing them, I knew I would do anything and everything to make them stop."

I sat there, unsure of what to say. This was some heavy shit. It was also the most you'd opened up to me in the six months we'd been living and working and fighting together. If you were a fine wood, it was like watching you peel back your own finish and veneer to reveal your raw grains and knots to me. I couldn't imagine having that kind of courage, Cole. I still can't.

You looked at me soberly. "Do you know how many people my family have exploited over the centuries? How many lives we've spent just so we could buy a nicer couch for our third sitting room?" The disgust in your voice was strong enough to turn my kelp roll bitter. "If you felt all that dumped on to your shoulders, how would you ever find a way to crawl out from under it?"

I leaned back in my chair and took a long breath. But when I thought back on how all that squared with everything I'd observed about you, it made sense. We'd talked about the guilt thing a few times now, because you always wandered back to it. Now, I was starting to get a clearer picture of why.

"You could have told me that before," I said at last. "I would've understood."

You shook your head. "I grew up in luxury. Every comfort I've ever experienced is tainted with blood and salt. You may be a shaman, but you—"

"Grew up the adopted daughter of the top player in the crooked game," I said, with a roll of my eyes. "Rich enough to build and keep a greenhouse full of tropical flowers in a cold, waterless city. You ain't the only one trying to balance a scale here, Cole. Hate yourself for it if you want, but it'll take a lot more than that for me to."

For a long second, we sat there together. Much as I didn't

like silences, I let this one breathe. Let the spirit fill it with the soft, eerie horns it was piping into your ears and mine. Let us and our city just *be* for a moment.

"I thought I would have to do something drastic to break the machine," you said eventually. "That's why I wanted to fight alongside you. I recognized immediately that you and I could do great things together. But standing there in the park, surrounded by all those salters, hearing their voices raised as one ..."

"You're thinking Binh could be what breaks the machine?"

You nodded fervently. "It's not another vision, just a feeling. But I believe he can be the actual change that Driftwood City needs. He could give the people roses every day."

Your sudden passion surprised me, but it was hard not to smile as I watched you. I didn't like the mopey Cole all that much. This version of you, the one with a clever glint in your eye and hope in your voice, was a lot more to my liking.

"Your fathers won't take this strike lying down," I said. "Binh will need some help."

Another kelp roll disappeared into your mouth. "He will," you agreed.

"Well, you're the mastermind." I gestured to our rain-flecked window, and the glowing city that stretched out into the dark. "What do we do first?"

That fervor had spread to your eyes, and the evening light turned them into twin amber flames. You turned them to look out over the home that was about to become our battleground.

"Anything and everything."

Part Three

The Second Revenge!
The Strength of the Blue
Rose

9

Now

Age 30

Zephyrs got their name because whenever anyone asked one where they got their information, a zephyr was obligated by their Guild to smirk mysteriously and reply, "I heard it on the wind." For three solid centuries, they were respected tradespeople on the Slats. It was a difficult line of work to break into—not like anyone was just gonna give a novice zephyr a few secrets to get started with. But once a zephyr did start to make a name for themselves and get the Guild's blessing, they could look forward to a career where, in Driftwood City's famously rocky economy, they would always do pretty well no matter what.

Of course, they were also painting all kinds of targets on their backs, because no one likes a fucking tattletale.

This particular tattletale was named Pamin. They made their home and office in a little tin shack in a scrapyard at the waterfront of the Shoots. The whole place looked refreshingly allergic to all your urban renewal. There was no fresh paint, no new bamboo streets, no new lamps. The inside of their home was even more disorderly. If there was a flat surface, it was covered in stuff. Dossiers, books, boxes, piles of trinkets and foreign coins, even something that looked like a bag of sawdust. I might've called it a mess, if I didn't get the feeling that there *was* a system—just one that only made sense to its owner.

The owner in question eyed me disdainfully over the bare feet they'd propped up on their cluttered desk. At first sight, my trigger for disrespect had gone off. But Diwata had spelled it out for me more clearly: they just didn't like shoes. They were Samnati, like you: brown skin, brown eyes, silver hair. Theirs was tied up in a red, grease-stained bandana. And thanks to four years in a place that had foxes, I could find it in me to say they had a foxlike face, which was currently scrunched with dislike.

"A Thorn Orphan, Diwata? Whatever you're about to ask me for, I hope you're ready to hear me say 'no.'"

I decided it was better to skip the part where I tried to deny it. "Ain't you even a little surprised that I'm alive?"

"It's my job to give, store, and take information, not interpret it," they said. "Surprise is unprofessional." They regarded Diwata again. "I take it she's the one you grew up with? Tenny the Red Rose?"

Diwata nodded once.

"And you want me to help her, even though you've sworn pahingán against her?"

I took a step forward. "Who said she wants you to help me?"

"Well, I'm sure she didn't bring you along for moral support," said Pamin, who didn't look all that concerned by my looming-and-snarling routine. "I'll take a guess: you already killed the Yellow Rose. You're responsible for that ghastly injury sported by the Black Rose. Now you're looking to finish

120

that job, plus do for the rest, and you want information to help you along the way."

I bristled at their dismissive tone. "I thought you didn't interpret information."

"I said it's not my job to interpret information." They smirked. "I do that as a hobby." They slipped their feet off their desk, then clasped their hands together thoughtfully. "Red Rose, tell me what zephyrs used to do when someone made an enemy of the Guild."

My teeth set. I didn't like power plays. "We all know—"

"I know we all know," Pamin cut across me. "But you're not in a position to say no to me. Otherwise, you would've gone to literally anyone but a zephyr."

I shot a look at Diwata. She shrugged: *Hey, it's your meeting*.

Fine. So I was on my own here. "The Guild would put together a file of all that person's weaknesses and secrets, and then make sure that folder found its way into the hands of their worst enemy. I think the official zephyr term for it was 'a dick move.'"

They leaned forward on their bony elbows. "And do you know where the Guild is today?"

I shifted my weight from one foot to another. "We had no way of knowing what—"

"The gangs always listened to whatever we told them," Pamin said quietly. "Right up until we tried to tell them we weren't helping the most well-informed outfit in the crooked game ... you." Their smile was joyless. "Our little strategy didn't work when everyone else decided that their worst enemy was us."

"You can't lay that shit at the feet of the Thorn Orphans," I snarled, my hackles raised. "We never told anyone the Guild was giving us our information. We always got it ourselves."

"Oh, I know," they breezed. "But when the other gangs

121

started slaughtering us just because they were desperate to bloody your nose ... where were the noble Thorn Orphans, defenders of the downtrodden and champions of the people?" Slowly, they rose. They were tiny, but I felt a ripple of unease anyway. "We were people, Red Rose. We were downtrodden. And you let us die. As far as I know, there are only four zephyrs left in Driftwood City, and the only reason we're still here is because the Blue Rose hasn't got around to us yet."

"Then do what the Guild would've done," I said fiercely. "Give me everything you've got on her and let me take care of the rest."

"They killed you once," Pamin said. "How am I supposed to believe that you'd do better the second time around?"

Diwata cleared her throat uncomfortably. "She's good for it, Pamin. We fought on opposite sides of a war, and no one knows you like an enemy."

Those two sentences seemed to carry more weight than the total of everything I'd said. Pamin's anger lowered from a boil to a simmer.

"This, I don't understand," they said, sitting back down and gesturing between the two of us. "I'm not Biranese, but I've been around long enough to know pahingán is a pretty serious thing. You've been bound by blood to kill her, Dawa. And the Governor's reign hasn't been so bad for us. So why are you making her case now?"

I opened my mouth to stop Diwata from speaking. It was always a dangerous thing when a zephyr started asking questions. Benilda taught us you were never supposed to give them information for free.

But Diwata held up a hand. And while I might've bitten her fingers off for that in a previous life, this time I shut up.

"You want the answer," she said, "you give us something in return."

122

Pamin looked taken aback ... and then very pleased. "It's nice to know there's one person left who respects the zephyr's trade. In exchange for that information, you'll get to ask me a single question about one of your targets. And considering how I feel about the Thorn Orphans," they added with a sharp look at me, "that's very generous."

"Dawa," I said, ignoring the glare she gave me for using that nickname. "I ain't letting you pay my tab for this."

"You get to learn my answer," Diwata said, still talking to Pamin. She jerked a thumb at me. "And she doesn't."

"Hoy!" I shouted.

Pamin rose to their feet again and offered out a hand. "Done."

"Just a fucking second!" I shouted, even as Diwata shook it. "I came here to sell you my fists, not my sister's secrets! You can't just—"

"Ten," Diwata said with a strained kind of calm. "Zephyrs only accept three kinds of currency: cash, information, or favors. You don't have any of the first two, and they were never going to take a favor from you when your credit's no good. I knew I'd be offering before we ever set foot in here. Now, shut up. Pamin, give me a pen and a piece of paper and I'll give you your answer."

They produced both from their desk, and Diwata stepped forward. As she bent to write her answer, I wrestled with the temptation to peek over her shoulder. I was tall enough. It would be so easy.

And then, she folded it up and passed it over to Pamin. They examined it for a moment, then slipped it into an envelope without reading it and slid it into their desk drawer.

"How do you know what she wrote is true?" I said.

"It could be because Benilda Lacanilao taught her daughters—or at least two of them—to respect the zephyrs," said Pamin. "Or because Diwata knows that I'm perfectly capable of carrying on the Guild's tradition for dealing with threats, and you both live in a city full of enemies. But the real reason would qualify as information, and I don't believe in free samples."

My fists curled up tight at my sides. Here at home, I constantly felt the absence of my old powers like my tongue would feel a missing molar. But right now I was particularly missing the days when I would've been able to sing with the city, and have it pipe its secrets into my heart.

"You want to be sore about it?" Pamin went on. "Be sore about it. That doesn't get you my trade for free. You Thorn Orphans thought you were too good for everyone else in the crooked game. But if you don't take the time to build credit with folks, don't be surprised when they don't trust you to levy a debt. Now," they said briskly, holding up one finger, "your sister's entitled you to a single question about the Blue Rose. Ask it carefully, and I'll answer as truthfully as my information permits. If I don't know the answer, I'll tell you and let you ask another until you hit on one I do know."

I nudged my glasses up my short, narrow nose. "What's the weakest point of her armor?"

"No one knows that." They narrowed their eyes. "And you knew I wouldn't."

I shrugged. "Since you don't want ours to be a relationship of trust, I had to check."

"Your sister bought a truthful answer," Pamin said. "Do that again, and I'll take it as a personal insult. Now ask your real question, Red Rose."

I nodded. I'd had a minute or so to think it over since negotiations had begun. There were a lot of things I already knew about Anjali, which actually clouded the issue more. What things could I trust to still be true? What might have changed in the past four years? What might have never been true? It was all too much for a single question to sum up.

I steadied myself. I needed to focus on the practicalities. "What bathhouse does she use these days?"

Pamin closed their eyes. Thought a moment. Opened them.

"Ishitani, in Oakyard," they said. "If you have anything further to trade for the times and days she tends to use it ..."

I shook my head. "That'll do." I already knew plenty about Ishitani Bathhouse.

My business concluded, I sank into a shallow but respectful bow. Any deeper, and it would just look like I was patronizing them, and people like a kiss-ass even less than they do a tattletale. "Thank you for the information. I'll get out of your hair now ..."

"Just a second." They leaned down to reach for another drawer in their desk. I tensed, and sang my power into the two small slats of driftwood I had hiding inside my coat sleeves. If they were about to try something on me, they'd end up with a skullful of birch for their trouble.

But Diwata didn't look concerned, and she was just as experienced a throat-slitter as I was. So I forced myself to stay still as Pamin plunked down a dusty old box of polished ash.

I froze. I'd seen that exact box before. I knew the patina on its metal corners. I could still picture the bedroom where it had occupied a permanent place under the bed.

"Where did you get that?" I breathed.

"Pham Binh Cong's cousin Thanh was one of us," said Pamin. "Shortly before he went, Binh gave this to Thanh in the hopes that it would find its way to you. Thanh gave it to me, suspecting that the Pham name would put him in the same danger that ultimately befell his cousin ... correctly, as it turned out."

"Him and half the Cuongvanese on the Slats," Diwata said with a smirk.

I ignored them both. As if sleepwalking, I moved forward

125

to the box. When I stood directly in front of it, I glanced at Pamin. They shrugged.

"Won't lie: I'm curious to see what's in it myself," they said. "The last will and testament of labor's fallen champion."

I raised an eyebrow. "You'd give that over to the woman who killed him?"

Pamin rolled their eyes. "You keep dangling this bait in front of my cute little nose, Red Rose, like you expect me to just hand you proof I'm some kind of idiot. Do you really want to test the limits of my professionalism any further?"

I glanced away from them. "Wanted to know what the wind had to say about it," I said quietly.

I caught just a shred of understanding in their narrowed, annoyed eyes.

"You seriously haven't looked in it?" said Diwata.

"Professionalism." They smiled at her in a way they hadn't even come close to with me. "Go on, then. Open it."

I made to reach for the box's lock ... and then stopped.

"That wouldn't be you looking for free information, would it?" I asked.

They looked up at me like ... well, a fox in a henhouse.

"You've got me," they said. "The spendiest coin for a zephyr is curiosity. How about this, then? Three questions, with follow-ups, about anything, if you let me see and read the contents of that box bequeathed to you by way of two zephyrs from the late Pham Binh Cong. That might just be the fairest price I've ever offered anyone." They extended a hand. "Shake on it, Red Rose?"

Diwata looked at me with surprise. I gathered that this wasn't the sort of offer that Pamin made every day.

Which is why it felt so good to look them in the eye and say, "Get fucked."

They reeled as if they'd been slapped.

"What?" I plucked the box off their desk. "You spend our whole meeting talking tough to me, and then you think I'm just gonna forget about it? Thanks for keeping this safe, but that's as far as our business is gonna go. Come on, Dawa."

She glared at me as I brushed past. I heard her mutter an apology to the zephyr, then storm out after me as we stepped onto a slick bamboo street. "What the fuck was that in there?" she said before the door even closed.

"I didn't need a lecture about the proud and noble history of the zephyrs and how the Thorn Orphans kicked them in the shins one time," I said. "They want to posture, they can see what it gets them."

"*They're a friend of mine.*"

"Not mine." I hefted the box. It felt surprisingly heavy. "And I don't owe them anything of Binh's. If he'd wanted them to see what was in here, he'd have left this to them, not me."

"Three questions," she hissed. "You could've had one for each of your old pals, or you could've asked three more questions about the Blue Rose and really torn her apart! All you had to do was let them read a few pages!"

"And all you had to do was let me pay for my information myself," I snapped. "You gonna tell me why you ponied up in there?"

She frowned. "'Ponied ...?'"

I rolled my eyes. "It's a land animal. Makes a lot more sense back in Biranba."

"*I know what the fuck a pony is.*"

"What I'm saying," I said, "is if how you throw your information around is your business, then how I keep mine is mine. Got it?"

Even coming from a town where almost everyone smoked, it was still maybe the most angrily I've ever seen someone light a cigarette.

"Trust me." I reached for the lock. I only needed to take a peek now; I'd read it properly later. "I did the smart thing, walking away from that deal. Who knows what kind of information Binh kept hidden in here?" I inspected the latch. It was held in place by a twistable brass knob, and as far as I could tell it hadn't been turned in years. Whatever else Pamin was, they were definitely as professional as they claimed to be.

"You don't know that," Diwata snapped. "Pamin has all kinds of info. Maybe they could've given you context for whatever you find in there."

"Please," I said. "Whatever message he wrote me, you can bet it'll be worth more than any three little questions I could ask Pamin. I don't trust them, and I don't need their help."

And then I twisted the knob.

My heart raced as I wondered what I'd find in there: a heartfelt letter? A mysterious map? A stack of emergency cash and a gun? This morning, I hadn't even known that the man I loved had left me a last will and testament. Now, I was going to get to hear his voice one last time.

I sucked in a breath, flipped open the lid—

—and found myself staring at an old, chapped boot.

I blinked.

Diwata glanced down into the box over my shoulder. "At last," she deadpanned. "All the treasures of Driftwood City, laid bare."

10

Eleven years ago

Age 19

Though I'd had my share of bedwarmers, and warmed a few in return, I hadn't exactly gone on what you'd call dates. I'd been in the same bars as folks I wanted to see naked, and either charmed or let myself be charmed into the kind of night where it happened. But small talk? Courtships? Holding hands on the boardwalk? All a new thing for me.

So I was surprised when Binh said, "I want to do something nice with you."

I stirred under his sheets. "You mean that wasn't nice just now ...?"

"It was more than." Fondly, he stroked my hair. He reached for his cigarettes. "You mind if I ...?"

I wasn't wild about the habit. Tatay Indawat's vice had given him bloody lungs, and the smell of smoke always shot me back to the fire. But it was his house, and my fingers and toes were still tingling, so I shrugged.

"Anyway. It's all been more than nice, Tenny. But it's been nine months, and I want it to be something else."

129

I sat up straight. This didn't feel like the kind of conversation to be lying down for. "You and I don't exactly keep normal hours."

"I know," Binh said.

"I've liked that we haven't let this get in the way of all the good stuff we're doing."

"I know," Binh said.

"And I think—"

"I want to take you on a date, Ten," said Binh. "Like I said, this has been more than nice. But I want more than 'more than nice.' I want to try this with you. You're the only..." He exhaled smoke, but I could tell it was just to give him a second to get his words in the right order. "I've wanted to be in this fight ever since I was old enough to march. You're the first person who's ever made me think about what my life might be like if it's ever won. And if that's not something you want to do, that's fine. I respect that." He gathered his knees under his covers, so they were up into his muscular, tattooed chest. "But if that's the case, it's probably better for me if you and I don't keep doing this."

And then he waited for my answer.

My first thought was that he was trying to trap me in a jar like some kind of rare bug. It made me want to rip the covers off, throw on whatever clothes I could find regardless of who owned them, and get the hell out.

But by the Great Bird's pointy beak, Cole, I wanted to learn more about the man who was brave enough to try it.

"Say I said yes," I said eventually. "What'd you have in mind?"

I stared up at the bathhouse. "This some kind of roundabout way of telling me I smell bad?"

He grinned and rested a fond hand on my shoulder. "That

130

wilted rose in your coat is all the hint you need. Come on. You'll see."

The bathhouse he'd picked was a friendly little place that had been running for fifty years. The family behind it had a few famous bathhouses across the sea in Honton, but three of its lesser cousins had banded together to start one right here on the Slats of Driftwood City. In both Slatspeak and Hontonese, their name was painted over the doorway in exquisite black ink: ISHITANI.

In a lobby that smelled faintly of lemons, all three Ishitanis waited for us with big, welcoming smiles.

"Hello," said the one standing in the middle, a plump young man with thinning hair and friendly eyes. The city sang his name to me: *Ishitani Kazuo*. I started to get other details about him, but I let them fade into the background of my focus. No point in prying if I didn't need to. "It's an honor to have your patronage tonight, Mr. Binh. Yours, and your"—I felt his eyes linger on my Biranese face—"guest's."

At my side, my hand clenched into a fist.

Casually, Binh hooked an arm around my waist. Instinct told me to pull away, but only for a moment. It didn't feel like he was trying to stake his territory. If he had been, I would've snapped his wrist.

"Given how tense things are between the salters and the Biranese community right now," he said cheerfully, "I think it's more important than ever for us to show our Biranese neighbors that they're still our neighbors."

Kazuo's throat bobbed. "Of course. No one knows better than a bathhouse master that we're all human ..." He added a sheepish laugh, and I had a lot of fun returning it with a dead-eyed stare.

"An hour, as agreed?" Binh said, reaching for his wallet.

I raised an eyebrow at him. Bathhouses were run-of-the-mill

kinds of places. Getting the royal treatment at one was unusual. What did he have planned for us in here?

One of the other cousins, a soft young woman named Kiyoko, held up a hand to stop him. "There'll be no need for that, Mr. Binh."

"Don't start," Binh warned. "Every worker deserves to be paid properly for their work."

"We agree," Kazuo cut in, eager to get back on Binh's good side. "So think of this as your payment for your work."

And then the three of them bowed in unison, before two of them pulled open the doors leading further into the bathhouse.

"Their patrons are all salters," Binh said as we headed deeper in. "A neighborhood place like this, you get close to your customers. And a lot of them—"

"Got lost in the fire, yeah," I said, tapping my ear. "The bathhouse is telling me all that. It's also telling me that we're in here alone."

He sighed. "I should've told you not to use your powers. Spoils the effect." Another sigh. "Well, come on. Might as well see it for yourself, then."

The bathing chamber had three pools: a small one for cold water, a small one for hot water, and a large one in the middle with warm water. Clouds of mist swirled up invitingly from all of them, even the cold pool. Normally, all three of them would've been full of people taking their weekly baths, stretching out and catching up with each other about life. The tiled walls and floors would've echoed pleasantly with their voices. But instead, the whole place was empty just for us.

I stared at it in shock. I hadn't realized it until that exact moment, but I'd never seen an empty bathhouse before. I turned to him with a surprised grin on my face. "And here I thought you wanted this thing of ours to be more than just getting naked together."

He smiled appreciatively, then knotted his fingers with mine. "I didn't exactly have a plan for what I wanted to do once you'd said yes. This was what I came up with. Call it a promise."

I took off my glasses. They were getting too steamed to use. It made Binh's face blurry, but I could fill in the details from memory. "A promise of what?"

"Two things." He held up a pair of fingers, then immediately ticked one off. "That we're gonna make it so every salter we're fighting for can have their own private bath someday if they want, just like the folks up on the Rock." He let the second finger curl back down. "And that when it comes to fighting the fight and loving each other, we can do two things at once."

My hand dropped away in shock.

Benilda had never said she loved me. Shown it to me plenty of ways, but there's power in just hearing the words. Same went for my sisters. None of the salters I'd worked with had—why would they?—and it wasn't like you had, either. I hadn't heard someone say those words to me since my mom.

Binh took a respectful step back. "If I didn't tell you," he said, "you would've figured it out eventually." He tapped his ear. "I wanted it to be on my terms."

I stared at him.

His confidence faltered. Quickly, he looked away from me. He indicated the pool beside us. "Did you ... still want to get in?"

Slowly, I broke into a smile. It lingered as we shucked our clothes and lowered ourselves into the water.

And when I woke up next to him the following morning, it was still there.

11
Now

Age 30

I left Binh's boot with Diwata when I went out that evening. I'd checked the heel and toe for hidden compartments, just in case Binh had slipped me an actual note, but I hadn't been surprised to find nothing. The boot was recognizably Binh's; there was no mistaking the chapping and scuffing. And if he'd left it specifically for me, I knew exactly what he'd wanted me to do: use my shaman powers to read it. Buried somewhere in its old leather were memories that Binh wanted me to see.

Binh. Clever fucking Binh. With a medium like that, there were only two real risks in play: that it might get intercepted by the one person who could read it besides me, or that the boot might get mistaken for trash and tossed. So of course he'd left it with the zephyrs. They were a source of information you'd never taken seriously. Of course you'd never think to look for something of his among them. Binh had thought of everything.

Except for what to do if his idiot girlfriend went and lost her powers.

I'd tried to read the thing anyway. I'm sure you're smirking at the thought, Cole—me sitting in Diwata's front room, head bowed and eyes closed, cradling an old boot like it was my firstborn. And I'll even admit something stupid: a part of me believed I might be able to crack it. Maybe, I'd thought, being in the city for a few days was all I needed to jump-start my old connection to it. But whatever you'd done to my powers in the boathouse that day held fast. I was still a woman who had absolute control over a few dozen square feet of old driftwood and shit all else.

And less each time, I thought. Roulette's lucky bullet had destroyed a few feet of birch, and my encounter with the Monster had left me without my lucky birchwood necklace. I'd need to be more careful if I wanted to have any left when I finally faced you.

Or better yet, have something even better up my sleeve. Maybe something Binh had left me.

So as I traveled downtown, I tried to reason my way through what he could've hidden in that damn boot. But that's where I ran into the classic problem of not knowing what I didn't know. This was an old, comfortable boot. He could've worn it anywhere. And he *had* worn it everywhere. It could've been witness to literally anything he'd been a part of while wearing it. Pretty much the only thing I knew for sure was that it hadn't just been one last love letter. That, he would've written in ink for anyone to see. No, whatever he'd left for me, it was something you'd deemed him worth killing over. And that meant I absolutely had to have it.

But first, I thought as my boatway ferry pulled up alongside the pier at Ugyen Yangchen station, I had to kill Anjali the Armored.

And before I did that, I had to make sure she wouldn't smell me coming.

I didn't pick the Ishitani Bathhouse, but I made sure to stay in the neighborhood. I wound up somewhere more modest, where the wall bore spots where the algae had been freshly scraped away. And I didn't stay soaking for too long, but I made sure to at least enjoy it a little. Nothing else about my night was going to be all that fun.

I emerged from that basin a new woman. I'd been carrying grime and sediment on my body that had come here all the way from the airship, from Biranba. The dirt under my fingernails, I'd earned in the kitchen of that small Malañong diner. And the faint sheen of grease that was now gone from my hair, hadn't all come from my pores. Now, I was refreshed. Completely a thing of Driftwood City once more.

Years of practice had made me a pro at weaving my braid together. When it was done, I tucked it up as best I could under my bell-shaped hat. No point in tipping Jali off.

I gave my top a stealthy sniff after I redressed, then wrinkled my nose. That would be the next order of business, once I got my hands on some spare coin. But when I headed out for Ishitani with my heavy driftwood trunk dragging behind me, at least I didn't look like something that had washed up alongside it anymore.

It was the first time I'd been out by myself since my encounter with the Monster. I'd watched a tiny sliver of the city go by through Diwata's narrow window, but it was nothing like being out on the boardwalk. You'd always communed with the city by sitting up in our Kelptown apartment and meditating. But this was how I did it, and it felt great to be doing things my way once again, with a chill in the air and the sun on my back.

At a newsstand, I took a moment to leaf through the day's papers. There was some day-to-day stuff that probably would've been interesting enough if I had time. But the only urgent news story I found was an announcement from your office that you were appointing Housing Minister Ngo to be the city's temporary head of Transportation.

With curiosity, I eyed the inset photograph of you two. At a podium was slender, beautiful Knife-Edge, his waist-length black hair frozen as it fluttered in some breeze. He'd exchanged his old black Thorn Orphans longcoat for a fitted, high-collared tunic with elegant floral embellishments on its right breast. The photograph was in black and white, but I knew the fabric of that tunic would be a bright, vibrant pink.

And standing just behind him, there you were. A shadow in the photograph cut a dark line across the top half of your face. I couldn't see your silver hair, or your calculating brown eyes. But I could see your straight posture. Your hands frozen mid-applause. And, of all things ... your smile. I knew your smile like I knew the city streets. But the expression you wore on your face in this photograph was an unfamiliar and practiced thing.

I scowled at the photograph. The perfect little son your fathers had wanted you to be ... you'd been him all along, hadn't you?

"Hey." Over the top of my paper, the guy behind the newsstand counter glared at me. "This ain't a library, you know? No more free reading for you."

I nearly snapped at him. But in a flash, I remembered what Binh would've had to say: *The worker is never the enemy, because their survival is never a crime*. And he was right.

Didn't mean the guy wasn't also a prick.

I slapped the paper down into the wrong bin. As I turned away, I caught the glint of something shiny and metal in his hand. My fighting instincts flared up: was he about to throw down with me over that? And sure enough, he was holding up a short-bladed knife. But as I started to sing to the birch boards woven into my trunk and feel their grains come alive, he produced something else with his other hand: a whole ripe mango, whose green-red skin he began to peel off.

I let my song die, and my driftwood trunk settled back down. I gaped at the fruit in his hand.

Mangoes had been prohibitive in Driftwood City as long as I'd been alive. The only reason I even knew what they were was because Nanay Benilda had always paid top coin to have them shipped in for her to eat. I didn't even really develop a taste for them until my stretch in Malañong, when you could buy them for pocket change from pop-up stands on the side of the road.

But now, here was a newsstand owner casually eating one. And from the sweet, tangy smell that filled the air, it was a damn ripe one, too. Plus, there was no mistaking the ease with which he carved around the mango's pit. This should've been an unfamiliar fruit for someone with his lot in life, and it clearly wasn't. Whatever magic you were working on the city's economy, it was having enough of an effect that a worker could now afford an exotic fruit habit.

I let that knowledge settle, but it didn't settle well.

I wondered what secrets I wasn't learning about Ishitani Bathhouse as I drew near the blue wooden arch standing ten feet out from its doorway. It was built to mimic a Hontonese resting shrine, with a sloping roof of clay that had been painted the color of seawater. From little vents and chimneys cleverly hidden in the claywork, welcoming curls of steam bled skyward. In isolation, it would've looked like an inviting country retreat. In the middle of a loud, stinking city, it had the air of a very nice tourist who'd got themselves good and lost.

I did a winding loop of the place, making a note of which alleys connected where, and which had dead ends. I caught sight of the loading dock in the back. Counted how many parking spaces were out front, and how accessible the streets were to large convoys of vehicles. This was the police chief I was about to fuck with; I had to assume that company would arrive fast, and in bulk.

It was easy enough for me to remember the layout of the bathhouse. Neither the front lobby, the changing rooms, the back office, nor the actual bathing room would give me somewhere to lurk. So that meant waiting outside and following Anjali in. A lot trickier, since the Armored was sharp. There was a more than decent chance she'd see me coming. But it was my best choice. So for old times' sake, I hoisted myself up on to a nearby rooftop to lie in wait.

Back in the day, I climbed buildings like a squirrel climbs trees. The city would sing to me exactly where I needed to put my hands and feet. Boards would catapult me a dozen feet in the air at a time. I had been lithe and fast, more of a shadow than a person as I scaled walls and drainpipes. But those days were far behind me, and I didn't know what was the bigger cause: that I was missing most of my old shaman powers, or that somewhere along the way I'd stopped being invincible and twenty-two.

By the time I hauled myself over the lip of a rooftop down the block, I was wheezing and spots were popping in front of my eyes. My hands took turns massaging my throbbing wrists.

"*Why,*" I wheezed, "*did I always do this? There were* stairs."

I collapsed on to my back, my chest heaving as I stared up at the night sky. It used to have stars in it, thanks to the patchy light grid. But while the streets below were now well lit once the sun set, the trade-off was a sky wiped as clean and dark as a chalkboard.

As I gathered my breath, and ignored all the formal complaints my body was lodging against me, I hummed a song.

Down in the alley where I'd left my driftwood trunk, the remnant of spirit in its fibers lifted its voice in reply. Neatly, the wooden box floated up through the air and deposited itself at my side. I kind of wanted to just sit there for a while, but I'd already spent a long time with Ishitani Bathhouse out of my line of sight. I had to get moving.

I hummed another song, and the driftwood warped itself apart until the constituent boards made up a single long, heavy, thick plank. And when I changed my tune, that plank stretched itself into a bridge to the next roof over. I scurried across it, keeping as low as I could and humming for the driftwood to curl up on itself behind me. I had four or five more of these roofs to cross, and it would only get riskier the closer I got to the bathhouse itself.

By the time I hunkered down on the rooftop adjacent to Ishitani Bathhouse, it still took half an hour before a sleek black police car pulled up to the curb. My whole body tensed as the driver, a uniformed officer, got out and came around to the badge-emblazoned passenger door.

The Anjali I'd known had worn her hair long and dark, with threads of azure silk woven into it. She'd worn dresses in every shade of blue, so that she always looked like an inviting pool of water. And when we'd gone into battle together, she'd always sported a madcap grin. Even when her face was hidden by her blue steel visor, I'd always been able to hear it in her voice.

But the woman ducking out of the car was small and severe. She'd exchanged her sapphire dresses for the muted dark blue of a career policewoman. Her long hair had been tamed into a tight, neat bun, with only a single stray lock running down the side of her face. And her mischievous, gleeful smile was nowhere to be seen. Even from up here in the dark, she just looked tired.

At the sight of her, my chest got tight. Either my ribs were shrinking, or my heart was about to explode. I caught myself breathing hard, remembering the sound of heavy metallic footsteps on blood-soaked birch. Fresh as a day-old wound, I relived the hopelessness and rage I'd felt when my eyes had first picked out her armored silhouette in the dark.

I wanted to stay up there. Not just until she left, but for the rest of my life. I didn't want her to know I was right there, didn't want her to know I was alive. Anything to avoid looking Jali in the eye again.

But that fear would get me killed. So I forced myself to watch her. I remembered my rage. And I drove that rage into myself like a nail that would hold me together even as I threatened to twist myself apart.

She strode up to the bathhouse, flanked by another pair of badges, while their ride drove off. I added that to my mental clock: at some point, that guy was gonna come back.

I stared at my hands until they stopped shaking. Took a deep breath. No turning back now.

The clever thing would've been to slip around the back, wedge the door open, and skulk my way into the bathing room proper so I could stick a splinter through her heart and call it a day. If I did it quietly enough, the guards out front wouldn't even hear anything. They wouldn't notice something was amiss until one of them went in and found their boss facedown in red bathwater.

But you were the clever one, Cole. Not me.

The moment the Armored and her entourage disappeared into the bathhouse, I counted to a hundred. And at a hundred and one, I began to sing again.

The driftwood flowed around me again, shaping itself into stairs that built themselves just before my feet landed on them, and unmade themselves the moment I stepped off. By the time

I set foot on the boardwalk again, the driftwood had folded in on itself to reform into my huge, heavy trunk.

The two officers were sitting in the lobby when I slid the door open.

"Ma'am," the first officer said as I entered. "You can't come in—"

"It's her!" the other guard said, going for her gun.

I swept out both hands, humming a sharp little arcane melody as I did. My trunk split into two rams, each flying to smash into an officer apiece. Both badges went down hard, one of them bleeding from his temple. I stepped past him, unconcerned. I hadn't been gentle, but I hadn't been brutal, either. Only one person needed to die tonight.

The attendant at the front desk yelped and put her hands up. I ignored her and strode right past, to the twinned sliding doors that led to the bathing room. As I got close, my glasses fogged in the hot and sticky air.

For just a moment, my steps faltered. I wasn't in Ishitani Bathhouse anymore; I was seven years old, approaching the greenhouse with my hand in Benilda's. I was twenty-seven years old, roasting in the heat of a cramped diner kitchen. I was eighteen, and all around me my comrades screamed as they burned.

But then I was back in the moment as I put a hand on each door and threw them wide open. I stepped past the threshold and into a huge bathing room. The floors were warm white stone, the walls rich dark wood. Steam floated all the way up to a high ceiling with bare wooden rafters. Water steadily streamed into the basin from the long nose of a stone seahorse that reared up in the corner of the basin.

And there, up to her neck in blue water, enveloped in roiling clouds of white steam was—

"*Anjali the Armored*." My voice carried to the farthest corners of the room.

Her hair was still up, but her arms had been raised for her to let it down. When she saw me, though, she gently let her arms slide back under the surface of the water. She looked at me like a person would look at a gun in someone's hand.

"Tenny." She glanced around at the bathhouse, as if seeing it for the first time. "Cornering me on a field where I'd have the fewest advantages. You were smart about this."

I wrestled with my pounding heart as I strode in, leaving the doors open behind me. The steam fled out into the lobby, so only a little of it clung to the lenses of my glasses. "You had to know this day would come."

"I started counting down to it once we heard about Roulette," she said. "I suppose you believe you deserve an apology."

I came to a stop at the edge of the pool. "I deserve a hell of a lot more than that."

"I know. And I also know that there's absolutely nothing I can say now to change your mind about what you're going to do to me." She exhaled. "Even before I knew you were still alive, I've spent the past four years walking through this world with the knowledge that I deserved to die for what I did to you that day."

I hadn't realized how badly I'd needed to hear those words from her, Cole. But them hitting my ears felt like balm on a burn. "I'm not looking to be cruel here, Jali. Just balancing the scales. This ain't about me."

A flicker of confusion, then immediate understanding. "Binh."

"Binh," I agreed. "You tell me why you all killed him, and I'll make it quick. I don't intend to do that for anyone else." Four years ago, she'd been the only Thorn Orphan to offer me mercy. It seemed fair to give her the same.

143

"From what the coroner in Malañong said, Roulette died quickly. Though maybe that's just because he was better at dying than you." She grinned, unafraid. "I never thought I'd see the day he actually beat you at something."

Instinct and habit told me to laugh. At least to smile. In my four years away, I hadn't met a single soul who'd made me do either as easily as Jali. The temptation was right there, like the sweet scent of rum under a drunk's nose.

But I forced myself to remember the way boathouse planks and human ribs alike split beneath her steel gauntlets. I remembered how her offer of mercy didn't extend to actually helping me when I needed her most. And once I did that, it became easy to not give any more of myself over to Anjali the Armored.

"What did Roulette say when you confronted him with this question?" she asked.

"That if I let him go, he'd come back with me and help me kill you all."

"Probably good that you didn't believe him."

"Yeah. And it ain't like I needed his help anyway." A knot had tied itself in my chest when I'd walked into the room. The longer we talked, the tighter it pulled. It was getting hard to ignore. "Now, are you gonna give me the answer I want, or what? Why did Cole want Binh dead? And why ...?" I hesitated. Almost didn't ask her. But fuck it. This was going to be the last conversation we ever had. "Why'd you do it? Why'd you throw in with him over me?"

"I'm going to stand up now," she said. Before I could give her permission to, she did, and waded out of the water. "I'm going to put on a robe, and we're going to talk this out."

"I thought you said you weren't going to change my mind." But even so, I didn't move as she glided over to the side of the basin and pulled herself out.

"I'm not." She shrugged on a sky-colored robe and cinched it shut. "I saw what you did to the Black Rose. I know exactly how much mercy you have left in your heart for us. And I know the promises kept in the meantime won't be enough to change your course, either."

"Then why do you think we can 'talk this out'?" I said. "You didn't want to talk it out four years ago in the boathouse. Cole gave you a shiny new suit of armor, told you to turn it on my boyfriend, and you didn't hesitate. *And even if you did,*" I added, raising my voice when she opened her mouth, "*it doesn't change the fact that you still went and fucking did it!*"

I watched the words hit her like a lash, but I kept going.

"And then," I said, lowering my voice, "you just went on with life like it was fine. You think this is the kind of thing we can talk out? If you really feel so fucking bad about how things went down, why didn't you try to make it right after I was gone, huh? Why is Cole still alive?"

Silence hung as heavily between us as the bathwater steam.

"Yeah, there's no denying that," she sighed eventually. "I guess you've kind of had four years to rehearse your airing of grievances, haven't you?" She steeled herself. "You do deserve to know the truth."

That knot in my chest tightened even more. Of all the Thorn Orphans, living or dead, Anjali was the one I trusted most to play me straight. "Yeah?"

She nodded. "Cole brought us together and told us that Binh was going to undo everything we'd worked to build and crown himself the Slats' new boss. Now that he'd established his victories against the Rock, he was going to disavow us and give up all kinds of key information about us: our identities, our addresses ..."

"Sounds like something straight out of the Zephyr Guild's playbook."

"Yeah, a classic dick move." She started to slowly pace the side of the steamy basin. "He told us we had to remove Binh as quickly as possible. And when I asked why you weren't there, he said ..." She hesitated. "His words, not mine. But he said you couldn't be trusted, and that if you found out we were coming for Binh, then we should expect the worst."

I gritted my teeth as I imagined you tugging at everyone's strings and making us dance however you liked. You'd been right about me; that was exactly what I'd done once Binh was in danger. But betraying the Thorn Orphans? Binh would never do that. Binh would never bet against me.

"And then," Anjali continued, "he gave us gifts. He told us all of them were imbued with a bit of his spirit power, so each one would be able to go above and beyond whatever we'd used before."

I thought back to the revolvers that Roulette had carried: *Genuine bamboo, harvested straight from the Shoots*. You would certainly have influence over that. It was a new trick to me, though; I'd never known you were able to do that, and I'd never thought to try myself.

"And let me guess," I said. "Now you couldn't turn against him even if you wanted to, right? That why I didn't come back to find out one of you just caved Cole's head in one day?"

"You don't understand," she said. "You weren't there."

"*I wonder why*," I spat.

"I'm serious, Ten. He was different after that. The day after the boathouse, he strode right out into City Hall plaza and announced he was taking over. And then he pointed up on to the Rock, at the old Pak estate, and he just ... snapped his fingers." She did it herself, and the sound pinged off the tiled walls like a stray bullet. "The whole house ripped itself right off the side of the Rock. It rolled all the way down the slope and crashed at the foot of the Slats. No survivors. And no one who wanted to challenge him, either."

I'd heard that much by reading the Biranese newspapers later. But it was different, hearing it come from Jali. For one thing, I'd known that your parents weren't in the picture anymore, and I'd known that you had destroyed your old house. But I'd never really realized that you'd made both things happen at the same time.

"He led a whole procession over to where the house had landed," Anjali went on. "Spent the whole time talking about what the new Driftwood City was going to look like. What it'd mean for everyone. And then when we got to the wreckage, he said he was going to build a memorial to the Driftwood City that had come before, because after that day it would be a memory and nothing more."

As she spoke, I could hear your words on her tongue. You must've made a hell of an impression; the Armored was a lot of things, but poetic wasn't one of them. "What'd he make?"

"A statue." Suddenly, she looked uncomfortable.

I did my best not to loom, but it's hard when you're as big as me. "Of who?"

Her lips thinned. "Binh."

"*You fucking* ghouls!" I roared, rounding on her. By the fucking Bird, Cole. She and I had been so close to something here. "You murdered him! And then you propped his corpse up to use, like some kind of . . . I don't know, *prop*?"

Her eyes narrowed. There was that hardness I remembered, the steel within to match the steel she wore. "We did more to make his dream come true than he ever could," she said. "Thanks to us, and thanks to him, Driftwood City is united and strong."

Anjali smiled again. It wasn't the full-bore, double-barrel

kind of grin I was used to seeing her with, but it was something. I hated the way it loosened that knot inside me.

"I'm ashamed of what I did that day, and what I haven't done since," she said. "But I've also done good things in the past four years. For instance"—she folded her arms over her chest—"standardizing radios as police equipment. It really speeds up our response time."

As if on cue, I heard sirens and screeching brakes outside. Lots of them.

And just like that, the knot in my chest was tight enough to choke the light out of the sun.

I glowered at her. I started to sing to my driftwood, but I couldn't use it to kill her yet. Any moment now, the law was gonna come through with their guns blazing.

"How much of all that was true?" I asked.

"Every word." The Armored looked at me with grim satisfaction. "I said I deserved to die. I didn't say I was going to let you kill me. I just think it's fair you go to your grave knowing the truth ... or at least, most of it."

"Most of it?"

She held up a finger. "One key piece to turn the puzzle into a picture." She let her finger drop to her side. "I have always trusted in my strength. If you want the remaining truth, Tenny ..." Her smile vanished, and now she looked at me not as a friend, but as a warrior. "Then show me yours."

From the lobby, a live grenade skittered in across the stone floor, thin coils of smoke trailing from one end.

From beyond it, boots thudded and gun safeties clicked off.

And I opened my mouth to sing for my life.

12

Twelve years ago

Age 18

"Do you know something, Tenny?"

We knelt next to each other on the damp warehouse floor.

"What's that, Cole?"

Rough-woven ropes bit into our wrists.

"I think tonight could have gone better."

Someone pressed a gun into my back. "No talking."

She was a foot soldier of the Silver Tide Tong, Tsunatown's top player in the crooked game. Like everyone else in her gang, she wore a sharp black suit with a shiny silver tie. One of her identically dressed colleagues chimed in with rapid-fire Tsunese.

The woman laughed, and there wasn't a damn thing I liked about the sound of it. "You want to know what they said?"

"Something about your mom?"

Her pistol's butt hit me in the back of the head, and my vision exploded with stars. My glasses flew off my nose and skittered along the floor.

"*Really?*" you muttered to me. "'*Your mom?*'"

"Doing my best over here," I hissed, unable to hide some real annoyance at you. After all, it was your fault we'd wound up here in the first place.

As rough hands hauled me back upright, I felt a trickle of something wet on the back of my head. Blood. My anger rose like precious steam in a kettle, but I held it back. The only way I was gonna get through this was if I pretended to be like you. I turned to the blurry shape that looked like the Tong who'd hit me. "You mind grabbing my specs for me?"

The humming of the city told me what she'd do just a moment before she actually ground my glasses into the floor under her shoe. Honestly, I should've seen it coming, as much as I could see anything without my glasses.

I scowled at you. This close, I could only barely make out your sheepish expression, but I knew you well enough to sketch in all the details on my own.

"What are you mad at me for?" you hissed. "She *stomped on them!"*

"This was your—" I started to say, but another hit to the back of the head shut me up.

"No. Talking."

The warehouse door slid open, and right away the city told me who had joined us. One of them was Tsao Tai, the scarred, balding leader of the Silver Tides, whose smugness hung around him like the smell of oil hangs around a frycook. And one of them was a hired bodyguard whose arrival was heralded by her thundering, hissing footsteps. She was a small Karuntan woman wearing an assortment of chunky plates of armor. I knew they'd been painted bright blue, and I knew the paint job was marred with the bullet dents and knife scratches made by all the people who'd failed to end her life. I couldn't see that now, but I knew it because I had a partner who never skimped on his homework.

"I wanted to make sure you really were the Thorn Orphans before I watched you die," Tsao Tai said. A sour-sweet smell seeped from his mouth as he spoke. I recognized it from the street markets: candied garlic. "Now that I see you're practically children, I almost want to have my soldiers executed alongside you. You've spent months leading them around by their noses."

Threads of tension tightened all around the room, a ghostly garrote on every throat.

"The soldiers of the Silver Tide Tong who have failed me will have their whole lives to atone," Tsao Tai continued. "You will not have the same opportunity." He nodded to the brown-and-blue blur to his left. "Kill them."

I'll admit: I felt the smallest flutter of fear in the pit of my stomach. The city usually knew its shit, which meant you and I usually knew our shit. But it wasn't infallible. Still, you'd been so convinced that this was our best way forward. And you were convinced because the city had told you so. Far as I saw it, I had no choice but to trust you.

"Hoy," I said. "You're Anjali the Armored, aren't you?"

"Name and job description," she confirmed proudly. There was a metallic ring to the edges of her voice, as it echoed off the sides of her own blue helmet. "You a fan? I like meeting my fans. They're always so earnest."

"I recognize you, from my days running with another crew," I said.

"Well, this *is* a surprise," she said after a moment, laughing. "The runaway Lacanilao is a Thorn Orphan, huh?"

Surprise erupted around the room. The Tongs muttered fearfully to one another in Tsunese. I didn't need a translator to get the gist of it. In Driftwood City, the name Lacanilao was a universal language.

"Is this true?" said Tsao Tai. "That girl there is Nanay Benilda's runaway?"

"The very same," said the Armored. "Now that I've seen it, I can't unsee it."

"Then leave her alive," he said. "We'll return her and enjoy the reward. The other, though, you can kill. He's worthless."

You did a better job of biting back your laughter than I did.

"What're you doing with these chumps?" I said to Anjali. "I know you and the work you've done. You're a real merc. And I know they don't have the juice to pay your fee."

"Stop talking to her and crush his skull already," Tsao Tai snapped.

"I wanted a shot at the very best," Anjali chirped, as if she hadn't even heard her boss. "And from everything the wind tells me, that means the two of you."

I grinned, then focused on the humming threads of the city's power around me. "And do we live up to our reputation?"

Knowing her like I do now, I have to imagine she shrugged. "I mean, not really."

I surged to my feet.

The music in my head kicked to life: not gentle strings, but bold brass. When the city said *Kick*, my leg shot out behind me and folded a Silver Tide in half. When it said *Duck*, I dipped just beneath a firing pistol, then headbutted the shooter's hand just as they fired a second shot. Instead of hitting me, their bullet sent another Silver Tide spilling to the floor. Even as they tried to bring the gun back around to me, I stomped down on their instep hard enough to feel something crack, to the tune of the city's cymbal crash.

"What are you doing?" Tsao Tai shouted. "Someone kill her!"

"But Nanay Benilda—! said one of the Tongs.

"Forget Benilda! Just shoot her!"

But I could feel her eyes on me as I tore through one Tong

after another. I could see already, glasses or not, that she was going to wait until she was the only one left standing. This was someone who trusted her own strength above anyone else's. And I'd just given her the ultimate bait: a chance to test it against me.

Bullets flew around me, but the city's song told me where to step so they would only hit air. I didn't have my hands to fight back with, but that didn't matter. I had my heavy boots that could break bones. I had my shoulders, broad and strong enough to send Tongs toppling. I had my head, hard enough to withstand your best ideas.

That last one, I brought down into the pistol-whipping woman's face with a particularly satisfying snap of her nose bone.

Which left just me and and our guest of honor.

"Impressive," she said. "And all with your hands tied behind your back. But I know you didn't need to do that."

I shrugged, then let my bonds fall away from my hands. I'd gotten tired of playing pretend anyway.

"You idiots!" Tsao Tai screeched. "*Does no one know how to tie a knot?*"

"Ain't their fault." I shot him the kind of grin that usually made people shit their pants. "No lock can hold me and no cell can keep me."

The Armored pointed a gauntlet your way. "What about that one?"

I smirked. "Him? He's better at other things."

"*Hey!*" you said from the floor.

"Ah." The Armored sounded as pleased as a cat with a bird in its mouth. "I'd wondered if it was like that between you two ..."

"*Other other things*," we chorused.

"Well, I'll admit I didn't see the night going this way, little

153

Lacanilao," she said. I heard the little gears and actuators in her armor hiss and grind as she planted her feet. Clearly, she was trying to present an immovable object against my irresistible force. And that squared with what I'd heard about her. She was unbeatable in combat because anything you threw at her would just break like waves on a rock. "But I can't say I'm disappointed anymore. Do you promise to come at me with everything you've got?"

I nodded. "You've earned it."

And then I snapped my fingers.

The floor underneath her rose up like a wave of wood and unceremoniously dumped her on her back. She landed hard with a surprised shout, and wasted no time trying to right herself. But her arms couldn't bend back that far. So she just squirmed in place like an upturned turtle as I slowly approached her.

She grunted and tried to swing a gauntleted fist up at me, but I pinned her arm in place by stamping my boot down on it. I heard the little servos in her armor grinding and whining, but her suit hadn't been built to articulate when she was on her back.

"All that heavy armor," I said. With my other foot, I nudged her visor up so I could look into her eyes. Or more accurately, so she could look into mine, because I still couldn't see shit. "What's it like to actually feel that weight?"

"That is enough!" Tsao Tai roared. "You will—"

But by then you were on your feet, your own hands free, a fallen Tong's gun in your grip. "We will do a lot of things, Mr Tsao," you said. "But you won't get to see any more of them."

You'd come a long way from the distraught, vomiting wreck you'd been the first time you took a life. Tsao Tai's body had barely collapsed to the floor, and already you were at my side. "Can you manage for long without your glasses?"

154

I nodded. "Well enough for this." I regarded the prone warrior beneath my boot. "You like to test your strength, right?"

This close, I could see Anjali clearly for the first time. She was older than me, but still a youngish woman. Without a trace of fear, she stared back up at us. "Just do it, will you?" she said. She had the rancid glower of a sore loser. "Gloating is so fucking tacky."

I nodded. "All right, Cole. Reckon we should go ahead with what we came here to do."

And then I stepped off her gauntlet and offered her a hand.

She stared at it in disbelief. "What the hell are you doing, little Lacanilao?"

"I ain't a Lacanilao anymore," I said. My tone was sharp, but I held out my hand anyway. "Just Tenny now."

I saw her head bob. "So what do you really want with me then, Tenny?"

"You like to pick a fight with the biggest, meanest motherfucker in the room, because you like the way folks look at you when you come out on top," I said. "Far as I'm concerned, that makes you a woman after my own heart. So what if I told you I was here to offer you the ultimate test of your strength?"

"A fight to the death against an enemy so powerful, it's never been defeated in all of human history," you added.

Through blurry eyes, I watched her disbelief flower into curiosity. At last, she took my hand in her cold blue gauntlet. "Who is it?"

I hauled the newest Thorn Orphan to her feet. By the time she was standing again, I wore a mad grin to match her own. "The world."

13

Now

Age 30

Quick as a thought, my driftwood shaped itself into a dome and clamped itself down over the grenade.

I braced myself for fire, but all I saw was the ghost of a bright yellow flash of light. When I willed it back to my side, I saw it had been blackened and singed. Shiny bits of metal stuck out of it. Just a flash grenade, as I'd suspected. They knew their commander was in here. They weren't about to risk her life with any heavy hardware. Even so, I was glad I'd snuffed it out. I'd already fought the Armored without my eyes once. I had no desire to do it again.

I glanced behind me for just a moment to see Anjali darting toward the back. I gritted my teeth, but let her go. If I tried to pursue, I'd get a bullet in my back. Better to face the badges pouring in from the front. I knew, with a sinking feeling in my gut, I'd probably see her again in a few minutes. And I knew she'd be dressed for the occasion.

"Fucking badges," I growled, breaking into a run. "Never know how to read a room ... !"

With a bellow, I charged straight into the front foyer, where the badges were kitted out in riot gear: blue breastplates, blue bucket helmets, black rifles. They looked less like law officers and more like an army on the march. They'd fanned out to enter the room. From the way they hesitated when they saw me, the last thing they'd expected was a counterattack.

"It's her!" one of them yelled. "Open—!"

I raised both my hands like I was about to conduct a symphony. And from the bathing room behind me, my collection of driftwood shot into the room, fragmenting and splitting into individual missiles. The air was alive with driftwood and screams and gunfire and song, always song.

I didn't hesitate as the first shots rang out. I charged on ahead until I was in their midst, a blot of red in the thick of blue. Driftwood pinged off pounded steel and snapped bone. But while the city's spirit helped me cover a lot of ground at once, none of them hit so hard as me.

I missed the city's song telling me how to dance so that every punch would hit home, and every enemy bullet would strike only air. I had taken for granted the days when I could close my eyes and trust that the spirit of Driftwood City would conduct me to victory.

Now, the music I heard from the driftwood wasn't the kind I could dance to, not like that. But luckily, the steps I remembered from the old days were good enough. By the time the first officer swiveled his gun my way, I was already stepping past it. My fist collided with his face just as a chunk of flying birch slammed into the back of his head. His helmet rang like a bell as he crumpled at my feet and I moved on.

Another was already in my sights. It took me two blows to crack her defenses open, another three to send her spilling to the floor. As I moved on, a flying chunk of driftwood hammered down to make sure she stayed where she lay. But by the time a third officer stepped to me, my punches were coming slower. His club grazed me, when before it would've missed me completely. And this guy took me seven, eight, nine blows to knock down.

Already, I could see the problem. Taking on the Monster or Roulette had been one thing; each of them was just one guy. Now, I was up against a dozen. And even though I was being strategic about it—using my driftwood to isolate them so I could do my takedowns one at a time—the fact was, it'd been a long time since I was the Tenny who could've eaten all these badges for breakfast.

In all my memories of fights like this, I'd fought on anyway. I'd used my reach, my strength, my powers, and I'd always come out on top. And habit told me to battle it out anyway. Even diminished, I was still better than these glorified guard dogs. It'd be harder than before, but I could still do it, I told myself. I wasn't the Red Rose anymore, but I was still fucking *Tenny*.

It wasn't the police I remembered in that boathouse, though, standing still and doing nothing as my blood mingled with Binh's.

So I switched gears and went for efficiency. I aimed for throats. Joints. Noses. Crotches. Anything that broke easy. If it got them to stop fighting, I hit it with everything I had. When they tried to withdraw out of my reach, I sang to my driftwood and it battered them back into striking distance. It hammered at their gun barrels and sent their shots flying wide. It allowed me to fight with a dozen fists, plus two.

By the time the last one fell, I was breathing hard and grinning big. I'd done a lot of things in my life that made me feel more alive, but by the Bird, none of them ever approached the high I got from walking out of a good, honest scrap. It'd been my favorite part of our fight for freedom, Cole: the actual fighting.

"*Now*," I said to the collection of groaning, beaten officers that lay at my feet. "I've left you all alive. Don't waste that gift. Stay out of my way." I narrowed my eyes at the front door. Heavy, metallic footsteps boomed from just outside. "Only one person needs to die tonight."

She didn't open the doors; she barged straight through them like they weren't even there. Around the woman who'd been my friend was a cocoon of sapphire-colored steel twice as wide as I was, and nearly as tall. Huge pauldrons bore the symbol of the Blue Rose, while her bulletproof breastplate was splashed with the ornate logo of the Meyongphirin Metropolitan Police Department. Her visor was tilted up, but I knew it could slide back down and render her a faceless blue juggernaut.

"I see you haven't lost a step," she said. "I'm grateful I'll get a real fight out of you before the end. Stand down, officers," she added to her squad, as if I'd left any of them in a position to help her. "I'll handle the Red Rose myself."

I sang low and steady with my shaman's breath, and all the floating chunks of driftwood in the air flew back to me. My skin crawled at what I was about to do, as old memories clawed to the surface. But I steadied myself; this was the only way I could go toe-to-toe with the Armored and win. So I willed it to reshape itself around me: a breastplate of birch. Two huge gauntlets: one weathered and brown, the other black and freshly singed by that flash grenade. I'd lost wood in my fight against the Yellow Rose, so I didn't have enough to cover any more.

But it would do.

You're here, I reminded myself, as memories of the coffin seared through me. *That place is a memory, and one you survived*.

My stomach didn't settle at all.

Anjali eyed me appreciatively. "That's a neat new trick."

159

She pointed a gauntlet at me. Atop it glinted the double barrels of a built-in gun. "Won't do you much good, though."

I clapped my gauntlets together in front of my face as a thick wooden shield, willing the spirit energy inside them to harden its grains against the impact. It was probably why I kept my face when the first round took me off my feet and sent me flying back into the bathing room, skidding hard across the floor. But I didn't have time to groan and collect my wits; I had to roll out of the way as Anjali's follow-up shot reduced the floor beside me to splinters.

I came up in a low crouch and barreled straight for her. My whole body sagged forward under the weight of my top-heavy armor, and I could feel my lower back muscles throbbing already. I ignored it; I had to move fast, before she could reload her gauntlet gun.

Sure enough, as I burst through the steam, she was ejecting the spent cartridges. She looked up in surprise.

I grinned at her as I ran faster.

And she calmly leveled her other gauntlet at me and fired.

I skidded to the side just in time. The shot punched a huge hole in the wall behind me. But then I was inside her range of fire, cocking my wooden gauntlet back for my counterpunch.

She got her visor down just in time, and my blackened gauntlet skidded across the smooth steel surface. My next hit was straight on, though, and Anjali staggered back from the force of it. And with each blow I landed, I felt something crackle through the energy I had in my grasp. It was as if I were trying to play my song, and every few notes someone was chiming in with a car horn.

I recognized the backlash of that spirit energy, though. I was striking whatever power you'd imbued this suit of armor with. To fight her, I reminded myself, was to fight you.

I got in two or three more free shots before Anjali started to fight back. I'd made a few dents in her armor and scratched the paint, but clearly I hadn't slowed her down any. As I wound up for my next hit, she swung her gauntlet into my chest like a hammer. I staggered back hard, gasping and choking. My improvised armor was tough, but it didn't have any padding. Even with its protection, I couldn't take a ton of hits.

But without it, she would've caved in my sternum, so I couldn't be totally ungrateful.

"I can't help but notice that the room isn't coming alive to murder me," Anjali said. Water collected and beaded on her armor the longer we stayed in the steamy room. "So the Black Rose was right; you don't have your powers anymore. At least, not like you used to. *Very interesting*." She planted her feet. "How long do you think you can last against me while you're wearing that lumberyard?"

I didn't tell her my answer. I showed her.

She stood her ground and let me come to her. This time, I didn't go for the big targets; I aimed for the elbow joints, with their little gears and servos. I lashed out at the pneumatic bars steadying the backs of her knees. She tried to swing back at me, but I could dodge circles around her. The Armored was meant to outlast things, not outmaneuver them. And each time I landed a blow, I felt that little shock of feedback and wondered if you were sitting in an office somewhere and feeling it, too.

But the harder I fought, the more I felt my strength bleed away from me. The heavier my feet got. And I wasn't the only one to notice.

"You chewed through an entire squad of my best before you ever touched me," she said, her words interrupted every time one of my blows clanged across her armor. "And you aren't used to fighting with that much weight on your back. Come on, Tenny. Did you really think you could keep this up?"

161

I staggered back, breathing hard. My face was flushed, my glasses fogged, and stray hairs were starting to fall into my line of sight. I wanted to snap a one-liner back at her, but I just didn't have the breath.

"You're fighting me with the driftwood that was your coffin," she went on. "But Driftwood City's heart has always been the water, not the wood. That's what Cole thought when he forged me this armor from the hulls of our city's boats. Wood lays out in the sun and rots away until it gets replaced. But those boats are always in motion. They're more alive than the streets ever were, and it's with their power that I'll endure and end you. 'Wood is good,'" she recited, "'but steel is—'"

"'—real,'" I finished grimly.

Her words cut through my defiance. It wasn't like watching the Monster shrug off blows that should've laid him out flat. This was an old friend calmly laying out exactly what would doom me to failure. The Monster and Roulette had been comrades and colleagues, but Anjali had been more than that. It was why she'd been the only one to offer me mercy when I lay bleeding at your feet.

I expected her to make another attack on me, but she stopped. Gears whirred inside her suit of armor, and then her visor slid back up. My heart sank. I recognized the way her smile was fading. She was preparing herself to finish me.

"I ... am genuinely sorry," she said. "I thought about you every day. The others ... well, you know how they are. I never could talk to them like I could talk to you. And while I've led my officers on dozens of raids, I would've traded even the best ones to have you at my back again."

A memory hit me: bullets streaming off Anjali's breastplate in a shower of sparks. And as the fire died, I sprang out from behind her to deliver the Thorn Orphans' reply with my closed fists.

I'd finally cobbled together enough breath to respond. "Will you miss me once you put me down for good?"

"Of course," she said simply. "I loved you like a sister, Tenny. There'll never be another you."

I'll be damned if I didn't believe she meant every word of it.

"Ready?" she asked.

I nodded.

She slid into a fighting stance.

And I came for her.

Once again, I swung at her as hard as I could. I kept hammering away at the same spots, hell-bent on creating a weakness. It was the only way you could win against someone as armored up as Anjali. But unlike last time, she didn't just let me lay into her. Now, she moved far faster than she had before.

I barely got my gauntlets up in time to block the first blow, and I had to leap back to avoid the second. I felt wood creak and splinter under the impact, as the force of it rattled through the grains and into my bones. Old wounds came alive all over my body, memories that ached as if they were fresh.

I turned from her and broke into a dash, back toward the main pool. She was quick to follow, sensing she finally had me in a desperate position. I turned around just in time to see her charging at me, shoulder-first. The sigil of the Blue Rose grew in my vision until it hit me like a sky-colored truck.

This time, I couldn't stay on my feet. I went skidding hard across the scarred-up floor of the bathing room. My entire torso was alive with pain. And when I looked down with wincing eyes, I saw that my driftwood armor had splintered from the sheer force of her hit. When I tried to sing to the wood, its fibers warbled brokenly back to me. I felt my hold on it fade. I should've been able to control the broken pieces, but I guessed it had something to do with the fact that her armor was imbued with your power. The same thing had happened

163

with the driftwood that had been hit by Roulette's bullets, after all.

But it wasn't like I had time to scientifically test it. Jali came to stand over me with two thundering footsteps. I knew the next blow would squash my head flat.

"Never known you to run from a fight, Tenny," she said mildly. "Maybe the first new thing you've shown me."

Pain flared through my chest as I coughed. "I always had," I wheezed, "the best ass in the Thorn Orphans ... so you're welcome for the view."

Anjali chuckled. "Fuck you for making me laugh." She was still smiling, but I saw sadness glitter in her brown eyes.

"Jali," I said. "I'm done for. You need to kill me so he won't. Give me that mercy you promised me four years ago."

Anjali sucked in a long breath. At last, she nodded.

"Thank you ..." My voice trailed off, my breathing more labored. "Don't let me go to my grave without knowing the truth ... Look me in the eyes. Tell me why ... you really killed Binh."

She'd been preparing to move, but at that request she froze.

"No," she said. "Trust me, Tenny, you don't want to know. It won't bring you any comfort on your way out."

"Jali," I rasped. I blinked back tears. "This is ... me asking. Please ..."

For two, three, four heartbeats, I lay in the shadow of a still and silent blue colossus.

And then she said, "Binh had to die because he learned the truth."

My head whipped up sharply so I could meet her eyes. "What? What truth?"

I could see her trying to figure out if the words she spoke in this room would magically find their way back to your ears

164

somehow. At least, that's what I assumed; who the fuck else would a woman like Anjali the Armored fear?

But then she looked down at me with fresh resolve.

"He learned," she said, "that Cole started the fire."

And my entire world spun right off its axis.

I understood what each of those words meant on their own, Cole, but stringing them together and giving them meaning ... something about that just made my whole brain short-circuit. There was no way. There couldn't be a way. I had suspected any number of things, and that never would've made any version of any list.

Cole started the fire.

No, I told myself. *She's lying.*

She might be, a second voice chimed in. *But if there was one Thorn Orphan who'd actually tell you the truth on your deathbed ... which one would it be?*

"I really didn't want you to find out this way," Anjali went on. "I warned you it wouldn't make your passing go any smoother. But now that I've told you, I can deliver you from this pain. One last favor for an old friend."

I gulped. Took a deep breath. "Remember," I said, "the night we met properly? When we ... were in the opposite position?"

"I do," Anjali said. "I remember feeling the weight of your power. Now, you'll feel the weight of mine." She gestured to her heavy steel boot. "And to think, you ambushed me here in the hopes that I wouldn't be wearing it."

She brought her huge foot down on to my face.

My wood gauntlets shot up from my sides, grabbing it an inch away from my nose and struggling to hold it there. My arms shook and my hands screamed with fatigue. I grimaced with the sheer effort of pushing back against her armor and its mechanical strength.

"That's not," I grunted, "why we're here."

And then, with a burst of song to lend strength to my gauntleted arms, I pushed her as hard as I could to my left.

Toward the big, deep basin of warm bathwater.

The one I'd maneuvered her next to.

You see, Cole, I'd fought alongside Jali many times. Even though she was wearing a new suit of armor, the same old principles applied. She could take hits from the front, from the back, and even from above. But she had always been vulnerable to sudden changes in her footing. I couldn't control the floor anymore, not like in the old days.

Not unless I made myself the floor.

Once I'd figured that out, all I'd had to do was lure her into a position where I could use that ... while getting her to tell me the truth.

I staggered to my feet as she sank straight to the bottom, facedown. I could see her below the froth and chop, frantically reaching for her straps and releases with those big, clumsy gauntlets of hers. Despite my resolve, a knot hitched itself in the pit of my gut. This would be the hardest part of the night.

Her armor was heavy enough to keep her sunk. But I had a specific favor to repay tonight.

With a few notes of psychic song, the driftwood shed itself from my arms and snaked down through the water. Each one wrapped itself around one of her arms, and clamped her wrists into place at the very bottom of the bathing pool. She thrashed, but not powerfully enough to break free. And the longer I waited, the more and more still she became, until she didn't move anymore at all.

Just in case, I left the clamps on her arms for a full minute more after she stopped thrashing. And when it was finally done, I bowed my head and whispered: "*Roses every day.*"

Solemnly, I traced the sign of the pinion in the air, to mark

166

the passing of a friend and an enemy. I didn't really believe she was going to walk forever in the shadow beneath the Great Bird's wings. But Benilda had been a believer, and she'd drilled in some habits that I'd come to accept would never go away.

Inconvenient feelings gnawed at me as I recalled my driftwood to my side. Ones I knew I was gonna have to sort out later. The woman at the bottom of that basin was probably the only person left in the entire world who'd given a genuine shit about me. When I'd looked into her eyes, I'd seen belief and remembered friendship.

But I'd also seen the face of a comrade who'd betrayed me, just to hang on to the armor that made her feel special. At least she'd done me one last kindness before I'd killed her.

My rage moved on from Jali. And like fire catching, it found you.

My stomach roiled as I turned it all over in my head. Why would you have started the fire? It'd been your inheritance. Your future. There was no reason for you to light it up. And what was more, I'd seen you during the fire. The terrified young man streaked with ashes and tears ... he hadn't looked like an arsonist to me. Neither had the champion you'd become, the fierce fighter for workers' rights known only as the White Rose.

But at that, I stopped. Had that been ferocity?

Or all this time, had I been seeing the work of a guilty man?

It was too much. I could barely keep it all inside me, and I still had to get away.

But one thing was certain, Cole: even if I didn't understand, even if I couldn't see the how of it, even if I didn't want to ... I believed her.

I staggered out into the back alley with significantly less driftwood than I'd walked in with. I eyed what I had left: half of it normal, the other half charred black. Definitely not enough to turn into a trunk anymore. I might've been able

167

to disguise it as a guitar case, at most. At this rate, I wasn't going to have nearly enough left over to kill you. I'd have to be more careful about how I used it to handle Knife-Edge Ngo and Mhap the Monster, because there was no way in hell I was going up against you with nothing.

But before I got to them or you, first I had to get through the squad of badges that were waiting for me at the end of the alley.

"*Freeze!*" one of them shouted, leveling a rifle my way. I glanced behind me. No way out. And in a lane this narrow, I'd be awfully hard to miss.

Now, Cole, I know what you're probably thinking. You're probably thinking this looks real bad for me. You're probably thinking that as good as your old buddy Tenny is in a fight, even she can't take down a dozen guys by herself, especially if they've got guns and armor. You're probably thinking that the only reason I got myself into a situation like this is because I had a rock-solid exit strategy from the get-go.

And I'll tell you what:

I wish to the fucking Bird you were right.

So I had no choice but to put my hands up and obey. If I got them to come close, I could take them out. And they wouldn't open fire just yet. My life was safe as long as they didn't know that I'd killed—

In the distance, a radio crackled.

"Jali," I groaned, "you absolute *motherfucker*."

"She killed the commander!" one of the badges yelled. "Light her the fuck up!"

It was a matter of one split second.

A split second as the police shouldered their rifles.

A split second as I stared into death's steel-bored eyes.

A split second as I tried to sing my remaining driftwood into a shield so I could make a suicide run of it.

168

A split second as I wondered what the hell that noise was.

And a split second as a truck plowed right through the ranks of officers.

I gaped. I'd learned to be good at expecting the unexpected, but no one could've expected that.

The truck's side door clunked open. And then Diwata poked her head out and shouted, *"Get over here, you idiot!"*

I had a lot of questions.

All of which could wait a second.

As I breached the mouth of the alley, I saw other officers running toward us, readying their weapons. I leapt on to the side of the truck and grabbed on to its metal frame. "Go!" I shouted.

"You're not inside—!"

A gun barked and the driver's side mirror shattered.

"All right, I'm going!" Diwata yelped. "Hang on!"

"What the fuck do you think I'm do—?"

She threw the truck into a hard reverse, and it was all I could do to keep my grip. As Diwata whipped us around, one of my feet came free of the side and dangled out in the air. Wind and momentum and flying bullets and the chill of the night all tried to wrestle my fingers loose.

But I kept my grip as we sped eastbound.

14

Fourteen years ago

Age 16 (almost)

"Give it back," I sighed, reaching for the lumpia Diwata had snatched off my plate. I was only fifteen (for the next few hours, anyway), but already I was almost as tall as the twins. I knew when I was done growing, I'd be the one looking down on them.

It'd be a nice change of pace.

"You're forgetting the magic word," taunted my older sister, the worst person in the entire world.

I rolled my eyes. "Fine. Give it back, *bitch*."

"Is that any kind of way to talk to your até?" Diwata said, mocking hurt. She kept the lumpia just out of my reach.

"Dawa," said Dalisa from the other end of our long, live-edge tigerwood table. She had a cup of tea and the finance section of the *Meyongphirin Blue Star*, like always. At twenty, she was definitely an adult by now, but I'd been watching her do this since she was eleven. "You should give it back."

"What's she gonna do?" Diwata laughed. "Hit me?"

"Yes," Dalisa said as I threw my punch.

Diwata spilled from her chair, but she was up on her feet in an instant. The lumpia rolled away, forgotten by both of us. Diwata had murder in her eyes, while mine danced with excitement. A tussle with até Dawa was just what I needed to start my big birthday off right.

"Tenny." Dalisa still hadn't looked up from her newspaper. "You should stop before this turns into a fight."

"She made it a fight," I said, with a grin that I knew would set Diwata right off. "Shouldn't start things she can't finish."

"No, she shouldn't," Dalisa agreed. "But if you make it a full fight, then I'll have to join in." At last, she set her paper down so she could meet my eye. "Would you like to guess whose side I'll take?"

I scowled at her. Nine years I'd been living with them, and I still felt like a cuckoo in their nest. The two of them were so close with each other, and it wasn't like that shocked me. But they'd never let me in as their third sister, not really. They called me all the right honorifics (or at least, Sasa did), but it never went any deeper than that. By my eighth birthday, I'd stopped trying to play with them. And by my sixteenth, I'd accepted that as far as they were concerned, the Lacanilao family had two daughters and one very tall pet.

"No fucking point in it now, anyway." I sat back down. "Lumpia fell on the floor. I ain't eating that."

Lumpia was the kind of treat we only got on special days. Benilda had the juice to buy us whatever we wanted, and lumpia weren't especially expensive. But as she liked to remind us every single time she served it, they'd been hard to come by when she was a girl. Restricting them to special occasions was supposed to remind us of where the Biranese in Driftwood City came from. And even at sixteen, I could appreciate what message that sent. But I would've appreciated it a hell of a lot more if I could've got a bite of lumpia out of it.

171

The three of us ate in sullen silence until Benilda swept into the room like a spring breeze. She wore a bright green wrap dress, its glossy folds brilliant against her brown skin. A maid followed her with a hat the size of a salad bowl, adorned with so many feathers that the milliner might as well have kept the original bird in one piece. All three of us rose dutifully, but the old lady was all smiles as she swept toward me.

"Anak!" She kissed me once on each cheek, touching my long braid with fondness and approval. "I'm sorry this morning has been so busy. Maligayang bati." She'd never missed a birthday lunch before, but in previous years she'd had Indawat to cover for her while she dined with her girls. Now, she had to do it all herself.

When she offered me her hand, I pressed it to my forehead. Her skin was cool and damp, as if she'd just washed her hands. "Thank you, Benilda," I said.

With her bright red lips, she pointed to the platter of lumpia on the table, next to a near-overflowing vase of pink roses. "You need to eat more, or people will say I starve you."

The words and tone were kind, but she didn't need to tell me twice. And this time, when I grabbed one from the platter, Diwata kept her hands to herself.

Benilda took her seat at the head of the table. Behind her, the maid respectfully laid her hat on a waiting rack. "Now that you're sixteen today, anak, there's something we must discuss."

Diwata glanced at me, while Dalisa dutifully rose. Benilda raised a chubby hand. "Stay, Sasa. This is for six ears, not two."

Dalisa frowned thoughtfully, but sat. I could see the questions passing silently in the air between the twins. Neither of them looked my way, and I tried to tell myself it didn't bother me.

Benilda took a moment to choose her words. "A life is not just what you do. It is what you build. There's a word for it: legacy. Do you know it?"

Dalisa nodded, while Diwata and I both shrugged.

"It will surprise you all to learn that I am not a young woman." Benilda's smile glinted like ice in the sun and melted away just as quickly. "Sooner than you think, my hands will no longer be steady or strong enough to guide Birantown toward the future it deserves."

Once again, Dawa and I were on the same page here. I could tell she had the same question on her mind as me: where was all this going? Sasa, on the other hand, had a knowing look in her eye, her mouth hidden behind thoughtfully steepled fingers.

"With Indawat gone, I am thinking more of how the next few years will go," Benilda said. "And there needs to be a plan ... one I will announce tonight, in front of all my captains." Her rings clacked as she drummed her fingers on the tabletop. "But here, among family, I will tell you first: Cheza, the new head of the family will be you."

"Congratulations," Dalisa said with a respectful nod, just as Diwata shouted, "*What the fuck?*"

The glare Benilda gave her was like drawing a knife: sharp and sudden. "Now you see why I told you now, in here, and not in front of everyone else." The whole mood of the room shifted, enough to turn the lumpia stone cold. "When I say it before a room full of raised glasses, you will be silent and smiling."

"Tita Benilda, you can't be serious!" Diwata shouted.

"I do not tell jokes about family, Dawa." Benilda was using her calm voice, the kind that scared me way more than any of her shouting ever did.

Diwata didn't take the hint, and ignored Dalisa's sharp look at her. "She ain't blood! She didn't even take the Lacanilao name!"

"Tonight, she will," Benilda said with a confidence I sure as hell didn't feel.

Dawa's chair hit the floor with a *thunk* as she shot to her feet. "Me and Sasa were your brother's," she snarled. "The same blood you got in your veins, we got in ours. What the fuck happened to the Nanay Benilda that was all about family?"

Benilda sat with the still patience of a flower that knew it would outlast the cold. "My brother would have sold you both for another pipeful of opium. Daning Tenlonghari? She fought with me. Bled with me. Built with me. *She* was the only sibling I ever really had." She slid Dalisa's teacup over to herself and took a sip before continuing. "Family is not blood, and blood is not family. Now sit down."

"*No*," said Diwata.

"Dawa," Dalisa said sharply. I jumped; the other twin had been so still and silent, I'd almost forgotten she was there.

"Don't 'Dawa' me!" said Diwata. "All you ever do is keep your head down! I ain't gonna let her treat us like this! If anyone should be head of the family, it's you! You're the only boss I'd ever follow!"

My head was already spinning, but even through that fog of confusion I saw her point. There was no denying it: Dalisa was smarter than me. Done better in school, that was for sure. I would've at least thought I'd do better during our exercise classes, but she'd been one of the only kids at school who could beat me at fencing.

It was more than just the grades she pulled, though. She had good relationships with every major player in the family organization. She already oversaw the family's books. And she'd earned the respect of all the major players in the crooked game in her own right. Dalisa was the clear choice.

"Tita Benilda does not want me to lead," Dalisa said quietly. Even the calm she wore was eerily like Benilda's. "I choose to respect her wisdom."

"A good answer," Benilda said, briefly warm again. "You will be Cheza's right hand, helping her run the important things. And you ..." When she regarded my other sister, she went right back to being icy. "You will be her left hand. When there are enemies that rise to face our family, you will curl into a fist and strike them back down. But to be a good left hand, you must obey. So, Diwata: sit. Down."

Diwata glanced to Dalisa. Her sister's expression was serene as a painting of a bowl of fruit. Frustrated, she looked to Benilda, cold and impatient. And then, she turned to me. "What about you, neh?" she snarled. "You've been awful quiet. You having fun over there, birthday girl?"

I didn't know what to do. I had no love for Diwata. But even if she'd never been anything but horrible to me, she had a point. Not only would Dalisa make a better head of the family, but there was another layer to it.

One I didn't want to admit to anyone.

But I couldn't spit in Benilda's face, either. She'd taken me in when no one else would. She'd clothed me, and fed me, and given me as much of an education as I'd allowed myself to be given. And besides that, she was also just not the kind of person you said no to.

So I did something I'm pretty sure you've never seen me do, Cole: I shook my head, sat still, and shut the fuck up.

Benilda narrowed her eyes. "Family is the only reason I have asked you several times to sit down. I won't ask another, Dawa."

For just a moment, Diwata looked like she was going to cave. I didn't know why, but I found myself praying to the Great Bird she just would, for once in her life.

175

"*No*." She planted her feet. "Dalisa should be running things after you. Not this fucking parasite."

Only I noticed the disappointment flit across Dalisa's face.

"Dalisa," Benilda said calmly, "hold your sister down."

With a soldier's swiftness and precision, Dalisa was on her feet and behind Diwata. "What are—?" was all Diwata managed to get out before her twin expertly forced her to bend over the table. Diwata screamed and struggled, but Dalisa pinned her with an elbow between her shoulder blades. In her flat eyes I saw a machine: unstoppable and patient.

"Hold still," Dalisa said flatly. "This will be over faster." And then she looked again to Benilda, fighting to keep her sister down as she awaited orders.

For the first time since she'd told me about my birthday present, Benilda looked to me. "You will be making these decisions someday soon, anak. What price should she pay for disrespecting family? For disrespecting you?"

I was having trouble doing anything but stare at my sister, pinned and helpless. But I knew I needed to give an answer, so at last I found my voice.

"None," I said. "She didn't do anything worth punishing. She wasn't disrespecting family; she was sticking up for it. Ain't that what you always say you want us to do?" My whole mouth was dry, but my palms left sweaty streaks on the polished tigerwood tabletop.

Benilda regarded me now, her lips going thin and red as a razor's slash. I'd given her the wrong answer. "I still have things to teach you," she sighed. She picked up Dalisa's heavy metal teacup, downed the rest of the tea, then clanked it heavily against the table. Satisfied with the noise it made, she nodded to Dalisa. "The right hand."

"*No!*" Diwata shouted, still struggling. But Dalisa's position was too good. Diwata made the table rattle, but she couldn't stop Dalisa from pinning her right wrist down.

At last, Benilda stood. She was a short woman, but she loomed over the prone Diwata like an executioner. "You will be Cheza's strong left hand, Dawa. But to be a left hand ... you must appreciate left hands."

I heard bones splinter as the teacup came down. Diwata howled loud enough to fill the entire grand dining room from floor to ceiling. Benilda gently set the cup back on the table. She nodded again to Dalisa, who at last let her sister go. Diwata crumpled to the floor, clutching at her hand. When Dalisa moved to help her back up, Benilda shook her head.

"Let her help herself," she said. "She has to learn that a left hand alone will not pull someone up."

So Dalisa and I had no choice but to watch as Diwata clumsily picked herself up off the floor and staggered out of the room, holding in sobs of pain as she cradled her hand to her body.

"Cheza." Benilda's voice sounded almost sad. "You will have to do many hard things like that, to build what I've built. But those hard things will lead you here." She indicated the huge dining room around us, with its bounty of food and waiting servants and freshly watered vase of roses. But as I looked around at it, it didn't feel magnificent. Just empty.

I didn't feel like eating lumpia anymore. I didn't feel like eating ... anything. I figured I'd go to my room and try not to think about what I'd just seen. But when I got to the hallway, I sensed footsteps behind me. And when I turned, Dalisa stood right in front of me.

"You should have chosen a price." Her voice was machine-tooled steel: smooth. Flat. Cold.

"I didn't want Benilda to do that!" I protested. "I didn't want any of that!"

177

She ignored me. "If you had been strong enough to choose a price, you could have chosen something fair. But you were too weak to trust yourself. And that weakness took my sister's hand."

My mouth flapped open and shut, but I couldn't find the words. What the hell did Dalisa expect me to have done?

She brushed past me, uninterested in an answer. "Be worthy of our service."

Maybe it was just the sight of her walking away, but I managed to find some of my temper. "Or fucking what?"

"There's no 'what.'" She didn't look back, didn't stop walking. "It's just what you have to do."

I watched her go. There was a desperate, clawing kind of energy in my chest, but I had no idea what the fuck to do with it. I'd been here nine years. It wasn't like I hadn't seen firsthand what Benilda did. I knew who she was, had known since I was in diapers. Everyone in Birantown knew it.

I'd just never thought that she would want me to be the same kind of woman.

At least, that was what I told myself then. But you and I can be honest here, Cole, since there's nothing left for us to lie about.

I know how my story looked from the outside. A girl grows up in the baddest gang in all the Slats, and walks away from the throne when it's offered to her. She decides she's gonna prove she's better than the family that raised her, so she gets a job doing honest work in a factory, like regular folks. If I'd been the Thorn Orphan to strut for the press instead of you, I'd bet Roulette Wu on the luckiest night of his life that they'd lap me up like milk.

But can I tell you something, Cole? Something I've never told anyone?

I didn't walk away because I didn't want it.

I walked away because I wanted it more than anything.

I saw how Benilda ran things. I saw the respect she got, that she could walk anywhere on the Slats without fear. I'd noticed the way things immediately turned around for me in school nine years ago once word got out who'd taken me in. And now the fantasy was right there in front of me: I wouldn't have to answer to anyone. And if anything about my world wasn't the way I liked it, I could beat it into shape. It was the ultimate birthday gift: a life where all my problems had simple, direct solutions. I'd always thought Dalisa would get the top spot. But the second it'd been offered to me, something hungry inside me had licked its chops.

Younger me was a fucking idiot, Cole. But younger me also saw that feeling and recognized that it scared the shit out of her. So I have to give her some credit.

I didn't run away that night. I played the part, and I let Benilda introduce me to the entire Lacanilao crime family as Cheza Lacanilao, her daughter and heir.

And the next day, I walked out of that house. In an alley, I cut off my braid.

And Tenny Tenlonghari cashed out of the crooked game.

15
Now

"Sheltering a fugitive?" There was a crack in Pamin's front door, and their sleepy voice crept through it like a spider. "I'm starting to feel like you're taking advantage of my good nature, Dawa."

My crime was less than an hour old. The press wouldn't have it yet. It should've been impossible for Pamin to know already. I guessed they were just that good.

"We don't got anywhere else to go," Diwata said. "Things got real bad, real fast."

They sighed. "Just like I told you they would."

We stood outside Pamin's shack. Piles of metal stood around us, stained azure by the moon overhead. Just looking around, I caught sight of truck chassis, roofing sheets, and ...

Boat hulls.

I bit the inside of my cheek. I was under strict instructions not to open my mouth, and for once I felt like obeying. During that whole episode at the bathhouse, I'd been able to use adrenaline and stress to keep everything at bay. Now, though,

I had nothing to escape into. I felt like I was standing in a huge empty room after a party, staring at the holes in my world where my friends had just been standing. I was hearing the faint echoes of music, the ghosts of their laughter, the rush of water as they thrashed and thrashed ...

"You think I'd bring this to you if I had another choice?" Diwata was saying. "We ain't trying to make your life hard. We're just trying to not get dead."

He learned that Cole started the fire.

"I'm a zephyr. I traffic in information. Do you really want to throw your lot in with me?"

He learned that Cole started the fire.

"You don't just sell information, right? You conceal it, too. Like you did that box you got left by Binh's cousin."

He learned that Cole started the fire.

The two of them were still haggling and negotiating, but I wasn't there. I was seeing my old friend thrash as her own armor drowned her. Feeling the satisfaction and heartbreak collide in me over and over, like a tide and a shore daring each other to be the first to quit.

And the noise above all it, over and over: the seven words that could turn my world upside down.

"*Hoy.*" An irritated finger-snap right in front of my eyes, and I was back in the moment. Diwata was giving me a hard look, but I was surprised by the faint concern I saw behind her eyes. "You all right? You look like you're gonna pass out, and I ain't letting you do that to me again."

I blinked once. Twice. "Fine," I said.

He learned that Cole started the fire.

My breath rattled like a door loose in its rail. "I'm fine."

I didn't want to believe it, Cole. Even after everything you'd done to me, I didn't want to believe I'd been that wrong about you.

But.

But hadn't you straight-up told me once, in your own way?

I thought I would have to do something drastic to break the machine.

Wasn't that you coming clean, only I didn't see it?

And if I knew perfectly well that you'd ice your own best friend, Cole, then why was I having a hard time believing you'd do it to over three hundred strangers?

Pamin's door slid open a further inch. Now I could see the blue moonlight on their sly face. "Are you sure revenge is a game you've got the stomach for, Red Rose?"

They knew I had killed Jali. They knew the police were after me for it. But even they, good a zephyr as they were, couldn't have known what really had my stomach roiling. And I wasn't about to let them in on it.

So I wrestled myself back into focus. And with a calm, clear voice, I said: "The Blue Rose is dead. I killed her, and I'd do it again." But even saying it kicked up something cold inside me. For over an hour now, the world had been missing my friend. She'd tried to kill me a couple times, but she'd also been the only one to honor me with the truth. I hated her. I missed her. I was glad she was dead. I wished she was right here next to me. It was all too fucking much for a single person to hold.

I gritted my teeth and tried to shake it all off. I had to make peace with this. If it was taking this much out of me just to have killed Anjali, how the hell was I going to survive killing you?

"Pamin," Diwata said. "I'm coming to you hat in hand here."

"I know. And I value our friendship. But I'm not in a position to make enemies. The only thing keeping me safe from them right now is that they all have better things to worry about than little old me. If I let you in, I shoot right to the top of their priorities. And that's just heat I can't accept.

I'm sorry, Dawa, but I have to look out for myself here. I told you exactly what would happen if you walked out that door tonight. If you ignore the weather report, you can't get pissed when you get rained on."

Dimly, I registered that just before riding to my rescue, my sister had been here. I wondered what business she'd had with Pamin at this hour.

Diwata looked like she was going to object again, then let it go. I saw a familiar bitterness in the way she looked skyward. I wondered how many times she'd had doors shut in her face like this since she'd lost the juice behind the Lacanilao name.

"Fine," she said at last, with a voice that sounded like burned coffee tastes. "Let's go, Tenny." She turned, but I stayed still.

"Will you shelter us in exchange for information?" I said. "Info you're free to sell to whatever bidder you want, with no fear of reprisal from me."

Diwata whipped back around in surprise, as Pamin slid the door open slightly more. "It would have to be quite the secret, Thorn Orphan."

"Tenny, what the hell are you—?"

I ignored Diwata. "Three days of shelter for me and Diwata both. And in exchange, you get something to tell the whole city about me."

There was a pause. And then, from the shadows inside, a slender and callused hand emerged into the naked moonlight. "It's a deal, Red Rose."

I took it and shook it. As our hands bounced, I mentally flipped through the secrets I had left to offer. There weren't many, and I was definitely keeping one of them to myself. When I eliminated that option, it basically left me with only one.

I let go of their hand. Breathed in deep. And then I said, "I don't have my powers anymore."

Silence greeted the admission. Honestly, it was about what I'd expected.

"Cole suspects, but doesn't know for sure," I said. That maybe wasn't strictly true, based on what Anjali had said to me. You had known how to suppress my connection to the city, but I had to believe even you didn't know you'd cut me off for good. "You're the only person who has absolute certainty. All my miraculous powers are gone."

"Are you fucking *serious*?" Diwata snarled.

I ignored her. I'd have to deal with her soon enough, but I had to finish buying our way in. "I only have a little bit of power left—over the driftwood that was used to send me to a watery grave. And I've lost most of it already. Here's what I've got left."

I'd sung my driftwood into a series of heavy rings wrapped around my forearms beneath my coat sleeves. With a few hummed bars, they slipped free of me and joined together until they were a long, narrow staff of weathered birch with black-burned splotches. I took it in hand and leaned on it. By the Bird, did that feel good.

"Once I'm out of this driftwood, I have no power left at all," I said. "Each of my encounters with the Thorn Orphans has cost me more and more. I don't know how much I'll have left by the time I finally face the White Rose himself. But other than this, the only weapon I've got up my sleeve right now is a bad upbringing."

And that was that. With the kind of business this zephyr did, I was sure by morning every badge in the city would know that they could come at me without fear. My reputation had been my armor. Whatever fights I got into from now on, I'd be fighting them naked. But at least I'd be alive to fight.

I leveled a stare at the darkness beyond their doorway. "So is your word as good as you say it is?"

A pause.

And then they said, "I'll get some tea on."

I'll give my até credit: when it came to confronting me, she at least had the decency to wait until morning.

Pamin's front room wasn't cozy by any stretch. Bits of scrap metal hung from the walls, and when a breeze blew through the place they clanked like Hell's own wind chimes. I'd slept the night on the bare floor, while Diwata had made do with the lumpy couch. I hadn't had a mattress under my back in so long, I was actually starting to dream about the small, hard one I'd tolerated on the airship ride over here.

Near as I could tell, Pamin's low, scratched-up tea table also doubled as their dining-room table, because I couldn't see any higher furniture anywhere else in the place. I sat cross-legged at it, biting into a kelp roll just as Diwata sat down across from me with a set jaw and a steaming mug of lapsang in hand. She wore an old grey tank top and a bright white hormone patch on her bare shoulder.

"If you're looking for an apology," I said through a mouthful, "you ain't gonna get one." I wasn't even looking at her. My mind was still on last night. Jali's confession had kicked open the door to so many hows and whens, and I was trying so hard to understand them all.

"You made me a promise if I held off on pahingán," she growled. "You take your own revenge, and then I get to take mine. But how do you expect me to get what's mine if you don't have the power you need to keep your end of the bargain?"

I avoided her gaze so I could pick at a piece of kelp roll. "Already did for two."

"You killed one by *luck*." She put her cup down so heavily, the tea nearly sloshed out the top. At the noise, I saw her own right hand tense for just a moment. "And the other," she went on, "I had to rescue you from. Just in case you forgot. By the time I brought you here last night, you could barely fucking stand. I don't know what was up with you two, but killing her knocked something loose in you."

I leaned back so that my hands rested on the long slab of driftwood that I'd molded into a crude support for my poor old back. "Roulette Wu was a guy I kinda liked. Knife-Edge Ngo was a guy I respected. Mhap the Monster was, and is, a fucking asshole." My fingers tightened their grip. "Anjali the Armored was a true friend."

"That don't change the fact that you needed my help," she snapped. "Why the fuck didn't you tell me you were powerless?"

"'Cause if I did," I sighed, "you wouldn't have done the thing I wanted you to do."

"You know, say what you will about how they do things in the old country," Diwata said, "but there's a reason we have a whole separate word for pahingán instead of just calling it 'revenge.' There's supposed to be honor to it. Truth. Proper rules, so folks know we ain't just animals clawing and biting at each other's eyes." She leaned forward across the table, eyeing me with disgust. "When we came here, our honor was all we had."

"Your lips move, and Benilda talks," I said with a roll of my eyes. "Stow the honor talk. I've lived plenty long without mine." I was starting to get hot around my eartips, but damned if I was gonna let her notice. "And what do you even know about how they do things in 'the old country?' At this table here, one of us has actually been there, and one of us is you."

"Just 'cause I've never been, don't make me any less Biranese than you," she spat. "I can't believe I let myself trust you. I should've sold you back to your pals and died a rich woman.

186

I should've stood there and watched as you choked on your own vomit on my fucking stoop. I should have killed you for leaving me alive."

I threw my hands wide. "So what then, Dawa? You gonna take your pahingán now? Balance the scales, right here in your friend's living room? A room I paid for?" I made it sound like a crazy move, but she was well within her rights to grab a knife. I'd made a promise in bad faith, and that made my life forfeit under the rules of pahingán.

But if that was how Diwata really wanted to go about this, I wasn't about to make it easy for her.

She snarled in disgust at me, and somehow it stung worse than plain old anger. "We're under my friend's protection right now," she said. "You think I'm gonna spill your blood under their roof? Just 'cause I want to do something, don't mean I gotta do it right then, Tenny." She leaned back, looking at me with naked disdain. "Don't even know why I tried to talk this out with you." She rose. "Our whole life, this is how you've been. Something's going on, and you just wander in and start kicking things over until you're the tallest thing left."

"I never asked to be a Lacanilao," I called to her retreating back.

She was fumbling with her cigarettes as she made for the front door. She paused in the threshold to light one up. Exhaled a cloud of grey. "You never were," she said, then stormed outside.

I shrugged. It didn't sit great with me that she was pissed, but I also had bigger problems to worry about. Because even if she was pissed, she'd also made a good point: how the fuck was I going to handle the next three Thorn Orphans, the way things had been going for me? And more to the point, Cole, how was I gonna survive killing you?

I didn't have long to think it over in silence. The slap of

bare feet on the floor announced Pamin's arrival a moment before they entered the front room. "Enjoying all the free information?" I said, and hated how sullen it came out.

"Oh, that didn't tell me anything I didn't already know," they chirped. "This kind of thing is my favorite information: interesting. Insightful. But not marketable. All my clients always want to know about the places that make their target feel safe: their favorite restaurants, theaters ... bathhouses."

Their tone wasn't judgmental, but I felt judged anyway.

They peered idly out their window at the grey morning. "They never think to ask about the people who make them feel that way ..." They sighed, then jerked their head down at the length of driftwood that lay next to me. "So how does it all work? For people like you."

"That'd be a very rude question if our positions were reversed."

"But they're not," Pamin said, "so it's fine."

I eyed them. "You're expecting information for free?"

"You can have some real breakfast if you tell me," they said with a shrug. "It can't be good for you, subsisting on nothing but kelp rolls."

"One of my deepest secrets, and all you want to offer me is breakfast?" I said.

"You must be better off than I thought," they said coldly, "to take food for granted."

I scowled. This was shaman shit we were talking about here, Cole. You and I both held it close to our hearts. I know for sure that you wouldn't have given up even the smallest secret about it for a bowl of rice. Even now I could see you in my mind's eye, folding your skinny arms over your equally skinny chest and glaring at Pamin with all the dignity your uptown breeding had lent you.

But while your paranoia had served you well over the years,

188

you weren't the only voice in my head. Meals were how Benilda had conducted business and built up support in Birantown. They were how Binh had kept the salters' morale up when things had gone bad during the strike. People had spent the past few centuries making the whole world complicated, with things like money and machines and nations and family. But somewhere at the start of it all, when the first folk had crawled out from under the Great Bird's wings and into the light, they had been hungry.

And so, my gut reminded me, was I.

"Imagine knowing everything you know, and everything every other zephyr ever knew," I said. "Except, you don't know it like you know other stuff. It's not books in your head that you have to pull off a shelf and page through until you find the right line you were looking for. It's an orchestra that always plays exactly the song you're in the mood for, even if you don't know what your mood is."

They considered all that. For the first time since I'd met them, they looked like they were smiling at me, rather than smirking. "It must have been the best feeling in the world."

I shook my head.

They raised an eyebrow. "Really? Then what was?"

Out the window, the Rock's shadow loomed behind a thin sheet of grey morning clouds.

"Finding out I wasn't alone."

Actual breakfast turned out to be fish with gull eggs, fried together with some chopped leeks and garlic over a bed of freshly steamed white rice. It was the kind of breakfast I'd actually been used to eating every single morning during my stint in Malañong. And not dissimilar to the ones Diwata and I had grown up with in Benilda's house ... or that you grew up with on the Rock.

But you'd been the richest boy in town, and my family had been the top players in the crooked game. Breakfasts like these weren't supposed to be an everyday thing for an information broker-turned-junker. It was the mango at the newsstand all over again.

"An entire generation of Driftwood City kids who can actually have regular protein in their diets," Pamin mused as they served up food for me and Diwata. "They'll all be towering over their parents by the time they hit puberty." They eyed me, a solid seven inches taller than them. "I guess that makes you what the poets call foreshadowing."

I rolled my eyes, took a bite, and had to stop myself from crying at how good it tasted.

"What do you think, Red Rose?" Pamin said slyly. "I've been told I serve a mean fry-up."

"Yeah?" I said. "By who?"

They swirled their tea in Diwata's direction.

Dawa ate in polite, cold silence. As something sweet and brassy and cool piped into the sitting room through Pamin's radio, her spoon clinked against her bowl like a syncopated cymbal.

I let Pamin fill the space with their idle chatter. As they mused on about how much they loved breakfast, and the little extra steps they took to ensure good flavor, I considered my next move. Since I was saving you for last, the two options I had left were Mhap the Monster and Knife-Edge Ngo. Neither was a soft option: Mhap was an unstoppable brute and Knife-Edge was a clever bastard. And it wasn't like I expected either one to sit on their hands, either. While I was coming for them, they'd be getting ready.

The truth was, I hadn't made up my mind about which one was going to die next. So instead of picking one, I decided on a third option. I was going to get to the bottom of why Binh had left me that boot. Clearly, he'd meant it to be a weapon.

Diwata had been right; if I wasn't going to have my powers on my side when I faced you, I needed to be able to use whatever Binh had left me. And now that I knew why Binh had died, I was certain I knew what truth lay hidden in that boot's sole. But since I didn't have the ability to summon visions anymore, I was gonna have to get my information the old-fashioned way.

I considered the remaining source available to me: the one whose help I'd been too afraid to seek until now. I thought about the stories she'd spent four years hearing about me. I winced. Even before I'd known about your lies, Cole, I'd been dreading this conversation. Now that I knew what kind of a table you'd set for me, this whole thing had gotten a lot more ... well, thorny.

But by the time I got up my courage to head out to the truck anyway, I found that the boot was missing from the back seat.

"Looking for something?"

And when I turned around, I saw Diwata was wearing mismatched boots. One I knew to be hers, and one meant for a foot much bigger.

"*Take that the fuck off right now*," I snarled.

"You want to keep information from me?" said Diwata. "Fine, keep it. And I'll keep this."

I stormed toward her. My spirit hummed a furious song, and from within the house I heard my driftwood respond ... but it didn't come to me.

"Trying to whistle for help?" she said. "You might have the best, most dangerous lumber in the city at your disposal, but it's still just wood, Tenny. And this scrapyard's full of boxes and chains. Last I checked, it can't bust through steel, can it?"

Sure enough, I could feel it straining against something. Why hadn't I noticed before? I bared my teeth, like a dog who'd just spotted a stranger in her yard. "I could still take you without it."

191

"If you're sure about that, then feel free to come at me." With the flick of a match, her cigarette glowed to life. She took a fresh drag, and waited.

I did the math. She had that boot, and the sight of her wearing it was enough to get me seeing red. But she'd already thought ahead to neutralize my powers. And before the fall of the Lacanilao family, she'd been Benilda's top throat-slitter. We'd both been out of the crooked game for a while, but I wasn't about to bank on the hope that Diwata had lost more steps than me. Even in my prime with all my powers, I never would've picked a fair fight with her if there'd been the option to have an unfair one.

When I didn't move, she nodded with grim satisfaction. "That's what I thought," she said. "So let's you and me have a conversation. I held off on pahingán because of information that you gave me, that I trusted. Now that I know you lied, your life's forfeit to me. So I want you to look me in the eye right now and give me one reason why I shouldn't take what I'm owed."

I seethed inside. Back when I'd been a full shaman, I'd just made things happen. Back when I'd been adopted by the Lacanilaos, things had just happened for me. Since when did everything in my life have to be such a fucking negotiation?

"Killing me wouldn't be worth your trouble," I said.

"After what you took from me?" said Diwata. "Think again."

"I'm so close to finishing what I started."

"Two out of five ain't close." Another drag. "It ain't even halfway."

"I gotta avenge Binh—"

"*And you think my sister matters less than your favorite source of dick?*" Diwata roared.

I didn't realize how many steps I'd taken to close the distance with her until I saw the knife appear in her hand like magic. "If that's seriously all the reasons you got," she said with deadly quiet, "then we're done talking here."

I was so furious, I couldn't even scrape together the words to defend myself. Avenging Binh was the whole reason I was putting myself through this shit, especially now that I knew what Binh had died trying to do. But it wasn't like mentioning the fire would do much to change Diwata's mind. She'd been on the other side of that fight in the first place. And besides, it wasn't for her to know. It was mine, to hold close until I understood it.

So how could I possibly get her to see how important this was, if she didn't already see it? She didn't know you like I did. She didn't know how important it was to do this the way I was doing it.

My brain snagged on that idea: *She didn't know you like I did.*

"Fine," I said simply. "You want the real reason you shouldn't take pahingán now? You want the full truth, since you're so bent out of shape about it?"

Her knife glinted in the low morning sun. But she didn't move any closer.

"When Cole killed me last time, he waved off offers from every other Thorn Orphan to finish me off. When one of them stepped forward to do it anyway, he told them they'd be next if they took another step. Before that, almost all our operations ended with him committing the coup de grâce on whoever our target was." I reached for the memory of what Anjali had told me just the night before. "And what did he do when he finally took over the city?"

Her gaze flickered to the Rock. I didn't know which exact spot she was looking at, but I could guess. "What's your fucking point?"

"Cole is a guy who's not just willing to get his hands dirty;

for him, it's necessary. He looks out his window and sees a world so broken, the only way he trusts it'll ever get fixed right is if he drives in every nail himself. Why do you think I came back, instead of hunkering down in Malañong and waiting for him to come to me? Because I knew he'd do anything to smoke me out and pin me down so he could finish me off for good. He would drop dozens of bodies just to get the chance."

"So what?" said Diwata. "You think I'm supposed to be moved by your heroism? Your selflessness? You trying to tell me your little crusade is saving lives? None of that matters in pahingán, tanga."

"I know what pahingán means," I snapped. "What I'm trying to say is, think on the kind of man I just told you about. Think on how bad he wants to be the one to finish me off. And think on what he'll do to the person who takes that from him."

She measured my words over the course of a long, thoughtful drag of her cigarette. "You're lying to live."

I shook my head. "I'm done lying to you. No secrets left for me to keep."

Give me credit, Cole. It was almost true.

"But his Thorn Orphans—"

"Are his lackeys. They're supposed to do what he says. They're supposed to bring me in alive so he can finish me off. But he also knows they've gotta fight for their own lives at some point, and that I ain't the gentle and understanding type. If one of them got me, he'd be pissed but he'd cut them slack. You, though? What makes you think he'd go easy on you ... the last Lacanilao?"

She looked like she'd just swallowed a mouthful of medicine.

I nodded to the knife in her hand. "That's the last explanation I've got for you, Dawa," I said. "So what's it gonna be now?"

She glowered at me, then dropped her cigarette to the ground and crushed it beneath the boot she'd stolen from me.

"I'm keeping the boot," she said. "And you're not leaving me behind anymore. We're killing the Thorn Orphans together, and then afterwards we'll see where we stand. Those are my terms, and they ain't up for negotiation. You don't like them, we'll settle this right now and I'll just take my chances with the Governor."

I didn't see any trace of compassion or patience in her eyes. I saw someone counting down how long she had to wait until I wasn't her problem anymore.

But it was also me who'd dragged her into this mess in the first place.

"Fine," I said. "You keep that boot on. Enjoy running in it."

The smirk she shot me was joyless and sour. She considered the boot on her foot. "So, you can't use your little wizard visions on this thing anymore."

"Not a wizard," I said.

"Well, you have a staff, so I don't know what you expect from me," Diwata said with a shrug. "But even though you can't do your magic tricks anymore, you came out here looking for the boot, which means you still think there's some information you can get from it. So I figure that gives me two options here: either you were gonna get blazed out of your mind and stare at this boot for a while, or you were going to take it to someone who you thought might help you. Someone you think would actually know more about Binh than you, since you don't have the answers on your own."

I stood there, stock-still and hating how transparent she made me sound when she laid it out like that.

But at least she was letting me carry on the fight. I was gonna find out from the remaining Thorn Orphans how you'd masterminded the Unified Utilities fire. Maybe even get a why, if I could. And then I could finally balance the scales for Binh and rest.

"So," Diwata went on, "who're we going to see?"

Part Four

The Third Revenge!
The Cunning of the Pink Rose

16

Twelve years ago

Age 18

The Lacanilao family's criminal empire ended when Benilda lost a war against the Thorn Orphans. But the first battle of that war, she won decisively. We didn't even realize we'd lost until it was far too late.

When Binh declared his mass walkout, you and I started planning. There would be power outages, we knew. Water shortages. Probably riots and unrest. In the months we'd been active, we'd done a good job of curbing bootlegger influence here and there. But this was on a bigger scale than anything you or I had ever done before. There were probably gonna be casualties. The Rock would bring in strike breakers and scabs. And of course, with the legal water market frozen, it would be a jubilee for every bootlegger on the Slats.

It was a question of which would be the bigger threat to the people of the Slats: the Rock, or the players of the crooked game. And when you and I discussed it, I came down hard on the side of Benilda.

"I know how she works," I said to you. We were in our

199

Kelptown apartment, in what was our living room during the day and your bedroom at night. You sat cross-legged and calm on the floor, while I paced a circle around you. I'd been at it long enough, I was pretty sure I'd carved a groove into our floorboards. "She didn't get to be the top operator in Driftwood City by sitting on her hands when an opportunity washed up on her shore. She'll let this strike go on as long as it needs to, if she gets rich off it, and it'll bleed the strikers dry. We need to send her a message, Cole: 'Touch this, and it'll burn you.'"

"You know," you said serenely from the floor, "if you gave me a chance to get in a word edgewise, you might be surprised to find that I agree with you."

I turned around. You sat with your eyes closed, like you were meditating. "Do you?"

You didn't open your eyes. "It's complicated."

"That's your answer to every damn thing, ain't it?" I started up my pacing again.

"Isn't that what our new friend always says? 'Every thread you pull has another side?'"

"'End.'" I'd come to know that line well. Binh had a few catchy slogans—the better to put on signs and banners, or sneak into fiery speeches—but that one was my favorite. It could do a lot, that phrase. He trotted it out when he wanted to remind people about things like unity and balance. He dropped it into speeches when he wanted to instill courage.

And now, in the context of striking back at greedy factory owners, it was a neat little threat.

"I don't disagree that the Lacanilao family is our first priority," you said, and at last you opened your eyes to look at me. "I know my family as well as you know yours. They'll be happy to wait this out. They don't think much of the people of the Slats. They believe that at the first sign of hardship, every-one down here will fold and turn on the Brethren. Proving

200

them wrong will make them far more likely to come to the negotiating table. And the faster we accomplish that, the more generous they'll be with their terms."

I frowned. "So what's the problem, then?"

"Would you mind sitting with me, please? If I try to follow you any more, I'll get a headache."

"You're not even looking at me."

"I can *feel* you pace. It's so much worse. Now, come on. I thought we'd agreed that I was supposed to be the broody one."

A reluctant grin broke on my face as I sat opposite you.

"Part of my eagerness to face Benilda Lacanilao first is because I ..." You looked like you were really wrestling with whatever you were about to say. "I'm terrified to face my fathers again. I haven't seen them since the day of the fire. And despite how discreet we've been, I would be amazed if they didn't know what I've been up to. Even with our formidable powers ... I'll be honest, Tenny. I don't know how well we'd fare."

"Come on." I pointed to the window. There wasn't actually a direct line of sight to the Rock, but that didn't matter. We both knew what lay out there. If you picked a direction in Driftwood City and started walking, you'd end up one of two places: the Rock or the sea. "They're just a couple rich guys."

"We've talked about this before. In many ways, finance is a more formidable power than anything you or I possess." You stretched. "Particularly since neither of us have possessed meaningful finances for a while. Humor me," you added when I opened my mouth to object. "Will our powers put food on tables? Will they inspire people to march in the streets with the mark of the rose on their signs and banners? Or will people only do that if they smell prosperity and security in the air?"

You have this way about you, Cole, where you're talking

about something and you know you're right. You don't smirk, like I would. But you do this thing where I can see you trying not to. Back when we'd first started running together, it was one of my least favorite things about you. Now, though, I'd come to appreciate it as something that only you would do.

"Fine," I sighed, leaning back on to my elbows and ass. "What's all that got to do with Benild—? Ah."

"Yes," you agreed. "'Ah.' If we're really going to make an open move against the Lacanilaos, I want to make sure you'll be able to handle it. It's not a judgment on you. It's—"

"No," I said. "I get it." And I did, Cole. I really did. It's true; at first, my temper had flared up like a grease fire, and my whole face had gotten hot as you called my guts into question. I would've socked anyone else for saying it, but you weren't anyone else. "Making the opening move to a game's a whole lot different from having the stomach to see the thing through to the end. And this ain't the kind of game we can win in one move."

I saw relief in the way you looked at me. I was always touched when a big-picture guy like you remembered the little things like a person's feelings. I know it ain't easy for you.

"We'll never bring balance to Driftwood City if we're not balanced ourselves. If we declare ourselves against Nanay Benilda ... are you ready for what might happen? The Biranese people in this city might shun you. Your own family will certainly gun for us. I know that right now, as things stand for me, I wouldn't be able to face my fathers. Can you face your mother and your sisters? If you say yes, I'll believe you. I just want to hear you say it."

A knot clenched in my gut. It was true; I didn't want to make enemies of them because I knew what they were capable of. I'd walked away from the crooked game, but I'd learned to play it from the very best. And in the time I'd been away, I'd kept my own tabs on what the family was getting up to. Dalisa was an unparalleled negotiator and investor. Diwata was the most feared soldier on the Slats. And Benilda was sharp as ever, even as she crept into old age. Even with our powers, the Lacanilaos would be a tough nut to crack.

But besides that, I couldn't help remembering the other things: warm family dinners. Huddling together on particularly rainy nights. The annual Festival of First Flight block party, where all the streets in Birantown shut down and Benilda personally cooked for an entire adoring neighborhood, and everyone who came for food paid their respects to her three lovely daughters.

Sitting on her big bed and telling her about my day as her stubby fingers deftly wound my long hair into a shining, beautiful braid.

I swallowed hard. Steadied my breath. Ran my fingers through my short black hair.

"I couldn't do it alone," I said at last. "But I ain't alone, am I?"

When I looked into your eyes they were deep brown and shining, like rain-slicked oak.

The next night, we fired the opening shot to end all opening shots against the Lacanilao family. We had to split up to cover all the ground, and even then it ran us ragged to do it. But we were sending a message, loud and clear: no one was gonna make any money tonight. So roads ripped themselves up underneath delivery trucks and sent their precious water bleeding out on to the Slats. The windows of speakeasies and dispensaries blew themselves out like a hurricane had hit them from the inside. And if any roving toughs crossed my path, I laid them out good and left them in the gutter. In the morning, they would wake and lend their voices to the story we were trying to tell: Benilda Lacanilao had finally lost her grip.

When I showed up at my final target in Birantown, I saw folks going about their night. Word was probably only just starting to filter back here that all across the Slats, the Lacanilaos were under attack. Amid all the colorful dresses and suits of the folks on the streets, my eye snagged on a splash of white. You stood there, waiting beneath the canopy of a rice-colored umbrella, looking about as chewed-up as I did after all the running around we'd been doing. The city hummed with excitement around us, like it was warming up for the next set it was about to play.

"You shouldn't have to do this part with me," I muttered as I approached you.

"You said you couldn't take them on alone," you said. "And even if you could, I never would let you."

I wanted to scowl at you, but I found my lips pulling themselves the other way. "The hell would I do without you, you prissy idiot?"

"Probably die." You shut your umbrella, then pulled a fresh white flower from your coat pocket and pinned it to your lapel. "Roses every day."

I nodded in solemn agreement as I did the same with a rose the color of fresh blood. "Roses every day," I agreed.

And with that, we headed for Nanay Benilda's house.

We strolled through Birantown with the intention of walking right up to that gate and commanding it to tear itself off its hinges. We were going to smash in all the windows. Make every water pipe burst and flood. And I was even ready to turn that glass greenhouse of hers back into sand and watch every leaf under it blacken and curl. It might not end the Lacanilaos, but it would take them off the board for a good long while. And without a backdoor source of fresh water, Driftwood City would turn real pro-Brethren, real fast. It wasn't a winning move, not on its own. But it'd cut all our opponents off at the knees, and they'd have to scramble hard to get back up.

But as we approached, something changed in the air. The city moved through me like music, and with each step closer we took, it descended deeper into a minor key.

We stopped walking at the same time.

"I feel it, too," you said simply.

I held out my hand. You took it. And when we touched, our powers harmonized. Awareness swallowed us both, and knowledge fell right into my head, fully formed and certain.

"She's in there," I said, nodding to the house. It'd taken a long time for me to stop thinking of it as *my* house.

"But nobody else is," you said grimly. You turned to me. "Not even the twins. Where are they?"

And right when you asked the question, the city told us both.

For a long moment, we stood there and stewed in the sheer weight of our defeat.

Gently, you squeezed my hand. "If you still want to go in," you said, "I'll stay with you. We can see this through to the end."

I glared up at the roof I'd grown up beneath: steep-gabled and sun-bleached. And just beyond it, there was the familiar glass dome of Benilda's prized greenhouse. From somewhere within the depths of that greenhouse, I knew she was waiting for me.

I let my hand fall away from yours. My sharp awareness fell away with it, leaving me standing in a muted, sepia kind of world.

"No fucking point anymore." I glared up at the house one last time, then turned to go. "We already lost."

*

Our defeat was immortalized in print the next morning, splashed across the pages of the *Meyongphirin Blue Star*.

RUTHLESS RADICALS ROUSE RIOT

is what it screamed up at me, right above a photograph of a huge knot of salters brawling in the middle of a street near the picket line outside the Plant. And while Binh was nowhere to be found, thankfully, the same couldn't be said about his younger sister, Phuong. She was front and center, skinny as a broom, the camera flash clearly capturing her signature Pham family nose. The photographer was a real son of a bitch; he'd caught her right as she was swinging her sign at someone like it was a plywood ax.

The photograph was damning enough on its own, but the article underneath it made no secret out of which side it was on. For paragraph after paragraph, it described brutish scenes of greedy workers trying to terrorize and extort the good and noble citizens of Driftwood City, all in bone-snapping detail.

I glanced quickly at the byline. "Fucking Kueiyang," I growled, slapping the paper down on our dining table. "And his fucking headlines."

"He's paid very well to write those," you sighed. "I would know."

"Is he really?"

"I mean, well for a journalist."

We were in our front room, illuminated by daylight and electric bulbs. The power was back on, even as the strike raged in the streets. I glowered up at them; their mere existence was a further reminder of how badly we'd fucked up. It turned out that I'd been right about Benilda; she was never one to sit on an opportunity. But I'd been wrong about which opportunity she would seize. Instead of using the chaos to fill her pockets,

Benilda had done the last thing I'd expected: thrown in with Plant management.

So while we were off smashing up her empire, she'd given orders to all the Biranese salters on the line to walk off and get back to work. It'd been a big gamble, betting that the Biranese would side with her over the Brethren. But this was exactly what Benilda had been building her entire life. All those block parties. All those little gifts. All those chats with shopkeepers when she made her rounds through the neighborhood. She'd built a community that would have her back in tough times. It didn't matter that she was a shark; she was *their* shark.

Meanwhile, the peaceful picket line had turned into a full-on riot last night when the Biranese walked off. Kueiyang's report claimed that the salters had turned violent to stop them from breaking ranks. But when I looked at that photograph again, it was easy enough for me to recognize the woman Phuong was swinging her sign at. She was only half in frame, but there was no mistaking the leaping fish tattoos on her raised forearm.

The plan had Dalisa written all over it. Diwata really had been right about her.

"Quite interesting, to see such an about-face from the *Blue Star*," you said. "Just last week, it was railing about the danger of outsiders like the Biranese. Now, to hear him tell it, all the greatest patriots in the city come from Birantown." I could tell you were trying to lighten the mood, but I wasn't having it.

"I don't see what she gets out of this, though," I growled. "As long as the Plant's up and running, and her own people are working it ..."

"They'll have the favor of the most powerful and wealthy people in the entire city," you said. "I'm certain that right now, the Lacanilao family is being very well compensated for their cooperation. Whatever they're getting paid, it's certainly cheaper than a full workforce at the Plant."

I didn't doubt that you knew down to the last coin how much it cost to run that place.

"And now," you added with a sigh, "brave and devoted citizen Benilda Lacanilao can talk about the horrible violence endured by Birantown last night, all at the hands of angry salters who resent the Biranese for their work ethic. She didn't lend credence to our story; we lent credence to hers." You tapped a finger thoughtfully against the table. "What I don't understand, though, is the long game. She has to know my fathers see her as nothing more than a useful thug. What could she want from them that she couldn't get herself?"

This time, I was the one who knew the answer. It felt like she'd been telling me the answer my whole life. "Benilda's always going on about building something. Something that'll outlast her. I'm gonna guess your folks offered her something all her bootlegging money can't buy: legitimacy. The real thing. The Lacanilaos, proper peers of good society. She'd go to war for that."

"And do an excellent job of winning it, it seems."

The sheer unfairness of it all threatened to smother me under its giant, elegantly feathered hat. "We've shown her our tiles." I hung my head. "She'll know this was me."

"Yes," you said absently, as if most of your brainpower was taken up with calculating the magnitude to which we were good and fucked. "She will certainly connect the dots. Perhaps that's why your family and mine are working together in the first place."

The thought had crossed my mind, but it felt more solid when you put voice to it. Between the two families, the Lacanilao clan and the Pak clan knew everything there was to know about us.

"We could try again," you said mildly. "Certainly, it doesn't hurt for us to curb the influence of this city's criminal element during times of unrest."

But I shook my head right away. "Last night took nearly everything out of us. Maybe we can do that again tonight, and another few nights besides. But eventually, it'll take too much of a toll on us. One of us will get sloppy. Probably me," I admitted bitterly.

"I wasn't going to say anything." You gave me a weary smile. "What are you proposing, then?"

I almost backed down right then, but it was too late. I'd already broached the topic. I held up the newspaper again and pointed at the photo: not at the fight in the foreground, but at the assembled ranks of striking salters behind them. "We've done good stuff, you and me, but we're still only two people." In my mind's eye, that teeming greenhouse glittered, its dome still intact. "If we want to really plant a garden that can produce roses every day ... we're going to need help."

Your eyes shone even brighter. "As it just so happens," you said, "I've been scouting out some talent. I was going to bring it up with you."

I was surprised to hear you'd already been thinking about this. Maybe a little hurt you hadn't brought it up with me sooner. But mostly, I was impressed that once again you'd thought of everything.

As you started naming names, I leaned in to hear you better.

17

Now

Age 30

The door slid open after I knocked on it three times. The woman who stood there was four years older than the last time I'd seen her—now almost as old as I'd been when I died. She'd changed: her hair had gone from plain and long and black, to close-cropped with streaks of red. Hints of tattoos peeked past the wrist and necklines of her simple black dress. And the eyes that widened with surprise had an air of age about them now, even though they'd never totally been innocent.

But she was still skinny as a broom.

"Hoy, Phuong," I said with an anemic wave of my hand. I glanced at her own hands, empty of an iron fire poker. "Thanks for not trying to hit me this time."

"Tenny . . .?" She staggered back from the door in disbelief. Her gaze slid past me, where the creak of the steps told me Diwata was approaching.

"You weren't kidding," Diwata grunted. "They got the same face and everything. Hi, I'm Diwata," she added with a cursory bow. "We, uh, took a picture together once."

"I know who you are." Phuong's voice trembled with equal parts hatred and disbelief. "You're—"

"Supposed to be dead, yeah," I said sheepishly. "I guess it runs in the family."

"Two dead brownbacks washing up on your front step," Diwata said. "With that kind of luck, you should run out to the nearest cardhouse and play a hand of high-stakes pektong."

Phuong gaped at both of us. But when her gaze came to settle back on me, I could see the barest beginnings of tears gathering in her eyes. When I blinked, I felt the same. How could I not, Cole? I thought I'd never again look into soft brown eyes that caught the light just so, or watch a thin pair of lips pull up into the sad smile that was a Pham family trademark. If you'd spent years missing those, and then one day they all jumped right out of your memory and back into your life ... wouldn't you cry?

Well, I guess I got my answer when you and I finally saw each other again, didn't I?

"Phuong," I said carefully, "I know the stories they've told about me. About what I did. I wanted you to see my face when I told you they aren't true. They pinned it on me 'cause I wasn't there to defend myself, and they succeeded 'cause I wasn't there to defend him." I talked about him so freely around everyone else, but looking at a face so much like his, it was difficult to make my lips and tongue form his name. "I'm sorry to drag you into all this, but it's important. Maybe the most important thing any of us will ever do."

In the corner of my eye, I clocked Diwata shooting me a skeptical look.

"I'm here for information that I think could help me avenge Binh once and for all," I went on. "If you let us in, I promise you: I'll explain everything."

*

It's a hell of a thing, Cole, how even the smell of a place can get to you. Binh hadn't lived here in four years. But the exact combination of dust and old wood and cigarette smoke all hit me at once, hard as a punch in the gut. I didn't need the city to tell me the history of this place; I could feel it in the echoing voices in my head and in the warm phantom fingertips roaming my body.

I shook my head to clear it all away. I was only half-successful.

Diwata and I sat on a saggy brown leather couch in the living room. I'd taken off my boots out of respect for the home; Diwata had left hers on, no matter how much I'd glared at her. I remembered this couch well; I'd helped Binh haul it up the stairs on a hot day, then collapsed on to it with him. We'd been tired and sweaty and we'd basically had to peel ourselves off it with a spatula. But the living room wasn't half as warm or welcoming today.

Diwata picked at a spot on the armrest where the leather had chapped. "This house," she muttered. "Drier than a bread sandwich in here. I bet I couldn't walk up the stairs without getting a fucking nosebleed." She pulled out her cigarettes. "Hoy," she said as Phuong came back in with tea. "Got an ashtray?"

Phuong set down the tray. I took in the sight of the old mugs with familiar chips and cracks in their blue glaze, and caught myself smiling. That was Phuong for you: always a perfect hostess, even under fire. "We don't smoke in here," she said stiffly.

Diwata tapped her nose. "Could've fooled me."

I admired the gentle steeliness of Phuong's voice as she replied, "Anymore."

She took her seat: a squashy green thing with a scratched wooden frame. The floorboards around it bore their own scratches from years of dealing with its clawed feet. It was weird, seeing how she sat; like Binh, she liked to lean forward with her elbows on her thighs. "How long have you been in town, Tenny?"

"Near on a week," I said. "Ran into Roulette out in Malañong and it turned bad. By the time I killed him, he'd already let everyone know where to find me. Way I saw it, I figured I might as well take things in hand myself instead of let them dictate the terms. We both know how that worked out last time."

Phuong was remarkably calm as she accepted this explanation. "And you?" she said, turning to Diwata.

Diwata's eyebrow raised. "You're doing a pretty good job of rolling with this. I didn't take it nearly as well when a dead person turned up on my step. Look at how well you're handling two."

"I don't really have much of a choice," Phuong said simply. "I'll save all my screaming for later."

"I appreciate someone who can repress like a champion." Diwata grinned, but it wasn't a happy look. "We like that, over in the church of the Great Bird. But as for why I'm here? When little Tenny came back, she needed a friend. I was the next best thing." Her yellow-stained fingers drummed against her thigh irritably.

Phuong sipped her tea calmly, but the slight tremor in her hand betrayed her. "And now you need to expand your operation? Is that why you're here? Because I'm afraid I'm not much of a killer. And if you think this isn't one of the first places the Governor will have people look ..."

I shook my head. "Last thing I want's for you to get wrapped up in this Thorn Orphans shit. Binh got too close to it, and we know what happened to him." The rest of that truth nearly came tumbling out of my mouth, but I held it

213

back. I'd promised to tell her everything, and I wanted to. But I couldn't, not with Dawa in the room. I'd have to wait for the right moment.

"This business is just for me to settle," I continued. I jerked a thumb at Diwata. "Only reason this one's involved at all is 'cause of some Biranese honor stuff you don't need to worry about. I promise: you won't have to get any blood on your hands."

Phuong drew herself up and folded her arms in her lap, neat as a napkin in a fancy restaurant. "Then what *do* you need from me?"

Diwata propped up her booted foot on to the tea table between us all. The kind of breach of etiquette that would've lost her a tooth if Benilda were still kicking. "What can you tell us about this?"

I didn't know it was possible for Phuong to sit even more stiffly, but people are full of surprises.

"Binh left it for me," I said. "He meant for me to read some kind of vision off it, but I don't got my powers anymore. Whatever he left on it, I think it's what Cole had him killed for." *All still true*, I assured myself as I went on. Binh's blood deserved the truth from me, so that was what she'd get, even if I had to leave out some stuff for the time being. "In the days leading up to his death, did he ever tell you anything about what he was up to? Did he meet with anyone unusual? Go anyplace strange?"

Phuong didn't answer right away. She just stared at the boot. As if Diwata wasn't wearing it, she reached out and ran a thumb across its scarred sole. "Those marks are from walking on broken glass," she said, more to herself than to either of us. "When the strike breakers threw bottles at us and we had to keep marching."

Diwata suddenly got very interested in the bottom of her teacup.

214

"He always said we wore our history on our feet," Phuong sighed.

"Yeah, he said a lot of real great things." I leaned forward. "But I need to know what he said to you about what he was up to. Who he was meeting with. What he was trying to get at. He was digging into something about Cole, I know it."

"Tenny, I want to help you," Phuong said, "but you have to see this from where I'm sitting. I've spent four years not knowing what to believe. The official story never squared with the Tenny I knew, but there's so much about you I never really knew in the first place."

My temper shot up like a fever. "You thought I could be capable of—?"

"*I didn't know what you were capable of*," Phuong snapped, her prim manner slipping for the first time. "I watched you rip up streets with your mind, walk across the city in five steps, and kick gangsters into the sun. How was I supposed to know who you really were when you only ever let me see the Red Rose?"

I was so angry, I was getting dizzy just sitting there. I'd expected a little skepticism from Phuong. I hadn't expected this. "I showed *him* who I was."

"And I'm not my brother," Phuong said. "No matter how much you want me to be."

"You really believe Cole's story." Blood pounded in my temples. From the lengths of driftwood hidden in my coat, I heard a faint song in furious, jagged phrases. "You really believe I killed Binh."

"I told you: I don't know what to believe."

"Do you *want* to believe me?" I asked.

She stared at me, stiff and silent.

This wasn't going at all how I'd wanted. I didn't want to fight Phuong, but everything she said was hitting all my little triggers. It was as bad as Diwata's cigarette smoke. The more I tried to focus on the moment, the more that moment slipped past me.

Jaws of doubt snapped shut around me. This had been a mistake, Cole. Coming here had been a mistake. I was the kind of monster who could watch one of her own friends drown and do nothing. Of course people would believe I'd murdered my own boyfriend. They were seeing through the person I tried to tell them I was, to the woman who was loathsome enough to get herself killed by her own friends. Didn't matter if my brain knew there was a reason behind it all that had nothing to do with me. A cold spike of logic shot right through me with an elegant and terrible point: *Your own friends thought you were worth killing to cover up a mass murder.*

"I get it." A voice cut through all the crashing, colliding instruments between my ears. Diwata.

Phuong glared at her. "What would you possibly know about it?" she spat. "You're a gangster. You preyed on the workers we were trying to protect. If you'd had your way, you would've been the one to kill my brother."

Diwata pulled her foot off the table and planted it back on the floor. "I ain't gonna apologize for being on opposite sides of the war, or for living the life I was born into," she said. "But I know what it means to wake up one morning with a sibling, and go to bed that night an only child. And unlike yours," she added, "Tenny actually killed mine. Or did you not notice that there used to be two of me, and now there ain't?"

Phuong opened her mouth, then shut it. Opened it again. Shut it, and this time kept it pressed closed and tight.

"Answer me, straight-up," Diwata went on. "You think there's really any chance the woman you're looking at here actually killed Binh?"

Phuong looked hard at me. "I want to say no," she said at

216

last. "I want to believe that my brother didn't love his own killer. But I just ..." She trailed off. "He was everything to me. If I help you, and it turns out Cole was telling the truth, then I'm betraying Binh's memory and the people who helped avenge him."

"*Then why the fuck did you even let me in here?*" I roared.

She flinched, but didn't falter. "Because I sat here and let him tell me his story. You deserved at least that much."

I didn't need her help understanding who *him* was.

My stomach lurched as I eyed the couch underneath me. How many times had you sat on it? Had it just been the once, or had you been by again and again? And even if it had only been the one time, how deep did the traces of you in these cushions run?

"Fine, then," I said. Hanging around a zephyr had put me in the mindset to tell tales. "You want to hear my story? I'll tell you about how Binh died. I'll tell you everything you want to know."

Next to me, Diwata stirred with interest.

"But after I'm done," I said, "you're gonna tell me what you know about Binh's last dealings."

Phuong shook her head. "I'm not a zephyr, Tenny. I'm not going to trade with you. You're going to tell me the truth about my brother's death because it's what I'm owed. A finger to help balance the scales."

I frowned.

But I answered her anyway.

18

Four years ago

Age 26

Did you ever bother to learn my side of things after it was done, Cole? Did you ever trace back the bloody footprints and see how I'd come to be fighting against you that day? Had you been surprised to see me there, throwing everything I had at the Thorn Orphans?

Or had you been hoping for it?

I was at home when the call came through. The city's energy flickered around me before the telephone even rang. It only ever did that when Binh was calling. And something about the way that energy felt to me . . . I just knew something was wrong.

"Tenny," he wheezed when I picked up. He didn't have my powers, but somehow he knew it would be me to pick up, and not you. All he'd said was my name, but already I could tell that he was in a bad way. He sounded out of breath, and Binh wasn't the kind of man who got out of breath easily. "You need to know—"

"Where you are," I finished for him, standing. "Let's start with that."

"No, Ten." He wheezed. "You need to—"

I reached through the city. Most of the time, it took me a bit to find a specific person in the entire city; I couldn't sift through them all like you could. But Binh was special. Over our years together, I'd formed a kind of connection that stretched between him and me like the notes between either end of a scale. And as I traced those five notes, the last one came to rest on a boathouse. On Beech, near where it hit Kombu. "I'll be right there."

"Tenny—" said Binh, but I'd already dropped the telephone receiver. I didn't bother replacing it in the cradle; I was already running for the front door.

I didn't know I'd dressed for my own funeral.

I threw the apartment door open. As I did, I wove together the strands of spirit energy that connected the two separate parts of the city, and knotted those threads together. And when I stepped through the threshold of our door, I didn't land in our buildng's hallway; I emerged miles away in a dark boathouse where I could smell blood on the air.

In the low light, I could just make out hulls gently bobbing in the water. The deck under me swayed gently as the water lapped at it from all sides. The sound would have been calming. But I couldn't feel calm. Not when the city was screaming through me that something was wrong, very wrong.

"Binh!" I called into the dark. Already, my heart pounded. Since the end of the Lacanilao family, no other big crime organizations had stepped up to cause trouble in Driftwood City. Anytime one tried, the Thorn Orphans stomped them into the Slats until they didn't get up again. So we'd been in a holding pattern with the Rock, gradually wearing away at their support while we prepared to make our next big moves.

So who would possibly have Binh this scared? Had your fathers finally decided to turn up the heat on this cold war of ours? Or was it someone even you and I couldn't see coming?

"*Binh!*" I shouted, even louder, and strode into the dark. I let my consciousness flow through the boards and walls of the boathouse and then bounce back to me, like a dolphin in black water. I quickened my step. I had to find him.

There. The city pointed me right at him, the north to my compass. I crossed the boathouse floor so swiftly, my boots barely even touched the ground. I darted past thick wooden beams until I reached the boat docked closest to the huge front doors. There, crouched below the deck railing, was proud labor leader Pham Binh Cong. Only, he didn't look the least bit proud, now.

The city continued to scream its warning at me: *something is wrong*.

"Hoy!" I shouted, and Binh leapt up with a yelp and threw a punch. I ducked it easily, then threw my arms around him. Out of instinct, I breathed deep and took in his familiar smells: sweat. Smoke. His aftershave. But mingled in with them: that inescapable scent of blood. When he pulled me into an embrace, a shiver went down my spine; his huge, muscular arms felt weak around me.

I broke our embrace. "What're you attacking me for? Didn't you hear me trying to call you?"

There was just enough light for me to see the haunted look in his eyes. "Couldn't be sure," he gasped. "Not 'til I saw you."

I shook my head. "Couldn't be sure of what? I'm the same woman I was when I woke up this morning. Now come on, let's get you out of here."

"Too late." I got the feeling he wasn't really even talking to me anymore. "They're already here ..."

I had just a second to realize that maybe all my shouting hadn't been the best idea.

Shafts of light punched through the solid walls of the

boathouse. Outside, gunfire echoed. And the wildest thought crossed my mind as the first bullets zipped past:

Don't I know those guns?

But no. They couldn't be.

With a shout, I curled my fingers into a fist. Whoever these people were, they weren't gonna take me down without a—

That was as far as I got before the entire boat jerked under our feet. One moment, it was floating hull-side down. The next, it capsized.

The water swallowed us with cold, black jaws. I flailed, unable to tell which way was up. I hadn't had time to take a good breath; already my lungs burned. If I opened my eyes, the saltwater would claw them out of my skull. It was no good. And even if I could swim up, there was still a whole fucking boat on top of us.

Something threshed the water next to me. Binh, I knew it. I could still hear those notes connecting us, their music so clear even as the ocean flooded my ears. I jolted. He was already in a bad way. He wouldn't survive long like this. I grabbed his thick wrist and focused. I had to do something.

Through the city, I channeled myself into the water around us. It took extra focus, focus I didn't have. Water was always harder to work with than wood or steel. But Driftwood City was nothing without the sea. It defined our home's every limitation.

And if it was part of the city ... then it was mine to control.

A current frothed up around us, strong and solid as a wall. And then we were breathing again, because the water had spat us right out into the air. Behind us, the boat smashed down on its nearest neighbor with a catastrophic crash. But I'd never given much of a shit about property damage. I wasn't gonna start now.

Binh landed hard on the deck, but the groan meant he was

still alive. He wasn't in ideal shape, but I'd take it. I landed hard, too. Water ran off me in streams, and clung to my hair and glasses. I breathed hard, and had to blink fast to keep the water out of my eyes. But at least I was on my feet.

The boathouse had more light in it now. While I was underwater, the front doors had been thrown open. But I wasn't eyeing the worn old boards, or the signs with all the rules about boat owner conduct, or the neat little rows of boats bobbing in their stalls like racehorses in a stable.

I had eyes only for the Thorn Orphans.

They weren't the friends and comrades I remembered. Knife-Edge wasn't carrying blades of steel, but rather ones of glowing pink stone. The Armored wore a shiny new carapace, like she was a sapphire beetle. Roulette Wu leveled a pair of revolvers, their handles wrought in bright yellow bamboo. And when I tried to lay eyes on the criss-crossing black tattoos on Mhap the Monster's body, my gaze kept sliding off them.

Despite my confusion, I faced them with a straight back. "You all mind explaining what you're doing here, trying to kill my best guy?" My voice shook with barely contained rage.

The four of them exchanged glances. Roulette was nervous, the Monster downright gleeful. Only Knife-Edge was cool and calm.

With a *clank*, Anjali's visor slid up to reveal her concerned face. "We've got a job to do here today, Tenny. Not a good one. We don't expect you to help us. Just stand aside and we'll take care of it. *Please*."

But her kindness just had me more pissed off. "Why the fuck are you trying to kill Binh?"

"Orders to that effect," Knife-Edge said simply. He gave his glowing pink knife a showy twirl with a spidery hand. I didn't like the idea of finding out what that blade could do to me.

My eyes narrowed at him. "Who gave them?"

The Monster's black-tattooed lips stretched into a cruel smile. "Only one person gives us orders."

Of course. Who else would they have listened to? But even if it was the most logical answer, I still felt like the floor had opened up and plunged me back into the water. That couldn't be possible. You and Binh were friends. You'd always gone on about the idea of us fighting two fronts of the same war. And even if you two had a falling out, you knew what he meant to me. So what the hell was going on?

I'd been your best friend and you'd been mine for years now. I knew you never did anything without a reason. If you'd sent the Thorn Orphans after Binh, it hadn't been on a whim. And you'd never steered them—or me—wrong before.

But when I looked at the man I loved, ragged and soaking wet, his normally brave face drawn tight with fear ...

I planted my feet in front of Binh and stared the Orphans down one by one. "Next one of you takes a step toward him gets a city thrown at you, and I ain't gonna feel bad about it."

Roulette's fingers flexed on his guns.

Knife-Edge twirled his blades again.

The Armored disappeared behind her visor with a clank.

And with a defiant grin, the Monster took a single step forward.

"*Binh, run!*" I shouted to him, and charged. It didn't matter that I was unarmed and outnumbered; the city was my weapon, and I was the city's. The two of us were one, and one fist beat four fingers every time.

Bullets screamed through the air, from both Roulette and Anjali. But the city felt them coming, which meant I felt them coming. My body moved with the liquid ease of a bow across strings, and no lead touched me. An urgent burst of music told me to look out behind me. Sure enough, I could hear the thudding basso of the Monster's footsteps in the dark. I stomped the floor, and the boards sprang up to hurl him right back out the door into the daylight.

With a wide sweep of my hands, I summoned up a wave of water from below the floor and hurled it at the remaining three Orphans. Roulette got swept right off his feet, but when the water cleared I saw that Anjali was standing right where she'd been, anchored by her heavy armor. Front-facing pressure wouldn't do it with her, I noted.

Already, I was thinking of how to efficiently take out my own friends. I really am a piece of work, huh?

Next to her, Knife-Edge knelt. I saw he'd anchored himself by stabbing both his blades into the wooden floor of the boat-house. When he straightened up, the gouges he left behind in the floor glowed around their edges and oozed smoke. My eyes widened behind my water-flecked glasses. Where the hell had he gotten those?

"Nice new toys you've got there," I said. "But they ain't gonna save you."

I stomped again, and once more the boards rose up to try and shake off Knife-Edge like they had with the Monster. But with a casual swipe of his pink blade, he carved a whole line of floorboards neatly in half. And before I could make another move, I was tumbling head over ass, courtesy of a punch from Anjali's hydraulic arms.

With a scream, I was back on my feet. She'd never been able to hit that hard before. Never been able to move that fast, either. Upgrades all around, then. Not a great look for me.

Before I could press my attack, Roulette unloaded on me again. I zigged and darted and leapt from boat deck to boat deck, trying to stay ahead of his fire. I was drawing on the city to keep me moving, but even my body had limits. I'd used a decent amount of juice to get myself here, and still more to get us out of the water. I needed—

A shape unfolded from the darkness in front of me, huge and strongly built. His punch folded me like laundry. Worse, he'd hit me in the exact spot Anjali had. The blow made me hesitate for just a second, and that was long enough for a bullet to bite right into my shoulder. Pain seared through me as I spun from the impact and hit the deck hard.

"You should've used more restraint," the Monster snapped at Roulette. "You could've hit me."

"Yeah, well, I didn't, now did I?" Roulette said, accompanied by the jangle of his boots. I caught sight of him raising his revolver at me. "Now I'll just—"

He didn't get to finish his sentence. He crumpled to the deck, courtesy of the boat oar that had just belted him around the head. His yellow hat fluttered down to land next to him.

With a roar that only could've come from someone desperate, Binh aimed his follow-up swing at the Monster, who stepped confidently into the fight.

"*Binh, no!*" I shouted, trying to get to my feet. A warm stream of blood ran down my arm, and I knew it'd be giving me a whole lot of trouble in a moment. "Get out of here!"

A crushing weight forced me back down on to my stomach. A blue steel boot pressed hard on the space between my shoulder blades. "Tenny, please stay down." Anjali's voice echoed inside her helmet. "Let us do this, and you won't have to—"

Another snarl grated my throat raw, and I shoved up with all the strength I had left. I felt iron dent under my elbow as Anjali fell off me. The city rushed to reinforce my tired muscles and cracking bones, and I knew my body was running up a tab that'd be hell to pay off. But right now, I just needed to survive. Just needed to make sure Binh did.

Needed to make sure we lived long enough to get an answer out of you.

Binh and the Monster were almost the same size. And even though the Monster was a better fighter, Binh looked like he was holding his own. But I knew better. The Monster was playing with him. Letting Binh get confident, so he'd leave himself open. This was why he was a monster: he knew how to crawl under your bed, knew how to wait until you went to sleep, knew that nothing could protect you from him once you did.

A rope slithered for the Monster's ankle, like a tough-woven snake. By the time Mhap realized what was happening, it had already lifted him into the air and slammed him hard to the deck. That was the thing with him: the fucker wasn't half as scary when he was off his feet. I slapped him against the deck once, twice, three times, as the wood splintered from the sheer impact. On the fourth, he stayed down.

Binh leaned hard on his oar, and breathed harder. With light in the place, I could finally see how bad a shape he was in. His handsome face was bruised and bloodied. An ugly red wound threatened to devour his stomach. The Thorn Orphans had already done a number on him before I'd come in. He must have just barely gotten away, then used that time to place a last-ditch call to me. He hadn't even known I'd been home.

Well, I was going to reward that trust.

By killing everyone for him.

"Ten," he said. "It's Cole. I've been trying to tell you. He—"

The knife tip sprouted from his throat like a pink weed. The blood that touched the blade sizzled and filled the air with a thick, acrid stench. He fell, revealing a triumphant Knife-Edge Ngo.

And something at the very core of me tore in half.

I don't even remember exactly what I asked the city for. I think I just asked it to make everything hurt.

Patches of ceiling rained down: on me, on the boats, on the

Bird-forsaken Thorn Orphans. The deck rolled as if an earth-quake were coursing through it, radiating out from the spot where I stood over Binh's body. Below us all, the water roiled and hissed. I could sense the Thorn Orphans trying to contain me, but they couldn't get close. Even with their neat little tricks and fancy new toys, they were all nothing. I had the power to crush them all, and our years of friendship wouldn't save them from me.

I.

Was going.

To kill.

Everyone.

The city and I lashed out as one. We delivered Driftwood City's vengeance for one of its brightest, cut down too young.

But through the haze of my rage, something finally clicked for me: I was duking it out with a gunslinger, an armored warrior, an elegant knife-fighter, and an inked-up brute.

And none of them could make a boat capsize.

As if on cue, I felt something smother my power, like someone had pressed a pillow over my soul. The boathouse stilled as my power was abruptly wrestled away.

Panic surged through me. I'd had my powers since our eighteenth birthday. I'd forgotten what it was like to be without them. And I could just feel it inside me still, as if we were reaching for each other with too-short arms.

Another blow from a tattooed fist. Another kick from an armored boot. My whole body rocked with the impacts, as blood splattered across the boathouse floor.

And all at once, I knew I would die if I stayed.

With the desperation of a cornered animal, I surged to my feet and tried to run.

Only, my feet felt like they were made of lead. I hadn't real-ized how much the city had been propping up my body. With

227

that connection gone, I could barely move. But I couldn't give up; I had to survive. If I didn't survive, how would I ever avenge Binh?

But even as I tried to duck into the water and escape, I felt icy fingers close around my heart. Faintly in my head, the city began to pipe a familiar song: one half of a harmony I knew all too well.

It belonged to you, writ in a minor key and scored by the click of your boot heels against the red-splattered wooden floor.

And that, Cole, was when I collapsed, with more of my blood outside me than in.

19

Now

Age 30

By the time I finished my story, Phuong was crying. Shit, so was I. Diwata was dry-eyed, but there was no mistaking how tightly her fists were clenched. The look on her face was one she reserved only for her enemies, and for once it wasn't aimed my way.

The silence that fell after I was done made me all kinds of uncomfortable. But for once in my life, I let it happen. I'd had four whole years to chew on this without choking. I figured I could give the two of them a minute.

Phuong was the first to speak. She sucked in a breath to steady herself. "Okay," she said at last. "I believe you, Tenny."

I could've melted into a puddle from the sheer relief. I hadn't realized how much weight I'd been carrying these four years, all balanced on the question of this single conversation.

"Thank you," I said at last. "You don't know how afraid I was to look you in the eye and tell you all this. I ... I failed him, Phuong. He called me for help, and I wasn't able to save him." I caught myself very intently looking down the barrel of my empty teacup.

"And you're trying to balance the scales," Diwata said impatiently. "We all get it." She picked up her leg again and plunked her booted foot back on to the tea table. "What's it going to be, Phuong?"

Phuong stared at the boot. She hesitated. Then: "I don't know where he went in his last days. He kept a lot from us."

I tried my best not to visibly deflate in front of her. This had always been a long shot. But it had also been my only real shot. Short of beating you up and making you do a shamanic reading on the boot for me, I didn't know how else to unlock Binh's last secrets.

"Seriously? Nothing at all?" I asked. I caught Diwata's eye and saw her giving me an alarmed shake of her head. I understood: *Tone it down.* I wanted to glare at her to fuck off, but I stopped myself. I'd tried to push Phuong hard before. It'd been Diwata, not me, who'd actually got through to her.

Wrestling myself back under control, I went on: "Before he ... Before, did he at least mention that he was looking into something?"

Phuong shook her head. "He always kept an odd schedule. 'The fight for justice doesn't have business hours,' and all that. But I assumed he was planning union stuff. Organizing the Brethren. Seeing ... well, you."

Disappointed silence settled over us like dust.

Abruptly, Diwata rose. "I'm gonna go have that smoke now," she said. "None of you lock the door on me, all right? I don't wanna kick it down to get back in."

And before either of us could stop her, she left.

Phuong stared after her. "So that's ... your sister?"

We both know the truth is a bit more complicated than that, Cole, but I was tired. I nodded.

230

"And *she's* the one you went to when you first arrived in town?"

"Didn't want to go to anyone," I said. "This was supposed to be a nice, private revenge, simple and clean. But my landing didn't go so smooth, and I had to go lay up somewhere."

She nodded, with the kind of patience that just sort of killed me inside. "Then why didn't you come to me?"

"I don't know if you would've liked that."

"But once you'd told me the truth like you did just now, I would've helped you," Phuong pressed. "Why didn't you reach out before now?"

I swallowed hard. "You really need me to say it? You know why."

She shook her head. "I don't blame you—"

"*It ain't about blame*," I said, sudden and sharp.

She leaned back in her seat carefully.

"I know you don't hold it against me," I said, more carefully. "But you have to know by now that I hold it against me. A lot. And I've thought about it every single day for the past four years.

"I had the power to do anything, Phuong. In six short years, I helped change everything about the way Driftwood City had worked for near on a century. And I still wasn't able to save him. You think I was gonna be able to face you, when I've been carrying that shame around like a bullet in my gut? The only reason I'm here now is because I got no other choice. If I had my way, I would've made it so you never had to think about me ever again."

She'd looked away from me while I was talking, her head bowed toward her lap. Her hands curled into fists, bunching up her black skirts in their grip. "How selfish do you have to be?" she asked softly. "How selfish do you have to be, to think like that?"

231

Her words were sharp and surprising as a bullet zipping past my ear. "What?"

Her gaze snapped back up to me. "You think you're so special, so important, that you could've saved him just because? I liked you as much as I could know you, Tenny. And you made my brother happier than anything. Even his cause. Even his family." She rose. "Hate yourself if you want. I wish you wouldn't, but I can't stop you. But even if you do ..." Her face grew hard. Her skinny hands shook at her sides. "You don't get to decide how I feel about you. Not ever."

This was a completely different Phuong than the one who had greeted us at the door, or even the one who'd sat across from me a few minutes ago. Hearing the truth seemed to have shaken something loose in her. The earnest glint in her eye when she looked at me now ... that was all him, Cole.

"I ..." My throat felt raspy. "I ..."

"You don't have to say anything," Phuong said briskly. "You're here now. And you want to make things right. That's enough for me. I'll help you."

I was jolted out of my feelings. Once again, looking up at her face felt like seeing Binh smile at me again. It was like feeling the sun for the first time after four years of night.

"I thought you said you didn't know anything," I said carefully.

"And I was telling you the truth." She took a breath, like she was steadying herself. "But that doesn't mean I have nothing to offer you."

As Phuong led us upstairs, Diwata leaned into me, reeking of smoke. "I see you got what you needed," she said in Biranese. "You're welcome."

I considered sniping at her awful accent, but stopped myself.

Instead, I scraped together my own Biranese and asked her: "How did you do that back there?"

"Do what?"

I glanced up the stairs at Phuong. There was no way she couldn't hear us, but she seemed to get that we were having family time.

"She was shutting down when I tried to get information from her," I went on. "But you got her to open back up. She wouldn't be leading us up here if you hadn't known how to talk to her. How did you do it?"

Diwata chuckled. "You know what your problem's always been, Tenny? You think you're not people."

"The fuck is that supposed to mean?"

"Look at Benilda. She got folks behind her because she spent time with them. Same with Binh. Old Suriwong Pakuanjangnambhar was powerful, but he had folks fighting for his money, not for him. You and your pal, the Governor ... you're the same way. All high-handed. No time for folks unless you need something from them. Just going on, doing what's best for everyone, and expecting them all to get out of your way and let you do it. Sometimes you just gotta fucking talk to people, Tenny."

"It ain't that simple," I bristled. I was thinking of that kitchen in Malañong, and the people I'd shared it with.

Or, if I went back further, two girls in a greenhouse who didn't have time for a third.

"I didn't say it was simple," said Diwata. "But it's how things are. And you don't get to cheat your way out of it, just 'cause you're a wizard."

"Near as I understand it," Phuong called from the top of the stairs, "neither Tenny nor the Governor is a wizard."

At the exact same moment, Diwata and I realized she'd answered us in Biranese.

233

Phuong cast an amused glance at us over her shoulder. "Everyone on the Slats speaks at least a little nowadays."

That was a hell of a thing to hear. It'd never been good to speak Biranese outside of Birantown. And after the Biranese salters had turned scab, even Birantown hadn't been safe.

"And I took a special interest anyway," Phuong went on. "Once upon a time, I thought it would've been a nice way to make my future sister-in-law feel welcome in our family."

Standing a few steps below her, I felt the tips of my ears burning.

"Now, are you coming?"

Diwata and I both cleared our throats, then met her up at the top.

The top floor had once been a separate apartment, as had the middle floor. But as more of the Pham family had entered the workforce, they'd been able to pool their funds and buy out the other tenants in the building. Now, all three floors were in the family. But I could tell from the gloomy air about the topmost stair that this level didn't see much use.

"Most of the others are out of the house now," Phuong said. "Sometimes one of them will drop in when they're nearby and it's late, but I'm the one who keeps the lights on."

"What're the others up to these days?" I said. With Binh gone, there were now four left, including Phuong.

"Nothing worth telling the wind," she sighed, turning to focus on the door. "Anh left town altogether. Works out on an oil rig somewhere and sends back money. The rest are all over the Slats. Honestly, I'm glad of it. Now that we're all grown, even a house this big can start to feel small."

I frowned. By now, their youngest sibling, Duc, would've only been fifteen. But then again, I'd left home at sixteen to join the workforce. And I guess even in good times, Driftwood City was the kind of place where a childhood couldn't last that long.

234

From her skirt pockets, Phuong produced a small ring of keys that I recognized with a jolt; Binh had once carried a set just like them. "And when others come through, the first two levels are always enough for them. So this one, I've mostly just used for storage."

With a click, the lock gave in. The room she led us into was both dusty and musty. I could see where it had once been a place for people to live, but there was no furniture; now, there were just boxes and boxes piled on top of one another, lined up the narrow walls and reaching all the way to its low ceiling.

"I'd hate to meet the widow that lives here," Diwata sniffed, stepping in and peering around. She sniffed the dead, musty air. "*Lived* here."

The bland smile on Phuong's face told me exactly how much she appreciated my sister's commentary.

"You still haven't told us what's up here," I said. "Did Binh keep some kind of diary?" He'd never told me about one. But then again, he'd written more than a few manifestos. And he'd been in charge of writing all the press releases for the union. I guessed it wouldn't have surprised me to learn that he'd kept one all along, and I sure would've been curious to know what he'd written about me.

"He kept a lot of things," said Phuong. "I don't know what might be of use to you. But your connection with him ran deep. I'm sure if there's anything in these boxes that can help you, you'll recognize it right away." She checked her watch. "I have to straighten up some things downstairs. We can leave you to your searching."

Diwata raised an eyebrow. "I'll stay up here."

"Actually, I could use your help moving some furniture," Phuong said apologetically. "Normally I wait until Duc is around, but since you're here ..."

An image flashed through my head: the newspaper

photograph those two had shared all those years ago. The thought of them teaming up to move a sofa was so funny, I had to bite my lip to stop myself from laughing.

Diwata eyed her for a moment, then grunted. "You good up here?"

I nodded. There were so many boxes in here, and I never had your gift for paperwork. But there was something so tantalizing about the thought that somewhere inside them, pieces of Binh lingered. And if I found enough of them, maybe I could reconstruct them into one last portrait of him.

So as the two of them disappeared back down the stairs, I shrugged off my coat. The driftwood hidden inside it clunked heavily against the floor. Now that there was so little left, it was a lot easier to carry around. And thanks to Diwata's little stunt earlier, there was no way I was ever letting it out of my sight again. It couldn't help me much for this task; it wasn't linked to the room around us. But it could at least play me soft music while I worked.

As much as you and I leaned on our shaman abilities to do a lot of big stuff, it's honestly the little things I missed the most about my old powers. Kicking up a street was great and all, but being able to change traffic lights with a blink was way more useful day-to-day. And while I definitely did miss being able to leap from rooftop to rooftop with the moonlight splashing across my back, my coat fluttering behind me like a cape, I would've happily traded it for the ability to psychically sift through all these boxes in five seconds flat.

I picked up the nearest loose box and opened it. I didn't have time to be dainty about it, so I just dumped its contents right out on to the floor and squatted to sort through them. Dozens of copies of the same old manifesto. The ink on them was aged and cheap and came away on my fingers in little black flecks. The paper was soft and pulpy, like all the stuff

236

that came out of the underground paper mills. Legit sources of paper always charged markup, so Binh got cozy with as many private pressers and millers as he could while he was leading the Brethren into action.

Those were relationships that had ended up paying out big. During the strikes, his biggest advantage had been his ability to get information out faster than the Rock. He'd learned from that hit job in the *Blue Star*. With every union action after that, the Slats heard the Brethren's version of events before they heard anyone else's. The Lacanilaos and your family had both worked very hard to gag the Brethren's whole press operation, but they'd never come close. Usually, the Brethren stayed one step ahead whenever a location was compromised. And when there wasn't time to get away, the printers could always rely on help from someone with a rose in their coat.

You and I had learned from our failure, too.

As I moved on to the next box (more pamphlets), I caught myself turning over what Diwata had said to me on the stairs. My first instinct was to push the thought away. What the fuck did she know about how I acted?

Yeah, Tenny, a voice in my head chimed in. *She only grew up in the same house as you and lived through every major event in your childhood and fought against you on the other side of a union war. What could she* possibly *understand about you?*

I scowled at that part of myself for being such a little shit.

The thing was, the more I thought about it, the more sense it made. By design, the Thorn Orphans had always been a spanner jammed into the complicated machine of Driftwood City. We'd both agreed that it was for the best, since it gave us the most freedom to act, and making real change required a hell of a lot of freedom. But no one had ever marched in the streets for the Thorn Orphans, had they?

I let those thoughts go round and round in my head as I

went through box after box. With each one, I kicked up huge clouds of dust, and soon enough it clung to my glasses and hair. But other than dust, I hadn't found much. There were Pham family photographs, more manifestos, and what looked like Anh's childhood art projects. It wasn't like I expected to find a folder with *ALL COLE'S DARKEST SECRETS* written on it in pink marker. But I couldn't help the swell of disappointment in my chest. By the time I reached for a heavy box at the bottom of the stack, the sun was hanging low in the sky, bright and big and heavy as a ripe mango.

I pried it open. I'd expected more stacks of paper, but instead I found a collection of books. A small smile broke over my face. I didn't recognize a lot of their covers, but I did recognize their spines. Binh had always kept his proudly on display, to counter the idea that salters weren't smart enough for any other lot in life. All my splashiest memories of him were of us on the picket lines together. But there were smaller ones I cherished just as much, of us lying together on that couch downstairs while he and I each read from our own books.

Five books deep, an old friend appeared: a tattered copy of *Our Small Important Lives, and Other Meditations in Verse*. I started at the sight of it. It hadn't been my favorite collection (you know how I feel about Sunjuklantung's work when he gets all sentimental, Cole), but it was one Binh and me had enjoyed reading together. It had been secondhand when he'd picked it up, and time had yellowed the pages until they were the color of teeth. I cracked the spine, figuring I'd treat myself to a break and read over one of his odes to early morning in Oakyard. But when I started to thumb through the pages, something slipped out and fell to the floor: a folded-up piece of paper. For half a second, I let myself believe it was one last message from Binh, hidden in our favorite book. But when I unfolded it, all I saw was a years-old shopping list.

238

My heart sank, but I tucked it into my pocket anyway. Until I'd laid eyes on it, I hadn't realized how much I'd missed the familiar curves of his handwriting.

I got up and stretched. It'd been hours, and I hadn't found anything. Time to call it, at least for today.

"Hoy!" I shouted, thundering down the stairs in my holey socks. I'd spent enough nights here to know that they'd hear me, even from two floors up. This lovely old building was echoey as it was drafty.

"Didn't find much," I called, hitting the second-story landing. "But maybe if I start it fresh in the morning ..." I made to step on to the final set of stairs leading down to the ground floor—

—and ducked just in time as a blade of pink crystal passed right over my head.

I braced myself against the wall of the landing and kicked out behind me with both legs, and my feet connected with a wiry chest. Knife-Edge—come on, you knew who it was, Cole—staggered back into the room he'd just tried to ambush me from.

Knife-Edge Ngo looked as smart as a storybook prince. His long black hair fell down his back like a shiny dark curtain, and his cream-colored áo dài was immaculately tailored. Tossed stylishly about his neck was a long pink hand-knit scarf, to match the jeweled pin of a pink rose in his lapel. His narrow, well-groomed face lit up with triumph. "This jacket costs a fortune to clean, Red Rose," he said, but he didn't look put out about it. "I hope you're prepared to pay for it."

The room I'd kicked him into was a mirror image of the third-story apartment. This floor, Phuong clearly took care of, because none of the furniture had dust. Things seemed neatly arranged. And until a moment ago, the door had been neatly slotted into its sliding groove in the floor. I got the sense that this was an extra place for people to crash; the floor was largely empty, but three futon mats were rolled up and piled in the corner. A large green rug lay in the center of the room, a huge lily in a small brown pond.

"Knife-Edge," I snarled. In my head, I saw Binh dying over and over, but I forced myself not to lose it. If he sensed the slightest weakness, he'd pounce on it. "What are you even doing here? Where's Phuong?"

"What, you thought this was all going to be one-way?" he said. "That we'd all just sit back and wait for you to pick us off one by one?" He rolled his eyes. "Please. I don't have time to be assassinated. I have a job now."

My snarl deepened. He hadn't answered my question. And I was running out of patience while Binh's murderer stood right here in front of me.

"Now, I know you didn't bring your fists to a knife fight," he went on. "So why don't you get it over with and summon your little pile of kindling already?"

I'd been hoping to catch him off guard, but there was no point in playing dumb with Knife-Edge. Of all the Thorn Orphans besides you, he was the one I could rely on to have done his homework.

"Fascinating," he said, as I sang for the pieces of driftwood and they came running. They floated into the room to surround me. "But Mhap had led me to believe there was a lot more of it. I guess it didn't survive your encounter with the Armored." The lack of a question in his tone set my teeth grinding. He noticed, and hefted his knives invitingly. "I wonder how much of it will survive me."

I folded my arms over my chest. "Enough to balance the scales for what you did to Binh." I'd kept it from Diwata, Pamin, and even Phuong, but faced with Knife-Edge the truth just rolled right off my tongue. "But not before I make you tell me why Cole lit the fire."

240

His eyebrows knitted into an amused slant. It was only the tiniest hint of surprise, but I had to take what I could get with a sharp fucker like Knife-Edge Ngo. "Anjali shouldn't have told you that. She's lucky you killed her before Cole could."

I ignored him. "Binh died for that truth, so you're gonna tell me what it was. And if you don't give it up easy, I'll have fun getting it out of you. You don't want me to have fun, Knife-Edge."

For just a heartbeat, fear flickered in his eyes.

But then it died so abruptly that I knew it'd never been real in the first place.

He chuckled. "You're good at the scary talk, Tenny, but I've had years to watch you work. You're not patient enough to draw this sort of thing out. You always draw the shortest, straightest line between yourself and what you want, then sprint like hell for it. And even though I know what you're about to try, you're going to try it anyway." Showily, he twirled his knives. "So I think I'll just take my chances."

My six pieces of driftwood molded themselves into sharp points and flew at Knife-Edge like arrows. I didn't want to face those knives up close, so it was better to keep my distance and overwhelm him. But he met my driftwood with a grin and another twirl of his blades.

My driftwood came at him fast, but apparently working at the Ministry of Housing was a great way to keep in shape. I tried to hit him from all sides at once, but his knives turned into blazing pink trails of light as he spun them around himself. Every time I tried to get past his defense, I'd only hit the flat of a crystalline blade. With each hit, I felt a tiny clash of energy. Your spirit was flowing through those knives, just like it had Anjali's armor.

There, I saw. An opening amid his unbreakable defense. His twirling blades were fast, but he was falling into a pattern.

241

Twice now, there was a point in that pattern where I saw him leave his throat wide open. It was only a second, if that.

But sometimes, a second was all I needed.

When it came up again, I willed a single splinter to break away from the other five and shoot right through it. It was a narrow window, but his elegant throat was bare, and my revenge was sharp and thirsty.

There was a flare of pink light. A screeching sour note in the song that stretched between me and my driftwood.

And then my needle of birch clacked to the floor, neatly cut in two. I felt my hold on it dissolve, and the music in my head grew fainter. I remembered when the streets would play me symphonies; now, it barely felt like a trio.

I pulled the surviving wood shards away, and he let me. Of course he would; Knife-Edge never made a reckless move. He seemed perfectly content to keep his twin blades leveled at me as I carefully stepped into the room. We'd made a pretty decent amount of noise, but I didn't hear anyone coming for us. The silence tied my stomach in knots.

"Where's Phuong?" I growled again. And then, after a moment: "My sister, too?"

Knife-Edge Ngo arched an interested eyebrow. "So it *was* her. I'd suspected, but we hadn't confirmed it yet. Is it Diwata or Dalisa? And how in the world did you manage to keep her a secret from us all these years? Honestly, I'm quite impressed, Tenny. You never really did the whole 'subtlety' thing."

"Will you *stop talking*?" I snarled. I pointed my driftwood splinters at him like five loaded guns. "Where the fuck are my sister and Phuong? What did you do to them?"

"I'll level with you," said Knife-Edge. "I'm not totally sure what happened to ... Diwata? I'm going to guess it was Diwata. Your face didn't change before, when I said Dalisa's name. But I don't know what happened to Diwata, because getting rid of

242

her wasn't my job." His smile was its own kind of knife twist. "That was for Phuong to do."

"The fuck are you saying?" I barked. "You made her—"

"I didn't have to make her do anything," he said. "She kept you busy while she called me to help her get rid of the monster who killed her brother." He let his knives drop to his sides, but I wasn't fooled. The moment I tried to move on him again, he'd have them up and buried in my guts. I watched him carefully for any shifts in stance, any hint he was about to make a throw.

"She told me herself," I growled, "that she didn't believe those filthy fucking lies. And I'm going to make you pay for telling them."

"Then how did I know to come here, Tenny? I'm a smart fellow, but I'm not psychic."

The truth of his words pressed into me like the tip of a blade. "If you were really smart, you would've come with backup."

"Backup didn't save Anjali," he said lightly. "Besides, why would I need it? You don't have your powers. And I knew you would be alone. Even when we fought together, you always fought alone."

I'd had enough. Coming at him from a distance was just going to give him a chance to whittle away at what little driftwood I had left. Maybe I could bank on him losing a step, but I was willing to bet I'd make a mistake first.

So instead of a second round of firing, I stretched out my hand, and my five remaining shards of birch merged themselves in midair, their grains twisting together like the strands of a rope. I sang to them, coaxing them into a new shape: a long blade with a straight back and a wide, curved edge, its length shot with black spots of char. It was a bolo—technically a knife, but a hell of a lot closer to a sword if you ask me, Cole. The Biranese invented it to split branches.

But it'd do just as well against a neck.

Knife-Edge raised an elegant eyebrow. "Do you really think you can beat me at my own game?"

I took a few trial swings with it, satisfied with the weight. "It'll be really funny when I do."

"I'm the foremost expert on edged weapons left in the city, and I know that because I killed all the others. Before I was a Thorn Orphan, I kept up a decent body count on modern battlefields without ever touching a gun." He leveled his knives at me, washing his face in a faint pink glow. "What about you?"

I pointed my bolo at him. Shrugged. "Did all right in gym class."

I charged for him. I couldn't let him dictate the pace of this fight, not when he had all the advantages. I didn't even know if my bolo was going to survive a round with the sapphire knives. Your spirit power running through them let them cut through anything and everything. I was focusing everything I had on resisting those blades, but I had no idea if it'd even work.

Well, I thought as I took my first swing, *too late now*.

We met blade to blade. I forced my spirit through every grain of driftwood in my bolo. It was like singing an octave higher than my throat could handle, the kind of singing that jumps right into screaming. As twin sapphire blades clashed with mine, I felt the gnawing teeth of your power trying to bite its way through my bolo to me. But by the fucking Bird, my power held.

He actually seemed pleased. "Do you know the last time my knives were actually tested?" He pressed hard into my blade, trying to force it back toward me.

I clamped a hand down on the back of my bolo and pushed back. "*It's gonna be right fucking now.*"

I slipped back and took a wide swing at him. He blocked with one knife, then used it to work his way past my guard so he could thrust with the other. But by then I was already sidestepping him, bringing my bolo back around to chop at his head. I did it fast enough that I almost caught him, but then he was dipping beneath my blade with a swirl of his bright pink scarf.

Round and round we went. He was lithe and practiced, me wild and brutal. He didn't grin when he fought like Anjali did; to him, fighting was an art to be perfected, and every duel was a recital on a stage. He wouldn't smile until he reached the end of the concerto and was greeted with bloody acclaim. But I could see so clearly the way his eyes danced with each swing and slice and nick-of-time parry.

I wasn't feeling the music. I heard it as I made my attacks, and felt it hum through me when I blocked his. But it was so diminished from what it had been, and it had already been pretty barebones when I'd arrived in town. I had old memories of swordplay, and I had the kind of killer stamina you could only get from a life of grueling diner double shifts. But I couldn't press my advantage any farther than I already was. I got past his guard occasionally, but I never scored any real hits. And the whole time we dueled, I felt like a mouse being batted between one paw and another.

More than my body, the fatigue was starting to eat away at my spirit. I only had whatever energy was trapped inside those old, gnarled grains of birch. Through you, Knife-Edge could draw upon the entire city as a battery. Could you feel it? Was it taking the same toll on you? Or was it just a shadow of a feeling, like the sense that you'd forgotten to do something today?

He stepped back and put his blades up, and I found I was too tired to just run at him. A few of his hairs had fallen out of place, but his suit was still irritatingly immaculate, minus my footprint on his chest. He hadn't even broken a sweat.

"We're making an awful lot of noise," he mused. "Don't you think if Phuong were coming to help you, she would have done it by now?"

"Phuong would never do that," I snapped. "And even if she did, it's probably because you've got her siblings or something."

"The surviving Phams are fine," he said, mild and detached. "Or at least, if they're not, their problems have nothing to do with me. I imagine Phuong wasn't too happy to see you. But out of pure curiosity here, Tenny: I don't suppose that at some point in the conversation, she suddenly changed her tune and became enormously helpful, did she?"

The truth of his words hit hard.

"Besides, I don't do much wetwork anymore these days," he was saying. "Haven't you heard? I'm the Minister of Housing now."

"Does every Minister of Housing get those?" I said, nodding to his pink knives. The floorboards under the living-room rug groaned as I shifted my weight.

"They were a present for my promotion," Knife-Edge said. "Shaped from the sapphires that were this city's glittering foundation."

"So that was all, huh?" I said softly. "All it took for you to turn on me was a new set of toys? And now, thanks to those things, he owns you."

He shrugged. "Binh was your boyfriend, not mine. And as for Cole owning me ... you forget: the knife has never been my true weapon."

And then he dropped to his knees, plunged both of his knives into the floor, and then viciously drew them apart from each other. A clean, burning line carved itself through all the weathered old floorboards.

Too late, I realized that as we'd fought, Knife-Edge had been carefully maneuvering me to be the one standing on the rug.

Too late, I remembered the way the floor had creaked and sagged under my weight.

"Knife-Edge, you absolute *motherf*—"

The floor fell away like a trapdoor.

20

Twelve years ago

Age 18

"Yes, of course I've heard of you," said the man known from one end of the Porcelain Sea to the other as Knife-Edge Ngo. He was in his early thirties, which at that time seemed ancient to you and me. And he was a good deal better put together than either of us. His pressed suit, the color of tuna sashimi, looked like it belonged at a Rockbound gala, not in this small neighborhood prayer house.

People of all faiths washed up in Driftwood City. There were folks that worshiped the Divine Bureaucracy, or the spirits of their own ancestors, or even the potential held by their own future selves. There were folks that worshipped the sun and stars, and folks that gathered weekly to contemplate the endless nothing they believed was waiting for them after death. If you were Biranese like me, odds were good you grew up believing in the Great Bird. And even if you stopped believing, the way most Biranese kids did when we grew up, you still caught yourself swearing by the Bird in tight spots anyway.

Knife-Edge Ngo's choice of meeting spot had been a small

church to Shokulak-Tauna, a sea god from the warm northern islands. The silk scrolls on the simple wooden walls depicted him as a jolly, wild-haired fat uncle, bobbing in the ocean waves like an island, his big belly gently offering his worshipers up to the warmth of the sun. There was no worship going on right now, so there weren't any blue-robed clerics up at the altar. But even in the absence of worshipers, I could feel the love and faith emanating from this place. It was like notes from their hymns and chants had been trapped in the grains of the floorboards, and now the city's voice in my ear was absentmindedly humming along. Sitting there on the mostly empty wooden bench, I thought the place was beautiful.

I also thought it was a weird-as-hell place for an assassin to hang out.

"Roulette Wu and Anjali the Armored run with you now, don't they?" Knife-Edge Ngo went on. He spoke at conversational volume, his smooth voice echoing all the way up to the temple's low, ornamented ceiling. "Well, I suppose she doesn't *run*. I never really understood that—advertising to everyone how big and slow you are. But I guess it works for her ... and now she works for you. Isn't life funny that way? All the circumstances in the known universe, lining up just so I could make a single bad joke."

You took a break from disdainfully eyeing the décor to share a disdainful look with me. I'd heard Knife-Edge Ngo was as sharp as his weapons of choice. I'd heard he was deliberate about how he presented himself. What I hadn't heard was what a damn motormouth he was.

By now, I was good at reading your moods, so I knew despite your stoic face that you were amused. Me, a little less so.

"So what else have you heard about the Thorn Orphans, then?" I said, leaning forward to rest my elbows on my thighs. "What's the word on the Slats?"

249

He gave his long hair an elegant toss. "The general consensus is that you want to drag the rich out of their homes by their genitals, light them on fire, and give their money to the unwashed mob."

"Ah, not exactly," you said, at the same time as I said, "*Fuck yeah.*"

"And speaking as a concerned citizen," Knife-Edge went on, "it feels like you're doing a fine enough job of it as it is. A full-on strike? A full-on race war to go with it?" he added, with a nod to me. "To say nothing of the plummeting confidence in the city's outside investments. There isn't a Silver Tide Tong running Tsunatown anymore, and rumor has it that you're going after Nanay Benilda next. So that would beg my first question: what's put the notorious Thorn Orphans in a mindset to recruit?"

"As the effects of our actions ripple out farther and farther," you said diplomatically, "we find that the ripples flowing back our way are commensurately bigger. And so, we require additional help to meet the additional demand our success has created."

"Also, we're looking to drop serious bodies now," I added. It was a dynamic you and I had worked out ahead of time: you played genteel, while I played the thug. It'd work toward his expectations of us. "Word is, you're good at that."

Of course, our word had come from the city. But so far, it'd been two for two on the help it had found us. Who were we to start doubting it now?

"I had heard that, yes," said Knife-Edge. "Which leads to a second question: what is it you believe I can do for you, that the likes of Anjali the Armored and Roulette Wu can't? I don't know if you've heard, but guns aren't exactly my thing."

I flexed my fingers. "Maybe you've heard that they ain't exactly ours, either."

I hadn't done anything, but Knife-Edge eyed my hand curiously. "I've heard a lot of rumors. Only a few of which are consistent from telling to telling."

"Well," I said with a grin, "they're all true."

"I'd like to reverse your question," you said. The sun caught your silver hair as you leaned forward curiously. "It seems like the most backwards thing to do. Here we have a city rapidly devolving into a battlefield, and yet you stride into it each day with nothing more than your grandmother's finest cutlery. The odds should be against you every step of the way. And yet, you've already had an illustrious and profitable career as a mercenary, while so many of your contemporaries have not been so fortunate. Do you attribute this specifically to your skill with blades?"

I saw his eyes light up as you flexed your conversational skill. Clearly, this was not a man who was used to people who could spit out a little flair. When he leaned back in his bench, there was no mistaking the shift in the way he sat. He was further away from us, but he'd opened himself up. His legs had been crossed, but now both of his feet were on the ground. You had his full attention.

I smiled to myself. I'd known you would.

"Oh, fun. So this *is* a job interview." His mouth slanted into a thoughtful grin. "So you do want me to become a Thorn Orphan like the others, then?"

"Sure do," I said. "Won't find any fairer employers in town. Might even say that's kind of a big deal for us. But first ... you gotta answer the question."

"I've seen what you wear. I doubt you could afford me."

"Standard we hold ourselves to," I bristled. "We don't dress any better than the people we're trying to help." I really didn't like his attitude now. I remembered back to my childhood in the Lacanilao house. I'd always taken Benilda at

251

face value when she called herself a community champion. I'd never paid any mind to all her glimmering jewelry and fancy hats, never thought much about my huge solo bedroom, until embarrassingly late in my life.

Knife-Edge didn't appear to have the same idea. "That all sounds very noble of you," he said. "But I've done my time among the poor. I have no desire to live like an ascetic. I'm a mercenary, not a monk, you see?" He nodded to the house of worship around us. "All evidence to the contrary."

"I've found," you said gently, "that dress code is the sort of thing that gets discussed with an employer after they become your employer."

"And clearly you're interested or you would've told us to fuck off by now," I chimed in. "So quit jerking us around and answer already, got it?"

Once again, Knife-Edge smiled appreciatively. "Well, I wouldn't want to upset the Red Rose, not when I know what she could do to me." His smile took on an edge, one I recognized immediately. It said, *But I could still take you*.

The smile I gave him in reply was really more an excuse to show my teeth.

He splayed his arms across the back of the pew and thought a moment. "Firearms have cheapened every life they take. Anyone with more than an hour's experience can point, click, and completely erase everything that someone is, was, or might be." He said it lightly, but the tension just beneath the surface of his voice was impossible to miss. I couldn't imagine him and Roulette getting along all that well.

"My real skill is that I know how to look at a situation, find a weak point, and apply exactly the right amount of pressure to it to produce my desired outcome. You know your friend, the labor agitator?"

"What about him?" I tensed, ready to throw a punch.

252

Knife-Edge didn't appear to notice. "We're both Thuotami. Thuotam spent three hundred years under Tsuna's thumb. Twice, we tried open war, and twice we were defeated: crushed by our own resources, turned against us by overwhelming Tsunese numbers. The Tsunese bureaucracy was too efficient, too well run for its grip on the country to be loosened, even when its roots were far away, over the southern mountains. So, do you know how we got rid of them?"

"Please tell us," you said, at the same time I said, "*Get to the point already.*"

"We eventually realized that the secret to Tsunese power was communication. They had the best postal system on the entire mainland. Their records were immaculate, with multiple copies kept in different locations. So the servants in governing houses studied those messages closely. Learned how to imitate every important officer's voice and hand. And when the final uprising started, official sealed letters went back to Tsuna with specific instructions of where to bring their armies, all signed and properly accounted for. So the invading army came and made camp right where it was supposed to ... half a mile from a dam the Tsunese had built." He grinned lazily, as if he had been part of the victory himself. "Not a single soldier escaped the flood alive. Fifty thousand, wiped out in an instant."

"Sounds like your people used one big gun, not a knife," I said.

"The river wasn't the weapon, the same way the knife isn't the weapon," said Ngo, suddenly serious. "The weapon is my mind. That's what I trust in, not my steel."

You and I exchanged another look.

"As our operations expand," you said eventually, "we had thought that someone strategically minded would be an asset."

"Considering how badly you got sandbagged in the press, I'm certain that's true," Knife-Edge said. "I feel like asking a question now. You mind if I do that? I'm gonna do that. What makes you so sure I want to work with you, then? You've admitted you can't offer me much."

"We rob folks who've got a lot for us to steal," I said. "That doesn't work for you?"

"Ah. Payment by commission. I suppose you'll also tell me all about the excellent exposure I can look forward to."

"The Thorn Orphans present the ultimate strategic challenge for you," you said. "At this very moment, we're faced with an overwhelmingly powerful foe whose grip we're attempting to break for good. Our will is there, but our advantages are limited. So we are attempting to, as you say, create our own weak point."

"And once we do," I said, "we're gonna plunge a knife right into its fucking heart."

Knife-Edge pondered this. "That's not the answer I expected from you," he said. "I thought you two would try to cloak this whole thing in idealism. Appeal to my moral compass. But framing it like a compelling puzzle ... you really did do your research into me, didn't you? Impressive. Oh, and this whole routine of yours ..." He gestured vaguely at the air between us. "That's good, too."

You arched an eyebrow. "What do you mean by that?"

"I thought you were hoping to recruit me because you liked how my mind worked," Knife-Edge said. "Don't be a poor sport if I'm smart enough to spoil your game. You're playing your parts—brutish Red Rose, smart White Rose—to try to put pressure on me, right? Or do you always let him speak, Red Rose, then sneak in with your little addition like it's punctuation? Because I imagine that would get awfully repetitive after a while."

For the first time since we'd sat down with him, I smiled genuinely. I'd been getting tired of playing such a grump anyway. "Reckon he's got us pegged, Cole." I turned to Knife-Edge. "We tried not to be obvious about it, but we needed to test that famous brain of yours."

"Chicanery aside, though, our offer was sincere," you chimed in. "We want to bring down a machine built on cruelty and exploitation. And between the activism of the Brethren of the Salt and our own clandestine efforts ... we actually have a real shot at it. Maybe once in a lifetime."

Knife-Edge shrugged. Guy was determined to play the heel, I guess. "Sounds like you want to build a world that doesn't have a place for nasty men like me."

"It don't have to," I said. "The world can always have a place for you if you help build it." I leaned closer to him. "This is your town. Ain't you tired of the same family making all the big decisions for it? Don't you wanna be a knife in their ribs? Don't you wanna be the one on top?"

He cocked his head as he considered it.

"Without you, we may win," you added. "With you, our victory would be certain. We need you to help us. That intellect you trust in? We want to trust in it, too."

He stroked his chin thoughtfully, then adjusted the collar of his shirt. "You showed me a piece of yourselves and trusted that I would notice," he mused. "I do admire that. And there's something to be said about the puzzle you've put before me here ... What happens if I refuse?"

"Well," I said, "you say you've heard of us and what we can do. You really wanna be on the other side of a battle we're in?" I grinned like a shark. "I wasn't totally play-acting just there."

Knife-Edge nodded, considering this.

"You say you have a keen analytical mind," you said to him. "I'm curious. Just one more question, if you'd indulge us. You've now seen us operate on a very limited scale, and heard about us on a much larger one. Given that limited knowledge, assess our strengths and weaknesses."

Knife-Edge laughed: not a polite chuckle, but an actual laugh that undercut his poised demeanor. "Oh, that's easy," he said, eyeing us both. "Your greatest strength is your unpredictability. No one knows exactly what you can do, so people believe you can do anything ... and it sounds like they might be right. It's made the crooked game more interesting than it's been in a depressingly long time. Why do you think I accepted your invitation so readily?"

I nodded, more to myself than to either of you. He wasn't wrong.

"As for your weakness ..." Knife-Edge continued, "I didn't notice it until I saw you both here face-to-face, talking with me. But once I saw it, it was impossible for me to unsee. One so close to you, neither of you has even noticed it. And even after I tell you what it is, neither of you is going to do anything about it."

I could tell he wasn't going to just come right out and tell us; he was going to drag the question out of us ... I guess because he thought he could. But I wasn't going to give him the satisfaction. I wasn't the most patient person in the world, but I could sit here silent on this bench until—

"What is it?" you asked. I could feel the threads of the city around you tense with curiosity. Apparently, our third partner was curious, too.

Overhead, the visage of Shokulak-Tauna smiled down at us. Knife-Edge smiled back up at him.

"Each other."

21

Now

Age 30

I gasped back to life, and my body collected on all its deferred pain payments at once.

Thinking was like trying to walk through tar, but frantically I checked myself: I could move my toes. My glasses were on my face. I was bleeding. I could hear the faint song of my driftwood, far away from me. Panic seized me: had you suppressed my powers again? Were you here, the one standing over me?

But no. I didn't hear the telltale click of your boots. And there was no mistaking the flowery scent of the man here with me.

I was lying on Phuong's living-room floor in a mess of plaster and wood. Just a few hours ago, I'd been sitting at her low tea table; now, it was crushed underneath me. I'd hit it hard enough to telescope the damn thing into the floorboards. The air was thick with dust, but none of it seemed to have polluted Knife-Edge's neat cream áo dài.

"It's quite something, Tenny," he sighed. "Telling someone

257

exactly what mistake they'll make, warning them what will happen to them if they make it ... and then watching them make it anyway."

Lying on the ruins of that table, I gasped like a fish on a monger's counter. Plaster dust stuck to my open wounds and settled on my glasses. Breathing was pain. Existence was pain. All I could do was lie there and stare up helplessly at the exit wound I'd just left in the ceiling.

"Years of fighting alongside you gave me a lot of opportunities to learn from you. Your ways are poetry—their confidence, their grace, their power, all moving in harmony. A thousand fighters could come and go through this city, and none of them would be able to touch you ... including me."

I winced as I tried to gather my thoughts. He was about to finish me, unless I thought quickly. I reached for the driftwood I could still sense, up a floor above me. Its song was faint, but it was enough for me to grasp on to. I screwed together my concentration, and sang out a desperate song.

"But your weakness was your own strength," Knife-Edge went on. "You're still used to fighting like you can't lose, so you rushed right in and allowed me to maneuver you, confident you could steer things the way you wanted. All I had to do was lure you on to the floorboards I'd already cut, and—"

On one final high note, my fallen bolo zoomed up from the floor and flew straight down through the hole at Knife-Edge. I could picture its hardened birch tip sinking into his back. I could hear, so clearly, the rattling sound of his breath as it rushed from his punctured lungs.

But his hair and áo dài both fluttered as he whirled around. His pink knives traced a glowing X in the air.

And the last remnants of my driftwood clattered to his feet, the music dying in my ears.

"*No!*" I wanted to scream, but I didn't have the breath for it. It came out as barely more than a rasp. All I could do was stare helplessly at the scrap wood inches from my face. Heartbeats ago, I'd felt something alive in those fibers, heard its notes sing with each swing of my bolo. Now, I could feel only the faintest thread of connection left with the wood that had once been my coffin, and it wasn't strong enough to lift it again.

For the very first time since I'd stepped on to this path, a horrible thought crossed my mind, inescapable and solid: Binh's murder would go unavenged.

"Interesting. So your hold on it really does dissipate when it comes into contact with shards of Cole's power. I wonder why that is. But then, I've never professed to understand shamanic matters." His knives hung casually at his side, but I knew any second he'd tense again and it'd be all over for me.

"That's your fucking problem," I growled. The sheer totality of my failure threatened to swallow me up like another ocean. "Never can just ... beat someone, can you? You gotta ... run ... your fucking mouth, too ..."

"Ah. You're wondering why I don't just get on with it already and kill you." Knife-Edge studied one of his knives like it was something interesting he'd just plucked off a store shelf. "Because unlike you, Tenny, I did not come here today with only one outcome in mind. I'm a man who likes to keep his options open. So, would you like to discuss how you can walk out of here today?"

I stared at him in disbelief. This had to be some kind of trick. Another floor Knife-Edge was waiting to cut out from under me.

"As you've correctly surmised, our gifts link us to Cole." He held up one of his knives, like I was suddenly gonna not know what he was talking about. "So I can't move against him directly. But just the same, I've grown rather tired of watching my city step in time to a single man's vision. So … how about it, for old times' sake?"

I couldn't help but keep staring. There was still a faint ringing in my ears, but surely I couldn't have misheard all that, right?

"Ah. I guess your brains are probably still addled from your fall. Allow me to simplify, then: if I let you go, I expect you to go out there and kill Cole. I'll give you his location, somewhere he's relatively unguarded. I can't help you any more directly than that, but I trust you would know what to do from there."

And then he dropped one of his knives. It landed point-first in the floor and immediately sank all the way down to its steel hilt. And he offered that newly freed hand to me.

It was a trap, I thought. It had to be a trap. The moment I put my hand in his, he'd tighten his grip so he could bring his remaining blade down on my wrist or elbow. He just wanted to defang me before he gift-wrapped me and presented me at your feet.

But he relented and put up his hand. "I understand, you're skeptical. I haven't given you a ton of reasons to trust me." He glanced up at the hole I'd fallen through. "My bad."

"If you wanted my help," I snarled through gritted, bloody teeth, "why did you fight me?"

"To stop you from getting any ideas, of course," Knife-Edge said, like it was the most obvious thing in the world. "I took something precious from you, and you hold grudges like a bucket holds rain."

At last, enough strength had returned to my arms for me to force myself to sit up. My bones and muscles all screamed at me exactly what a bad idea that was, but I couldn't keep baring my throat to him. I snatched up half of my useless wooden bolo and held it up.

"So your genius plan to get me to kill Cole for you," I said, "was to get rid of the one thing I had that could kill him?" The piece skidded across the floor when I chucked it back down, and then lay there quite still.

"Oh, I think you're being awfully uncharitable to yourself here," Knife-Edge said. "Didn't I say, even from the very first, that Cole's actual greatest weakness was you? I've pitted myself against you before, Tenny, but I've always believed in you. Why do you think I made sure to be so thorough about this?"

My scrambled mind was still analyzing this from every angle it could. But the harder I looked to find a trap, the less it looked like one. That was the problem when dealing with someone like Knife-Edge, though. Never could tell what was what with him.

"If you're really on the level," I said, "then let Phuong go."

He rolled his eyes. "Will you come off that already? She sold you out, Tenny. When I heard you were coming back, I knew she was one of the people you'd seek out. And we Thuotami do stick together, just like you and your fellow Biranese."

"Then she knows what you did?"

His smile turned cold. "I assume by now you've already told her. I'll have to deal with that."

"She lives," I said quickly. "No matter what, she lives. Enough Phams have died for this."

A satisfied glimmer in his eye. "And at last, we're negotiating."

"She lives, and so do I." I narrowed my eyes, trying to guess his game. "I kill Cole, then take my leave, while you ...?"

"I don't need to sit on top of the Rock," Knife-Edge said with a shrug. "I just know that 'one man, one vote' isn't a system that'll work for our city in the long run, and Cole won't be eager to let go of what he fought so hard to get his hands on."

"And you can turn on him, just like that?" I said, but

261

stopped myself. "Guess I shouldn't be surprised, huh? Friends don't mean much to a man like you, do they?"

His eyes took on a strange, muted glint. "You don't understand how much more dangerous I would be if I were brave enough to have friends." He held out his hand to me once again. "But perhaps I could start."

I stared up at him. I wanted so badly to have the spirit here, whispering the truth in my ear. Instead, I just had to weigh him as best as I knew how. He was offering me a clean, straight path to my revenge, and then a chance to walk away after and live whatever life I had left.

But unlike when Roulette had made me this offer, I found myself believing that Knife-Edge was on the level. And more importantly, that he'd actually give me the help I needed to keep up my end of things. The realization felt like poison to me, but there was no denying it: accepting his offer was the only smart move.

And there was something else there, too: an ache to have a comrade again. Someone to fight by my side. Fighting with Knife-Edge wasn't like fighting with you, Cole. But it would be better than the lonely battle I'd been fighting for so long.

At last, my hand slid into his.

He beamed down at me. "Thank y—"

And I smiled right back as I yanked him down to the floor.

His knife was ready to gut me, but I twisted my body out of the way while my fist folded him in half at the waist. As his knife sank effortlessly into the floor like the other one had, I threw all my weight back toward his arm. I was rewarded by the snap of his wrist, and the cry of pain he let out. He collapsed next to me, rolling on to his stomach.

In a flash, I was up and he was down. His unbroken hand went for one of his dropped knives, but I slammed my foot down on to his other wrist as hard as I could. The bone gave way with another scream.

"*What are you doing?*" Knife-Edge yelled, his voice shrill with pain and fear. "*I was telling the truth! I offered you everything you wanted!*"

"You did," I said grimly. "And I know you would've given it to me, too. And then, you would have expected me to live in a world where Binh's killer was still breathing."

He shook his head, as if he just hadn't heard me right. "You don't understand! You're throwing away your only—!"

I seized a fistful of his sleek black hair and slammed his face hard into the floor. He fell silent, except for his shallow, pained breaths.

"This is gonna hurt, and I ain't gonna feel bad about it," I said, before kicking him over on to his back. "Now, I know what you think I'm throwing away: the smartest option. But taking my heart from me? You were always gonna die for that." I kicked the other half of my now-worthless birchwood away. "And then you had to go and take my soul, too."

Up until this point, the fear in his eyes had been like fire: immediate and alive. But as I spoke, I watched as it turned into something colder. More distant. And I wasn't surprised.

Knife-Edge was too smart to hope this might still end any other way.

"So . . . another interview, then . . .?" He was breathing hard, and his broken front teeth made him whistle when he spoke. I'm pretty sure even I couldn't have beaten the pretty out of a man like him, but he wasn't so elegant now. "And then no matter what . . . I tell you, you'll . . . kill me."

I nodded. "I will. And don't act like you're surprised about it, Knife-Edge. You and I both know this one was a long time coming."

I figured his head was still clouded. But even in his unusually dull eyes, I recognized a glint of fear. Not the wild animal kind that'd make Knife-Edge dangerous; the measured kind that showed he respected me.

"You want to know ... why Cole started the fire," Knife-Edge said.

"More than that," I snapped. "I know Binh got killed because he confronted Cole about it. And he wouldn't have done that if he didn't have proof. I figure Cole had you all get rid of it. So you're gonna tell me what it was."

Knife-Edge chuckled.

"What?" I snarled. "What's so funny?"

But Knife-Edge just kept laughing, his bloodied face aglow with amusement.

"Stop laughing," I growled, "and *answer me!*"

But even when I drove my fist right into his handsome face, he still chuckled. "I ... I overestimated you, Tenny," he said, his voice ragged with pain and laughter. "I thought you would always understand him ... better than me ... but you don't know Cole at all ... do you?"

I grabbed him by his scarf and yanked his face close to mine. "What the fuck are you talking about, Knife-Edge?"

"You thought ... Cole would trust the proof ... to us?" Knife-Edge rasped. "Just hand us the tools ... someone else had tried to use ... to destroy him?" His voice threatened to break into laughter again. "Who do you think he is, Tenny?"

Rage crashed through me like waves. I wasn't even pissed at Knife-Edge. I was pissed at myself. Because by the fucking Bird, Cole, he was right about you. The moment Knife-Edge said it, I knew he was telling the truth. You never would've trusted that task to someone else. And I should've known better.

"Can you prove that Cole lit the fire, Knife-Edge?" I said quietly.

One of his eyes was swollen shut, which made it look like he was winking as he smirked up at me. "What do you think?"

I nodded, then reached for the pink crystal knife sticking out of the floorboards. "Then there's no reason for me to keep you alive."

As I pulled the knife free, I noted that the crafting on it was downright artisanal. The handle was polished steel, with elegantly worked rose and thorn motifs that bore no hint of tarnish. The blade was the most gorgeous shade of pink I'd ever seen, with not so much as a notch in its edge. It glowed from within, fire frozen in its facets. Was that a portion of you at work, Cole? When I plunged this blade into Knife-Edge's throat, would you feel it like the gentle tug at the other end of a long, pink thread?

I was surprised by how heavy the thing actually was. Knife-Edge was a hell of a lot stronger than I gave him credit for. It was probably a lot of fun to swing around.

Well, I guessed I was about to find out.

"You always did like symmetry," I said. "I don't know if this knife was the one you used to kill Binh ... but it's definitely gonna be the one that kills you." I tightened my grip and held it high. *"Roses every day."*

I didn't hear her, so much as feel the weight of someone new entering the room. "His life's not yours to claim, Tenny."

"Phuong." I didn't turn around. "You've got a hell of a lot of nerve, telling me what to do after you set me up like that."

"You told me yourself that he was the one who killed Binh." Phuong's voice sounded steady. All the warmth I'd heard before had bled away. "That makes his life mine."

"And you sold me out to him." I kept my eyes trained on Knife-Edge. "That makes your life mine after I'm done with him."

"I'd been told for four years that you were Binh's killer,

and he approached me with a promise of revenge." Her voice shook with anger. "Was I supposed to say no?"

"You were supposed to believe in me!" I shouted at her. Beneath me, Knife-Edge recoiled from the sudden noise. "You were supposed to trust that I'd never have hurt Binh!"

"I couldn't be sure," Phuong said. "And I'd already lost too much to bet on the wrong side. So I agreed to his offer. I heard you out. And I made it so that no matter who survived, I would get my revenge. If you don't let me take it, you won't like what I take instead."

While she was talking, I ran the numbers myself. Sure enough, it held together. She'd been the one to send me up to the attic, to root around in Binh's trash. And she'd made sure to get Diwata away from me before Knife-Edge showed up.

Slowly, carefully, I turned to face her. She stood in the doorway to her ruined living room. Her hands were at her side: one empty, one holding a small gun. She stared back at me with hard, decisive eyes.

"You could've tipped me off," I said. "Could've given me a chance to prepare. I could have died today, Phuong."

"And if you had, Knife-Edge would've rewarded me for bringing you in," Phuong said. "But now that you've won, I can make good on your promise myself: justice for Binh." She tightened her grip on the gun. "Step away from him and let me do this."

I didn't move. "You think now I'll just stand aside and let you have your way?"

"What would you have done?" Phuong shouted. Her gun hand trembled. Rage, not hesitation. She was getting dangerous. "You mattered to Binh, which means you mattered to me. But my family matters more. And I'm willing to bet yours does, too."

Diwata stepped into my view, her hands on her head. She had a bleeding gash on her forehead.

"Ten," she muttered, "gotta say it: your friend Phuong sucks shit."

"I don't want to hurt her, Tenny," Phuong said, leveling the gun at my sister's head. "But I will if you don't do the right thing here. Let me balance the scales with the monster who took my brother from me, and I won't have to take your sister from you."

I measured her posture: stiff. Straight. Serious. It was the kind of look I'd seen on Binh many times before. He'd had it when he'd declared war on the Plant after management had started offering more money to its non-union staff. He'd had it when he'd stood before the assembled union at the dawn of the strike, and told his brethren that there'd be no more beating of Biranese strike breakers. He'd had it when he'd looked into my eyes, brushed away a stray lock of my hair, and told me for the first time that he loved me.

It was the look of someone who meant what they said.

"This situation is fraught for everyone," Knife-Edge said carefully. "If I could offer up a potential solution—"

In a single swipe, I took off his head.

All at once, the sick-sweet stench of sizzling flesh and marrow hit me. I dropped the knife, and once again it landed blade-down in the floor, easy as if it were carving a cake.

I turned slowly back to Phuong, matching her gaze with one of my own. And I saw that Diwata—furious, disbelieving Diwata—was completely unharmed.

I stepped off Knife-Edge's body and started to limp toward them. "Put the gun down," I said. I didn't need to put any salt on it to make it sound serious; my tired voice gave the words plenty of weight. "I'm done here."

Phuong held the gun level with Diwata's temple. Her lip began to quiver. Tears pooled and flowed down her angular cheeks. She reminded me of the shards of a priceless vase. "*He was mine*," she whispered.

"Ten," Diwata said, "I don't know what the fuck you think you're doing here—"

"*He was mine*," Phuong said again, loud enough to fill the small living room all by herself.

"Different bits of Binh belonged to both of us." I didn't falter in my step. "And Knife-Edge managed to kill me, too. Can you say the same thing?"

"*He didn't* kill *you!*" Phuong screamed. "*You're standing right here!*"

I was now close enough that I could have reached out and snatched the gun from her if I wanted. I didn't bother.

"Maybe he didn't kill me." I shrugged. "But I died that day, just the same." I nodded to my sister. "We're going, Dawa."

When she hesitated, I put a hand on her shoulder and calmly steered her toward the door. I made sure to turn my back on Phuong. I couldn't ever bring myself to harm her, even after what she'd done. But I knew her well enough to feel certain that my disdain would cut her.

"Tenny . . ." Diwata said through clenched teeth.

"We've got nothing to fear," I said, loud enough for Phuong to hear. "Except for the Monster, anyway." And just like that, I tasted fresh air again, Driftwood City-style: seafoam and sawdust.

I didn't spare Phuong a final glance as we left her. The easiest way to say goodbye is to not, and I'd had my fill of hard goodbyes.

Diwata led us a whole block, digging into her pocket for the keys. And when we arrived at the truck, she neatly dropped them into my hand.

I stared at them. "I don't fucking know how to drive."

"Then you learn, and do it fast," Diwata said coldly. "I'm done with you."

And she took off, walking.

"Hoy!" I tried to run after her, but found the best I could manage was a decently paced hobble. "Dawa, wait! Are you seriously mad about the thing with Phuong back there?"

Diwata sped up.

"I knew we had nothing to worry about!" I called after her. "I know her too well! She never could've hurt you! She couldn't have even hurt me!"

"When we went to visit my old friend," Diwata said, "they didn't turn on us. They made us breakfast. *Breakfast*, Tenny."

"How could I have possibly known she was going to do all that?" I had to strain to keep up with her now.

"I never tried to play you." Her words fumbled around the cigarette she'd stuffed into her mouth. But at least I caught up when she stopped to light it. "Not fucking once, Tenny. Even when I wanted to kill you, I promised I'd do it when we were face-to-face."

I rolled my eyes. "Don't give me that crap about pahingán . . ."

"*It ain't about pahingán!*" Diwata roared, and I felt every set of eyes swing our way like searchlights.

"Keep walking, assholes!" I shouted, my volume matching Diwata's. "This is family business!"

That would've drawn stares in a lot of places. But this was Driftwood City, so they actually listened to me. Still, I heard more than a couple of them mutter "brownback" as they left. The word didn't have the same sting it used to. If anything, I felt a savage kind of pleasure from hearing it. You might have slapped a new coat of finish on Driftwood City, Cole, but even you couldn't sand away all the ugliest bits of its people.

Diwata dropped her voice. "You think this is about some old-country honor shit? Breaking news, Tenny, I ain't ever

269

been to the old country. That's *you*, remember? All I know is the way we do things here. You and I were supposed to be partners. But when she had a gun on me, you decided you'd rather roll the dice on my life than miss out on a chance to get even."

My shoulders rose like hackles. "They took everything from me."

"And she could've taken what you had left!" Diwata said, shoving me. *"But you didn't even hesitate!"*

I made to shove her back, but stopped myself. For one thing, I wasn't confident about my chances of beating Diwata in a straight fight right now. But I could also see that I'd let this go too far. I had to rein it in before something broke for good between us.

"Hoy." I put both my hands up. "I'm sorry, all right?" I let out a big, heavy sigh. "There. I said it. I know that's what you've been waiting for. I'm sorry I got you mixed up in all this. And I'm sorry I played a dangerous game just now. But you've gotta trust me. This is my world. I know how it works. I know where everything is. I know where we're going, and I can see how we get there. We're close, Dawa. *So fucking close.*"

The sincerity in my own voice caught me off guard. At the start of my little speech, I'd worn my pleading tone like a coat. But somewhere along the way, that coat had become as natural to me as another layer of skin. With a jolt, I realized the truth. And in the kind of rare moment you would've been proud of, Cole, I told her.

"I need you. I can't do this without you. Help me, Dawa. You're right. I ..." Saying the next words was like spitting up stones, each one catching in my throat on the way up. "I need my sister."

I knew how dicey it was, invoking sisterhood. But I needed her to see that I meant it because I did, Cole. I really did. The past three Orphans, I'd taken on by myself. And I'd gotten my ass beat up or ambushed every single time. Now, I'd spent my last driftwood, and with it the final shreds of my power. Finishing this on my own had been unlikely before; now, it was impossible. I needed someone at my back. Someone I could trust no matter what. It'd taken me way too long to realize. Stupidly long to realize. But when I'd been at my highest, I'd never been alone. I'd had the other Orphans. I'd had the spirit of Driftwood City. And I'd had you by my side. If I wanted to rise high again, I needed help now.

She only hesitated for a second before I saw a light go out behind her eyes. "If you're not gonna use that truck," she said dully, "give me the keys back. 'Cause you and me are done."

"No, we're not," I said. "You still gotta kill me for taking out Dalisa, don't you?"

Her fists clenched. Then, suddenly, they were at my shirt collar, and her fury-twisted face was inches from mine. I didn't fight back.

But just as quickly as the rage had descended on her, it dissipated like a fog. She let me go and stepped back, shaking her head. "You know what?" she said. "Fuck it. You can just get away with it. You get a hall pass from me. Go live your life and die young, Tenny. When I read the headline about you catching a bullet, I'll consider the scales balanced." She crushed her cigarette right on to the Slats, then sat down next to it.

"The fuck are you doing?"

"Giving you these," she grunted as she removed her mismatched boots: one hers, one Binh's. "So you and I never have to talk again. Give me yours, and we're done."

I stared at her in disbelief. Then, at the familiar old boot standing straight up next to her.

Reluctantly, I unlaced mine and traded with her right there on the curb.

She was done tying her laces before I was. She got right up and started walking. Not even a goodbye.

"*Hoy! Dawa!*" I shouted, as she drew further and further away from me. "*Come on! You've made your fucking point, all right?*"

This time, no one looked at me. Including Diwata. It was like I wasn't even there.

"Diwata!" I called, but it was too late. She'd already disappeared around a corner.

Damnedest thing, Cole.

Diwata didn't shoot me, didn't stab me. Didn't wrap my spirit in a chokehold, then smother me in a coffin and drop me into the ocean's dark jaws.

Didn't turn three hundred and fifty brave souls to ash.

Didn't turn the kindest, brightest man I ever met into bloody meat.

But when she left me there, it hurt just as bad.

22

Eight years ago

Age 22

Knife-Edge Ngo had been correct when he put his finger on our greatest weakness, Cole. I hate to give the bastard credit, but he had us figured out right away.

And unfortunately for me and you, he wasn't the last one.

You told me later that they'd taken you at dinner. That was how I knew Benilda really fucking meant it. To her, meal-times were sacred. It was a hospitality that no self-respecting Biranese person would breach. She was a bootlegger and a murderer and a collector of opulent hats, but she also liked to think of herself as a woman with a code. And one of the solid tenets of that code was, *No playing with your food*.

But they'd caught you out in the open, courtesy of a drugged cup of tea. You'd been too unsteady to use your powers, and then you hadn't been awake at all. Once they'd had you hooked up to an IV meant to keep you under and safe, I'd got the telephone call.

"Come home, anak," Benilda had said simply. "Come home, and your friend will be able to leave it."

You saw the aftermath of my fury, Cole, when you came home safe the next morning. But you didn't see me in the thick of it. Our chairs, upturned. Our lamps, smashed. Our shelves, emptied out on to the floor. And the whole time, I strung together every single curse word I could think of, in every language I'd ever heard in my short life, at the top of my oversized lungs. I only stopped when I realized I had pried our dining table out of its place on the floor, and had been ready to hurl it through our big round window out of sheer rage.

It was like clearing a poison out of my system. I let the table fall hard to the floor, ignoring the scuffs it'd created. I released a long, hard sigh, and it felt like breathing fire. Destroying our apartment wasn't going to get you back.

But Benilda . . . we'd supported the Brethren against her strike breakers. Beat up her lackeys and ambushed her soldiers. We'd hijacked her trucks. But we hadn't moved directly against her since the night of our first defeat. I'd done everything I could to avoid it, and you had been a good enough friend not to push me on it. Whenever any of the other Orphans tried to bring it up, I didn't have to be the one to shut them down. You always did it for me.

I don't think I ever told you, but I always appreciated that.

I guess she'd decided to make the first move after she'd figured out I wasn't gonna. She'd finally found the one thing that could bring me to the table on her terms. I'd been stupid to assume she wouldn't. And now I was there in our ruined apartment, drowning in shame because it was my fault you were in this mess.

The city's little limitation on us—that protection it gave us from each other's powers—had been a lifesaver when we needed privacy. Now, it worked against us. I couldn't find you when I closed my eyes and wove my consciousness through the threads of the city. If I could have, it would have been as easy as opening a door from our apartment, scooping you up, and carrying you back over the threshold like you were a sleeping baby. But no matter how much I begged the city for that little favor, it wasn't about to give it to me.

After I hung up on Benilda, I almost picked up the telephone again. It would've made sense for me to call in Roulette, Anjali, Knife-Edge ... even the Monster. And the Bird knew I wanted to call Binh. If I'd asked him to, he would've set all the Brethren marching behind me to help get you back. I knew once he found out about this, he'd be pissed I hadn't told him. He would have wanted to do something.

But, I thought as I donned my long black coat, I didn't want him to do anything.

I wanted to do everything.

Rather than just appear in her study, I emerged from a door down the street. I was dressed in full Thorn Orphans regalia: the black coat, the flatcap, the carpenter's mask, the red rose. And I walked right down the street in broad nightlight, hands in my pockets and a five-note melody on my lips. Inside, I seethed. But an angry Tenny wouldn't scare Benilda. She had weathered all kinds of tantrums from me. A calm Tenny, though? A collected Tenny? A casual, whistle-while-she-strolls Tenny who made every light burn brighter as she passed it? That, I knew, would strike the proper chord.

I strode into Birantown with my face visible and my head held high, and Birantown recognized me as Tenny, native daughter. The smells welcomed me, and the sounds serenaded me with blaring brass and soaring strings and deafening drums. But the folks on the street recognized me, too: as the Red Rose, and they kept their distance from her.

275

I moved among my people like a shark through minnows.

The guards at the front gate of the house sprang to attention when they saw me approaching. They shouted to each other in a mix of Slatspeak and Biranese. I heard the groan of iron on iron as they began to slide the gates open for me.

Bad luck for them that I didn't feel like waiting.

I thrust my hands forward, their backs to each other, and jerkily parted them like I was prying open the jaws of a beast. At once, the gates threw themselves wide for me. The guards shouted again, but no one went for their weapons. No doubt they knew that if they shed a drop of my blood, even by accident, their life was forfeit. It would just be a question of whether me or Benilda collected it first.

Dalisa and Diwata waited for me in the front foyer. Diwata stayed ramrod stiff, while Dalisa bowed low. "Welcome home, Tenny," she said in a voice as cool and tempered as steel.

There's something funny about coming home again, Cole. When it's not home anymore, you see it for the first time. Until that day, I thought I'd grown up in a palace. But now, I saw paintings so clustered together that they bled into one another as a generic cloud of art. I saw furniture with shiny details, but no rhyme or consistency in their shapes and colors. It all looked less like a queen's castle, and more like a magpie's nest. Now that I'd seen firsthand the kind of people Benilda was pretending to be, I could see how far removed from them she actually was.

I glanced around the receiving hall. I'd played here so many times. Accidentally knocked over vases with my too-long teenaged limbs. Tracked in sawdust on rainy days. Hell, I remembered this place even better than the house I'd lived in before my mom died. And if I let myself listen, I knew the city would sing me all kinds of histories and stories about how much blood lurked under the black-and-white tiles on which I stood. But home, Cole, was the green roofs of Kelptown. It was a small one-bedroom flat with a big, round window, creaky wooden floors, and a young man with silver hair who slept on the couch.

"Where the fuck is she?" I said.

"You'll find her in the dining room," Dalisa said evenly, "awaiting your arrival. She's made pancit for you. I would advise tempering your language, but it's your choice."

Diwata didn't say anything, but she didn't have to. I knew exactly what kinds of words crouched behind her clenched teeth.

Neither of the twins tried to make small talk as they led me down the familiar hallway to the dining room. I didn't even need them to lead me, but I guessed I couldn't just burst in. The whole way down, I didn't pay notice to the vases of roses or the hanging art; I was probing the grounds for any sign of you, even though I knew it was probably pointless. Benilda would never make it that easy for me. You were the only hold on me she had left.

So instead, I let the city's song fill my ears. Tonight, the melody was small and urgent. It was a horn, brought alive by short, sharp breaths from phantom lips. But while it set all my hairs standing, I took grim pleasure in knowing that the fear I felt wasn't mine. This whole building was drenched in fear. Of me.

Good.

When we reached the dining room, the twins each took hold of a door and slid them open in perfect unison. I slipped my hands into my coat pockets, so no one could see the sweat on my palms. "She's got you two well trained," I said.

"We always aim to show Benilda our gratitude for all she's done," Dalisa said.

I made sure my voice was hard and sharp as a needle when I replied, "And yet I'm still her favorite."

Diwata opened her mouth to say something back, but snapped her jaw shut again when Dalisa shot her a look that was both flat and forceful. Satisfied, I passed between the two of them, waiting for a knife between my shoulder blades the whole way. But it never came, and I stepped into the dining room intact.

Benilda was seated at our long tigerwood table with its live edges. The chairs were all neatly arrayed around it. And standing in the very center was a violet mother-of-pearl vase with a dozen red roses standing tall.

True to Dalisa's word, a huge ceramic platter of sauce-stained rice noodles sat in front of Benilda, the top covered in curly pink shrimp. My traitor stomach growled at the sight of it from the sheer nostalgia alone.

"Anak." She stood. She wore a shiny black silk hat with an entire stuffed red bird perched on its brim. Her short, stubby arms spread in welcome. "How I've missed your beautiful face."

I took three steps into the room and stopped just short of the table. "Where's. Cole?"

"There will be time to discuss that," Benilda said, indicating the chair next to her. It had been pulled slightly away, just waiting for me.

I ground my teeth. No choice but to play Benilda's game until I knew what she wanted.

"Prove to me he's alive," I said.

"Your special ... thing? That you do?" Benilda said. My powers weren't a secret from her anymore, but it was weird to hear her talk about it so casually. "Can it tell you when someone is lying?"

I grunted. "It can."

She met my gaze calmly. Smiled. "Your friend is alive and safe."

I studied her while listening for any break in the melody, even the slightest sour note.

At last, I nodded and crossed over to the chair she'd left open for me. "Tell me what I need to give you for you to let him and me walk out of here again."

At the far end of the room, the twins shut the doors and came to stand dutifully behind Benilda like guard dogs. Dalisa was calm as ever, but Diwata glowered at me as I took my seat.

"This war of ours," Benilda said, as Dalisa began to serve us each portions of pancit. "For two years, it's gone on. You have drawn my blood ... I have drawn yours ... and I think it is fair to say that we've both fought it well."

"If you're talking about the struggle of the salters for fair pay and a better life," I said, "then I would say we're hand-ily winning right now." The smell of the pancit twisted my stomach into origami, but I held firm. Rejecting her hospitality would send her a clearer message than my words could have.

Even so, I decided to throw more words into the mix. "Public opinion's come back around to the salters, now that all those nice business owners have remembered who buys all their goods. And they're tired of rationed water and blinking lights. You want me to say you played well? Fine. You played well. But you're out of winning tiles."

Benilda shrugged. "There is winning, and there is winning." It was hard to tell if she actually knew something I didn't, or if she was just fucking with me because parenthood had taught her how. "We could fight it forever, and when it is finally over neither of us will be rich enough to justify the cost."

I pulled out a sneer. "All that big talk about serving your people, but it always comes back to that with you, doesn't it?" I spat the last word: "Money."

"Yes, anak, I want to make money," Benilda said with a roll of her eyes. "If the world ran on seagulls, I would have your sisters out there day and night with the biggest nets they could find. But it runs on money, so I do what I need to do to make money."

A memory floated to the surface of my mind: a day at the start of our friendship, when a certain Samnati smartass had told me something similar.

"And while you wrinkle your nose at money," she went on, "what do I do with it?"

I scowled. "Buy longer fingers so you can reach more pockets."

"Do not make that face at me," said Benilda. "You don't know what it was like when I was a girl here. When your lola—"

"She wasn't my lola," I snapped. Time to twist the fucking knife. "Same way you're not my mo—"

"*We fought and bled so a Biranese girl like you would be free to roll your eyes at us*," Benilda lashed back, her voice hard and sharp as a brandished blade. "The Lacanilaos, we made things better for everyone else. We made the streets of Birantown safe, from the gangs and the badges. We got tourists to buy from Biranese businesses, eat Biranese food at Biranese tables. Biranese hands carried to the Slats the water they needed. And when the people here came to our streets looking for blood, it was Biranese hands that shed it. But all that costs money. So I go out into the world and I make money."

"By becoming the Rock's pet."

"By giving my people all the jobs they could want," Benilda said. "With better pay than any salter has ever had. Have you seen the streets of Birantown, anak? Have you seen how the Slats here shine?"

"What about the rest of the city?"

"When has the rest of the city cared about us? Fuck the rest of the city." She shrugged. "A person must choose where to build the wall of her garden." She helped herself to a big bite of pancit. "But I don't want to tend the Rock's garden anymore, anak. And I know you don't want to fight me. Remember: I called you here to end the war between us."

I raised an eyebrow. I knew there was a catch coming, but Benilda's word was ironclad. If she was only going to let you go, then I was gonna bring the whole house down on us. But if I could get her to promise more than your safe release ... this was at least worth hearing out.

"I will let your friend go," Benilda said. "And I will command all the Biranese salters to go home and join the picket lines. I will give the word, and plunge Driftwood City into darkness. That should put enough pressure on the Paks for your boyfriend to get his big win at last. I will even help provide water to the salters and their families until they go back to work."

I glanced at the twins to see if I could read anything off them. Neither of them gave me anything, except for Diwata's constant, low-simmering rage.

"You would help the people that killed Sion Atlak?" I said.

"You should know me better by now," said Benilda. "For the right price, I will do almost anything."

I sighed. "And what do you want in return?"

"The same thing I've always wanted."

Somehow, expecting it didn't make it any less surprising.

Apparently this was a plan she hadn't run by the twins, because both of them reacted in surprise: Diwata's, full-bodied and outraged; Dalisa's, restrained and calm, but unmistakable if you knew her like I did.

Benilda paid her other daughters no heed. "You have never had my blood, but you have always had my heart, anak. This empire was only ever meant for you. My price to give you everything you have ever wanted ... is for you to give me the same. Now, doesn't that sound fair?"

281

I could only stare at her in disbelief. "This whole time ...?" I said, my voice suddenly weak. "All of this was just to get me back?"

"Family is everything," she said. "The future of the Lacanilao empire should rest in the hands of a true Lacanilao. The daughter of my heart. The most precious flower I ever tended. My favorite rose."

I glanced back at the twins to see how they were taking it. Diwata looked like she was actually fighting back tears of rage. Dalisa had taken on a faraway, resigned look. She may not have expected tonight's turn, but she'd probably taught herself to make peace with it a long time ago.

Both of them remained still.

"You talk about wanting to do good, wanting to do more," said Benilda. "Here. I'm giving you more power than you've ever had. More money, more people, more resources. You'll be able to do more as a Lacanilao than you ever could with your little gang up in Kelptown."

I sat there, frozen. I'd had a solid minute to process the offer, but I still couldn't believe it. I should have spat it back in her face right away. I should've snapped my fingers and caved the roof in.

But instead, my hand lay limp on the table.

Kindly, Benilda slipped hers on top of mine. Her palm was warm. "You have been an impressive girl, Cheza. Now, be the woman I've always seen in you."

And she smiled at me.

It was just the distraction that stopped me from seeing the knife until it was too late.

With coldly adept hands, Dalisa drew a perfectly straight line across Benilda's throat. The old woman gasped, more with surprise than pain, as her blood and breath raced to see which could flee her body first. Her pancit was stained red, and she fell forward into her own ruined dinner.

I jerked my hand away with a roar, and it came away covered in warm, sticky blood. Benilda's hand flopped on to the table. Her fingers—the ones I could almost feel braiding my hair—twitched like a hanged man's legs.

Diwata recoiled with a shout as all around us, the doors slid open. Guards flooded in, most of them foot soldiers I recognized. All of them had guns in hand.

And all of them pointed their weapons ... not at Dalisa with the knife in her hand, but at me.

The sight of them snapped me back to life, at least a little. I tensed, but didn't rise. Any sudden movements, and I might scratch someone's itchy trigger finger. And there was still the matter of you, drugged up and tied up somewhere. I couldn't risk any harm coming to you. So I had to sit there and wait for an opportunity. Next to me, the body of the woman who raised me grew cold.

Fuck, I realized. One of the last things I'd told her was that she wasn't my mother.

Fuck, I realized. Why did I care so much? I'd hated her and everything she stood for.

Fuck, I realized. That didn't matter.

"*Sasa!*" Diwata's whole body shook. "*What did you just—?*"

"Benilda was no longer the right person to run this family," Dalisa said, calm and cold. Methodically, she wiped her bloody knife clean on the back of Benilda's dress. "Her decision making was becoming increasingly erratic, and there was far too much on the line to allow her to damage us further. I'm sorry I kept it from you, but I sought out the opinions of the other captains. The feeling was unanimous: the Lacanilao family needs new leadership."

Diwata's eyes darted to Benilda, and then to me. She looked

283

as if she wanted nothing more than for the clock to wind back a minute.

"And you think that person's you?"

"No," Dalisa said. "I don't."

And she flipped the knife into the air, caught it, and presented it handle-first to her sister.

Diwata and I both stared at the offer, freshly cleaned of blood.

"I've spoken with every captain," said Dalisa. "They all agree that we need a strong leader to take us into the future. And none of us can think of a stronger leader than you."

Diwata gaped at the knife. But rather than take it, she turned to look at me. "What are we supposed to do about her, then?"

Dalisa turned to me. "Tenny," she said carefully. "I know what you're capable of. Whatever you may think of me, I know you'll believe me when I tell you that I respect the power you wield. These soldiers are under instructions not to fire unless you try to use it. If you don't, you will be allowed to leave peaceably, with the location of your friend. We neither seek, nor do we desire, a quarrel with you and the Thorn Orphans."

"Then why get me involved?" My words were slow and clumsy. I still felt like I wasn't completely there. I couldn't look away from Benilda's body, from the blood still pumping from it, from the last meal her hands had made. "Why do this tonight?"

"You were a way to get her guard down," Dalisa said. "Something in front of her that she would pay all her attention to. I'm genuinely sorry to have involved you, but it was the only way."

I might've sat there for another minute, Cole. Another five, another ten, another hour. I knew I wanted to get up. The city was singing for me to get up. And I knew that if I got up— slowly, calmly, with my hands where folks could see them—it

284

would put me on the shortest, straightest path to rescuing you. But the haze I was in ... I felt like nothing could really cut through it.

And then Dalisa said, "Please understand: tonight's events were always meant to be a matter settled between family."

I have zero doubt Dalisa had a plan to deal with me in the long run. She had a plan for everyone. She was like you that way.

But as my soul screamed the opening note of my most furious song—

—as the city's voice rose to meet mine—

—as the floor split beneath me—

—Dalisa's plans, like grass beneath a frost, withered.

Hey, Cole. Wanna hear something I've never told anyone?

I used to wonder how you could've possibly been taken so easily. We'd spent years avoiding the Lacanilaos, and they were the toughest crew in all the Slats. So what had changed? You didn't have the best street smarts, but you knew how to survive out on the Slats. And you had the city at your back. Sneaking up on you should've been a damn hard thing to do. Taking you in alive should have been a hell of a battle.

But now I know you better.

Now, I wonder if losing the battle was how you won the war.

Part Five

The Fourth Revenge!
The Faith of the Black Rose

23

Now

Age 30

There's a funny thing about the way your head gets wired
if you were raised with religion, Cole. Doesn't matter if you
walked away from it, and doesn't matter how hard you
slammed the door on your way out. When things get tough
on you, you'll come crawling back. It's been a good long time
since I thought I was walking in the shadow beneath the Great
Bird's wings. But when I'm dodging bullets, sinking into the
black ocean, or even just hoping my opponent's pektong hand
is worse than mine, Their name always finds its way to my
lips.

There's a hundred gods worshiped in Driftwood City. I
know you never put stock in any of them, even before we
got our powers. The gods were something immigrants brought
along on our ships to keep us warm, but your family had long
forgotten how it felt to be cold. That was how I knew, when
I passed out in the main sanctuary of an eyrie, you wouldn't
find me. Coming here was a strategic decision.

Mostly.

I stared up at an unfamiliar ceiling. I'd just laid myself out on a backless bench to sleep off my wounds and exhaustion, but now it was morning and I was lying on a soft prayer mat on the floor in a different room. I found my glasses folded atop my coat in a pile next to me, and when I put them on I saw walls of the same deep red oak that the outside sanctuary had been made of. So at least I was still in the same place.

As I shuffled out into the sanctuary, it struck me how weird it was to be in this place after having actually seen Biranba. Eyries had always had all the traits I imagined of a Biranese space: round windows, to satisfy our ancestors' obsession with arches. Tall wooden pillars with wide tops, to act as symbolic perches for the Great Bird. But now I could see that the roof here was steeper, to keep off the kinds of snows Malañong could never see. Those perch-pillars were made from red oak, not the dark and glossy kamagong that grew all over the islands. And of course, there was no mistaking the jagged script of Slatspeak on all the signs, compared to the rounded and curving calligraphy of Biranese writing. This place didn't feel Biranese at all.

A priest was wiping down the windows. Their head was shaved perfectly bald, though the bandage on the back of their head told me they needed an initiate with a steadier hand to do their upkeep. Over their plain green jumpsuit, they wore a necklace woven with feathers of all different colors. The higher up you went in the clergy, the more prestigious the feathers you got to wear. But all that was lost on me, since I didn't know shit about birds.

"I guess I've got you to thank for the roof and the bed." My voice echoed across the open, empty sanctuary like a too-sharp note at the heart of a chord.

They stopped wiping their window. Set their rag down. "Don't be too quick to thank me," they said coldly. "You stink of shit, and it was scaring my initiates. I dismissed them for the morning, for their own safety." They glared at me over round glasses, and I was instantly annoyed by how much more commanding they looked than I did. "The sooner you quit this place, the better for everyone."

"Hoy," I growled. "I get that this is your place and I kinda crashed in, but I've had me a rough week. If you knew who I was, you wouldn't be talking to me like that."

"Oh, don't worry," they said. They stepped down from their stool and faced me with the planted feet of a gunfighter. "I know exactly who you are."

A sweat broke out all over me. "Oh yeah?"

They couldn't have looked colder if they were naked in a blizzard. "You're a gangster," they spat. "The Governor makes bold claims about how he's taken care of the likes of you, but he's young. He doesn't understand that there will always be people like you."

"I ain't a gangster," I started, but I realized the blood on my clothes wasn't really helping things. Explaining that it wasn't my blood probably wouldn't help much, either.

They rolled their eyes, then walked over to the altar, which was carved with elegant feather motifs and the twin heads of the Great Bird. "Everyone's so quick to forget how this town used to be. But I don't forget the sight of blood on the Slats so easily. And all of you had the gall to say you were helping our community. Parasites, every one of you."

They withdrew sticks of incense from the altar, and began to light them.

"I remember the priesthood being friendlier when I was a girl," I said. I'd been up for all of five minutes, but already I could feel my temper starting to work up.

"Those priests served the Great Bird by shutting up and keeping their heads down." The priest hustled from pillar to pillar, slotting sticks of incense into built-in holders and lighting them. "I serve Them by creating the shadow of Their wings here in the world: a place of cool and calm and dark. A place of solace. A place with no room for the likes of you."

Blue-grey smoke began to curl in the edges of my sight. A cloying, sweet smell started to fill my nose, like rotting bananas. "If you hate me so much," I spat, "then why bother to take me in at all? Why not just hand me over to the badges?"

"Because I dislike gangsters," they snapped, lighting another incense stick to life. My head was starting to pound from the smell. "No matter what uniform they wear." They hurried along to the next holder in line. "I was bound by my vows to provide aid to an insensate woman in my sanctuary. Now that you're sensate, please leave my eyrie and don't come back."

I glared at them, but only for a moment. They had a point; this wasn't my house, and I was way past the point of being able to throw my weight around.

Besides, I couldn't think of any good comebacks.

As I turned to head for the front door, though, my head swam. All around me, curls of grey incense smoke groped for me like tentacles. The smell had been faint before, but suddenly it was the only thing: not the only thing I could smell, but the only thing in my world. I sat down hard on a wooden bench.

"What did I just tell you?" Their shoes clicked on the polished hardwood floor, and each step hit me like a kick in the head. "You don't get to treat my eyrie like your personal palace!"

I put up a hand to stop them. "It's the smoke," I managed to squeeze out. I looked up at them as they came to stand over me, incense and lighter still in hand. "Doesn't agree with me. I need a second, and then I'm gone, all right?"

They looked down at me.

And calmly lit the entire fistful of incense.

I was up on my feet and out the door before the smoke could take ahold of me. The chilly morning air was a stinging slap in my face, but I was away from the smoke.

I took a deep, clean breath before turning back to the open doors and shouting, *"You suck at cleaning windows!"*

It was the best I could think of, okay, Cole?

I tried to ignore the stares of the people on the street as I turned my collar up and stalked away. A stranger yelling wasn't uncommon on the Slats. Strangers yelled all the time here. Passersby yelled at each other, bums yelled at birds, and old men yelled at clouds. But I couldn't help feeling like the eyes of the entire city were on me.

That feeling of unease grew the longer I walked. I glanced around, looking for a source. But among the cars on the street, I didn't see police vehicles. Among the people around me, none were walking with the swagger that always gave away an undercover badge. And when my eyes lingered on the shadows between buildings, I didn't see Mhap the Monster's glittering black eye staring back at me.

Eventually, I was able to put my finger on it. My world had gone quiet.

Don't get me wrong, Cole. There was noise everywhere around me. Cars, chatter, humming power lines, squawking gulls, the groaning of the Slats underfoot, and the distant roar of the sea. It felt like they were all towers around me, caving in toward me all at once. But without the city's spirit underneath to give it shape, all that music just turned into noise.

You've never had a moment in the past twelve years where you couldn't hear it, have you? You probably don't even remember what it's like to walk the city and only see the very tip of it. When you're a shaman, nothing in Driftwood City is just what it is; it's a collection of things that it had been or

293

might have been, and the difference between the two was like seeing a square versus seeing a cube, if the cube had a million sides. And even without my shaman's senses, I'd at least had my collection of driftwood to give me a small reminder of that feeling. But my fight with Knife-Edge had cost me the last of my driftwood. So all I had left to dismantle your brave new world was my fists, my feet, and the silence.

I stopped walking. I recognized what I was doing. I was starting to stew, because this was what happened when I was left alone with my thoughts for too long. I'd been able to avoid doing it for most of my time back home because I'd had Diwata with me. I needed her back.

No, you don't, I snapped at myself. And I was right. I didn't need her. I didn't need anyone. I just needed to remember what really mattered: the three hundred and fifty-two souls in the Plant, and the one on the boathouse floor. My mission was to balance those scales, and I didn't need Dawa or even my driftwood for that. All I needed was the will to see it through.

On the corner ahead of me, a newsstand was opening shop for the day. I ambled up, ready to peek at the morning's headline, but stopped. At the top of today's edition of the *Blue Star*, there was a headline:

PUBLIC ENEMY NUMBER ONE

And above it was a lifelike sketch of a thin-faced woman with long, braided hair, glasses, and the kind of sneer you'd see on a villain from a motion picture poster.

On reflex, I started to read the opening sentences of the story, which said I was wanted for questioning in the murders of three city officials. But when I looked back up, the chubby old guy behind the counter was gaping at me, recognition dawning on his face.

My body didn't have much gas in its tank, but I took off at a full fucking sprint anyway as he cried out. Heads turned my way as I hauled ass, and I left them all behind. I didn't stop running for a full four blocks, and I would've kept going if the stitch in my side hadn't stopped me cold. But I was far enough away now that I could blend in to the cityscape again.

Even as I thought that, I noticed a wanted poster with the exact same sketch hanging on a lamppost.

I was wheezing, but I kept on walking. So, I thought, you'd finally decided to drag me out into the open. I'd expected it to happen at some point, but I'd been hoping to eliminate all the other Orphans first. Now, I'd have the entire city looking out for me, plus the Orphan I'd had good reason to save for last. You'd just put a clock on everything I did next.

I guess Diwata jumped ship at the right time, I thought bitterly.

But I stopped before I sank too deeply into that bitterness. I hadn't been paying close attention, what with all the trying not to die. But now that I had a quiet moment, I finally noticed it on the very edge of my consciousness:

A ghostly song.

For a wild moment my heart soared: somehow, my powers had come back.

But then reality set in. The song was too faint, too far away. To be a shaman was to have the spirit of Driftwood City alive in your heart. This had to be a remaining fragment of the driftwood I'd clung to. But where would I have left—?

The answer came to me before I even finished asking the question. I closed my eyes in resignation.

Well, I'd always planned to face Mhap next anyway, I thought bracingly.

Since my eyes were closed, I reached out with my consciousness. I didn't have the fine, precise control I'd had in my prime, but at least I could detect the last remaining sliver of my revenge. And I found it, sure enough.

I immediately saw the flaw in my thinking. I'd assumed Mhap would keep the splinter for himself. I should have remembered that he was a monster, but he was your monster. Clearly, he'd given it to you, because you would have kept it by the seat of your power.

And that seat just happened to be the one place in the city I feared to go.

I braced myself. I wasn't ready to face you. I'd wanted to slay Mhap first. Wanted you to feel as alone as I'd been, right before the end. But according to that faint song, you had your hands on what I wanted, and I was gonna have to face you sooner or later. I guessed the coin had just landed on the "sooner" side.

The eyrie was blocks away from me, but the stench of smoke filled my nose again as I headed for the edge of the Slats, and the answers that waited for me there.

The Unified Utilities Plant had first been built to treat the seawater surrounding Driftwood City, so the Pak clan didn't have to keep paying import costs on mainland fresh water. Vertical farming had come next, as another way to cut down on import costs. The fact that it'd made it possible for a working family to afford anything fancier than rice was incidental. Last of all came power, when the Rock didn't want to be left behind by the mainland. By then, it had ballooned to a massive size, and needed a crew of thousands to run it every shift.

It was the true rock the city was built on. But it was also something your folks could use to crush us.

Getting into the Plant was easy enough. The days of armed guards patrolling the grounds and standing at every entrance were long past. And even if you'd kept guards there, I still knew how to get into places without being spotted. I skulked closer and closer until at last I was in the huge shadow of the complex itself.

The fire had given your family an excuse to give the façade a refresh, so that it stood gleaming and white on the edge of the water like a palace. From its eastern wing, huge black cables the width of a person pumped out enough juice to keep the city's heart beating. From the western wing sprouted a collection of tall, round towers and silos. There'd never been anything like mangoes growing inside, but least our onions weren't bad. And criss-crossing the two wings and everywhere in between were networks of pipes that led back to the central wing, carrying the true unifying utility: water.

That sector was where I'd worked from sixteen to eighteen, desalinating ocean intake so we could turn it into power, food, or just something to drink. This had been the first and most important step Driftwood City had taken to being a truly independent city, not relying on supplies from the mainland just to keep its citizens alive. Even more than in other, more normal cities, water had always been the key to everything in Driftwood City.

Sure enough, true to what Jali had said, Binh's likeness stood out front, wrought in bronze. I waited until the coast was clear, then hurried up close to get a better look. When I neared, my first thought was that the sculptor had actually done a decent job. Rather than pretty him up, they'd kept all the blemishes and scars and rough-hewn features that'd made Binh, Binh. Even the way he stood—shoulders squared, fist raised, mouth open to raise his voice with it—looked like a moment of the real man's life had been trapped in metal. Under his burnished boots was a stone pedestal engraved with the words:

PHAM BINH CONG
Fighter, Hero, Salter
"Every thread you pull has another end."

The Binh I knew would've wanted the thing taken down. But he also would've appreciated being remembered in the marks left by a worker's tools.

I'd called it ghoulish when Anjali had told me about it. And I still thought it was, especially since I knew who'd put it up. But when I looked up at the face that had only lived in my dreams for the past four years, something deep in my chest wrenched anyway. I thought I'd cried all the tears I had left for him when I washed up with my driftwood on that fishing boat.

Staring into those gleaming bronze eyes, I found a few more.

I gave myself a minute, then got it together and headed inside.

As I crossed the threshold, I wondered if I had walked across some kind of shamanic tripwire. Were you expecting me here? The moment I stepped in, would some trap spring for me? Or was this a move so bold and stupid, you'd never expect it?

That one, I dismissed. You knew me way too well for that.

But as I walked on, something eclipsed even my fear of you, Cole. The farther I went, the tighter a knot my stomach tied itself into. Memories rose up like ghosts: sizzling human meat. Crackling fire and groaning machinery. Screams from my brethren. And smoke, always smoke. From the way my glasses kept slipping down my nose, I knew my face was covered in a fine beading of sweat. I glanced down at my hands: same deal. And my clothes felt hot and tight enough that my shirt collar was like a noose.

Fuck me, I thought. *Am I actually up for this?* I hadn't set foot in the Plant since the day of the fire. Maybe this was too much, too fast.

But I thought of Diwata, lying low after the mess I'd made of her life. Phuong, cowering in her ruined sitting room as the Monster loomed over her, questions on his tattooed lips. Binh, his restless spirit trapped in that monument you'd built to mock his memory.

I thought of you in the boathouse, digging down deep and finding whatever grit you needed to kill me.

And I resolved to be every bit as tough.

The most surprising thing about the state of the break room was that there was a break room. And it was more than just a place for an on-duty salter to catch a bite and a smoke. There were communal showers. Lockers. Hampers full of fresh coveralls. Somewhere, I thought, you must have had some serious laundry machinery installed, which I guess made sense. Where else in the city was someone gonna find this much fresh water lying around?

Remembering what the priest had said about me, I decided to roll the dice and shower off. I intended to keep out of sight, but if I did get spotted, I figured I should at least kind of look and smell like I belonged. And today, fortune was on my side; no one tried their luck with me as I washed away a week's worth of sawdust and grime. A few nodded to me as they took up showers nearby, but no one talked to me. No one even gave a hint that they might know who I was. Maybe it was how I hunched low, or how different my face looked when I wasn't wearing my glasses. But I didn't look like Tenny to these salters. I didn't even stand apart as Biranese, the way I might've back in the day. I was just someone else.

I emptied my pockets, then left my clothes at the bottom of a trash can. No point in coming back for them when I was done now. All I kept were my boots; otherwise, I swapped everything else for the grey coveralls of a salter.

As soon as I shrugged it on, I could tell this was one of the only things you hadn't bothered changing. Gotta admit, Cole: it felt good to be wearing familiar threads again. You'd never known me during this part of my life. But for two years, these greys had been every bit as much my identity as the red rose in my coat lapel.

I stepped out on to the Plant's floor in my mismatched, borrowed boots. Diwata was about my height, but had bigger feet, and Binh's had been even bigger, so with each step my feet knocked around inside them like loose change. I tried to focus on Binh's boot in particular, as if some long-buried shamanic sense would just click back to life and spare me this whole endeavor. I didn't fucking want to be here. The clank of machinery, the roar of the furnaces, the rushing of water, the echoes of screams.

But a memory wasn't a vision. And try as I might, all I got from the boot on my left foot was that it was just that: a boot. Old, broken in, and too big.

Without visions, the floor itself wouldn't hold anything of value for me. My only chance was to cross it and sneak my way into the executive offices, where records might be kept. Odds were better than good that if there was anything damning in them, you would've had them destroyed by now. But this was the only thing I could do. And if I could do anything ...

I didn't want to spend any more time on the huge floor than I had to, but running would've raised eyebrows, so I had to take my time while also looking like I had places to be. All around me, salters talked and joked as they worked the line on the floor and the catwalks above. But while I was dressed like them and walking among them, I didn't feel even the memory of camaraderie with them. If they knew who I was, they'd turn on me just like everyone else.

With each step, the faint song in my ear grew stronger. I could feel it leading me upstairs to the offices that overlooked the main floor. Yellow lights in the big observation windows told me I wouldn't be alone up there, but I could handle some scared paper-pushers. I just hoped I'd be able to handle you.

At the thought of those bureaucrats and all their files, I glanced down at my boots, another possibility occurring to me. I wasn't sure what I would find in the archive room; if Knife-Edge was telling the truth and you'd been the one to dispose of anything that could incriminate you, there'd probably be nothing left. But since I was already here, I might as well try to see if you'd missed something. You were good, Cole, but even you weren't perfect. And if you'd been just the tiniest bit careless ...

As I neared the head office, I felt the spirit's song ramp up. It was in there. I hovered in the hallway outside for a painfully long moment, listening for any sound of life inside. But I didn't hear the click of your boots, didn't see your slim shadow through the frosted glass. Without the spirit to help me, I could only guess, but I guessed the office was empty.

I closed my eyes, focused, and called for that fragment of birch to fly to my side. But after a long moment, nothing happened.

I thought back to how Diwata had handled me back at the scrapyard, locking up my driftwood inside something too heavy for it to move. I guessed you'd had the same idea. Well, shame on me for thinking you'd make this easy for me, Cole.

I regarded the main office door again as I came to a stop outside it. It had frosted glass, with glittering gold paint that told me it belonged to MANAGEMENT. So that meant, once upon a time in a previous life, this exact office had been your destiny. And after all your years of fighting against it, you'd gone and made it your destiny anyway. I didn't know whether to feel sorry for you, or ... okay, fine, I didn't feel sorry for you. You were a prick who'd done this to yourself.

Your door wasn't even locked. The office it let me in to was big, but not grand. A simple ebony desk, a matching ebony chair with a tall, stiff-looking back, and almost nothing else. No mainland university diplomas on the wall, no impressive-looking portraits. There weren't even papers on the desk. Just a black telephone so sleek it looked like it had come from the future ...

... and next to it, a small but heavy glass jar containing a polished shard of birchwood with dried blood on its pointy tip.

Greedily, I started for it. But mid-step, an important detail sank in about how you'd decorated your office.

I hadn't thought about it at first, because I was about as tall as people came. Every time I went into a shop, I looked at the shelves people forgot to dust. Every time I walked, my limbs tangled themselves up in whatever lay spitting distance from me. And every time I sat down in a chair, I always had to bend my knees just a little too much to be comfortable. You didn't have those problems, because you were short.

Which is why it was weird to see an ebony desk and ebony chair, both of them absolutely towering in size.

I closed my eyes with a groan.

See, Cole, I'd assumed you would trust no other person with stewardship of the Plant, not when it had been your birthright and the key to your glorious revival of Driftwood City. I'd assumed you'd keep my last piece of driftwood in your own personal care.

And I'd fucked up.

The door shut behind me, and I felt a familiar heaviness in the dark.

"Find what you were looking for, Red Rose?"

I turned around just in time to see the tattooed fist before it collided with my face.

302

24

Nine years ago

Age 21

The vision took me like sleep after a long day.

One moment, I was standing in a night market, testing mangoes for their ripeness. Folks were staring at me; they always did when I went out and about now. The salters' strike was in full swing, but the Biranese scabs in the Plant had kept the city's water and power limping along for months now. And depending on where a neighborhood's sympathies fell, that changed a lot about how the city worked for people who looked like me.

I tried to ignore them—both in general, and the specific glares I was getting at this night market. I knew if anyone tried to give me grief, I could make them regret it in a thousand ways. But even so, those little stares and murmurs chipped away at my armor, bit by bit. And that day, my armor felt thinner than ever. So I focused on the mangoes in front of me, and nothing else. Every one in the box was green, rock-hard, and overpriced. When I finally picked one, the scowling vendor would probably try to charge me extra. But if I got the right one ...

It wouldn't matter. Because suddenly, I wasn't in the market. I was standing on a street corner, watching a tired old Biranese man in grey Plant coveralls slouch his way down the street.

The city sang his name into my head. *Sion Atlak*, it told me. *Remember him. You'll need to.*

"*Hey! You!*"

Sion Atlak gave no sign that he heard, but there was no mistaking his quickened step. I glanced back and saw a tavern's doors vomit out a gang of riled-up drunks. They wore no uniform, but I didn't need one to know them as salters.

"*What's the matter?*" another of the salters called. She pitched her voice into a nasally impression of a Biranese accent. "*You no understand Slatspeak?*"

Sion was now striding as quickly as he could without flat-out running. From the practiced, calm expression on his face, I realized with a pang of sadness that he'd been in this situation before. Many times, from the look of him.

A rush of footsteps. Before Sion could change course, one of the salters zipped past him and put himself right in Sion's path. He was silver-haired—Samnati, then—and drink had turned his eyes the glassy brown of a beer bottle.

"I'm sorry," Sion tried in Biranese. "I don't speak—"

"Lucky for you, I speak Biranese," said the salter, and indeed he was speaking Biranese. His name fell on to me like a piece of ripe fruit: Rhuchut. "Why'd you ignore me and my friends when we flagged you down just now?"

By now, those friends were within ten feet of Sion and had begun to fan out. I knew exactly where this was going.

Sion seemed to realize there was no point in pretending further. When he next spoke, it was in Slatspeak. "I don't want any trouble."

"You got trouble the moment you put those coveralls on, Atlak," said Rhuchut. "You think I don't know who you are?

We all do. When we walked out of the Plant, you don't think we all looked around and noticed who stayed?" His lips peeled back from his teeth in an ugly, hateful snarl. "I always knew we couldn't trust you brownbacks."

Helplessly, Atlak put up his hands. "We're just trying to—"

He didn't get a chance to tell them what he was trying to do. Rhuchut kicked him right between his legs. The entire world went jagged for a moment as the city felt his pain. I gasped as it shot through me as well.

The other salters joined in now. They laid in to him with their heavy, salt-flecked boots, and my vision went to static with every breaking bone. At first, Sion cried out for help. But people on the street ran away from him, not toward. And then, a kick to his throat crushed his voice like a spent cigarette. He curled in on himself, but to no avail. The salters were out for blood.

"*Stealing our jobs!*" shouted one.

"*Foreigners!*" cried another, even as the city told me that Sion was Birchbarrel, born and raised.

"*Line-breaker!*"

"*Scab!*"

"*Traitor!*"

I knew it was just a vision, but the sound of splintering bone set my teeth on edge. All my nerves fired, and a cry rose out of my throat as I charged in to help—

And just like that, I was back in the market, a fallen mango at my feet. But all I could see were the residual images of those angry, drunk salters laying into the old man who was way past the point of fighting back, and who hadn't even tried.

My breath came hard and ragged. When I blinked, tears clung to the edges of my eyes. I wanted to collapse and cry, and I wanted to punch a hole through the world, and I didn't know which I wanted to do first.

"Hey!" the fruit seller shouted at me. "Pick that mango up, brownback! You're buying that!"

I ran for the nearest telephone booth, only to find the telephone already ringing. And sure enough, when I picked it up you were on the other end. "Did you see it?" You sounded as breathless as I felt.

"Yeah." It was only one word, but my voice was shaking. I'd been busting heads for three years now. And before my two-year stint as a salter, growing up in Benilda's house meant I'd seen plenty of violent shit I wasn't supposed to see. But even though all that violence—even the stuff I did—was ugly, none of it felt like that vision had. There had been pure, triple-distilled hate in every single blow those salters had heaped on to that helpless man. Even getting close to it in a vision, I'd felt scalded by it.

"Meet me at Pakuanjang," you said. I could feel the sourness of the name on your tongue. "That's where they'll take him. It's the closest hospital to—"

"No," I said.

"Tenny, he needs us," you said, unable to keep the irritation from your voice. "We ... this could ruin everything. We need to know how to make this right."

"I already know how," I said. "You tell the others if you need to. I'll get there in a bit."

And then I hung up the telephone, walked to the nearest building, and furiously began to climb its drainpipe.

The thing was made of slick steel, but that didn't matter. The city guided my hands and feet, to make sure my grip never faltered. When I hauled myself up on to the rooftop, it sang to the boards under my feet until they curled up and flung me off them like springs. And as I sailed through the air to another rooftop, I saw its shingles rising like arms to catch me. I cut a path through the Driftwood City sky this way, tracing

306

a straight line right across the map while everyone below me had to zig and zag.

Usually, using this much of my power at once would've tired me out. But when I really got focused on what I was doing, everything felt effortless. I wasn't using power; the city's power was using itself, and I was just the channel it flowed through. I swung off flagpoles. Skated over power lines. Sprinted across four-inch ledges like they were as wide as a boardwalk. In every single cell of my body, I felt an overwhelming drive to close the distance between where I was and where I was going. And when my boots touched the ground again, I was standing in front of the Pham family flat.

I didn't bother knocking on the door. I just angrily swept my hand aside. The lock clicked open by itself, and the door slid right open. Phuong immediately dropped the child-sized boots that she'd been polishing. "*Binh, run! They're here!*" she screamed into the back of the house, before recognizing me.

"Move, Phuong," I said, striding in right past her. I made sure to step over the pile of boots—apparently, all Binh's siblings were home from school and work. "Your brother and I gotta—"

Heavy footsteps, and then Binh thundered into the room, ready for a fight. He wore a white sleeveless shirt and a black flatcap, his suspenders dangling in huge loops from his waistband. But he stopped when he saw me. "Tenny?"

"*Binh!*" Phuong shouted. "You were supposed to run out the back!"

"I'll let you set me straight later," he said, catching the look on my face. He jerked his head back into the dingy flat. "Go make sure the kids are all right, will you? Tenny looks like she needs to talk with me."

Phuong glared at me. "Knock next time," she snapped, before sweeping out of the room to check on their younger siblings.

307

Binh turned to me. "What's going on?" he said. "Why are you looking at me like that?'

"You're coming with me," I said firmly. That same urge to be elsewhere arose in me, and the city played a furious crescendo in my ears. "Now."

And then I seized him by the shoulder and yanked open the coat closet.

I don't know why I did that, Cole. I had absolutely no reason to think that the coat closet would be anything but a coat closet. But the city told me to open that door, and I trusted what it told me. And when I slid that door open, it wasn't coats and linens I saw; it was a dingy hospital room with a bloody man in a too-small bed, surrounded by five of the six legendary Thorn Orphans: Roulette by the door, hands on his guns; Anjali, frowning at the evening paper; Knife-Edge, knitting a length of pink yarn; Mhap, looming near the window; and you, seated beside the bloodied patient.

While I'd been wrangling Binh, you must've assembled the other four. You all turned to me with surprise as I stepped out of a medical supply closet, dragging the city's foremost labor leader behind me.

All at once, everyone was shouting.

"*Shut it, all of you!*" I barked. My blood pounded through my head, and it was making my thoughts run together like paint in rain. "One at a time!"

The five of you all exchanged glances. For a moment, I didn't think any of you would speak.

But then Roulette said: "Were y'all hiding in that closet the whole time?"

"We ... we weren't," Binh said. He sounded dazed, and I guess I couldn't blame him. I was confused as hell myself, but he didn't have a city telling him everything was gonna be all right. "We were in the front room of my house, and then ..."

You were the only one seated, and now you rose from the rickety hospital chair. It was a refined, controlled movement, and the sight of it annoyed me. Just once, I wanted you to be off balance. You'd been the only other witness to Atlak's beating; I wanted to see that you were as furious about it as I was. "Tenny," you said, brushing a lock of silver hair out of your eyes, "did you just transport yourself here ... from Birchbarrel?"

I knew that I had, but it didn't really sink in for me until you put it into words. "I ... guess I did."

"How," you said, "did you do that?"

"Does it look like I fucking know?" I snapped. *"We got bigger problems."*

In a horrified daze, Binh drifted past me to the bed. At a nod from me, Anjali stepped aside to let him approach the beaten, bandaged remains of Sion Atlak. The man in the hospital bed seemed to have more blood outside him than in. His shattered limbs were all elevated and vised together. Patches of his greying hair were matted with still more blood. One eye was swollen shut; the other stared aimlessly forward. Between his split lips, I saw a mouth with more gaps than teeth.

But before all this, his face hadn't been all that different from mine. And that was what they'd looked for. My whole stomach seized with anger. These salters had been our allies, and now they were going after people like me.

"What happened?" Binh asked, his voice soft with horror.

"Your crowd," I snarled, "cornered him outside a bar and beat the shit out of him."

Binh whipped around. "How can you possibly—?"

"We both bore witness to it," you said, your voice far more even than mine. How, Cole, how could you channel that stillness of yours, even now? How could you look at the man in the bed and not feel roiling rage? "Not in any fashion that

309

would be admissible in court," you continued, "but do you doubt that we did?"

Binh dropped his head, his huge fists clenching. I knew him well by now; I knew the sheer shame of this was threatening to devour him from the inside out. But at the moment, I didn't care. *Fucking good*, I thought. He needed to feel shame. That was the only way I could get him to do what he needed to, to make this right.

"Do you know what this does to your cause, Binh?" you continued. "Do you understand how badly this compromises you and your position?"

"This kind of thing needs to happen," Binh tried. "This man was a scab. He forgot all workers are in the same boat. If he crossed a picket line, we can't be surprised—"

Before he could finish, I'd crossed the room and belted him across the face. He was a big man, and he went down hard. Fury and disgust filled me. This was the man I loved, the man I shared a bed with. And I'd just heard him try to say ... I could barely collect my thoughts. I felt like I'd caught sight of a completely different man wearing his face.

Roulette chuckled down at the fallen Binh. "Not wise. Not wise."

Anjali, leaning against the wall, gave me an approving nod.

The Monster, lurking near the window, just loomed as Binh pushed himself up on to his elbows.

"*When you need someone hurt*," I growled down at him, "*you. Call. Us.*"

Knife-Edge set down his needles and yarn.

"When he dies, the papers will make him a martyr. A hard-working citizen, made a victim by the lawless hordes of greedy strikers. The people who were on the fence about the strike will hop off it, and not to the side you're hoping for.

310

The people who were defending the salters will waver." Leave it to him to understand all the angles.

"And that doesn't even get into what Benilda will do next," Jali chimed in. "Your salters have put her in a position where she has to answer this."

"That *scab* there?" I said. "He's working the line because Benilda makes him. Probably got his life savings banked with her, since the normal banks like to fuck over Biranese accounts. Probably pays his rent every month to one of her lackeys. He's got no choice but to work, neh? If he doesn't, everything he spent his life building goes away, just like that. You want to tell people like him, folks who have barely the same as you, to walk away from that?" At last, I helped Binh up from the floor and led him to Atlak's bedside.

Binh stared down at the prone and bloodied form of Atlak. I could see him wrestling with what he knew I was prompting him to do. "What do you want me to do?" he said eventually. "Kill them? We're workers, not gangsters."

"That man was a worker, too," you said quietly. I felt a rush of gratitude for the calm, controlled fury I heard in your voice. I was the only Biranese on the team, but with you I knew I wasn't alone. "His name was Sion Atlak, and all he wanted was a life. He was doing his best to keep his."

"And once that life ends, how far do you think Nanay Benilda will take her vengeance, just so people know not to fuck with her?" I leaned down, really got in his face. "Who do you think she'll start with?"

Binh withdrew, fumbling for a cigarette. Irritably, he began to pace. "We had nothing to do with this."

"Tell her that yourself," I said, "when you hand over the four salters I point out to you."

He nearly dropped his lighter. "You want me to meet with her? And you think I'll walk out again?"

311

"It's the only way she doesn't come after you for this," I said. "You show up, you give her justice for one of hers so she can make an example. You thank her for letting you leave. Someday, we'll take her down. But until then, this is the world you live in. And in this world, that's how you make things fucking right, got it?"

In the corner, the Monster loomed like he always did. Threatening a figure as he cut, though, Binh had eyes only for you. "You want me to sell my own brethren to Nanay Benilda for the life of a scab." He didn't sound like he was fighting anymore. It was quiet. An admission of defeat. "Word will get out that I compromised on the cause for personal justice. You understand what that will do?"

"I don't believe you understand what's already been done." At last, you sank back in to your chair at Atlak's bedside. "This is how the Rock has stayed above everyone else: by turning them against each other while it slips its hands into all your pockets. If there's anyone who knows how they operate ... don't you believe it would be me?"

Binh swallowed hard and took another nervous drag. "You're still asking me to give up my own comrades," he said. "The rest of the Brethren might turn on me. There are far less reasonable people in the union. People who will do far less reasonable things to get what they want."

The Monster had been so still in the shadows, I'd almost forgotten he was there until he stirred. "There don't have to be."

Binh looked between the six of us, clearly hoping one of us would relent. But while I felt like we were more fragile than ever, at least for the moment we presented a united front. "Right." He nodded, tired and resigned. "Take me home. I've got some telephone calls to make."

I reached out to the city as Binh spoke. *Is that something you can do?* I asked it.

312

The notes of its song came back in reply: *Whenever you're ready*.

I glanced over at you, and saw you had your listening face on. You were trying to work out how I'd done this wild new trick of mine. I made a mental note to ask you about it myself the next time I saw you. I could do this shit, but damned if I ever knew how.

I swung the door to the medical closet open again. And instead of shelves full of medicine and scrubs, I saw a cramped little front room in a tall, narrow flat. "I'll be back," I shot over my shoulder, then dragged Binh through.

The music abruptly changed key, and I recognized the same leitmotif I always heard when I was walking through Birchbarrel. And sure enough, I was standing in Binh's flat again.

Air whistled past my ear in warning, and I turned around just in time to catch the swinging iron fire poker. Skinny little Phuong saw it was me again, and immediately dropped it. "I'm sorry!" she exclaimed. "I thought you were ..." She glanced at the closet, confused. "Okay, I don't know who I thought you were."

"Guess it's good to know you're quick on your feet when things go bad," I said, picking up the poker and handing it back to her. Hesitantly, she took it and then looked past me.

"Binh?" she said carefully. "What's wrong? What happened?"

Binh shook his head. He looked like he was still miles away.

"I'll be back inside to check on you and the others," he said, sliding the front door open now. Outside, a screaming city beckoned him.

Reluctantly, Phuong turned and headed back into the house. Binh jerked his head to indicate I should join him, and then sat down heavily on the top stair of his front stoop.

I sat next to him, wincing a little as I did. Now that the adrenaline wasn't flooding my system, I could tell I'd done something to my knee during my mad rooftop dash to get over here.

"I'm sorry," he said eventually. "I was afraid, and I said something I shouldn't have. Your peoples' lives aren't expendable, Ten. That belief has never lived in my heart. Please ... if you believe nothing else I say, believe that."

I didn't want to give him that, Cole. How could I know it was just a moment of weakness, and not his mask slipping at long last? And even if it had just been a moment of weakness, I'd heard him say something that had me rethinking everything I knew about him. It didn't matter that Sion Atlak was technically on the other side of the war. He was Biranese, like me. That Binh would think, for even a second, that that made his life worth less ... it filled me with disgust. And I wanted to hold on to that feeling. That anger in my gut was what I'd reached down into to find my new ability. It had carried me here swiftly. Right now, I felt like I could use it to melt the Rock into lava if I wanted.

But when I glared into that face I loved, I was glaring into a mirror. I saw disgust in the slant of his mouth, and in the light of the eyes he couldn't quite bring to meet mine. I didn't need the spirit's help to know who that disgust was aimed at.

The anger felt so good, Cole. It was a fucking drug. And in that moment, climbing down from that high felt like the hardest thing I'd ever done.

"Say something like that again," I said eventually, "and we're more than done. I will absolutely destroy you. Workers all gotta survive the same storm. But they ain't all in the same boat. Got it?"

He nodded. "This has grown into more than I ever wanted it to be." He used the stub of his old cigarette to light a fresh one. "I'm not a gangster, and I'm not a soldier. This was never supposed to be a war. I just wanted those greedy parasites"—he turned from me to jab his cigarette in the direction of the Rock—"to cough up what they've been stealing from us. Make a better life for everyone. Make sure that our comrades didn't burn up for nothing. I only started this fight because I wouldn't have been able to live with myself if I hadn't."

I hesitated, still feeling the heat from my last embers of anger. But I let them die out. "I know the feeling." I put a hand between his shoulder blades. Through the thin fabric of his shirt, I could feel the ridges of muscle there. But beneath his warm skin, I felt something more primal: how fucking tired he was.

"Most of us don't live our lives looking for a fight," I continued. "But all of us find one eventually. And once you find yours, all you can do is win it."

He nodded soberly as he absorbed that, his gaze fixed on the bustling night street outside. "I'll have my crew round up the four you point out. I'll make the offer to the Lacanilaos personally. Anything else? You ... know them, don't you?"

In the window, the reflection of his eyes met mine. He was furtive, in a way I wasn't used to seeing on men his size. Despite everything, it made me like him more.

"Yeah," I said. "I know the Lacanilaos. Better than anyone else on our side, I'd bet." Dimly, I realized my hand was still on his back, and I let it drop. "Benilda's a demon, but she's got her honor. You do this the way I tell you, and she'll respect you for it."

He nodded once.

"And once you do that, you get your Brethren under control," I said. "Because if this happens to another Biranese salter ..." I nudged him to turn around and face me again. I wanted to say this to his face. "I love you, Binh. Didn't even

315

think I could love another person this much." I caressed his cheek a moment before I kissed him.

I let us have that moment, then pulled away and found his eyes again.

"But if this ever happens again," I said, "I promise you: my love won't save you." I indicated the blood-colored flower in my lapel. "Instead of winning one war ... you'll be losing two."

25

Now

Age 30

"You're lucky he gave me specific instructions about what to do with you when I called him," said Mhap the Monster. "He's the only reason you're still alive."

I heard his words like I was underwater. My vision slid in and out of focus, and I couldn't hold on to a complete thought for more than a heartbeat at a time. I was aware enough to know I was sitting in a chair. I could feel the bite of steel cuffs, tight on my ankles and wrists. And though my vision wasn't at its sharpest, there was no mistaking the huge, dark man looming over me from the other side of a desk.

"The fuck did you do to me?" I groaned. "Why does my head—?"

"Simple blunt force trauma," said the Monster. "Liberally applied, and with enthusiasm. As I said, I was specifically told to leave you alive. I was also told I couldn't pay you back for how you ended our last meeting." He tapped his left eye ... or rather, the lid that lay over the empty socket. His right eyelid

317

was uninked, but his left one had been adorned with intricate black lines that formed the shape of an eye.

"I was, however, told that if you found a way to threaten me, I could defend myself . . . within reason." He leaned calmly over the desk. His desk, I guessed. "I wouldn't tempt me to test the boundaries of what 'reason' means in this scenario. You know exactly how creative I can be."

"You gonna keep spitting empty threats at me?" I rasped. My throat was dry, my tongue leathery. "Or are you gonna actually do something?"

"I'm going to hold you here while the Governor musters a protective detail and comes down to retrieve you," said the Monster. "That's doing something. But if you try to push me, I have permission to strategically break you until you behave."

I'd had enough of him. Time to put a hole in his head. I reached out for my wooden necklace charm, trapped in its glass prison on his desk. It was jammed against the bottom of the jar and the lid so that it couldn't actually move. And it was too heavy for me to just have it pick itself up and smash the jar open. Not like I could just reach out and grab it, either. But I sang to the fragment of spirit trapped in the jar anyway, hoping it'd show me what to do.

But I needed to distract the Monster while I did it.

"So what the fuck is a brute like you doing in an office like this?" I tried.

"Don't you remember what I told you back at the station when we last encountered each other?"

"You said a lot of shit." I struggled to keep my voice flat. I needed to steer him away from that topic, or he might think to look at the jar on his desk. "Cole and I loved to recruit people who talk too much."

"I said he entrusts all the most important things to me," the

Monster said simply. "He always has, when he wants them done ... properly."

I shouldn't have given a shit about which of us you liked better, but I bristled just the same. "You were a blunt instrument," I snarled. "Nothing more. A bomb we dropped on the stains that were too stubborn to scrub out."

He seemed more amused by the comparison than anything else. "When he took on the task of reforming the city, he assigned all of us tasks befitting our abilities. And no matter what you think of me, there's no denying I've succeeded. Do you really think you would've done better?"

I made a show of scoffing, even as I attuned myself again to the driftwood shard in the jar. I was done with delicate singing; time to fucking shout. With everything I had, I pushed—

—and the jar moved.

Just barely.

But it fucking had.

Quickly, I sketched out a new plan: stick to the old plan. Keep him talking, nudge the jar off the edge of the desk, and settle in for round two of our little scrap. I was gonna kill Mhap the Monster while tied to a chair.

"That was a serious question," the Monster said. "Do you really think you could've done anything better than I?"

I nudged the jar another eighth of an inch. Made sure to keep my eyes off it. "What?" I said. "You think I'm just gonna answer your questions?"

The Monster shrugged. "We have a while to wait. And if you answer my questions, I'll answer yours."

I narrowed my eyes. The Monster was many things, but never a liar. That made this offer of his a great deal more tempting than it would've been, coming from any of the other Orphans. And besides, it wasn't like I was going anywhere.

"Fine," I said. "No, I don't think either of us should be

319

touching a place like this. The Thorn Orphans weren't supposed to outlive our own revolution. But you fuckers killed the guy who was supposed to inherit it from us." As I was talking, something about what he said snagged in my brain. "Wait, what do you mean, we have a while to wait? Why ain't he walking through that door right now?" I'd invented teleportation, but I'd been nice enough to teach you. I'd even lived long enough to regret it.

"He didn't tell me," said the Monster. "He just said he would be here soon. I tried to tell him you had been rendered toothless, but he didn't believe me. So take some comfort in the fact that he still carries a shred of respect for you."

"Uh-huh," I grunted, as the jar inched closer and closer to the edge of his huge desk. It wouldn't be far now. "So, are you gonna ask me another question, or not?" I made sure to lay on the aggression. He wouldn't feel threatened by it, but he would make a big show of being amused, and that was more attention he would pour into me instead of my splinter.

True to form, he let out a low chuckle that was as dark and deadly as spilled oil. "Why did you come here?" he said. "You've been acting much too surprised to have found me, so clearly it wasn't to kill me. What really inspired your visit? Was it this?" I winced as he picked up the jar holding my splinter, and then set it down ... just a little closer to the edge of the desk than it'd been before. It might've been the first time in my life I was grateful to the bastard. "Or was it something else?"

How much to tell him? I guessed there was no harm in going with the truth. I needed to keep him focused away from the splinter in the jar. And besides, I thought, I might even get some good information out of it.

"I know Binh was investigating Cole when you all murdered him." I didn't bother keeping the venom out of my voice.

"And before she died, Jali told me what it was: Cole lit the fire. The blood of three hundred and fifty-two dead salters is on his hands. I came looking for proof." Anything to keep him from thinking about the jar on his desk.

At this, the Monster didn't appear to take any joy or satisfaction. I got just a single nod of his huge head. "He's had plenty of other blood on his hands, all in the name of change. Drawing your line at the fire is hypocritical, Red Rose."

I couldn't feel shock from the thought, because it wasn't like a bomb going off. It was the slow, sickening, inexorable burn of a fire climbing its way up the face of a building. I could cower on the roof all I wanted; the air would only grow hotter and brighter.

"How long have you known?" I risked a glance at the jar, as it nudged itself within an inch of the edge of the desk. This was going to be the crucial part, but it was getting harder and harder to divide my focus.

"Longer than the others," the Monster shrugged. "He had to tell somebody."

"And you didn't care?" I seethed. "Whatever happened to serving a righteous cause? You don't see how this taints every single thing we've ever done?"

For just a moment, I hoped I might get something out of him. Mhap was a lot of things, but he'd always been a true believer.

But instead, he shrugged again. "I've always put my trust in him. When he told me, I saw it as a sign that he had put his own in me."

I stared at him, the jar temporarily forgotten. My little shred of the city called out for my attention, but I couldn't divide myself anymore. If the Monster was keeping to his policy of telling the truth, then he spent every day in this office building something on a foundation of ashes and lies. The fact that he could just shrug it off was ... was ...

Well. He'd gotten the name for a reason.

"You've taken a couple turns, so I'll reclaim my time." He shifted, and his hand strayed dangerously close to the jar by the desk's edge. My whole heart seized as I waited for him to reach for it again. But then his fingers settled into place, mere inches from where the jar stood. "And because you took such liberties, I'm going to ask you a question with a big answer attached."

I glanced at the jar again. It was so close. *So* close. And maybe a big answer was exactly what I needed to keep his attention diverted from it.

I forced myself to meet his eye with a gaze like still water. "Go for it."

He nodded appreciatively. "I want you to tell me what happened after you died."

I think he expected to catch me off-guard with that question.

But instead, I answered it calmly.

"There was darkness," I said. "Water rushing in. I remember specifically telling myself, 'This is how you die, Tenny. In an unmarked saltwater grave, sent there by the only friends you ever had.'"

He grunted, amused.

"Oh, shut up," I snapped. "If you can't be melodramatic when you're walking right into death's mouth, when the fuck can you be?"

"I wouldn't know," the Monster said. "Death and I don't have that kind of relationship."

Keep running your mouth, and I'll change that for you, I thought, as the bottom lip of the jar crested the desk's edge at last. Just a little bit more, and it'd tip over all on its own. I renewed my focus, and it was like I was playing the city's melody faster and faster, in higher and higher keys, until the whole thing was just one big shriek between my ears.

"And then," I went on, "I woke up. I was on the deck of a fishing boat. The tide had carried me out to sea, and they'd caught me in their net. The captain had wanted to throw me back, once she'd realized I wasn't the catch of a lifetime. But once they saw their haul was Biranese, too, it was easy enough to get them to bring me back home. They wanted to toss the driftwood, too, but I made them let me keep it."

"And why did you keep it, then, if you didn't have any intention of ever coming home?"

My eyes flashed, sharp and deadly as a drawn blade. "I could still control and mold them," I said. "If you'd been through an ordeal like mine, are you seriously telling me you would've given up the one thing that still made you feel powerful?"

He leaned back in his chair, considering. Then he smiled. Again. In all the time we fought together, I didn't remember him showing me this many teeth. "That's the difference between the Red Rose and the Black," he said eventually. "You let people take your power from you. I carry mine with me wherever I go."

"Yeah, so did I, asshole." It was tricky. My words were all but inviting him to look at the jar half-dangling off the desk. Any second now, I could give it one last push and send it spilling to the floor.

"You came to Driftwood City with the coffin we buried you in," said the Monster, leaning over his desk. His shoulders stretched his black suit to its seams. "Attrition from the other Thorn Orphans slowly whittled away at the power you had left. Now, you have almost none. And you think you can still dismantle our order with a glorified toothpick. You couldn't have before"—he held out his hand so I could see the black ink there—"and you certainly can't now."

Between the dark of the station platform and the dark of the boathouse, I hadn't really had a chance to examine his elaborate array of tattoos the last two times we'd met. But now, I could see what he was showing me. There were thick, patterned black lines up and down his palm, which I knew flowed out to cover the rest of his huge, muscular body. But now I saw new ones: finer black lines, visibly darker and threaded between his older tattoos. They didn't appear to be text of any kind, or even discernible symbols. After a second, I understood why: they weren't supposed to be. They were meant to imitate the curling grain lines of wood.

My eyes widened as a realization hit home for me.

"Your tattoos," I whispered. "That's how he bought you."

"They were not a price at which I sold myself," said the Monster, "but a reward for faithful service and loyalty. You've already seen for yourself how potent they can be."

I remembered wood splintering from his bare fists. His huge body, moving far quicker than it had any right to. Me, throwing some of my best blows at him, only for him to shrug them off and keep moving. The only reason I'd been able to wound him at all was because I guess you hadn't yet figured out a way to ink someone's eyeball. If I hadn't made that shot, Knife-Edge and Jali would probably have still been among the living.

I narrowed my eyes. "What are those tattoos made out of?" Each of the other three Thorn Orphans had had a gift made for them out of something that resonated with Driftwood City, so you could imbue them with scraps of your power. What bit of the city could you have possibly inked on to his skin?

Triumph flitted across his face. He looked as if, of all the questions I could've asked him, this was the one he'd been waiting for.

"What have I always believed in, Red Rose?" he said. "Institutions? Tools? Destinies? Unknowable spirits? No. I've always preferred to set my trust . . . in people."

Horror and revulsion spread through me like a rot.

You see, Cole, I understood: a city wasn't just the materials it was made from. There was something intangible about what its people brought to those spaces: the smells, the sounds, the soul. Their imaginations shaped all those raw materials in the first place, so that one city would have flat roofs and another would have domes. Of course you would have found a way to siphon off from the people of Driftwood City.

But my horror deepened as I realized how you could have possibly distilled people into tattoo ink.

Vomit welled up in my throat as I remembered bodies pressed on bodies. Skin crackling like fat in a pan. Mouthfuls of caustically sweet smoke. Screams rising, water in a kettle, me standing amid the flames and feeling like I was about to burst—

With one last shove, I sent the jar teetering over the edge of the desk—

—and into the Monster's waiting hand.

I stared in disbelief. He'd moved inhumanly fast. Faster than I could've moved when I was in my prime. And now he had the last shred of my power firmly in his hand. But how had he even seen what I was doing when it was in his blind spot?

He seemed to know the question on my mind. Once again, he tapped his empty eye socket.

Or more specifically, he tapped the eye tattoo on its lid.

"The power of Driftwood City's people flows through me," he said. "They give me strength ... and insight." He held up the jar. "Do you know how hard it was to pretend I didn't notice this happening?"

He closed his remaining eye. An identical tattoo on his other eyelid stared back at me. What, could he just magically see with his eyes closed, then? Was that why he'd been able to fight me so easily in the dark?

325

I strained against the cuffs that bound me to the chair. Something vicious in me wanted to take his other eye, and then work my way from there. I'd been all right granting the other three Thorn Orphans the dignity of a quick death. Not so for Mhap the Monster, the Black Rose. I wanted him to suffer to his last breath. He sat here every day, in this Plant, with the ashes of his own dead neighbors woven into the tapestry of his skin.

And you'd put him here.

"Let me out of this chair and see how this goes," I snarled at him, but I could hear the desperation in my own voice. I was spitting threats because I was powerless to follow through on them. But it was all I had left, so I poured everything I had into it. "Let's fucking do this, just you and me."

"It would never be 'just you and me.'" The Monster held up his hand, to show me his tattoos there. "I have the power of the people behind me. And even though you've deluded yourself into thinking you're fighting on your own, you've never been alone in your life. The Lacanilaos, the city's spirit, the Thorn Orphans ... you have no idea how much power the world handed to you like it was nothing.

"But do you know what, Red Rose?" the Monster went on, studying the jar in his hand. "I can understand why you're upset with me, now that you know what you know ... about my enhancements, and about this place. And I suppose that's worth certain considerations."

He gripped the jar tight. I thought he was going to hurl it at me, or at least the floor. But instead, he just flexed his thick fingers. Cracks erupted in the thick glass: small at first, and then spiderwebbing out in every direction, meeting each other and deepening.

In a spray of shards, the jar shattered, and my splinter hovered above his hand.

Immediately, I took my shot. He leaned out of its way, even

326

as I brought it back around to take another stab at him. The city's melody was alive in me, flighty and desperate and furious. He was underestimating me. I had to prove that it would be his final mistake.

"Anyone standing on a mountaintop will think themselves a giant," the Monster said, sliding his chair back from his desk. He batted my splinter away again, and its point stuck in the nearest wall. "And when they get so used to that mountaintop that they forget it's underfoot ... they forget how small they really are."

I gritted my teeth and let him talk as I wrenched my splinter free from the gouge it had made.

My next shot actually got him on his feet. He bent back grossly far, his spine suddenly made of rubber, and the splinter sailed over his head like a stray bullet.

"You believe yourself a brilliant soloist, thinking the dancing of your fingers across a fretboard can set the world aflame." The bastard didn't even sound like he was trying. "But you've had a band this whole time, and it's the only thing that's kept your notes resonating at all."

"*What the fuck do you know about it?*" I roared, as I willed the splinter to shoot for him again.

He ducked it with insulting ease. Despairing, I was starting to realize exactly how lucky I'd been back at the pier. If he could see me coming, he could answer me.

... Of course.

My next shot didn't go for him; it went right for the lightbulb above us. I knew the darkness wouldn't help me.

But the momentary flare of the bulb as it exploded ...

I channeled all of myself into the shard and sang for it to fly true.

And as white light swallowed my vision, I trusted the city to aim.

I heard the telltale sound of wood burying itself in flesh, and then silence fell over the dark office, gentle and deep as snow. For a long, painful moment, I heard only the gasps of my own breathing.

The desk lamp flickered on, courtesy of a huge hand yanking its tiny chain. In the faint light, the Monster seemed so much larger, his tattoos making him disappear into the gloom around him. In the half-light, he lived up to his name: something terrifying under your bed that you could never quite see. How many dozens of people had seen a sight just like this in the moment their heart beat for the last time?

He held up his hand to reveal a palm pierced all the way through. The narrow tip of the splinter was wet with his blood for the second time, and sticking out the back of his hand. He regarded me with perfect calm as his other hand reached up and pulled it out.

"This was the last piece of your power," he said, holding it up. I tried to will the splinter free, but his grip on it was far too tight. "The tool with which you would unmake everything Cole built. A necklace, right? An instrument of revenge that you literally kept next to your heart for all those years you were dead."

And then he clamped his fist down on it and crushed it into pulp.

When you'd severed my connection to the spirit, Cole, you hadn't killed it. I could still feel it just out of reach, as if we were on opposite sides of a window, pounding on the glass to get back to each other. I'd still been able to hear its song: muted and weak, but still enough to bring hope to my failing heart.

But Mhap the Monster did not have your deft hand. At his touch, the city in me died screaming.

Even when I was dead, Cole, I'd always had those tiny

remnants of it to warm me. When I was lonely in Biranba, it had sung me through diner shifts, giving me a rhythm to keep as I washed one dish after another.

The Monster had been right. I had forgotten how hollow my voice sounded without anyone to harmonize with it.

His huge hand opened, and lifeless fibers of driftwood clattered to his desk. Traces of spirit energy clung to them, but they were just the blood leaking from a fresh corpse.

"And with that"—the Monster cracked his knuckles. Each one rang out like a gunshot—"I do believe you've just given me a threat 'within reason.'"

26
Twelve years ago

Age 18

Your vision for the Thorn Orphans had always been so concrete. You'd determined that in addition to the two of us, we would need four others to stay nimble and flexible. Each was supposed to introduce a new element that could harmonize with what you and I already had, whether that was Knife-Edge's keen mind or Roulette's pure dumb luck. We consulted with the spirit of the city to seek out the people who had the qualities we needed. But Mhap the Monster was a special case.

He was the only one to come to us.

The strike was in full swing, but the Biranese scabs kept the Plant's basic functions limping along. It would be another year before we finally brought the Lacanilao empire crashing down like the glittering roof of Nanay Benilda's greenhouse. But while the Rock was paying her well to keep out of bootlegging and protect their scabbing workforce, they hadn't extended that same courtesy to the other bootlegger gangs of the Slats. According to you, they'd done the math and decided that all those little outfits combined couldn't put a real dent in their profits.

But they were just tall enough flowers for us to snip.

This time, our target had been the Moon Shadow Syndicate. "Syndicate" was a bit of a grand term for them; they controlled four blocks in the Shoots, and had a couple ties to a bigger Hontonese outfit in town. Honestly, they weren't that major. But the bootleg water market was crowded, as always. And their solution to distinguish themselves from the other gangs was their choice of allies: the union families.

Binh had brought me the first report of them a few months back. One of his buddies had been approached by a Moon Shadow with a cash-stuffed envelope and a promise of plenty more where that came from if he did them a favor when the signal came through. They couldn't have picked a worse target; he'd dropped the bribe straight into the union coffers and told Binh everything. But it had made Binh curious about how many of his other salters had been approached.

The answer, you and I discovered, was "a whole bunch." So far, they'd all been hired to do little things. Mostly, they'd been brought in to repair distilling equipment. But the strike had dragged on for months now, and things were getting desperate out there. It was only a matter of time before one of those salters was issued a knife along with their bribe, to bring to the next closed-doors Brethren meeting.

At a secret meet-up in the hidden back room of a boatway station, you, Binh, and I all agreed on the severity of the threat.

"A strike's like a siege," Binh said. He wasn't smoking, since the room was so small, but I could tell from the twitch of his fingers that he very badly wanted to light up. "Right now's the hardest part, after all the original enthusiasm has died down and people start to realize what they really signed on for. The last thing we need is for our Brethren to notice that some of their comrades are more well fed than the rest. There can't be solidarity while there's inequality."

"Do you have any idea what a talent it is," I said, "to talk like you write and not be annoying?"

He winked at me.

"Can we please get back to the matter at hand before I choke on a cloud of pheromones?" you said. You were so much shorter than the two of us, and running spindly fingers through your silver hair. "Binh is right. We already have too many things trying to undercut the integrity of the strike. If word starts to get around that your salters are just another gang ... We're already fighting enough of an uphill battle in the press."

"That'll never change," Binh sighed. "You really think the papers will ever print bad things about the rich people who own them?"

I felt the usual bristle of guilt from you.

"We've supplied you with every name you need," you said. "I trust that if you pay a visit to each of these Brethren of yours and lay out the case for why they need to stop ... they'll listen?"

Binh kept his tone polite, but there was just the barest flicker of annoyance in his bright brown eyes.

"I know how to keep my house in order, White Rose," he said, with a lot more venom than I'd expected.

"Hoy," I said. "There's no need to—"

"And what happens on the day you can't?" you fired back. I shot you a look, too. Why were you getting on him like this?

"I got us this far, didn't I?" Binh said, with the kind of calm that I knew meant he was really fucking pissed.

"Only with *our* invaluable—" you began.

"*I trust both of you to know what you're talking about,*" I cut in. You both shut up in surprise. "And I trust you 'cause I've

332

got a good eye for people. If I didn't, I'd be an asshole. Either of you calling me an asshole?"

You couldn't back away from each other because the little office didn't allow it. But Binh's chest was suddenly not puffed out, and you had color creeping to the tips of your ears.

"My apologies," you said eventually. You cleared your throat to buy yourself time to think of something to say. "This is just a particularly sensitive matter. Decisions made by the individual, especially at crucial junctures like these, can have all manner of ramifications for the whole. And in order for this to work, we must be unified."

"Well, I'll handle that within the *union*," Binh said, his cigarette-less fingers twitching at his side. The city played me a tense little melody as he spoke. "What do you plan to do to the Moon Shadows?"

I took his hand to still it. Stole the chance to look in his eyes again. "The same thing the Thorn Orphans do to everyone else."

He smiled at me like sun through a storm.

After he'd left, you and I decided to walk back to Kelptown. The strike had kept you and me busy enough as the Thorn Orphans that we hadn't had many chances to take in the city as plain old Tenny and Cole. But I didn't say anything to you as we walked. It fucking killed me, since there's little I like less than a long, awkward silence. But I was annoyed and I didn't trust myself to play nice if I opened my trap.

"It's not that I don't trust him," you said, apropos of nothing, when we were ten minutes into it. "I do. It's just that we can't afford for anything to mess this up."

I shrugged. "It's not just your fight, remember? You were the one who made the big push for us to throw in with him in the first place."

"I know. I know what I did in there was unworthy of me. It's why I apologized, Tenny."

333

"But that's not gonna stop you from trying to explain your-self to me now," I sighed.

"As someone who values his privacy, it's irksome to have a friend like you who can read me so easily." From your cautious smile, I could tell you were trying to lighten the mood. But I was still a little annoyed with you, so I didn't let you have it.

You realized my smile wasn't forthcoming, and composed yourself. "Order and discipline are how armies win wars," you said simply. "The other side has all manner of machinery in place to help it maintain order when times are tough. We can't afford even a single slip-up."

"You think Binh doesn't know that?" I said.

"I'm sure he's aware. But the fact that he allowed it to happen ..."

"You and I let plenty of things pass under our noses," I said. "It's a big fucking city. We can see into any part of it, but we can't see all of it at once. We can't know *everything*, Cole."

"We don't know that," you said. I was surprised by the fierceness in your voice. "We have no idea what our upper limits are, Tenny. I've experimented a great deal already, and so far I ... I don't believe we have any. Remember? If we can do anything, then we should do everything."

"Hey, easy," I said. "I'm with you, all right? You're just getting ... you know. Like you get sometimes."

You eyed me. "'Like I get sometimes?'"

"Yeah. You know, intense. Headstrong. Stubborn." I grinned. "Not like me."

For a moment, you looked like you'd been hit over the head. And then, you burst out laughing.

"When I think about ... what we can do," you said in a much smaller voice when you'd stopped laughing. "All that we're not already doing."

"We're doing plenty," I said. "So is Binh. And in this fight

334

of ours, he's not some ally or some convenience. He's our partner, same as the other three."

You frowned, more to yourself than to me. "He's not a
Thorn Orphan."

"Good," I said, and let myself chuckle to let you know I
wasn't pissed anymore. "He shouldn't be. Once we burn
everything down, someone's gonna have to figure out what to
do with the ashes."

The Moon Shadow stash house was nice enough to mark
itself for us, with an elaborately painted sign of a red moon
eclipsing the familiar silhouette of the Rock. They were a small
operation, but they were clearly trying to make themselves
look more legit. Even without the sign, though, I would've
recognized the mechanical, gearlike ways the air bent itself
in my ears as we approached. This, after all, was a place of
graspers and schemers.

We'd shown up with our new Thorn Orphans at our back.
You were currently going around the back with Knife-Edge
Ngo, so he could stand guard while you expertly dismantled
their distilling equipment. You two were soft instruments,
strings and reeds. Not like me and Roulette and Anjali the
Armored; we were booming drums and crunching bass and
braying horns. With skills like ours, there was no point in
trying to play sotto.

The three of us made a hell of a sight, strolling up the block
together. We'd held off on issuing uniforms just yet; you'd
wanted to wait until we had our full complement of Orphans.
So I was wearing the Thorn Orphans standard uniform, with
a freshly folded paper rose tucked in my lapel. On my left,
Roulette didn't walk so much as strut. He was still dressed for
battle on the frontier, with his wide-brimmed yellow cattleman and dusty amber coat.

And on my right, a clanking blue juggernaut who would barely fit through the stash house's front door.

"I think I should be the one to knock." Anjali's voice echoed from within the depths of her battle-scarred suit. Her breastplate had a new addition: a freshly painted blue rose. Her footsteps clanked heavily on the oak boardwalk. She held up a steel gauntlet, engines and pistons whirring from the simple gesture. "Look at this thing. It was made for knocking."

I flexed my fingers. Above us, a pair of street lights winked off and on and off and on again like festival lamps. "I don't know if you'd have the same effect."

"Someone sees me coming up their front walk, and you think they won't shit their pants?"

"I don't want them to shit their pants," I said. "We gotta be in the room with them, remember?"

"Keep fighting, keep fighting, you two," Roulette breezed. I wrinkled my nose as he blew out a mouthful of perfumed cigarillo smoke. He smiled at me with teeth as yellow as the rose pinned to his coat. "I got my own ways of opening a door." Showily, he twirled one of his revolvers.

A tinny laugh from Anjali. "You couldn't hit a lock with a key, let alone a bullet."

I smirked as Roulette sputtered to fire off a comeback. But my grin faded as the city abruptly changed the tone of its song. Before, the melody had been energetic but pleasant, like it was excited to see what came next. But something harsher had grown inside that melody like a tumor, and now it was all I could hear.

It was a leitmotif I would come to know well.

The door didn't need knocking on, or even in; it hung off its hinges already. In the front hall, bodies littered the floor, spent like the bullet shells that rattled underfoot as I stepped in.

"Hm," Roulette grunted, brushing his bangs out of his eye to take in the room better.

"What is it?" I said, eyeing the scene.

He pointed at the bullet holes ringing the door and nearby walls. "All the shooting's one way."

Sure enough, the far wall facing the door was untouched. I closed my eyes and asked the city to sing me a story. And I got it in a brief flash: strobing guns and shrieks of terror as a shadow moved among them, huge and deadly.

Down the hall, a door was propped open by the leg of the Moon Shadow who had fallen there. When I spread my consciousness through the floorboards, I could tell that there were plenty more where these bodies had come from. Right about now, I bet you and Knife-Edge were making the same discovery.

"Too slow, too slow," Roulette sighed. He hocked a glob of tobacco spit on to the bloody floor. "Bet whoever got here first already cleaned out the loot."

The city carried me an answer, swift as a telegram. "The loot's still here." I narrowed my eyes at the upstairs. "And so's the guy."

"What guy?" Anjali asked, but I was already sprinting ahead of her. The stairs were on our right. I leapt on to the railing, then vaulted over on to the next-highest flight of stairs.

As I bounced between two walls to scale the final flight of stairs, I faintly heard Roulette say, "I could do that, too, you know."

At the top floor, there were bedrooms—not just utilitarian bunks, but spaces that felt both lived-in and loved-in. My understanding of this place changed. The Moon Shadow Syndicate hadn't just been a criminal enterprise; to some extent, these people had been family. That wasn't supposed to faze me; they were playing the crooked game. When people like them won it, the whole city lost. The fact that they were family shouldn't have mattered at all. But my stomach seized up just the same.

The door to the rooftop had been left open, and silver moonlight spilled down through it. It fell on the access ladder, which had been left folded down. Fresh blood painted the steps. No denying it: this was an invitation.

You flickered into the corner of my vision like a white flame. The moonlight found its echo in your pale rose, and in the silver hair peeking out from beneath your black flatcap.

We didn't bother exchanging a greeting. "You know who he is?" I asked.

You shook your head and pulled your mask down from your mouth. "But I can't deny I'm curious."

I took just a second to eye you over. I wasn't honestly that worried about your embrace of the more literal ways to fight this war. You were a rich boy with a soft life behind you, but I didn't care about that. You'd chosen this life. That said it all for me.

Even so, this was on a whole different level. I'd known Benilda to torture people for hours when she wanted something bad enough, and they'd come away from her sessions looking better than the poor eyeless fucks downstairs.

Their maker waited for us on the rooftop. Though the night sky was huge, I still felt trapped by the stench of fresh blood. When I looked down at my feet, I saw why: it was streaked all over. Not randomly, either, but I couldn't make out the shape from where I stood.

The painter stood right at its center, a huge shape covered in tattoos that were darker than the night around him. "What's your deal?" I called to him. "You ain't Lacanilao, I know that much. So who brought you in? The Rock?"

"No one had to bring me in." His voice rang, deep and huge

as a black iron bell. "I'm as native to this place as you, Cheza Tenlonghari, and fighting just as hard to defend it."

I took a threatening step toward him. "That ain't your name to say."

"Do you agree, Mongkhul Pakuanjangnambharat?" said the monstrous figure.

"Hear that?" I said loudly to you. "Guy knows our old names, Cole. He's making a great case for his not leaving this rooftop alive."

I expected a quip from you. But instead, you just stood there, a thoughtful expression on your face. "You don't strike me as an enemy of ours," you said. "So what drove you to this?"

"The two of you have done great work," the figure said. "Surely, you can't be surprised that there are those who find it ... inspirational."

We'd dropped bodies, but I didn't remember inspiring anything quite like this. Before I could hit him with a decent comeback, though, you spoke up again. "Who are you?"

"I was born with the name Mhap." His voice was an un-rosined bow dragged across bass strings. "In some circles, I have another name. I'm sure your secret friend is just about to tell it to you."

Right on cue, the city whispered in my ear. "The Monster," I said. A jagged chorus ran through my head, and with it a vision of the Slats ringed in bloody footprints. Whoever this guy was, he'd been busy.

"You enjoy being known by that name?" you asked him. "Monster?"

I gawked at you. *"He's fucking covered in blood, and that's what you wanna ask him?"*

The Monster ignored me. "Stories always have monsters in them to teach children what not to do. Listen to your parents.

339

Be home before dark. Don't stray from the path. The monster is consequence."

"And whose consequences are you?" you said with a patience that was beyond me.

He grinned. "The children who've grown up and forgotten what happens to those who stray from the path."

"And you just appointed yourself, did you?" I snarled.

"Did the Thorn Orphans not do the same thing?" Mhap said evenly.

"We. Were. Chosen." The words came out of me tight as a noose. I hadn't shied from killing, but to my mind there was a whole lot of blue sky between what we did, and the slaughter-house downstairs. For this guy to try to put himself on our level . . .

"The gods blessed me with only one gift," the Monster shrugged. "I can't deny my purpose, so I will always be a monster. But with you, I could be a monster who helps bring about meaning."

I didn't take the time to parse that out. I was already done with him. This guy was giving me the fucking creeps, and I was keyed up for a good scrap.

"I know you've recruited others to your cause," he went on. "Consider the delivery of the Moon Shadow Syndicate my credentials."

I let out a bark of laughter. "You've gotta be shitting me," I said. "So you've done your homework. But you think anyone who throws our names around and has a decent kill count is Thorn Orphans material? We don't just kick doors in and do what we want, pal. We fucking believe in things. What do you believe in, huh?"

I wasn't sure what answer I expected. But what he said was, "I believe in roses every day. I believe in Driftwood City. And . . ." Gently, he dropped to one knee. "I believe in you,"

340

I'd taken a step or two forward while I was talking, and the light had shifted. Now, I could trace the curve of the line of blood at my eyes. And from the way it intersected with another line, I could tell exactly what flower he'd drawn on the rooftop in the blood of the Moon Shadow Syndicate.

I turned back to you. Other than those two questions, you'd been pretty quiet so far. Had the sheer violence actually gotten to you? Or were you waiting to signal me about something? But instead of any urgency on your face, I only saw that closed expression you wore when the machinery between your ears was hard at work.

"Cole," I said, "what're you getting off this guy? I ain't liking anything the city's had to say so far."

You frowned as you considered Mhap the Monster for another long second.

He knelt in the dark, silent and patient.

At last, you turned to me.

"We've hired mercenaries," you said eventually. "Ones we like, but mercenaries just the same. Think of how fiercely Binh fights, because of how fiercely he believes. Don't you think the Thorn Orphans could use a true believer, too?"

"What're you talking about?" I said. "Ain't it got two already?"

"We believe in Driftwood City," you replied. "But we need someone who believes in us."

I can't hate you for bringing in the Black Rose, Cole. No matter how bad you wanted it, you left that choice to me.

And I was the one who nodded at long last.

27
Now

Age 30

I was feeling the cold trickle of seawater as it piled up and clawed at my hair and clothes.

I was feeling the searing sting of the Monster's fist on my cheekbones.

I was lying on my back in a dark driftwood coffin, helpless as I sank deeper and the water seeped in.

I was lying on my back in a dark office, chained to a fallen chair, helpless as the Monster stood over me.

I was screaming for the city to help me and despairing when it wouldn't.

I was screaming for the city to help me and despairing because it could never help me again.

"You've always mistaken me for a cruel man, rather than a thorough one, Red Rose." He rolled his neck, and bones cracked like fireworks.

When he kicked me I went skidding across the floor, chair and all.

"But that said," he continued, "I'm going to enjoy this."

My ribs exploded with pain every time I moved. So I didn't move much during my days aboard the fishing trawler that had rescued me. I just stayed belowdecks, hoarding my driftwood.

Twice the crew had tried to take it from me. After the second time, they'd shrugged and left me alone. I knew I was lucky to get picked up by a nice crew. There were ships on the Porcelain Sea whose crews would've just cut my throat and been done with it rather than spare me the galley supplies. But I could thank them later. Right now, I had to take care of me. So I sat in that pile of driftwood, staring at the opposite wall. Wincing as pain played across my ribs like mallets on a zither.

Lifting my arms anyway, and willing the stumps of my power to slip into the worn and swollen grains of that driftwood, the only pieces of home I had left.

And listening, always listening for a spirit to raise its voice in answer.

My ribs exploded with pain as I came to a stop. With each breath I took, it felt like phantom feet were kicking me again and again.

"It's unfortunate that you thought you could know Cole's heart," the Monster said. "You had the barest of similarities, and you thought it made the two of you family."

I had to hack up some blood before my throat was clear enough for me to speak. "I," I gasped, "know who he is now."

"I've always known," said the Monster. "Who else could say the same?"

Another kick. I tried to fold my body in around his foot to grab hold of it like a trap, maybe twist his ankle. But I was too slow. Bursts of pain ran through my whole body as his steel-toed boot hammered me in the chest.

"Do you even know why he chose me, that day on the

343

rooftop?" said the Monster. "The others were chosen by your city, but I alone was chosen by Cole. Have you ever realized that before?"

Of course I'd realized it. But I'd always figured you had your reasons.

"I'll take your silence as a yes. But I don't think you know *why* he—"

"He picked you because you could take me," I rasped. "He chose you to become the Black Rose ... because he was scared of me."

You weren't there, but I could imagine how you would've reacted if I'd hit you with that. You would've shaken your head. Laughed it off. Then, come at me with those earnest eyes of yours and tell me from the bottom of your heart that it wasn't true.

All the classic signs you were lying.

A smile split his face open like a crack in a rotten fruit.

"Maybe you did know his heart after all, then."

Weeks at sea. Berth at Kolkalang. And me: chewed up. Dead-eyed. Short black hair, streaked white with salt. And dragging behind me a driftwood coffin.

The crew had asked me how the box had been put together before; there had been no nails to hold it together. The boards had been woven, somehow, they told me. When they asked me if I knew how that was possible, I kept quiet.

"You know," said the first mate one night as the crew was turning in, "we did pull you from the chop."

I raised an eyebrow sidelong at him. "And?"

"And," he said calmly, "you don't have to be such a raging asshole literally all the time."

I shrugged it off when he said it, and I shrugged it off as I dragged the new and improved coffin behind me. It was crude; the

344

ends of the boards didn't match up, and the lid didn't close properly. The nails were all different sizes, made from whatever I'd been able to scavenge on the fishing boat. When folks in Kolkalang port asked me what was inside, I invited them to see the nothing for themselves.

They always asked me why I kept it around. I told them I planned to fill it someday, and that usually got a laugh before they let me on through. I was unusual, but what harm could a single person pose with a big, empty box?

Every night, I unmade that box. Every morning, I remade it before hitting the road again.

And in the time that it was unmade each night, I continued communing with each grain. Listening to each moment of its history. Stretching my soul into a string on which I could pluck every song I knew.

All for the one night when, at last, I heard a note rise, and a single splinter of driftwood with it.

Through the haze of my pain, I could almost hear the music again.

There was no point in struggling, but I did it anyway. He'd done the cuffs tight, and it wasn't like I was gonna break steel with my bare hands. But maybe if I could break this chair ...

"Why do you let him use you?" I said. "You could—"

Another kick. I didn't go skidding this time, but I definitely felt something inside me snap. My words twisted into a shout of pain.

"Cole saw me for the monster I was, and he gave me a place in the world that wasn't beneath someone's bed." His voice was even and cool, like black glass. "How could you not understand that? It's like you told me all those years ago on that rooftop: I was chosen."

I pushed against the chair. Despite all the punishment it'd taken, the frame was still solid. Fuck.

"I'd spare him the pain of ending you if I could, but he's set on it. I disrespected his wishes once and paid for it." He tapped his empty eyelid. "But I'm going to bring you right to the very edge until he arrives."

He picked up the chair. I ain't light, and neither was the chair, but he held it overhead like it was nothing.

"That way," he rumbled, "all Cole will have to do is push."

He hurled me straight at the wall.

Night after night, I shot shards of driftwood at my wall. Once my aim was good, I started teaching myself how to work with more than just a splinter at a time. By the end of my first six months of exile, I could sing to it and it would twist into any shape I asked.

Once I could control the driftwood, I dreamed of nothing but taking it back home. And when I got there ... well. I had a whole lot of different fantasies about what I would do. But no matter what shape those dreams took, they all ended the same way for you.

Still, even I knew those fantasies wouldn't keep my stomach full between now and then. I needed to regain my strength. Rest. Really make sure I was ready for the big moment when it finally came. At first, it was just hauling shit at the harbor in Malañong. But that got to be hard on my back, and years of old injuries didn't help. I needed something easier on my body, or I wouldn't have anything left to spend ruining you.

That was how I wound up at that diner, washing dishes and chopping vegetables. I'd come in for my shift while the sun was still up, and leave under a starless sky each night, reeking of dish soap and fried garlic. And when I staggered into my dumpy little flat each night, my little shred of the city was waiting to greet me like a good dog.

Like a friend.

I was lucky; the chair hit the wall, not me.

Of course, I was still in the chair, so that didn't help much.

It was two hits, like I was caught between sets of chewing teeth. The wall on my spine and on the back of my head, which sent my glasses spinning away. And then I fell to the hard office floor again. This time, I couldn't help letting out a cry; my wrist had wound up pinned between the floor and the armrest, and there was only so much a small bone like that could take.

I was on that boathouse floor, bullets in my body and my own blood outside of it.

I was back in Malañong, trying to make a single piece of wood float.

I was on the floor of the Monster's office, watching through blurry eyes as my wrist flopped uselessly.

And always, always, I was screaming for help from the one thing that could give it to me.

I had no family. I had no friends. I had no one in my heart. All I'd had was my home.

When I'd begun practicing for my revenge, the desire to destroy you had roiled inside me like steam. Each night I came home and let that steam drive me like I was some kind of engine. I sang, and the driftwood danced itself into a million different shapes. I practiced my aim until I could pin a gnat by its wing. I sharpened my ears so I could hear even the faintest note being scratched on it.

But time passed. I came home from work and fell in to bed, letting the song from my floorboards lead me to a blank and dreamless sleep. My revenge was still a real thing, but it had become more distant. I had other things to keep me busy. Wasn't like you were going anywhere, after all. And given how bad you'd gotten the jump on me, more time to prep wouldn't hurt.

The steam slowed down. Settled into water.

And then, somehow, I'd been dead for two years. One day at the diner, I looked up from washing dishes (all that water ...) and realized I hadn't thought about you once that day. That I hadn't thought about you yesterday, either. That water had slowed and cooled even more and turned to ice inside me, and I realized that at last, I'd found stillness.

All I'd had to do was die.

My eyes snapped open. I didn't know what to do next, but I knew this: I would not go back to the stillness.

All this time, I'd told myself I was alone. But the Monster was right. I hadn't been, had I? In Malañong, I'd had my coworkers at the diner. My neighbors in the projects. And here too, I'd had people: Pamin, offering me a good deal right after I'd insulted them to their face. Diwata, taking me in. Suspending her pahingán. Bringing me to a zephyr. Rescuing me from the badges. Trying to pledge herself to my fight. And at every turn I'd pushed them away, because my heart had been lucky to survive the knife you'd plunged into it, Cole. I knew it wouldn't survive another one.

But you did. The thought wafted into my head like a faint snatch of song. And with it, the memory of a tearful Phuong, the gun in her shaking hand. *She didn't hesitate to stab you ... and you're still here.*

The heavy tread of the Monster's footsteps filled my ears. *For now.*

I squeezed my eyes shut with pain. Not the kind that came from snapped bones and twisted muscles. It was something deeper and older. A shame that had nested in my heart since the day you betrayed me. I had held on to the driftwood from my coffin, even as it dwindled in my ever-tightening grip. I'd been convinced that it was the only power I needed: my souvenir of that day, soaked in mine and Binh's mingled blood. And against Roulette, against Anjali, against Knife-Edge, it had been enough. Barely, but enough.

But it wasn't enough anymore. *I* wasn't enough anymore. And to survive the next thirty seconds, I was going to have to open myself up to one last old friend I'd been pushing away.

I didn't know what would work here, Cole. I've never been good at humbling myself. But I decided to do something wild, because I didn't think I had the option to do anything else.

I decided to trust you.

Or, specifically, to trust the man who'd told me that our powers had no limits.

Please, I sang to it. *Please help me*.

I felt the Monster's shadow fall on me like a rancid breath on my neck.

I expected indifference. Maybe contempt. I even expected nothing at all. And while I felt claws of terror dig into me at the mere thought, I forced myself to bear that pain rather than run from it. The spirit and I had been partners. Whatever it chose now, no matter how desperate I was, I had to accept it. I'd trusted it before when it had deemed me worthy of serving it. And I'd have to trust it now if it deemed me worthy of death.

I sang out, *I need you*, expecting silence in reply.

But instead, a voice rose to harmonize with mine, singing a single word in a crescendoing major key:

Finally.

The cracks were small at first. Voices and images and phantom smells seeped through like trickles of icy water into a wooden box. But already, it was so much more than I'd been used to carrying. The driftwood I'd brought with me contained only memories of the day I died. This Plant contained so many more.

There was no middle. The trickles were trickles, then a flood. I heard the *clang* of the first hammer striking the first nail to join the first two boards of this place. I smelled the stink of sweat as a ragged crew of salters entered their thirteenth straight hour of work. I tasted sweet, perfumed smoke as an overseer lit incense in her office, passing the time. And I saw one silver-haired descendant after another, all standing on a walkway and surveying what was theirs.

I heard screams and whirring machines and sizzling flesh and rushing water and chanted slogans and boiling blood and then there was ash, so much ash, filling my nose and stinging my eyes and coating my tongue and—

The scream ran through my throat, jagged as the teeth of a saw.

And somewhere beneath my own tattered and battered voice, I heard an ethereal orchestra play me a harmony.

"I'd expected you to be tougher," the Monster said. "That wrist is nothing compared to some of the injuries I've seen you suffer in the field. But I guess my colleagues did their part to chip away at your armor. I never respected them much, but they have my gratitude for that."

"You know ... how ... you're like them?" I grunted, as my head threatened to split in two.

He lifted a huge foot and held it over my hand, ready to stomp. "How?"

I gritted my teeth and forced myself to focus. "You all fucking talk too much."

I sang to the city, and Cole.

Cole.

The city sang back.

The office's wooden walls peeled themselves back like the skin of a banana. And from their depths, something black snaked out and wrapped itself around the Monster's

350

outstretched ankle. An electric cable. Three more shot forward to join it. And before the Monster even knew what was happening, I willed them to lift him up into the air, slam him into the ceiling, and then slam him back to the floor.

Again, I asked the city.

And again, the city sang.

His huge body made dents and splinters wherever it struck. I couldn't see them with my glasses gone. But I felt them, as real as fingers running through my hair.

I hummed another request: *The window*.

The city didn't answer me this time. Or maybe its answer lay in the sound of shattering glass.

The four electric cables snaked around the legs of my fallen chair and, working together, sat it upright. My head swam: from the bloodrush, from all the pain I was fighting, from the sheer weight of senses that I hadn't properly used in years.

I remembered the old magic. *No lock can hold me*, I'd always boasted.

And as I thought it, there they were: four little clicks. Four sets of metal cuffs clattering to the floor. I cradled my arm to my body, and stood. Though it was dark, the city told me exactly where my glasses lay. I put them back on, then limped over to the spectacularly shattered window to take a look at what I'd done.

Sticking my head through the ring of broken glass in the open frame was like sticking my head into the teeth of a huge beast. Out on the work floor, all the salters had stopped dead in their duties. I could smell the different reactions in the air: curiosity from the faraway crews, who were venturing in for a closer look. Confusion from the closer ones, who'd seen the window explode outward as a dark shape spat itself out of it. Panic from the closest ones, who were wondering what the hell could have possibly done that to their huge, powerful, invincible overseer.

He lay in a heap. A huge metal tank opposite the window bore a large, Monster-shaped dent; no doubt he'd hit it on his way down. It'd probably saved his life by slowing his fall, even a little. It must've, because when I looked down, I could see him trying in vain to push himself back upright. But a heavy, familiar leitmotif in the city's song betrayed the truth with its drumming. It was the beating of his heart, getting faster and faster.

The powerful were afraid.

I took a few steps back from the window. I closed my eyes and let a fresh burst of the city's song wash over me. I blinked back tears of relief as I listened to my old friend tell me where to go.

And then I sprinted right to the window and jumped.

I twisted my body so that it threaded the space between fangs of glass. And then, for the first time in four years, the legendary Red Rose was sailing through the open air.

It was a long drop to the floor, but the city had crooned to me: *Grab the chain*. And sure enough, I shot my good hand up into the air and closed my fingers around a thick link of iron chain I hadn't seen on my way down.

My whole body swung from it as the chain took my weight. My broken wrist protested, but I kept my face straight and stoic. My pain wasn't for others to see.

The city sang another note, and somewhere above a winch turned by itself. The chain lowered me gently to the Plant's main floor. By the time my feet touched down, a huge crowd of salters had gathered around the fallen Monster. A few had rushed forward to help him, but they all froze when they saw me.

With a grunt, the Monster shouldered his way free of the

work crews. I could see he was in a bad way. The tattoos on his body had made his muscles strong and his skin tough, but you couldn't tattoo bones and guts. He had to be bleeding from more than a few places on the inside. It wasn't that different from fighting Anjali, really; the armor he wore was his own skin, but it was my weapon as much as it was his shield.

He looked at me with dazed, disbelieving eyes. "How did you ...?"

"You wouldn't understand if I told you," I said. "You were never one of us. That was just a story Cole told you so you'd let him own you. You liked how powerful he made you feel. Of course you would be loyal to him for that." While I talked, my mind was paging through my memories of the boathouse. Trying to recapture a feeling. "If I couldn't give up what made me feel powerful, why would you?"

His amusement was pained, but obvious. "You've wounded me, but you haven't killed me. And no blow you can deliver will hurt like you want it to. Cole wove these protections himself. As long as they stand, you can't stand against me."

While the Monster spoke, I racked my memory. I brought myself back to the boathouse, trying to recall the exact feeling of you severing my connection. And as my mind tuned into the past, my ears tuned themselves into the present, listening for the soft discordant notes that played on the strings you'd tied around your pet monster.

His entire face twisted into a manic grin.

"He made me to unmake you," he crowed. "So what now, Red Rose, do you propose we—?"

I snapped my fingers.

And he collapsed with a scream.

I shot him an annoyed look. "I thought I told you," I said, raising my voice to be heard over his cries. "You talk too much."

He writhed at my feet. If his voice was volcanic glass, each scream was the sound of it shattering. It was gods-damned *music*, Cole.

"I-impossible!" he cried. "Y-your power—!"

"You were an idiot to tell me exactly what was sustaining you," I cut in coldly. "Especially if you knew that I could do everything Cole can. What he can give, Black Rose, I can take away."

If you hadn't felt my rebirth, you definitely felt me slicing through all those strings that tied you to your last puppet. You would know what had just happened.

Good.

I spied a nearby furnace. That would work just fine.

Calmly, I grabbed his collar and began to drag him behind me toward it. He was heavy and I only had the one arm to pull him with. But he couldn't resist me anymore, and I would make myself be strong enough for this.

As I neared the crowd of salters, a few of them started for me. I was dressed like one of them, but I sure as shit didn't feel like one of them. Not anymore. Without Binh to lead them, they'd lost sight of the real fight.

"*Do any of you know who I am?*" I bellowed at the top of my lungs. I was tired and beat up, but I had breath enough for this. "I was the daughter of Nanay Benilda Lacanilao. I was the love of Pham Binh Cong. I was the Red Rose of the Thorn Orphans. I was a salter, just like you. My name is Tenny." I gestured down to the Monster with my broken hand. "*And I came here to kill this absolute motherfucker.*"

Ripples of recognition fluttered through the assembled crowd of salters. I could taste their surprise, their shock, even the excitement of some. At Binh's name in particular, something warm flitted through the crowd like an unseasonable summer breeze. But all I really cared about was the fact that none of them had taken another step toward me.

"Anyone who lays a hand on me, loses it!" I shouted for everyone to hear. "This is old business, a long time coming. It doesn't need to be your business. But if you feel like getting involved"—I dropped my gaze to the salters directly in front of me, so they could look me in the eye and see how fucking serious I was. I met the gaze of one salter in particular: a young Samnati, with silver hair and a once-broken nose—"I will oblige you."

Despite the groans and clanging of working machinery, the moment felt long and quiet.

And then, at last, the Samnati salter in front of me stepped aside.

When they did, so did everyone else around them. More and more salters cleared a path, freeing up floor space moments before I set foot on it, dragging the Monster behind me. I felt them closing in around me, but they kept their distance. I listened to them murmur, heard the fluttering of fear in their hearts. They didn't know that I would never hurt them. On some level, that was painful; I'd thought my lifetime of service to their cause would be proof of what kind of woman I was. But on the other hand, the last thing I needed was for some idiot to try calling my bluff.

The temperature climbed as we reached the furnace. Beneath my hand, I felt the Monster groan and try to roll away from me, but I held fast. Without juiced-up muscles to hold his broken bones together, he couldn't fight me anymore.

"You wanna wear ashes?" I said, gesturing with my broken hand. The loading hatch for the furnace sprang open on its own. "I'll give you ashes. You wanna draw your power from the people? I'll make sure you're connected to the people every time they breathe deep." I grimaced with effort as I lifted him up higher so I could look him right in the eye. *"Roses every day."*

At the familiar declaration, he burst with laughter: a phlegmy, ugly gurgle from deep in his throat. Fear flashed through me. What did this bastard know that I didn't? But I pushed it aside. I'd broken him with a snap of my fingers. I was a full-blown shaman again, and within these four boroughs I could do anything. There was nothing he could do to hurt me anymore.

"You're wrong," he rasped. He favored me with a broken smile. "You can't do everything he can. You ... can't ... *build!*"

He surged with life and vitality. I could feel phantom impressions of his pain, even more searing than the open furnace. He mustered up all of his strength and hurled his full weight at me. I stood between him and the furnace's gaping, fiery jaws—

—so I stepped out of his way, then gave him a sharp kick in the back.

He fell in with a final scream, and the flames rushed to devour him. A tattooed hand, already charring and scorching black, lunged back out. But before it could get a grip, I waved my hand and the hatch slammed shut again. It muffled his screams, but not by much.

Quick as a knife, the sound came back to me: hundreds more screams just like his, as the fire chewed through strong, proud salters. But as quickly as they returned to me, I shut them out. This was different, I told myself, even as my stomach turned.

I faced the huge crew of salters staring at me, horrified. Everything I saw on their faces, I felt doubly in the way the city's spirit moved around them. I tried not to let it sting me. They just didn't understand what was going on here. But they would soon enough.

A disturbance jolted through me. Bows and fingers playing

across the strings of the city, their strokes getting smaller and tighter as the notes climbed higher.

A grin spread across my face like an egg in a pan as I recognized it.

You were here.

28

Twelve years ago

Age 18

Knife-Edge held up his long black boiled wool coat, inspecting it with a frown. "I don't know why I thought you were joking when you told me we would be wearing these," he sighed. "And yet, here I am."

"It's like we said at the time," you replied patiently. "We're fighting for the people. Until they can afford better, we don't wear better."

Knife-Edge's nose wrinkled as he considered the coat in his hands. "Black, though. Such a dull color. Black is what you wear when the only statement you have to make is, 'I have nothing to say.' Although I'm sure it will look lovely on *you*," he added with a smirk toward Mhap, who didn't stand in the corner so much as loom.

Mhap didn't rise to the bait, but his annoyed grunt felt like a threat of its own.

"That there ethos of yours ..." said Roulette Wu. I hadn't allowed him to light up his cigarillos in our place, so it bobbed

358

unlit in his teeth. "Reckon that's why we skimped on having ourselves a cool hideout, too?"

"Hoy, asshole," I said. "We lay our heads here. Show some respect for my home when you're in it, neh?"

Roulette put up his hands apologetically.

I sighed. "You ain't wrong, though."

The Kelptown apartment had been spacious enough when I was the only one living in it. A big comedown from the Lacanilao estate, but what on the Slats wouldn't be? When you'd moved in and taken up my couch, it'd become a bit tighter. Not that I minded. I liked living with you. Maybe you felt guilty about having servants your whole life, but you were always good about keeping the place clean. You were quiet. And it was good to have a friend sitting across the table from me every morning when I slapped some breakfast on a plate. So maybe snug was the wrong word; with you around, our Kelptown apartment had become cozy.

With all six of us, it was tight as a clamshell.

"Here's what I don't understand," Anjali said, casting a critical eye around our sitting room. Instead of her armor, she wore a sea-colored dress that flowed even more beautifully. "Your unit is a one-bedroom." She arched a mischievous eyebrow. "Some of my very favorite books revolve around this setup. So is this your way of telling us something about the two of you?"

"Of course not," you said.

"Why're you so stuck on that idea?" I added.

"I can't help myself," Anjali said. "You kids are so earnest. You have no idea how adorable you are together. If only the gangs knew who they were really up against ..."

"The crooked game *is* full of bleeding hearts," Knife-Edge said with a wry smile.

Roulette's hand casually draped across his revolver handle.

"There'll be a lot more of those to go around once we get going."

You leaned close to me. "I'm starting to have second thoughts," you groaned under the chatter, soft enough that only I could hear.

I grinned and clapped you across the back. "At least they're getting along, neh?" My eyes slid to the Monster, silent in his corner. "Most of 'em, anyway."

"This was your idea," you grumbled.

"That you'd already had without me." My smile widened. I couldn't help myself. The spirit's song was exciting that evening: propulsive as a march, and growing richer with each measure. More and more instruments were chiming in, and leitmotifs I had in isolation were colliding in harmonies and counterpoints. There was no way I couldn't smile with that in my ear.

That said, I was also smiling 'cause it was fun to fuck with you.

"I suppose we should discuss the matter at hand," you said. "We only have a few hours."

You'd only been speaking to me, but at your voice the Monster finally peeled himself off our wall and stepped forward. "What mission do you have for your Thorn Orphans?"

Knife-Edge was still inspecting his outfit with disdain, and Roulette had draped his across his lap. Only Mhap had immediately put his on. His was the biggest coat we'd been able to find, and even then his muscles still strained its seams. From within the shadow of his flatcap's brim, his eyes glinted like bullets in a gun.

I shot you a look: *Why'd we invite this guy again?*

Your mouth twisted. You put up a hand, and the room fell silent.

"First of all," you said, "I want to clear something up. We

360

may have recruited you, but this organization"—you gestured between me and you—"is not 'our' Thorn Orphans." You swept out a slender hand to indicate all six of us. "It's *our* Thorn Orphans. We're not some gang. We're a collective, and we aim for something higher than personal enrichment."

"The real fight going on right now is at the Plant," I chimed in. "The Brethren of the Salt are facing off against the Rock. Things are broken in Driftwood City, and this is the first real shot we've had at fixing them all. But it'll only happen if the Brethren win. So for us, until all this is over, the name of the game is this: make sure the Brethren win."

"Benilda Lacanilao's cooperation has allowed the Rock to keep things in motion so far, even with the widespread demonstrations." You picked up smoothly where I left off, just like we'd practiced. "But the Paks are growing tired of the prolonged strike. We've received reliable word—"

The four Orphans all looked at each other. Through the spirit, I sensed their curiosity. They all knew we could do something weird and special, but they were still hazy on the details. That, I knew, was a conversation the six of us were gonna have to have at some point.

"—that they've recruited strike breakers," you were saying. "Mercenaries from the Tsunese frontier, and the company is due to drop anchor at port tonight."

"I served me a couple tours out that way," Roulette drawled. "Place like that? It don't spit out pushovers."

"That's what we've gathered," I said grimly. "The salters out there ... they're fighters, but they ain't warriors. These mercs could mow right through the picket lines. Maybe scare the survivors into taking their places back on the line. If that happens, the Brethren lose." I shot a look at the collection of weirdos in my sitting room. "And what do the Thorn Orphans do?"

"Make sure they don't," Roulette said, then looked around at the others. "I thought we were supposed to say that all together ..."

"So you want us to strike out at the dead of night to ambush a company of hardened professional killers?" said Anjali. "Hardened professional killers who will probably outnumber us?"

Knife-Edge laughed. "Definitely outnumber us."

"If we let their numbers scare us," Mhap growled, "then we never had a place on the battlefield to begin with. Send me in alone, Cole. I'll paint the decks red with——"

"I didn't say their numbers scared us," Anjali said, annoyed. "I just wanted to make sure I understood exactly what we were going to be up against."

"The Thorn Orphans are in possession of assets and abilities that would be the envy of any mercenary company, no matter how experienced or deadly," you said smoothly. "But if I have to answer your original question directly: yes, Anjali, that's about right."

There was silence as they all considered this.

"Any other questions?" you said at last.

More silence.

Then Knife-Edge pointed at Anjali and said, "Why doesn't she have to wear an ugly coat?"

"My wardrobe is my whole thing, fancy boy," came Anjali's amused reply.

Knife-Edge gestured to his immaculately tailored áo dài. "*So is mine.*"

I caught myself grinning again. There was something about seeing them all together like this that filled me with hope. I didn't totally like all of them. Didn't totally trust all of them. One of them straight up gave me the fucking creeps. But I felt a growing certainty that Driftwood City had never seen anything like us before. And when we made our first strike tonight, no one would be ready.

"One more question, one more question," Roulette said. "You said our whole thing was to make sure the Brethren win." He leaned back, deep into the couch cushions. "What happens once we've done that?"

You and I exchanged a look. We'd talked about it. A whole lot. We had ideas, dreams. Scores we wanted to settle, scales we wanted to balance. But how much of it could we tell them? How much could we trust them with?

I gave you a nod. One I knew you'd understand: *Whatever you say, I'm with you.* It scared me, the thought of showing our hand to these strangers, even if the city's spirit had given us a good feeling about them. But if there was one person I knew I could count on even more than the spirit of Driftwood City, it was you.

Gratefully, you nodded to me.

On the dining table was a box from the neighborhood florist. You went to the table and picked it up, then turned around and flipped it open to reveal six roses. Each one a different color, each one waiting to be claimed.

"Let's worry about tomorrow," you said, "after we win tonight."

The papers wrote one story about what happened that night. Their account had searing reports of brave police and dutiful soldiers falling under cowardly ambush from a group of unknown terrorists. There wasn't any evidence that could lay the attack at the feet of the Brethren, but fucking Kueiyang spent inch after column inch throwing the suspicion Binh's way all the same.

But all across the Slats, the people told other stories: of the gunslinger who effortlessly shot out the tires of the strike

363

breakers' transport vehicles. The armored soldier who waded easily into their return fire, bullets pinging off her breastplate. The knife fighter who gracefully carved his way through strike breakers and badges without a scratch. The hulking brute who left a trail of snapped necks, gouged eyes, and far worse behind him. The way their combined ferocity drove the mercenaries and their police escorts back, circling up at the center of the Tsetsang Shedrap Bridge.

And the two people who, with matching gestures, made the bridge twist and splinter before it collapsed and dumped every strike breaker and badge into the canal to drown like rats.

Binh's picket line that day was unbroken. The Rock reeled, all its plans in sudden disarray. The people of the Slats kept whispering, and the story their voices told was loud enough to drown out the headlines.

And in a small apartment in Kelptown, the six of us laid the plans to bring Driftwood City even closer to the dream of roses every day.

Part Six

The Fifth Revenge!
The Heart of the White Rose

29
Now

Age 30

You'd mustered the entire gods-damned police force, it looked like.

Their cars and wagons jammed every road leading to the Plant. Their officers were putting up barricades around the entire perimeter, while a tide of dark blue assembled behind them. They cradled wood-stocked rifles, but I was surprised to see they'd also brought heavier hardware. I saw the kind of machine-gun emplacements that would've looked at home in a war zone, bolted to the backs of police trucks. And the city told me I could expect a whole lot more. Clearly, the Armored had been busy while I was dead.

I watched your army fall in from the roof of the Plant, my arms folded tight over my narrow chest. My long black braid whipped and snapped in the wind, and the metal arms of my glasses were cold against my temples. I'd been tempted to go back and get my coat and hat from the bottom of that trash can. But I'd decided to stick with my grey salter's coveralls for this. It felt like old times, going into battle dressed like the people I was fighting for.

My eyes scanned the ranks of blue below. Officers were hurrying to their positions, or already standing at attention. But I sifted through them for someone with a slow walk, the kind of person who didn't hurry because the world moved to his tempo.

And just like that, there you were.

Even from this distance there was no mistaking you. The police force was full of silver-haired Samnati, but you were the only one who didn't have a helmet on. And while your goons were all in blue, you were wearing your usual: something sleek and black, because you liked how it made your hair stand out. But even if you'd been dressed like one of them, you'd have been given away by the way they moved around you. Wherever you walked, folks got out of your way. I could see so clearly from up here what I'd never been able to when you were next to me: we were both idiots to have ever thought you could live without subjects.

Soon, though, you wouldn't have to.

You froze. And even though I couldn't really make out the details of your face from this distance and height, I knew you were staring right at me. I stood still for a moment and let you get a good, long look.

A familiar tune piped into my head as I stared down at you. And even though the melody was bittersweet, the fact that I was hearing music at all almost made me cry. I'd been so sure that if I'd tried to reach out, the city would've rejected me. The spirit knew me inside and out, and it knew I'd failed it before. Why would it help me now? I'd been so certain I'd never get to feel that connection again, and all the warmth and strength it brought me. So certain I didn't deserve it.

So certain I'd have to face you with only the silence at my back.

But now, I felt like an idiot. The beautiful song winding through me now was as much a part of me as my arms and eyes. It had always been there. If only I'd trusted it.

"Let's do this," I said to the empty air.

The ghostly song trilled in counterpoint. Power flowed through me, and I flowed through it, until I was not just Tenny, and it was not just the spirit.

We were Driftwood City.

And then I sang through that city and stretched myself into the radio units of every police car, and held by every operator in your ranks. They all crackled at once, and then their speakers carried my voice to you like the wind had done once upon a time.

"*All of you officers.*" I spoke out into the chilly air, but I could hear my words echo down below, half a heartbeat behind me. "*Know my name when you hear my voice: I am Tenny the Red Rose.*"

Maybe it was just a trick of the light and distance, Cole. But I thought I saw your little army shrink back at my name.

"*I'm here to settle things with your governor and no one else,*" I continued. "*Anyone who walks away now, I guarantee their safety. And anyone who stays ... I guarantee something much, much worse.*"

I let go of my hold, and waited.

Not a single officer broke ranks.

I gritted my teeth. How the fuck did you do that, Cole? I'd chewed up all your best. At least one of those grunts down there should've been scared shitless at the thought of facing me. How did a bastard like you manage to inspire enough loyalty in these officers to stand in my way?

Well, I thought with a wave of my hand, *I'll just have to make them see reason.*

I sang to the spirit again, and it moved through the façade of the Plant itself. Your folks had made it big and stately and white, but now I rearranged it on a whim. Pieces of the building jutted out into makeshift stairs. As I walked down them, they disappeared back into the façade behind me like fluid. Step by step, I made my way down to the ground, waiting for someone to dare open fire. I could feel the city waiting, too: lips pressed to a reed between movements, looking for the flick of the conductor's baton.

By the time I touched down on the Slats, no one had fired. But when I started walking toward them, I heard a chorus of clicks as hundreds of bullets slipped into chambers.

I reached for their radios again. "*Cole,*" I said, and heard my own echo. "*Don't be a fucking coward. You knew this day would come. Stop hiding behind these badges and take what's coming. Enough people have already died for you.*"

I couldn't see you through their ranks anymore, but I knew you were listening. I waited for them to part so you could face me one-on-one at last.

But after a full minute passed, you still hadn't shown your face. None of the badges had moved. And I was staring down a whole lot of gun barrels. But they hadn't fired on me, either. You probably thought I wouldn't actually make the first move, not with so much collateral on the table.

I fucking hate being underestimated, Cole.

I gestured with my non-broken hand and a rumble echoed through the Slats. Your army only had a second to look among themselves before a gigantic cloud of scalding steam erupted from the Slats beneath them. Shouts erupted across your line as furious white clouds exploded into the air. And as those shouts turned to screams, the guns finally began to roar.

370

I met them with a blast of horns and drums that would rattle bone. The ground that stretched between us was made of wooden slats that were thicker than a person. The spirit played a wild solo in my ear as those slats bent themselves upwards like they were reeds. The first wave of gunfire hit them, not me. An old trick, but there was a reason you and I had kept using it.

I heard something louder, and gaping holes exploded through my makeshift fence. Those damn heavy weapons. What the fuck were badges doing with that kind of hardware, anyway? I gritted my teeth from the effort it took to keep my defenses standing. The huge slats shrank in closer to me, until it was less of a wall and more of a shield. It'd keep me safe for a few more seconds, but even the strongest oak was still just wood. Hot lead would chew through it eventually. If I wanted to win, I had to push back.

So that's exactly what I did.

With a shout, I sent my huge oaken shield surging away from me. It rumbled across the Slats, skimming over them like a train over its rails. I watched with grim satisfaction as it slammed right through the heart of the police line, sending officers and vehicles flying. The entire street jolted, and nearby windows bowed and shattered in their frames.

Your troops were already in complete disarray, but they were trying to rally. One of the dark blue wagons zipped forward from the rest, its turret barking and blazing. I darted just in time to avoid the stream of bullets as they tore up the slats I'd been standing on like the footsteps of an invisible giant. I punched the air, and a splinter of driftwood shot straight for the officer crouched behind its controls. I clocked him right in the helmet, hard enough to send him tumbling from the back of the huge police wagon. The gun fell silent, but the huge thing kept charging for me, its engine baying for my blood and its front grille shining like teeth.

I stomped, and the road under its tires promptly flipped the whole wagon on to its back. It lay there like an upturned beetle, wheels spinning.

I charged past it on foot. Bullets tore through all the places my feet had just been. They should've been tearing through me, too, but nothing could touch me with the city's spirit on my side.

As I stampeded closer to their ranks, I saw the frontmost officers were now wearing masks that made their faces look like midnight-blue skulls. I recognized them from Roulette's old war stories. Gas masks.

A moment later canisters arced toward me, trailing thin streams of white gas. Whatever it was, I knew I sure as hell didn't want to breathe it.

They landed all around me, a drum roll of hollow, metallic *thunk*s. A huge cloud of the gas erupted. I closed my eyes, but tears clawed their way through my lashes anyway. I tried to hold my breath, but I couldn't keep it out of my nose. It burned on contact, and then I was on my knees and hacking up a lung.

Desperately, I reached for the ruined slats I'd left in my wake. Another burst of song from me, and a whole segment lifted itself up. Not like a wall this time.

A fan.

It slammed back down. A huge gust of wind swept over me, near strong enough to knock me on my face. All the gas fled past me, straight for the police lines. Return to sender.

Dark shapes in the fog. Badges, charging forward with shouldered rifles. Behind them, more vehicles. I'd never been to war, but I had to imagine it was something like this.

Their masks protected them from the gas, but it didn't let

them see through it. So when the first one emerged from the gas cloud, rifle barrel first, he didn't see me come at him sideways. I only had one arm to work with, but all it took was a hit to the bare spot between his helmet and his armored vest. As he dropped, I palmed his gas mask and yanked it right off his face, then jammed it on to my own. It set my glasses askew, and navigating the leather straps was hard with only one working hand. But I just needed to be able to breathe well enough to get through this and get to you.

I sprinted through a thick white bank of the choking gas. I couldn't see anyone until I was basically on top of them, but the city told me when there were footsteps in the mist. By the time I burst through the other side of it, maybe a dozen officers lay beaten, while the rest searched for a woman who wasn't there.

I hurled my stolen mask aside as a cry of surprise ran through the remaining police behind their barricades. I gritted my teeth. There were still a ton of them, even after my steam attack and the gigantic hole I'd punched right through the center of their line. This was all going well for me, but my frustration mounted. How much harder was I going to have to push before they finally gave you up?

Well, if they really wanted to defend you with their lives, I guessed it was time I obliged them.

"*Come out, Cole!*" I shouted again through their radios. Now, with all the officers still stuck behind me, I heard myself echo from back there, as well. "*Or I'll finish this!*"

But this time, I didn't wait for you to reply. I knew by now what kind of man you really were. You'd sacrificed all those salters to get what you wanted. Of course you'd hide behind a thousand police just to save your own skin. But I guess four years had been long enough for you to forget who I was.

Or maybe you hid now because you still remembered.

I stomped hard on the Slats, a mallet on a drumhead. Another rumble rang through the ground beneath us, but this time the pipes didn't burst (they could only burst once, anyway). Instead, all the Slats beneath your entire army wobbled, as though they were water and a wave was passing through.

And then the ground collapsed beneath them all.

Once upon a time, that would've dropped them straight into the ocean. The officers in wagons and trucks would've drowned for certain, and the heavy riot armor worn by the ones on foot wouldn't have done them any favors. But over the centuries, Driftwood City had built out its share of maintenance decks and tunnels.

I peered down into them now, where maybe two hundred officers lay groaning and dazed. Broken power lines sparked dangerously. Snapped water lines sprayed fine mist into the air. I was breathing hard, but I still found the energy to smile at the sight.

I looked upon them without pity. When I saw those badges tossed everywhere, bleeding and choking and screaming, I thought of their batons crunching the skulls of peaceful strikers on the picket lines. Their armored gauntlets smashing through Birantown shop windows. Their jackboots kicking over every bucket of rainwater they could find. Their bullets piercing the hearts of the people they were supposed to serve and protect. They had always been a hand around the throat of the people, and it felt good to break that grip finger by finger.

Thanks to the sharpness that the spirit lent my ears, I heard the click of your boot heels before I heard your voice.

"*Tenny!*" Across the gaping hole, you ran into sight, a protective detail of officers just behind you. "*That's enough!*"

At the sight of you, everything else in the world fell away. Rage pumped through me like venom. I felt it twisting the

374

melody in my heart, turning it into something minor and staccato. But even so, I felt a thrill. At last.

"None of this had to happen, Cole!" I called back. "This is on you!"

"Well, you can stop." You weren't shouting, but your voice carried across the gap just the same.

"Then come over here and settle this."

You shifted your weight. Didn't move.

"Fine," I growled. "Then I'll come over there."

Wood flowed past me like water, until it jutted out over the huge hole I'd opened up. You took a step back as the stretching wood touched the side of the pit where you stood. Other slats followed it, until a thick oak bridge stretched between us, with you and I at either end. You strode on to it. When your security detail made to follow you, you whipped around and held up a hand to stop them.

"But, sir!" one of them said.

You just shook your head, and then turned and kept walking. Satisfied, I followed suit until at last you and I stood together in the middle.

I hate to say that you looked good, Cole. Our four years apart had treated you a hell of a lot better than they had me. Your walk was smooth, no hint of a limp or a bad knee. Your back was straight, not bowed from the weight of old wounds. Your cheeks were full, even if you were still a skinny fucker. Your silver hair was swept neatly back, not a tousled nest. Your suit was patterned black silk, expertly tailored. It all had this cumulative effect; even though you were short, you didn't feel small.

Every atom in me screamed to lunge at you and be done with it. The only thing protecting your throat was a high-banded collar of black and silver silk. It would be so easy to end this. Everything I'd spent the past four years dreaming of, in the bloody palm of my hand ...

Did you know that's what I was thinking, Cole, when you saw me standing there?

Did you feel the same about me, when you saw the woman I'd become?

"Tenny." I heard the politician's edge in your voice. This wasn't the Cole I remembered. You were putting on a performance for your flunkies I'd chucked into the pit below us. "I want to resolve this without any further bloodshed."

"I've shed more than my fair share already," I growled.

"I'm aware of that," you said. "And I regret my part in that more than you can know."

"*Do you?*" I roared. All around us, fresh cracks splintered along the Slats. My voice boomed from every radio still in working order. Everyone else flinched, but you stood like a tree in a hurricane.

Time to end this. Time to cut you where you'd bleed most.

"You started the Unified Utilities Fire," I said. "You had Binh killed when he found out. You had me killed when I tried to save him. *Do you regret those things, too?*"

You held your hands open, fingers splayed. A gesture: you were unarmed. "I can't regret what I didn't do."

So. That was how you were going to play it.

I flashed a grin at you like it was the edge of a blade. "You thought you'd outsmarted Binh," I said. "Boxed him in. But he left me a little something." I nodded to my mismatched boots.

For the first time, you registered surprise instead of grim wariness. "A vision?"

I grinned wider, just to twist the knife. "He had you all figured out. And he knew just how to set you up for a fall. He even trusted that if you got to him first, I'd find a way to balance the scales for him." I gestured to the chaos around us both. "And what do you know, neh?"

Now was about the time I expected you to start with the

begging. I'd killed your attack dogs, beaten down your last defense, and called your game. I'd dragged your darkest, most shameful secret screaming into the daylight. I'd left you with nothing, just like you'd done to me when you dumped me in the ocean. And while I'd always known you to be a brave enough guy, I also knew you didn't shrug off the idea of dying the way some of our comrades did.

So, yeah. I was kind of hoping for a complete collapse of your dignity here.

But instead, you met my gaze and calmly asked me, "Have you watched it yet?"

I gotta hand it to you, Cole: no one else I've ever met has been so good at surprising me. But I regained my composure quickly. This was just a trick of yours to get into my head. If I slipped into a trance, you'd have someone put a bullet in my head. I was this close to ending you. I wasn't gonna let you fake me out at the finish line.

"So you haven't," you said calmly. I watched the fear behind your eyes vanish, and it infuriated me. "You really should."

"I don't need to." I took a step toward you, and felt you starting to gather your power. I reached out with my own, remembering what I'd done to Mhap in the office. "All I need to do now is kill you."

"You can certainly—" Your words were swallowed by a shuddering gasp, as if I'd just plunged you into cold water. I grinned at the sight.

"You were trying to keep me talking so you could short-circuit my powers, just like you did to me last time," I said. "But I've always thought any good trick is one worth stealing."

I tapped my foot on the bridge, and a slat of wood shot up and punched you right in the gut, hard enough to send you tumbling end over end like a coin. You landed hard right at the edge of my bridge, coughing as you forced yourself onto

377

all fours. It was a hell of a satisfying thing, seeing how easily a single hit could unmake your perfectly groomed appearance.

I didn't give you a chance to collect yourself. I channeled the solid, unyielding nature of the boards below me, and funneled it into my leg and foot as I came in for a kick. Once again, you went flying. This time, you didn't actually hit the Slats; you collided hard with the officers rushing in to assist you. You scattered them to the ground as you blew straight through them.

I was hot on your trail, singing to the city as I passed your bodyguards. Behind me, the wood grains reached up to wrap around their wrists and ankles, until they were all held in place by stocks it'd take a chainsaw to remove.

Which left me, at long last, with a clear path to you.

I treated myself to a wide, triumphant grin as I chased you down. The air was alive with your fear. You got off on being this city's shining silver champion. To be broken in front of everyone, by the living embodiment of everything you'd ever done wrong ... I couldn't think of anything you'd fear more.

Sure enough, terror blazed across your face. You were trying to run, but it was more of a limp after the beating I'd already given you. I grinned. You weren't even trying to fight back. You knew exactly how well that'd go for you.

It looked like you were headed for the front door of a laundry. I broke into a sprint. If you got through that door, you might teleport into thin air. The city's enforced blind spot between us meant that even I wouldn't be able to track you then.

But I liked how you were thinking. So as I caught up to you, I sang to the spiritual threads of the laundry's door. I threw a punch straight across your stupid face, and you staggered through—

—into a tailor shop, its guests squawking in alarm as I

plowed us both toward a utilities closet, which opened up into—

—a living room, where someone sat at a piano, plinking out the barest melody of the city's anthem, a song that had once belonged to you and me alone, leaping up from the bench as I kicked you through their front door—

—and you rolled hard into an empty room: a half-built home, tarp stretched over the wooden bones of its roof. And then, I recognized the elevated view from the window. High up, with the Slats stretched out before us. Beyond it, the sea was a huge, dark void, its luster stolen by the thick grey clouds overhead.

This was one of the new housing developments you'd had Knife-Edge building.

We were up on the Rock.

"Tenny," you wheezed. I saw now that you were clutching at your side. Your hair was no longer slick, but matted with sweat and dangling in unruly strands. A bloody red spot had begun to spread over the white of your left eye. "You've made your point. Please ..."

"*My point?*" I don't know how I had the breath to yell, but I found it somewhere in me. "This isn't a fucking *debate*, Cole. You took everything from me, and every thread you pull has another end. How could you have ever expected this to end any other way?"

"It doesn't have to!" you shouted. I could hardly remember the last time I'd ever heard you raise your voice. "Don't you see that yet?" You thumped hard against your side, as if you were trying to knock a rib back into place. "Please ... I've come so far and built so much. Don't take it from me. Let me make it yours, too."

"Yeah?" I said. The city flowed through me, but in that moment nothing made me feel more powerful than your naked desperation. I wondered if I'd worn the exact same expression when I was bleeding out on that boathouse floor. "You think you know how to build me a Driftwood City that could make me whole again?"

You didn't rise to the bait. Instead, your desperate expression turned grim, because you had figured out exactly what I was about to say.

"Build me a city," I growled, "with him still in it."

I threw a punch at the air. And like a mirror image, the floor itself rose up as a grainy wooden fist and caught you in an uppercut that took you off your feet. You landed hard on the half-finished wooden floor. You tried to get up, but I pinned you with a stomp to your gut. You folded in half like a dying bug, sputtering and gasping as your breath fled you.

"Do you know what it's like to die alone, Cole?" I stomped you again, and only a wet cough escaped you this time. "To feel the edges of your world rise up around you in every direction, until you realize you're standing in the palm of a fist closing to crush you? Do you know how it feels to watch all your friends step out of death's way when it comes for you? Do you know what it feels like now?"

Somewhere along the line, a gash had opened up on your scalp. A thin stream of red ran through your sweaty silver hair. Blearily, you nodded up to me. Your lips moved like you were trying to say something, but you still didn't have the breath to form the words.

I shook my head. "No," I said. "You don't. Because you still have more to lose."

I hauled you back to your feet, and now you didn't resist me at all. With another wave of my hand, the kitchen door of this half-complete home slid open. I chucked you through it—

—and watched you tumble down the gleaming white steps of the Unified Utilities Plant, while behind me its massive front doors slid open with a fresh spray of steam. On every step you hit on the way down, you left a red splash of blood. The farther you fell, the bigger they got.

At last, you came to a rest in a broken heap at the very foot of the stairs, right next to the pedestal where the statue of Binh stood. My grin stretched wider. You'd put together everything I needed to give you the death you deserved.

I guess we'd come out just as the salters were finishing their evacuation of the Plant. The Slats were awash with a grey-uniformed tide. Some were fleeing. Some were helping the fallen police, which was just about the last thing I'd ever expected to see. But when we reappeared, they all turned as one to watch me end you.

I took my time descending the steps as you tried futilely to pull yourself back up. By the time I reached the bottom, you had only just pulled yourself to your knees. You didn't look like you could climb any higher.

I listened to the city, waiting for you to play your counter-melody. I always played more forte, but you'd had an intricate way of plucking at the strings of Driftwood City. The way you would commune with the spirit ... Sometimes, it would all sound like noise to me, until things came together and I would realize I'd been hearing your melody all along.

But now, though, I heard nothing. Your fingers desperately fluttered along the fingerboard, but I'd already ripped away your bow. The strings stayed silent.

"Pathetic." For the first time, I noticed how Binh's boot rang slightly different against the oak boardwalk, compared to the one I'd borrowed from Diwata.

The look you gave me was pure defiance. When you spoke, you sounded tired as a man twice your age. "You've already taken everything from me that I can stand to lose. I'll let you take my life before you take anything else."

"But it ain't that simple," I said. "You're gonna admit to all of them now: you started that fire. You made sure three hundred and fifty-two souls were devoured in it. You're going to admit that Binh found out what you'd done, and you killed him for it. And then, when you've admitted to all of them that your shiny new world is just one big fucking lie ... then we can talk about your life. You may think you've lost everything, but you'll play a different tune once you start losing fingers. And toes. Eyes. There's a lot of bits a person can live without, you know."

"You'd torture me in front of all these people," you asked, "just to get what you want?"

"You tried to murder your own best friend in private to get the same thing. Whatever I am today, I'm what you made me," I spat. I could feel roiling emotions in the air from onlookers in every direction, but I shut them all out. As far as I was concerned, the only two people in the world right now were you and me. "Last chance, Cole. Start confessing now, or I'll show you and everyone else exactly how far I'm willing to go."

Your blood-blotched eyes met mine. "I'm never going to give you what you're after. Trim and tend this rose as you see fit, and be done with it."

There was no mistaking the sheen of panic in your eyes. You'd always lived in comfort, even when you were slumming it with me. Jumping from the warm lap of wealth and power, you'd been kept and protected by shaman power ... and by me and the other Orphans. Standing over you, I realized this was the first time you'd ever stood to truly lose something for good.

But the curse of knowing someone as well as I knew you, Cole, was that I instantly believed you.

I scowled down at you. "Fine."

I wrapped my power around the statue above you: the metal

remains of your family's mansion, twisted into an effigy of the man I'd loved. There was no better way to bring this to a close.

"*Roses every day*," I said, and then I snapped my fingers.

The statue of Binh sundered at its ankles.

As its shadow grew over you, you stared up at your bronze death.

But the hammer never fell.

Suddenly we were both surrounded by bodies. All around you, strong and callused hands shot up as one. Elbows buckled from the sheer weight of the statue ... but they held.

"*Hurry, Mr Governor!*" one of your rescuers cried. "*Get clear!*" She was a salter: older, and built with the kind of brawn I'd had in my younger days.

"*We've got this!*" shouted another: a young man whose slender arms shook from the effort of holding up the statue.

You stared up at them in disbelief. And I stared with you.

You were surrounded by salters.

It was taking more than a dozen of them to keep the statue up. Others were trying to lift you back on to your feet so they could carry you to safety. And still others were closing ranks around you, to stop me from getting any closer. But all of them wore the grey coveralls of true Brethren.

"*He's clear!*" someone else yelled. Sure enough, the salters had pulled you out from under the statue's shadow. "*Let it down easy!*"

The salters grunted as one, and the statue fell its last six feet to the Slats with a deafening *CLANG*.

And with Binh's statue fallen and prone, the eyes of every salter there turned my way. Their arms linked like chains. Their feet planted where they stood. Their jaws grimly set as they dared me to do something.

Rage flew through me, my hands straining from the sheer effort it took to keep them still. These people, these fucking people, didn't they understand what they were doing? Didn't they know what kind of a monster they were throwing their lot in with? How could they look at you and not see the man I saw so clearly?

"You don't know who you're defending!" I shouted at them. "Do you know what he did to me? To your families and your friends? Don't you want to know what he's too ashamed to tell you himself?"

The front line stood resolute. The salters behind them were starting to prod you farther away from me, though I could see you trying in vain to resist them.

"*He started the Unified Utilties fire!*" I roared. "*He used his powers to light it, then lock us in there with it!*" I pointed a furious finger at the prone statue. "*And Binh—*"

But my words were lost in a burst of shouting. And not the kind I was hoping for.

"You killed Binh!" someone yelled.

"*What?*" My whole face flushed with fury. "No, I didn't! I was trying to save—"

But someone else yelled over me: "You killed our City Council!"

"*They tried to kill me!*" I shouted, straining to be heard over the crowd's growing outrage.

"The Governor built my house!"

"The Governor gave me a job!"

"The Governor made the boats run on time!"

"The Governor fixed the streets!"

"*The Governor saved us!*"

I took a step back, and the heel of my boot scuffed someone else's toes. I jerked away, and saw that I'd been pressed in on all sides by salters.

All to defend you.

"*Move!*" I roared at them one last time. "*Don't make me—!*"

The first salter to the rescue, the leathery old woman, folded her thick arms. "I've seen what you can do," she said. "But you can't kill us all."

Helplessly, I stared at the salters. They glared back at me with thrice-filtered hatred. It was the kind of look they'd worn when they marched on the picket lines, brandishing signs and fists up at the Rock.

I could've drowned in the sheer unfairness of it all.

Movement in the crowd. Now, officers were stepping forward: not with weapons, but with handcuffs.

"Stop."

Your voice barely rose above a croak, but somehow it silenced the whole crowd. The officers froze where they stood.

"Sir," said one of them, who bore sergeant's stripes on their shoulder. "Let us take her into custody."

"There's no point," you said. "No lock can hold her and no cell can keep her."

"What are we supposed to do, then?" said the sergeant.

"Yeah!" called one of the salters. "Tell us what to do!" Cheers and questions arose in echo. I had no choice but to stand helplessly by as they all rallied against me.

You raised a weak hand, and everyone fell silent all over again.

"Leave her be." Your eyes were bloody and swollen, but there was focus in them yet. You turned them on me, and even though I was a foot taller than you, I suddenly felt very small. "She can't hurt anyone anymore."

You nudged the salters carrying you, and they turned and started to bring you toward the huge pit I'd gouged. The police turned neatly on their heels and formed ranks around you, creating an honor guard. Still more salters followed along, cheering you on.

Chanting your name.

385

And I had to stand there and watch as, for the second time, my city turned its back on me.

I didn't flee the scene, so much as sleepwalk away.

No one stopped me, not even the badges on the streets. Folk just got out of my way. They didn't look at me. Didn't make eye contact. I felt their glares like needles on the back of my neck. But that was all I was able to sense of them. Even though the spirit and its song were still with me, it felt like my city was withdrawing its touch.

I passed by blacked-out windows and hastily scrawled signs on doors that warned about suspended water service. At every street corner, traffic lights were out. Mostly, police directed traffic, but at one intersection I caught sight of a waitress doing it, waving cars on and barking orders while still wearing her tea-stained apron. Folks weren't honking their horns or shouting at each other. Everyone was being patient. Everyone was helping each other. Driftwood City was holding strong in the face of disaster.

And that disaster, I guessed, was limping along the streets of Oakyard in mismatched boots.

I could barely string my thoughts together. I'd been on the edge of everything I'd been working for, and somehow you'd found a way to turn things around and then hollow me out. I'd thought you'd left me empty before, when you'd left me to die. But at least I had the ice in my gut that demanded I settle things with you one day. Now ... what was there? I'd thought I was in harmony with Driftwood City. When had its people changed their tempo and key?

I gritted my teeth as the noises around me crept deeper and deeper into my head. It felt like they were scratching right on the wrinkles of my brain. All I could see when I blinked was an army of my former comrades, all ready to lay down their lives just to keep you breathing for another second.

Your words echoed in my ear like a taunt: *Have you watched it?*

I stopped. Looked down at the boots on my feet: right black, left brown. It had been a trick. Nothing more. Just another attempt to manipulate me, the way you had all those salters who came to your defense ...

But no, something cold and logical in me said. *It takes more than manipulation to get people on their feet like that.*

I knew, because I'd seen the way Binh himself could work a crowd. That wasn't manipulation. It was his Brethren, responding to hearing something true.

My stomach lurched as I turned and made for a rooftop.

Whatever memory was hidden in this boot, I wanted to be alone when I saw it.

30

Eleven years ago

I am Pham Binh Cong, first among the Brethren. When the Rock demands obedient silence, I am a raised voice.

And when it demands complacency, I am a raised fist.

The young man across from me in the kelp roll shop goes by a few different names. The White Rose. Mongkhul Pakuanjangnambharat. But the one by which I've come to know him best is Cole.

And not for the first time in our brief association, the two of us are having an awkward conversation.

"How did you end up with that one, anyway?" I say. "I've never heard any name like it." I'm careful to keep my voice pleasant. I know there's something up with the way he can read people. I'm not sure how it works, and for all I know, this extra effort to keep things level is for nothing. But I've seen this guy turn even the most tight-lipped bootlegger inside out with a glance, so I won't take my chances.

His smile is small, more a gesture than an expression. Cordial, but not friendly. "I met someone once, in a different life, and liked the sound of it. Its owner probably never expected it to take on a new meaning all the way here, across the Porcelain

Sea." He glances out the window. "But then again, neither did I."

He coughs: a clumsy bridge between pleasantries and business. I don't know everything about him, but I know he's had all the best training high society can offer when it comes to the art of conversation. For him to use something so blatant against me ... well, it makes me feel awfully satisfied to know I'm under his skin.

"I must admit, Binh, this is rather unusual," says Cole. "I obviously don't have the same rapport with you that Tenny does ..."

The thought of me having a rapport with a person like him makes my stomach knot with revulsion in a way it didn't last week. But I can't turn over that tile just yet. I have to be patient. If I'm too direct, he might do something desperate. Right now I'm building a trap, piece by piece. It will require patience, or else—

"You started the Unified Utilities Fire."

The accusation hangs between the two of us like a corpse on a noose.

When he turns to face me, the motion calls to mind a machine: something unfolding and clicking into place. Maybe gears in a watch.

Maybe a round into a chamber.

The silence endures long enough for the shop's owner, Auntie Vuong, to arrive at the table with tea, kelp rolls, and extra garlic sauce. She smiles at me, but bows to him.

After she leaves, he measures me with a long look, and then sits back in his cushy, moth-eaten booth seat. "Does she know?" I know it's not Auntie Vuong he's talking about.

The question catches me genuinely flat-footed. I'd had a whole speech prepared: a long chain of logic that started with

389

watching Tenny manipulate doors, and ended with me diving deep into the city's hall of records late at night.

"Just like that?" I say. Surprise has bleached away my anger, but some of it bleeds back into me as I continue: "You're not even going to deny it?"

He shrugs his skinny shoulders. "You know me and you know what I can do, Binh. I imagine confronting me was a scary prospect, even for a brave man like you. You wouldn't have done it unless you were absolutely certain. So why waste our time when we're both so busy?" He swirls his tea without sipping it, almost like it's a show of nonchalance rather than the real thing. "Before we can have a conversation about it, though, you have to tell me: does she know?"

I eye him. "Why does it matter if she knows?"

"Because," he says simply, "I need to know whether or not I'm a dead man walking."

A fierce kind of pride fills me. Damn right, he should be scared of my Tenny.

"She doesn't know," I say eventually. "Yet."

Relief visibly ripples through Cole. "Why didn't you tell her?"

I decide I'm done answering questions about my relationship. I lean forward onto my muscular, tattooed forearms. "Three hundred and fifty-two of my brethren, burned alive," I snarl. "I heard them choke as they tried to scream. I learned what it smelled like when their hair crackled and burned. I know you've probably got some magic trick you can do to stop me before I reach across this table and throttle you. So I think the question you should be asking me is, what's to stop me from trying anyway?"

"I suppose that *is* a question worth considering," Cole muses. "Why confront me? If you're so certain, why not tell Tenny and sic her on me?"

"Because ..." I clench my fist. I don't want to tell him. He doesn't deserve that information. He doesn't deserve anything from me. But he needs to understand what's at stake here. "I don't want you to die. I want you to leave town. Start a new life somewhere else. And never set foot on the Slats again. Do that ... and I won't have to break Tenny's heart."

Cole nods in understanding. "I see," he says. "You kept silent because you care too much. Or at least, that's what you tell yourself. Not a bad way to justify it, I suppose."

"You have no idea how much I care," I snap. I sit up straighter, making sure to loom over him. *"And you have no idea what that will make me do."*

I know the picture this paints of the two of us. Even if I slouched down as low as I can, I would still tower over this guy. Everyone in this place knows who I am. I've made myself the face of the city's labor revolution, a hero of the people.

But right now, I don't look heroic: I look fucking *scary*.

But Cole's not scared of me. "I want you to think very carefully about what happens next if you succeed. What does it accomplish, besides making you feel better?"

My snarl stretches even wider. I'm sure I look like I want to just take a big bite out of his throat. I feel nothing but disgust as I look at this pathetic little man. How is it that Tenny can't see him for what he is? "They were my comrades."

"And now they're something more valuable," Cole says simply. "They're a symbol. They're a foundation. And look at the great things you've built on that foundation."

"Are you trying to tell me—?" The plates rattle as my fist pounds the table. Heads swivel our way, and I immediately restrain myself. But even as I make myself sit back, I see the color has drained from Cole's face a bit. He was already leaning back, but now he sits stiffer, his arms held tight at his sides.

If only for a moment, I got to him.

Given what I know he's capable of, it's like seeing a god bleed.

When I speak again, my voice is low, almost a rasp. "Those were workers with families. Lives. Futures. They weren't yours to spend so you could buy ... what, even?"

"*This*." For the first time, Cole has lost his patience with me. There's something dangerous about the way the air tastes on my tongue, like stepping into a house and smelling gas. He points to the twin mugs of tea in front of us. "I bought *this*. Before the fire, Auntie Vuong could only keep up with the demand for tea by using bootleg water. If she only used legal taps, she would've had to charge more than her customers could afford. For *water*. Now, we didn't even order it. She just served it to us, *because she could*. You're supposed to be smart, Binh. You're supposed to be better than me. *How do you not see it?*"

I'm struck by how young he suddenly looks to me. He holds himself like an older man, and the light hits his eyes in a way that makes his fatigue shine. But his face is unlined like only a young man's can be. And that's not the only thing that makes him seem young. When he talks, it's with the kind of frustration you can only have if you haven't been in the world long enough to be tired of it. I'm not that much older than him, but those few years are a wide enough gap to need a bridge.

"So you get ... I don't know, magical powers or something," I say, "and your first thought is to make Driftwood City better. Fine. I can get that." On the tabletop, my huge hands clench into huge fists. "What I don't get is how you make the leap from that to burning my comrades."

"Do you know what would have happened if I'd sat quietly until I could claim my place as chairman, and then attempted to bring about change?" he says. "I would have spent a month enacting radical reforms. And then the board of directors would

392

have voted me out, installed someone to undo everything I'd accomplished, and you'd all be left worse off than you started. You may not trust me or my word, but surely you can see that's true."

I feel like a door's been slammed in my face. "So your next option was—"

"You're still not getting it." He puts his head in his hands. It's almost a convincing display. Except when he looks up at me again, there's something haunted about the way he stares at me. "The fire wasn't my first option, nor my second or third or twenty-eighth. It was the only choice I had. The only way I could actually build a better city for the people who call it home."

"You keep saying that. And I keep thinking about the sound your neck will make when I help it turn ways it's not supposed to go, if you don't get up from here and leave town right now."

The witnesses around us don't deter me. I can sort all that out later. The number 352 is tattooed on my arm, and it's a debt I have no choice but to pay.

"You have to understand how people like my family work," Cole says. "They tilt the world incrementally one way, the whole time telling you it's still flat."

"I know that," I snap. "I wrote the gods-damned book on labor in this town, so don't you—"

"Then you know the increments don't work the other way," Cole says simply. "Think about the problems your movement is addressing. They were always there, weren't they? And they've only worsened in living memory. Because people will let themselves adjust to whatever slope my family puts the world on. My parents let you hold union activity before, because they knew you'd be lucky to get a dozen people out of a staff of thousands." His voice is running dry, and so he pauses for a sip of tea. "After the fire, how many marched with you? And what have you been able to do with them at your back, now that they've woken up to realize they're in a fight for their lives?"

The ideologue in me wants to end this here. His whole point keeps coming back to one notion: that any number of lives are worth sacrificing for this vague notion of "a better future," as long as the lives sacrificed don't include his.

But ...

But I remember beating my fist against the pub wall in frustration after a dozen people showed up to the first union meeting, and four showed up to the next.

But I remember the way my crews would stand with me and call me a pal, until the time actually came to stand for something.

But I remember feeling like I was trying to swim for the surface, and drag everyone else up with me.

Now, the Rock is afraid of me. They've thrown scabs and strike breakers and even assassins my way, and they can't keep me down.

"Do you expect me to keep this quiet, now that I know the truth?" I say eventually. I mean it as a taunt, but I hate myself for knowing that's not really how I make it come out.

Cole hears it for what it is. "There's a reason I didn't kill you for trying to threaten me just now, Binh. Unlike some people we know, you're capable of seeing more than what's just in front of you. You can step back and see the big picture. You understand what's at stake. So I know you understand that if this information gets out, your entire movement will be discredited."

"The people won't just turn their backs on—"

"You saw how hard it was to get them to turn toward you in the first place. Do you really think they'll all stay, once you give the fence-sitters an easy out?" Delicately, he dips his kelp roll into the garlic sauce and takes a bite. "Your movement wouldn't die. But it would splinter. And my fathers know exactly how to exploit gaps like that. You're a good leader, but even you couldn't contain that."

The truth of it makes Cole's words land harder. I came into this fight wanting to be the good guy. There's no vanity in admitting it: I like being the good guy. I like knowing that I'm a force for positive change. And I entered this conversation playing that role. But what makes Cole slippery isn't that he's magicked his way into my head. It's that he understands me well enough to know what I want ... and how much I'll pay for it.

My siblings' faces flicker through my mind. Two of them were working in the Plant that day. Either of them could've been turned to ash by this madman.

But they weren't, a small voice whispers to me.

And thanks to the fights I've already won, their future doesn't have to be that Plant anymore. Not if they don't want it to be.

I wonder if he's read my mind when he says, "You don't have to like me or respect me. You just have to keep the secret, and everything we've built will hold."

My shame threatens to swallow me whole. But I tell myself it's something I'll have to wrestle with later. Now, I need to finish this negotiation. "I can't keep it from her."

He shakes his head. "Of course you can."

"She can do the same things as you, can't she?" I snap. "I don't know everything that's up with you two, but I know enough, so stop treating me like an idiot."

"She can read people, yes," Cole admits. "But we don't just magically gain insight, Binh. You have to ask about someone, and the world will provide. And that means as long as you can keep yourself under control, Tenny will never know the truth. She trusts you." The young man hesitates, then adds: "Perhaps even more than she trusts me."

I eye him with surprise as I detect the quiet note of pain in his voice. That doesn't square with my understanding at all. I've seen the two of them together. They carry on like twins: moving in time with each other, speaking in ways that feel almost harmonic.

"Believe it or not, there are limitations to our gifts." He finally eats the piece of kelp roll he's been holding. Takes the time to swallow it before continuing. "We can't read each other."

Tenny's never told me this. "Sounds like you have no choice but to trust each other, then."

"Precisely. She *has* to trust me. She *chooses* to trust you." The bastard manages to sound sad, the way he says it. "Do you see the difference?"

My despair gains a whole new dimension. It's tricky to pin down what I and Tenny have between us. It's not like we're destined for wedding bells anytime soon. But I deal with hundreds of folks every day, if not thousands, and she's the only one who gets me. I see her bravery and her sharpness and I listen to her talk about this city, and it all just makes me want to be a better man. To have to look into that face every single night and make the choice to lie ... to have to make it again every morning ...

I love her. I know her.

And that's how I know that if she ever learns the truth, she'll never understand.

"There's no shame in this," Cole says calmly, when my answer is clear.

"Is that what you tell yourself?" I spit.

"Sometimes," he admits. "It doesn't help." He leans forward. "Do you know what will, though?"

396

I take a big bite out of my kelp roll. Auntie Vuong made it perfectly, but I can't bring myself to enjoy that salty chew it has. I don't ask him what.

He knows I want the answer anyway. He raises his hand to signal Auntie Vuong for the check. "Winning."

The next time I see Tenny, I lie to her. Day after day, month after month, year after year, I lie to her. Each time, I tell myself it's for the cause. And each time I have to look into her eyes and do it, I feel a dagger drive itself a little bit closer to my heart. It takes years for its tip to inch deep enough to draw blood. But when it finally does, I decide two things: one, that I need to unburden myself at long last.

And two, that whatever judgment Tenny renders ... I will trust it.

31

Now

Age 30

After the vision subsided, I just sat there. Tried to puzzle out how this could've been some trick of yours. But I couldn't find any way around what I'd just seen. The only way out was through.

My stomach tends to turn in bad moments, Cole, but now I felt nothing in my gut. I felt nothing at all. Even the city's music had grown spare in my ears. It was like I'd been spooned hollow. There were things that could bring me back to the bad times in my life: the crack of gunfire, the stench of smoke. But this was the first thing I'd ever encountered in my four lost years that dug up the exact feeling of powerlessness I'd felt in the last moments of my old life. It was the kind of despair that made everything seem pointless: my fight for revenge, my fight for Driftwood City. My life with Binh, my life with you.

My life.

Do you know how this kind of despair feels, Cole? The utter certainty that you're living poison to everyone you meet? The equal certainty that there's only one antidote left for you, because no one else believes you're worth saving?

The inability to escape the thought that they're right?

I shook as I stood and walked right up to the rooftop's edge. I'd considered it back when I'd done for Roulette Wu. But I'd found reasons to weasel out of it then. Now, all those reasons were gone. The only reason I had to keep on living was if I wanted to. And I didn't. Not if living felt like this.

Taking the next step was easy.

This was the only right thing, I told myself as I fell. The brighter, happier Driftwood City rushing to meet me was proof that things could only get better once I was gone. After all, they already had once.

But even if that logic was airtight to me, it couldn't stop the song from rising in me like a scream.

It was pure, panicked instinct. But all the same, the building's fire escape unfurled like a carpet beneath me. I slammed into its black iron, and the impact jarred all my broken bones. I gasped and screamed at the same time, a lungful of air stuck trying to both come and go. I rolled over, cradling my broken arm against my body, twitching from the pain and breathing so fast my vision turned spotty. And when I had the breath to form words again, all I could manage was a half-sobbed *"Fuck."*

It was only dumb luck that let me find Diwata that first night back in town. She could've moved house, or even skipped town entirely. If I'd knocked on that seventh-floor walk-up and a stranger had answered the door, I don't know what I would've done. Probably gone to Phuong's, and we both know how that would've turned out for me.

Now, with my powers, it was easy to find her. I asked. The city told me. And when I pushed open the door to a half-built housing complex, I found myself stepping into the sheet metal shack where Pamin made their home.

I'd never been past their front room. I wasn't that surprised by what I saw here in the back: shelves overflowing with books and binders. More of them were stacked on tables, or even on the floor, where they'd joined with other stacks to make new tables, which Pamin had stacked with more books. When I scanned them, the city whispered what I'd find between their covers: newspaper clippings. Accounts. Compromising photographs. And an entire stack of plays, probably traded by their writer for something.

But I wasn't here for trade. I was here for the occupant of the bed. Well, occupants.

Diwata and Pamin separated with a yelp. Diwata grew resigned when she recognized me. Pamin, on the other hand, plunged their hand under their pillow and produced a gun. I stared numbly down its barrel.

"Put it down," Diwata sighed. "It ain't gonna stop her anyway."

"She's in my house, Dawa!"

"Yeah, I can see that," Diwata grumbled. "But she's got her powers back, just like you told me. Now, she's a storm we have to wait out." She flicked on a bedside lamp, and then reached for her smokes and lighter. I noticed the ashtray by her side of the bed was overflowing, while Pamin's side didn't have an ashtray at all. "Tenny, is it gonna penetrate that skull of yours if I tell you to get the fuck out of Pamin's house?"

"I got something to ask you, Dawa."

"And I told you last time: you and me are done. I got nothing left for you, you hear?" *Click*, her lighter opened. *Click*, it sparked to life. She exhaled smoke. "You had no right to come after me, and you definitely had no right to break into my friend's house to do it."

I folded my arms over my chest, careful of my broken wrist. "You don't sound that upset."

"Because I ain't surprised," she said. "This is what— Hey, put that down, would you? This is what you do."

Pamin reluctantly placed the gun in their lap, though I noticed they kept their hand on it.

"You come to a place, you see what's there, you take what you like, and you kick over what you don't. And when you're done kicking, you leave." Their foxlike face pinched sourly. "I'm not even your sister, and I know that about you."

"Stay out of this," I barked.

"You're the one who's supposed to stay out of *my house*."

Diwata held up a hand. "Tenny," she said carefully, "go wait outside. I'll be there in a few minutes. We can talk this out. And once I've listened to whatever you have to say, and said my piece on it, I never want to see you again. Got it?"

I was dimly aware that it should've hurt me, for her to draw that line between us. But there was nothing left for Diwata to take from me. So I nodded and swept from the room without another word.

For three minutes I sat out on Pamin's front porch, listening to them bicker. If I'd wanted to, I could've used my powers to listen in, instead of registering it all as dialogue-shaped noise. But I left them to it, and a few moments later I heard bare feet on the floor and the scrape of the door behind me.

Diwata had shrugged on a patchy striped robe, and she drew it tighter around herself as she came to stand over me. "I take it you heard all that with your wizard ears?"

I didn't rise to her bait. Shook my head. "None of my business."

"So you'll magically break into a house and hound someone who's done with you, but good to know you're not an eavesdropper."

401

Her words made my shame curdle in my stomach. "I wouldn't have come if it wasn't important."

She took her seat next to me. "That's the fucking thing with you, Tenny. Everything's important if you decide it is. And those weird powers of yours mean the rest of us don't get a choice in the matter. You get an answer you don't like, and you'll collapse the house on us. And don't tell me you won't, 'cause I've seen it." Her fingers twitched. "Survived it, even."

Even through all the wounds I was nursing, her honesty stung.

"So what do you want, then?" she went on. "It looks like you got all your powers back. The fuck d'you need me for?"

I hugged my knees close to my chest. "Do you know what happened today outside the Plant?"

"'Course I do," she said, jerking her thumb at the house and its scowling owner standing in the window. "You killed the Black Rose, stomped on an army of badges, then beat the shit out of the Governor while the whole city watched. And then you were surprised when the city didn't like that."

I bristled at her tone, but stopped myself from saying anything. I deserved it.

"I had him. He wasn't even fighting back. And then ..."

"A cross-section of Driftwood City's working-class heroes rushed to save him," Diwata said. "Even if I wasn't sharing a bed with a zephyr, it's all the radio can talk about tonight. You gave them the perfect story to run with." Her grin was a rueful, joyless thing. "You remember how we beat you during that first salters' march? We used the papers. And based on what we heard just on the evening news, you gave him everything he needs to beat you into the fucking ground. That what you came here to ask me?"

I shook my head. "The papers and radio wouldn't tell you how they were looking at me, Dawa. They weren't plants Cole put there to outmaneuver me. They were actually trying to save his life, and they were willing to throw themselves at me to do it."

"Why're you surprised?"

"What do you *mean*, 'why am I surprised?'" I said. "The folks of this town have never liked the people on top."

"Yeah, well, the people on top never looked out for them like he has," Diwata said mildly. "I don't even like the guy, and he's still done better for me than anyone else has." She patted her shoulder. "You seriously never thought about why Benilda and all the other big players lasted so long, even though they were ripping folks off? It's 'cause they gave folks a return on their investment. That's all your pal's doing in City Hall these days. Of course they're gonna side with him and not you, blowing into town like some ponytailed hurricane. It's nice, thumping your chest and shouting about your ideals and whatever. But most folks just want a leader who makes them feel like they're gonna be okay, and they'll look the other way on everything else.

"Is that what you wanted to hear from me?" She stretched. "'Cause we've been talking for a few minutes now, and you ain't any closer to a point, and I'm this close to going back in where it's warm."

I lifted my leg, so the dim starlight caught on Binh's boot. "He knew."

She stared at it. "Knew that you were a men's size twelve, or …?"

"*He knew about the fire*," I said. "He knew Cole lit the Unified Utilities Fire, and he kept it from me for *years*."

I'd been vaguely aware of Pamin lurking on the other side of the door, but now I felt them scurry off to write that down. I was so numb, I didn't even care about the piece of information I'd just handed them.

403

Diwata blinked. "That ..." She stared off into the dark for a moment. "There's a lot to unpack there."

"The Blue Rose told me right before she died," I said. "That's why I went to Phuong's house. I was looking for proof Binh might've left behind. But once I got my visions back, I saw it for myself."

Diwata sat there, rocking back and forth as she wrapped her head around what I'd just told her.

"The Governor started the fire ... to kick-start the strike ... to kick-start the revolution." Her tone reminded me of a marble winding its way through one of those elaborate machines that goes through twenty-eight steps just to serve you a bowl of rice. She leaned back on her hands and looked skyward, thoughtful. "It makes sense."

I started. "The fuck are you talking about?" Hearing Anjali say that had turned my sky into my ground. How could she be so calm about this? "In what world does that make any sense?"

"A plan that involves a whole lot of sacrifice, none of it yours?" She chuckled. "That's the kind of plan only a rich kid comes up with."

And just like that, it was my turn to sit there in silence.

"Why aren't you furious?" I asked her eventually.

"Well, if I was gonna make a list ..." She started ticking off fingers. "We were on opposite sides of that fight. I never liked or believed in the fucker, so this doesn't change how I feel about him. I can't deny that things have been better since he took over." She hesitated at her fourth finger, but only for a moment. "And besides, what's the point of getting mad? Folks like him have been doing this shit to folks like us since time began. It's how they got to be who they are."

"But the better Driftwood City," I sputtered. "It's all based on a lie!"

"Yup. Just like the old one," Diwata sighed. "And your golden boy Binh knew about it the whole time."

I barely stopped myself from lashing out at her. My vision was growing hot and red, and the spirit's song turned angry to match. But I kept my grip by hanging on to one thought: it wasn't Diwata I was pissed at.

"*Three hundred and fifty-two dead,*" I growled. "*I worked with them! I fought for them! And he spent his whole career campaigning in their memory!*"

"More like *on* it." She drummed her fingers on the deck thoughtfully. "So now I see. He was gonna finally tell you. The Governor killed him to keep his mouth shut, and then decided to pick you off while he was at it. It's the kind of thing a normal person would have to roll over for, but you're not a normal person. You can actually hit back if you want, and you just got your biggest stick back. So that brings us back to the question I asked you back in the bedroom: the fuck do you need me for?"

"How did you do it?" I asked bluntly. "When you lost everything you'd ever fought for in a single night ... how did you keep going?"

Understanding dawned in Diwata's eyes. Not the nice kind. "Let's get something straight. I watched my mother get assassinated, and then you killed my twin sister and burned my childhood home down, *and I ain't arguing with you about why*," she added, raising her voice as I opened my mouth. "But you're saying that's equal to finding out the sun didn't actually shine out your dead boyfriend's well-toned ass?"

"*It's not funny, Dawa!*" I was on my feet. My voice echoed through the scrapyard, but I didn't care. "Balancing the scales for him was the only thing I had left to do! And now, what the fuck was I even trying to avenge? Look around! Cole's made things better! For everyone! Even for you!" I gestured

405

furiously at the distant silhouette of the Rock. It used to have only scattered lights on its face, since so few people lived up there. Now, it was studded with the lights of distant windows. "He won, Dawa. And I'm having a hard time seeing around the idea that he was right. So what the fuck am I supposed to do now?"

Diwata stared up at me with a quietly appraising look. And then she said, "Did killing Sasa stitch up Benilda's throat? Put all her blood back where it was supposed to be?"

"What the fuck does that have to do with anything?"

"Balancing the scales is a lie, Tenny," said Diwata. I was a raging fire, but she had all the cool, unstoppable calm of a still ocean. "There's just what happens to you. And when something does, you can either move on or let it be what kills you."

I turned from her. "I've already been dead."

"Yeah?" she said to my back. "Sounds like you want to go back to your grave."

"Of course I don't," I snapped. "It was like being a prisoner, except the whole world's your cell." I found myself struggling for words. I knew what I wanted to say, but actually forcing myself to say it felt like I was prying some piece of myself apart. "I left the family behind because I wanted to be part of something better. When I left the Plant for the Thorn Orphans, same reason. Everything turned bad on me wherever I went. I was just a gear, getting swapped in and out of one rotten machine after another. Fighting's all I've ever known how to do, Dawa. And now I don't even know what I'm fighting for."

Diwata sat there a long moment, chewing on everything I'd just dumped in her lap. I stood there, feeling like I'd just ripped all my clothes off. In all the years we'd known each other and grown up together, this was maybe the most honest conversation I'd ever had with her. I was talking to her like ... well, like I used to talk with you.

406

"So ..." she said eventually. "What you're asking me is how I moved on?"

"*Yes*," I said, exasperated.

"Hoy, don't fucking take that tone with me, all right?" Diwata said. "I'm the one who should be pissed at you right now."

"Look, I tried to apologize earlier—"

"Not for *that*," Diwata cut across me. "I'm pissed because you didn't have to drag me into this shit. You could've found the answer anytime you wanted."

And she nodded to the mismatched boots on my feet.

I stared at them. Specifically, at the one on my right foot. Of course.

"You were wearing these that day?" I asked.

She nodded. "I ain't had the spare scratch to buy myself something really nice since you dealt me out of the crooked game," she said. "So I hung on to 'em." She shifted her weight a bit. "I don't got your wizard powers, but sometimes it's kinda nice to remember."

I studied the boots again. The one on my right foot was a good deal nicer, even with the years of wear and tear on it. The one on my left foot probably would've been worn down by now if it hadn't spent the past four years waiting for me in a box.

"Why won't you just tell me?" I asked her.

"I don't think I need to do you anything in the way of favors."

"Because I've got wizard powers?"

"Because you're an asshole." She got up and stretched again.

"Where are you going?"

"Where do you think?" said Diwata. "Back to my bed, where it's warm and my feet don't hurt. What, you thought I was just gonna sit out here and freeze my ass off while you played with a shoe and went on some kind of vision quest?"

I coughed. "I mean, not when you put it like that."

She smirked. If I didn't know better, I would've been fooled into thinking she'd liked that.

As she headed back inside, I sat back down on the porch. Opened myself up to the city: what it was, and what it had been.

And I asked it to sing me a song of my sister.

32

Nine years ago

I am Diwata Lacanilao.

For years, I've been Nanay Benilda Lacanilao's hand on the Slats, which means I'm one of the most feared players in the crooked game. I've commanded her troops to victories against the striking salters. And when those salters have gotten ideas about touching the folks in Birantown under my protection, I've reminded them that there are rules in this town.

Or at least, there were.

This morning, I'd had a twin sister. She was the other half of my soul. Quiet when I was loud. Thoughtful when I was brash. Patient when I was ... well, literally anything but.

Now, dead when I'm alive.

I'd had more: a mother. An aunt, according to any official record in my halls, but she'd cared for me like only a mother would, and hurt me like only a mother could. I'd had a small mansion, the envy of Birantown, with a nice greenhouse attached. I'd had the respect of every player in the crooked game, not to mention the fear of the taxpayers on the side-lines. And for all of three minutes, I'd even had the throne of a criminal empire.

All I have left now is Tenny.

The woman standing over me is three times as old as she was when I first met her properly, that day in the greenhouse. But even though she's taller, and she's wearing a bright red rose in her coat, it's something else, how much she still looks like that same little girl who decked me. She's gained a new gang, and a whole bunch of powers I don't really understand at all, but I can see the same fear behind her eyes even fourteen years later.

Above us both is a naked night sky; beneath, piles of debris and bodies. Somewhere under all this collapsed roofing, Benilda is still sitting at her table. Somewhere, pinned to the floor by a falling rafter, is Dalisa. And the woman who killed her and everyone else in the house is extending a hand to me.

I'm sure she's going to use some wizard thing to finish me off; we've never gotten along, so of course she's saved me for last. I've never been totally clear on how her powers work, so my imagination runs wild. Even without powers, I've done some pretty creative things to my enemies.

Instead she says, "You okay?"

I don't register myself taking her hand. I'm just aware that I'm on my feet again.

I let her drag me behind her. I'm barely even aware of where I am anymore. I just keep playing it over and over in my head: the knife across Benilda's throat. The blade, freshly cleaned, as my sister offers it to me. The rage of my other sister as she—

My heart hardens at that thought. *No*, I think fiercely as I glare at her back. *She was never your sister*.

A crowd has already gathered around the ruins of the Lacanilao house, but Tenny leads us around them and to the front door of a bakery. I can't understand what a slice of biko is going to solve right now. But before I can point this out, Tenny gestures and the door opens as if tugged by invisible hands. I gape: it's not a bakery I see on the other side, but what looks to be an empty apartment. It's small, and it's got an air of neglect to it. Just from the view in the window, I can tell it's higher up than the ground we're standing on right now. But before I can observe any more, Tenny yanks me inside and the door shuts itself behind us.

"What is this place?" I bring myself to say.

I have so many more questions and feelings, and they're threatening to escape from me in a way that'd leave an exit wound. So I need to start small.

"Place I keep on the side," Tenny mutters, flicking a switch. She seems distracted, like there's other shit on her mind. I don't understand how there possibly could be, but I'm also not in a position to argue with her. "Just in case."

"Just in case what?" I don't even register myself asking the question at first.

"*I don't know, okay?*" she snaps. "I just ... needed it. I slept better knowing I had somewhere to go."

I nod, then square my shoulders. "If it ain't too much to ask, I'd rather die somewhere else." It almost sounds brave. Almost.

She turns around in surprise. "What?"

"Ten. Come on. We ain't shared a house for a while, and we've been having us a big old fight, but don't act like a stranger."

She shakes her head. "Dawa, you ain't here to die."

"Then what? Be your prisoner?" Anger seeps into my tone, even though I know Tenny ain't the sort of person I'm supposed to get angry at. "The moment you leave, I'll just chuck myself out that window there."

"Will you give it a rest, Dawa?" Tenny says. "I ain't keeping you here. If you want to go after I leave, then you go. No one's gonna stop you. I just needed to make sure you got out safe, all right?"

411

The words hit me like a slap to the face.

"*Decades, Benilda spent building something for people like us!*" I erupt. "You walk out, and she still tries to offer it to you! You walk back in, and annihilate it with a thought! And then you get to go back to Kelptown and sleep all this off, but you've left me without a tomorrow. Do you understand that, Tenny? *Today, you ended my world.*"

I've closed the distance between us in three short steps. Tenny doesn't back down. Doesn't look scared, which is rare for a woman with my reputation. If anything, she just looks ... tired. The brim of her black flatcap shades the top of her face, but I know her too well. And as it happens, I don't give a fraction of a shit.

"You ain't keeping me alive out of the goodness of your heart, or 'cause you're better than me," I bark. "You're doing it for you. 'Cause you can't handle the thought of having to go through life as the last Lacanilao. Well, guess what, Tenny? You don't have to do that, 'cause you can't." My eyes narrow venomously. "You were never one of us."

She looks like she wants to say more to me. I glance around the little empty apartment, looking for some sign that the floors and walls are about to close around me like jaws.

But then her hands relax at her sides. She walks around me, back toward the door. "I'm going to find Cole. I'll find you in the morning."

She's almost out the door and on to some random street when I shout to her: "Don't."

She stops. Says nothing, but I know she's listening.

"Don't check on me. Don't try to find me. Don't ever put yourself in the same room as me again." I swallow hard, and then my tongue traces the outline of familiar words. Words I always knew the crooked game would make me say eventually.

"You spilled the blood of my blood."

412

She straightens up. Still doesn't turn to face me. "Pahingán." It's not a question.

I almost want to try to fulfill it right here and now. Dalisa's shocked face looms large in my head, like I'm watching her on a motion picture screen. And I can hear her in my ear, whispering to grab one of those knives off the kitchen counter and ...

But I don't. I let the long silence pass. And eventually, Tenny passes, too.

For weeks afterwards, I find myself staring at those knives.

They're lined up on a magnetic strip, like the kind in a restaurant. But none of them look like they're meant for cooking. If I had to guess, they're all probably trophies Tenny's collected from her busts over the years. I know she runs with an actual knife collector now. But I don't wonder why she kept these ones, instead of letting him have them. All peoples of the world invented knives eventually, but to the Biranese a knife is more than just a knife.

To me, Sasa is everywhere. But I encounter her most often when I'm looking at those knives. Those are the moments when her voice is so clear, I can practically feel the breath of her words on my neck. When I have my lonely meals of instant noodles in salt-water broth, I can see her across the table from me, healthy and whole. She's sitting, even though I don't have another chair.

And always, she has an invitation for me: *Pick up the knife.*

Sometimes, the invitation is to join her. More often, it's to pick up the sharpest one and go out on to the Slats looking for trouble. Specifically, trouble with a red rose on her coat.

There are days when she's easy to brush off. There are days when the temptation is overwhelming. She lost her life because she gambled on me. Every day I leave the pahingán unfulfilled is an insult to her memory.

One night, I get as far as the street corner before I turn back around and put the knife back on the wall with an unsteady hand.

I start seeing Sasa less and less after that.

I shave my head and get a job fixing boats. I was always a little interested in them, but it turns out I'm almost as good at putting boats together as I was at taking people apart. My back hurts at the end of a day, and sometimes I have to soak my hands after a long shift, and it seems like nothing can ever quite get the grease out from under my nails. But the boss pays me in cash, he pays me on time, and he doesn't ask what my hands did before they turned bolts in his garage.

I work every shift expecting a familiar silhouette to fill the doorway: Tenny, maybe, or one of the shitkickers she runs with now. She's kept away up to this point, but who knows how that mind of hers works? And even if she honors her word ... who's to say that silver-haired bastard will?

But the silver-haired Samnati who shows up one day isn't the White Rose; they're a salvager I've seen around. They're slight and short, and a little bit older than me, with a narrow and clever face. They've hauled in a fishing boat for me to break down, so they can sell off the scrap. But while most salvagers would just drop it off and leave me to it, this one sticks around. I'm relieved when they cut right to the point instead of trying to corner me with it. More than a few folks have learned the hard way what I do when I'm cornered, and my old habits die harder than I do.

"So," they say mildly. "This is an interesting place for Diwata Lacanilao to wash up."

My hand tightens around my wrench. "What did you say?"

"There's only a small number of folks like us across the Slats," they go on, nodding at my workbench. Sure enough,

I've left my pills sitting out there. I ain't ashamed of them, but I don't like giving folks a window into my personal business. "Fewer still that are Biranese. And fewer still," they add, "with arms like yours."

"If I'm who you say I am," I say after a pregnant pause, "then you know how dangerous it is to walk right up and talk to me like this."

They hold up their hands. "I've known who you were for a long time. If I wanted to let people know, they'd know by now. But I don't want to do that."

I frown at them. This isn't the first time I've been recognized, but every other time I've had to punch and stab my way out. "Why not?"

"Because," they say, "Nanay Benilda would listen to the wind, and believe what it told her."

Immediately, my understanding of the situation changes. "A zephyr," I breathe.

"One of the very last, the way things are going," they say darkly.

"If you want me to do something about that, I ain't your woman." I turn back to the boat hull. "I'm done playing the crooked game."

"No, that's not it." Smoothly, they step into my line of vision. "I wanted to let you know that there's ... a group. For people like us." They nod to the pills again. "Folks whose engine wound up in the wrong chassis."

"And why would I need a group?" I say, annoyed.

"Because everyone needs someone." They prod something into my view: a folded-up piece of paper.

I take it, smudging it with grease in the process. I don't need to bother unfolding it to know that it's a telephone number. Wordlessly, I drop it to the floor next to me.

They step back, putting their hands up again. "You might want to hang on to that number, just in case."

"I know you've got that scrapyard out in the Shoots .... Pamin Tuklangjinukmanir," I say casually. I leave two other pieces of knowledge unspoken in that sentence: *I know where you live* is the obvious one.

The less obvious one is, *I know you went very far out of your way to talk to me here.*

"Fair enough," they say, with another sly grin. It's obvious they understand me perfectly. "I look forward to hearing about my boat, then."

They depart with a bow.

After they're gone, I slip the paper into my boot.

The explosions up on the Rock echo everywhere in the Slats. Everyone's come out of their houses to watch the fires burn. And I, who've done my best these past few years to keep out of the sun, can't help but join them.

I'm up on my roof with my neighbors. All of us watch spellbound as the stately mansion of the Pak Clan tears itself free of the mountainside and tumbles down it, like a die across a felt table. I see it hit the Rock hard, but don't hear the crashes and crunches until a few seconds later. And I stare and stare until it dips out of view and crashes down on to the Slats.

Silence falls over the roof. Over the neighborhood. Over the whole damn city, as far as I can tell. Even Benilda at her most powerful never dreamed of taking down the Paks.

The neighbors are all muttering to themselves about what it could possibly be about, but I already know. My mind is full of roses.

When I stagger back downstairs into my apartment, I dig that greasy, folded-up piece of paper out of the bottom of a drawer, and get my coat. There's a telephone booth down the way from here, and given what's going on, I know there'll be a queue.

By the time my first meeting is done that night, the full story has broken in the news. The young man I know as Cole has declared himself the city's new governor. He's formally revealed the incredible powers I've always known about, and he's called the fall of his own ancestral house the first note of a new movement in the symphony of Driftwood City. And he's claimed that beloved labor organizer Pham Binh Cong is dead, and that he personally avenged the man's murder by his girlfriend, Cheza Tenlonghari.

It was shocking for me to read her name printed like that, plain on the page. I've never thought of her as a Lacanilao, but I've never really thought of her as a Tenlonghari either, or even as a Cheza. She was just Tenny. But that name was nowhere to be found. It was almost like the news story was about a different person.

I stay quiet while everyone else speculates about what this means for them. The tone in the air's not optimistic; it's always been pretty hard to get the Rock to give a shit about people with needs outside the baseline. Three months from now, after the first wave of hormone patches rolls into the clinics, they'll all be wearing white roses on their coats.

Pamin is quiet the whole time. That, I get. The Thorn Orphans made the zephyrs an endangered species. Of course they'd have mixed feelings about their former guild's greatest enemy up and crowning himself king of the city.

Sitting across the loose circle of chairs from them, I'm quiet, too.

"How much of it do you think is true?" they ask me afterwards, as the two of us sidle to a bar down the street. It's been many minutes since we were all talking about it, but I know what they're asking about.

"You think I'm just gonna up and tell you? What kind of a zephyr are you?"

They sigh. "You know, I got into this job because I like knowing things. I didn't realize until it was too late that I'd fallen into a trap."

I raise an eyebrow. "What trap's that?"

A weary chuckle. "When your life is your work, your work's your life." Their face softens. "You don't have to tell me if you don't want to. But this isn't a transaction."

I don't answer the question as the two of us walk in silence. But I turn their question over in my head with each step. I want to say one hundred percent of it is absolutely true. She killed my sister. She turned my birthright into rubble. Of course she'd kill her own main squeeze and wind up with a friend's bullet in her back.

Of course she would.

But by the time Pamin and I have claimed seats at the bar, and had a few beers, and we've maybe given each other some lingering looks over our latest round, I still can't bring myself to say "yes."

Later in bed, my tears ambush me. I hate myself for wasting them on her. And when Pamin lets it pass without a word, just a gentle hand between my shoulder blades, I hate them for seeing me.

One morning, I wake up next to Pamin and realize I haven't seen Dalisa for a long time.

Pamin and I have a good thing going. It isn't a full-time thing, but neither of us wants that. Pamin wants more than any one person could give, and I don't have enough to give anyone for long. But even when we aren't doing our thing, I enjoy their company. I enjoy the whole group, really, and even the folks I've met who aren't a part of it: their families. Their own friends. Sometimes, I'll go hours without remembering that I ain't the Diwata they think I am.

For so long, I hold on to that idea: that there's some "real" Diwata nested inside the boat mechanic I've become. The real Diwata would never spend hours on small talk with people about their little lives. She wouldn't go with them to driftball games, and shout when Sasaki throws an intercept for the thousandth gods-damned time. She wouldn't smile patiently as their children tell long, rambling stories about what they'd learned in school today.

But over time, that feeling drifts further and further out of reach. My days as a throat-slitter and shot-caller start to feel more and more like a motion picture I watched once, and then a dream I half-remember.

The lumpia I make myself for my birthday that year, with the newly abundant ingredients at the market, are not Benilda Lacanilao's lumpia; they're mine.

The dead woman on the couch is snoring loud enough to wake the actual dead.

She stayed on her feet just long enough to say hi, and then promptly collapsed. It took me some serious doing just to drag her in here. And now I stand over her, a mug of lapsang tea in one hand and a knife in the other.

She looks like hell. She's darker than me now, which I take to mean she's been holed up somewhere sunny. In her long-braided hair, faint threads of grey are starting to show: the steel of a hull beneath paint that's just begun to peel. But even relaxed in the hold of sleep, it's the deep-worn lines on her face that really age her.

I wrinkle my nose a bit at the stench of stale frying oil, and wonder if she's spent the past four years as a carny.

"You swore pahingán." Dalisa's voice doesn't point an accusation my way. It's just a statement of fact. That's all Sasa ever needed: the facts. I know she's not really there, but I see her standing next to me just the same. She's prim and coiffed, like she always was, instead of the pulped-up mess she became courtesy of the woman in front of me. She looks like someone who would've been the best player the crooked game had ever seen.

I nod. "I did."

"And she's come back to you, begging for death," says Dalisa.

I nod. "In a roundabout way."

"You have no reason not to put that knife through her," says Dalisa.

I nod. "I don't."

"Then you know what you need to do."

I do.

I really do.

But I can feel the phantom touch of a hand between my shoulder blades, and it's not Dalisa's.

33
Now

Age 30

It was like the reel ran out on a projector. One moment, I was standing over myself, holding cold steel and warm tea. The next, I was sitting on a porch, staring at my own two feet. Above me, the sky was turning pink around its edges.

I tried to stand, and it felt like my knees had rusted. Braced myself with my bad wrist, and immediately regretted it. Managed to get to my feet eventually, but I was still reeling from everything I'd experienced. I could feel fresh anguish in my chest, and I knew the pain had nothing to do with you or Binh or anything else that had happened to me in the past day. It was like opening my mouth to sing, and hearing someone else's voice come out.

Behind me, the door scraped open. Diwata stepped out, Pamin on her heels. They each had a mug of steaming hot tea, plus something else. Diwata had a cigarette, freshly lit. And Pamin was carrying a simple brown envelope.

I reached for the mug. "You didn't have to—"

Diwata leveled a stare at me as she calmly pulled the tea out of my reach and took a long sip. I let my hand fall to my side. Fair enough.

"I'm sorry, Dawa," I said. "You were trying to help me the whole time, and I kept shutting myself off from you. If I'd let you help me, Cole might already be dead." I hesitated. Drew in a big breath. I might not ever get another chance to say this to her. "And I'm sorry about D—"

"What'd it show you?" Diwata calmly cut across me. "Figure it must've been interesting, if you sat around to catch the whole thing."

I shot a look over her shoulder at Pamin. "I think it's family business."

Casually, Diwata slipped an arm around their waist. "Yeah, it is."

I looked between the two of them. "Why didn't you tell me they were more than just a zephyr to you?"

She snorted a puff of tobacco smoke. "Why didn't you tell me ... well, anything?"

I looked away. "It showed me what I needed to see."

"I swear to every god in every temple," groaned Pamin. "Are all Biranese this cryptic, or is that just a family thing?"

"You didn't find something new and latch on to it," I went on. "You made little choices. You chose to stay. You chose not to go after me. You chose your favorite zephyr. All those little choices ..."

"Until they added up to a life," said Diwata. "You wanna move past this? That's how. You build something new." She spread her arms wide. "I built this."

Pamin cleared their throat.

"*Metaphorically*," Diwata clarified. "It's that simple, Tenny. If you've got nothing left to live for, then at least keep living 'cause you're too selfish to die."

"But," Pamin said, "you're not just going to live for yourself, are you?"

I glared at them over the top rim of my glasses. "What do you know about it?"

"Wrong question to ask a zephyr," they said, their pale eyes dancing like sunlight on ice. "Especially a zephyr who knows you. Are you really going to let Cole get away with what he did to you?"

I bristled at the question. It still felt like none of their business. But I couldn't argue with my sister's arm around them. So I swallowed my objection and said, "But everything good he's done for the city ..."

"They weren't asking about that," said Diwata. "And they weren't asking about Binh either, before you jump to that."

"*I wasn't gonna!*" I said, too quickly.

"Then be straight with me," she said. "Could you really live the rest of your life letting him skate on this?"

"He lit hundreds of salters on fire just to get what he wanted," I said slowly. Beneath my words, I could hear strings and horns gently stirring. "Killed his own best friend for it, too. I can't trust a guy like that to run things. Who knows what he'll burn down next?"

"Well, there you go, then," Diwata said. "Sounds like you've got your way forward. Get out there and beat his ass again."

I shook my head and leaned hard against the porch railing. "It ain't enough to kick his ass. I did that. You know where it got me."

"The front page," Pamin mused.

I ignored them. "If I'm gonna do this," I went on, "I can't destroy him. I hate him, but the guy built something good. Something *actually* good." Admitting it hurt me worse than another go-around with the Black Rose. A realization hit me, and it almost felt like your words were coming out of my mouth instead of my own. "If I destroy what he built, it'll be up to me to build something to replace it."

Pamin glanced at Diwata. "Are all members of your family this self-involved?"

"Nah, this one's special. She was always like this, even before she turned into a wizard."

I glanced at the shoulder of Diwata's robe. Under it, I knew she wore a white patch. "You've always had something at stake if I won this. Why the hell have you helped me so much?"

"I fucking knew she'd ask," Diwata said, nodding to Pamin.

They held up the envelope. I recognized it from my first visit here. It was the one that contained Diwata's answer of why she was helping me against the Thorn Orphans.

"Zephyrs give information in exchange for three kinds of currency, Red Rose," said Pamin. They sounded businesslike, as if they'd just flicked some kind of professional switch in their head. "Cash, information, or favors. If you accept the onus of a personal favor from me, you can read what's in this envelope."

I stared at them. "You know if I really wanted to, I could just use my powers to find out now."

"I'm trusting that you won't," Diwata said. "What'll it be, Ten?"

I stared at the envelope. Even felt the faint echo of a song's opening notes as the city's spirit asked me if I wanted its help here. And by the Bird's pointy beak, Cole, it was tempting. You know how our powers get. It gets to be impossible not to use them, sometimes.

But I pulled back. Nodded. "Name your favor."

They shook their head, then handed over the envelope. "I'll name it after you've read."

With a shaking hand, I took it. Fumbled the thing open and tossed the envelope aside. The wind caught it and carried it off.

"You know I'm gonna have to pick that up later, right?" Pamin said, as I unfolded the piece of paper. On it was Diwata's familiar scrawl, big and sharp as a tiger's teeth:

The bastard tried to kill my baby sister.

It was only one sentence, but I read it over and over again until I wasn't even reading anymore, just staring at it. When I looked up at the two of them, they stood hand in hand, eyes on me.

"Cheza Tenlonghari," Pamin said. "The Governor, Cole, shed the blood of your blood. In exchange for this information, I charge you with this favor."

With her free hand, Diwata produced a mahogany-handled knife from her robe pocket. She flipped it adroitly and offered it to me hilt-first.

Here's the thing about pahingán, Cole. Pahingán is a promise, sure enough, but it doesn't actually mean "revenge" or "vendetta" or anything like that. If you take it literally, what pahingán means is "knife."

The same tool the Biranese used to tame the jungle, to hunt their game, to protect their own. The revered blade that the Biranese used to cut a big, cruel world into pieces that they could survive. When you invoked that knife, you were promising that you were going to use it to set the world right again, however it'd gone wrong.

So when my sister offered me her knife, Cole, she didn't need to tell me what the favor was.

Pamin offered me the traditional assistance of a Guild-certified zephyr: the lethal infodump known by all players of the crooked game as *a dick move*. But I turned them down. There was nothing they could possibly know about you that I didn't already know.

They offered me other information, but I had that covered, too. You know, what with being an all-powerful city shaman and all.

Diwata offered me none of those things; only new clothes. That offer, I took her up on.

So as morning broke over Driftwood City, I wove myself a path from Pamin's front door to the door of the topmost observation deck on the Rock. The woman who came through, you might've actually recognized: a black flatcap. A long black coat. A black carpenter's mask over her nose and mouth. And a paper rose, folded from a piece of old stationery, with a single word written within its petals.

The deck was made of white-painted sheet metal, with glass shields to protect tourists from the wind. There was even a little access tunnel, so folks could walk straight from the cable cars to the deck. According to the plaque on the wall, you'd built it right on the spot of your childhood home, with the promise that the space would now serve the public good. And once again, Cole, you delivered.

I guess you had seen our city from the sky, after all.

That sky, grey and pink with the morning, was dotted with airships. Beneath them, miles of oak and birch and bamboo reached out into the glittering ocean. All across them, elegant towers, and the sharp-roofed homes and tenements that huddled in their shadows. And when I listened on the wind, I could hear a thousand mornings starting in a thousand different places. It was like I was watching a gigantic machine spin to life, sprocket by sprocket and gear by gear. You and I had always thought of machines as big, scary, unstoppable things, whose wheels turned with cruel indifference. But there was nothing cruel about the one sprawled out beneath me.

I'd needed to see it before I went on: one last glimpse of the big picture before I dove in to fiddle with the details. Whatever

426

I built after today, it would have to be better than this. That was the price I had to be ready to pay for my revenge.

For a long time, I just stood there and let the sight of it wash over me.

If this was what I was fighting for, I thought, I couldn't go too far wrong.

I made sure to come back to the Plant under the cover of night, so no one would mark me. The pit I'd gouged into the Slats had been cordoned off, but no one was on duty to guard it. It occurred to me that you could have very easily repaired it with a wave of your hand, but you'd left it there. I guess it didn't hurt your story, having something you could point to whenever you wanted to remind people exactly what I was capable of.

I could sense the thousands of salters on shift inside the Plant's walls, and even some milling about outside on their mandated breaks. But a soft song from me, and all the outdoor lights gently bent away from where I was, until I was standing in a small blind spot of my own making.

It was pretty impressive, how quickly you'd put that statue of Binh back up on its pedestal. Your welders had done a good job; I could barely make out the seam where I'd snapped it off at its ankles. As I got closer, I could hear the echoes of the welding torches, and feel the residual heat of them on my cheeks.

But it faded as I approached the statue and my attention came to rest on Binh's face. In the dark, I had to fill in the details. Yet even though I had years of fond memories to help me, I could feel myself stretching his features in my mind's eye. Rough hands, robbed of the ability to gently run the length of my spine. Eyes, hard and brown and cold as uncut topaz. A flat, brutal nose. But those weren't what made him ugly to me. Binh had had a way about him that lit up every room he stepped into. As I studied the statue, I saw it all bleed away. And all that was left was … a guy. Nothing else.

I almost knocked him down again on sheer fucking principle, Cole.

But instead, I pulled a small scrap of paper out of my coat pocket: the shopping list I'd taken from the Phuong family home. The last scrap of his handwriting I'd had. Delicately, I folded it into a paper rose to match the one on my lapel. And then I laid it at his feet. My last respects before I turned away.

It was one thing to know he'd lied to me all these years. It was another to slip inside his memories and feel him make that choice, over and over again. But he'd tried to tell me the truth at the very end. Too late, and he hadn't quite succeeded. But he'd tried. And for that alone, I left him standing.

Maybe someday, if I survived the next few hours, I'd come back. And when I did, maybe the man on that pedestal wouldn't look like a stranger anymore.

I went to find a telephone booth. Instead of teleporting, I decided to look for one on foot. Savor the chilly air. Take in the sounds of the city as it came to a rest.

Also, I'd busted every door within three blocks of the Plant.

But eventually, I found one. As I approached it, the city told me that it was out of commission. When I asked why, it played a few notes that I translated as, *Some asshole had a tantrum.*

But even so, when I picked up the receiver, I heard ringing on the other end.

You let it go two more times before you answered. "Tenny."

"How'd you know it was me?" I said.

"No one else would think to reach me at this number." I heard wooden chair legs scrape on a floor. "Have you watched the vision Binh left for you?"

My fingers tightened around the receiver. "I did. You really thought it'd be enough to make me go away?"

"I hoped it would give you some perspective. However you might feel."

"'However I might feel' about getting left for dead, Cole?" I snapped. "Have I left you in the dark on how I *feel* about that?"

You didn't bother answering me directly. "If you're looking to try me again, I have an army of police who are eager for another chance at you. Or can I hope against all reasonable hope that you might want to settle things between us like civilized adults?"

Normally I would've risen to that bait. But now I knew to say, "Yeah, Cole, I do."

There was a shocked pause at the other end of the line. I tried not to savor it.

"Really?" you said eventually.

"I've already proven I can kick the shit out of you whenever I want," I said. "I mean, I always could. But that's not gonna balance the scales for me here. So let's you and me figure out what will."

Anyone but me would've been fooled by how even you sounded. But I knew how to listen for the signs of your effort. You were . . . I don't know. Hopeful, maybe.

I gripped the receiver tighter.

"Where?" you asked.

"Are you sitting where I think you are?" I asked.

You swallowed loud enough for me to hear. "I am."

"Then I'll come to you." I hung up without a goodbye.

I knew I'd be saying it soon enough.

Part Seven

Final Revenge!
The Justice of the Red Rose

34

Twelve years ago

Age 18

The first time I saw you was the morning of the fire: my eighteenth birthday. The day I became a shaman.

As I was taking my place on the line for the morning shift, I was wrestling with my own head. Since I'd woken up that morning, I'd been hearing music. I'd thought it would knock off once I got into the Plant, where all the machinery was at work. But it just played right on over all the grinding and whirring. And it wasn't just music. There was something else lurking just beneath the notes, and if I concentrated—

A friendly pat on my shoulder. It was Ramesh, one of my partners on the line. He was an old salter, the kind who'd been on the line since he was younger than me, and it showed in his wrinkled face and hands:

"Been trying to get your attention, Tenny. Look up there."

A whole group of folks came clanging across the metal catwalks above. I recognized your fathers right away: company president Suriwong Pakuanjangnambhar, silver-haired and powerfully built. He looked like the kind of person whose ass

433

could turn any chair into a throne. Next to him was his husband, Guan Ming Pakuanjangnambhar, elegant and shiny as a really nice knife. The third son of a Tsunese shipping tycoon, happy to be of use to his family somehow.

And between them was a needle of a man: small, skinny, and silver. Enter you, stage right.

You stopped and looked down across the floor. And even before we knew each other like we know each other now, Cole, I knew that you were looking right at me. And when I met your gaze, I heard that phantom melody resolve itself and start over again, this time in a major key. But you didn't seem to hear it, and it faded as you hurried to keep up with your fathers.

"I remember back when the clan's name was two syllables shorter," sighed Ramesh. "Get a good look at the little one, Tenny. You'll grow old working for him."

I tried the name. "Mongkhul Pakuanjangnambhar ...?"

"—at," said Ramesh. "You know why the Samnati do that to their names?"

"Why?" I asked.

"'Cause they're all daring someone to break their streak. Now, come on. Let's put our backs into it today."

Within the hour, Ramesh was ash. A lifetime of work for the company, reduced to curls of stinking smoke in my nose.

And I was fighting back to back with two new comrades.

"*There!*" one of those comrades shouted over the mingled roar of the fire and the salters it was devouring. Your fine black clothes were flecked with ash, your silver hair with soot. I didn't need to follow your slender brown finger to see. My other new comrade had already told me the whole row of water tanks were about to blow.

I ran forward, ducking and dodging past the salters trying to flee. A few turned to gape at me as I ran toward the fire, but

434

most just kept running. In the pit of my stomach, I let myself hope they'd get out alive. They couldn't do anything about this fire.

We, on the other hand, could do everything.

The huge brass water tanks were already full of hot water, but the outside heat had elevated their temp way past what the old things could handle. From the urgent tempo of the melody in my head, I knew in some deep, instinctual place that they were seconds away from turning into a cluster bomb. It would be steam and shrapnel everywhere. And anyone who was caught in that cloud would end up dead as Ramesh.

I didn't totally know what I was doing, but this was a power that taught us how to use it. When I thrust my hands out, I wasn't demanding that something happen, so much as asking the spirit for help. But when I reached out, I felt the valves on the tanks start to turn in response. I could feel the heat of their metal, the grit of their rust. When they twisted, steam spat into the air like a horn blast.

But I could only grab a few at a time. And when I tried to shift my focus to new ones, the ones I'd loosened up started to spit steam even faster as the pressure rushed into this new outlet. I could blunt the impact of a few explosions, but I couldn't stop them all.

"Hoy, rich kid!" I shouted. "I can't hold them much longer!"

You appeared at my side as if by magic, your hands already outstretched. More plumes of steam rose, but not enough to vent all the pressure before something ruptured.

"This isn't going to work!" you said to me. Your narrow aristocratic face was screwed up with concentration, but I saw a glimmer of something else in your eye: disbelief. Excitement.

"Well, if you've got any better ideas, we could use them about thirty seconds ago!" I grunted. The effort was starting to take a toll on me. It wasn't pain. More like fatigue, as if each

435

passing second was another hour I'd stayed up too late.

Your eyes took on a calculating edge. "The tanks are the surface!" you said breathlessly. "We need to go deeper!"

I felt you let go of the tanks, and I started to shout in protest. But before I could, you turned and sang your song to a different audience: the water pump beneath the workings of the floor.

And when you pulled that end of the thread, the other end moved.

Just like that, I felt something shift inside every tank at once. And then they were spewing their boiling hot water back out into the ocean. The old pipes groaned and creaked from the sudden change of temperature, but they held. It'd cook every fish within a mile, but I'd trade those fish for salter lives, any day.

"How'd you know to do that?" I wiped the sweat from my forehead, and it was instantly replaced.

"I have to know everything about this place," you said grimly. "I never thought it would be useful."

I sang to a locked emergency exit, and its doors flung themselves open. Salters flooded through it like steam from the valve. I saw them sporting fresh burns, dragging out the ones who couldn't walk anymore. Fury roiled inside me at the sight, but I found bitter satisfaction anyway. They would live. "Are you seriously complaining about being from the richest family in town?" I snapped.

"Point taken!" you said, then busied yourself dousing flames with a gout of water from a utility pipe.

I was surprised as I watched you work. Growing up in Benilda's home, I couldn't say I'd been poor. But you weren't just rich; you were wealthy, and my understanding of the wealthy was that they wilted like a flower when they got even a degree outside their comfort zone. But you fought the

436

flames with a cool and collected head. All your actions were decisive and controlled. I would've been fooled into thinking you knew what you were doing, if not for the look of surprise that crossed your face every time something happened.

"What do you think this is?" you called over the chaos.

It wouldn't be until the next day that I'd remember having read something about shamans for school, and the pieces would start to fall into place a little bit. So all I answered was, "Dunno! But its timing is good!"

I could feel deeper emotions on the edge of my consciousness: panic and fear and revulsion and all the things any normal person would feel as they stood in the middle of a blaze, breathing in their comrades' ashes. But I knew I couldn't let myself get bogged down in that, or I'd come to a complete stop. So I added: "Hell of a birthday present, though!"

"For you and me both!" you answered. "Up top!"

I already knew what you were talking about. We gestured in unison, and I felt our powers harmonize as we grabbed an unoccupied catwalk and twisted it into the path of a falling rafter. Steel ground against steel and set my teeth on edge. But it gave the salters below enough time to get clear before the rafter came crashing down to the workfloor.

I waited until the screeching of metal had died off before I turned back to you and said, "Happy birthday."

Fire by fire, flame by flame, we fought back. The song that flowed through us made our motions fluid and our purpose clear. And with each note we played, more salters were spared, and the more we starved the fire.

We were both breathing hard when the last flame finally died. Even though the power had flowed through me rather than coming from me, my muscles ached like I'd just danced a five-act ballet by myself. And yet, I didn't remember ever feeling more alive in my life. In time, the memories would catch

437

up with me and sour until I couldn't stomach them anymore. But in that moment, standing next to you, I relished the song of savage, primal pride running through me.

Your voice rose to meet mine. They harmonized, interlocking like the fingers of held hands. And as powerful as I'd felt before, with you I suddenly felt like I could hit a high note that would shatter the Rock to its core.

I nodded to you. "You're Mongk—"

"Cole," you cut in. You offered me a hand. "I prefer Cole."

It was a weird name. Didn't sound like any language I recognized. But I wasn't gonna give you grief over it. I took your hand, gripped it firmly in mine, felt the softness of your palm against my sandpapery calluses. "Tenny."

"Tenny," you said breathlessly, "we need to get out of here. Now."

I wondered at the time why you wanted to go, instead of basking in the hero treatment you might've received if you'd stayed. I wondered why you didn't want to run right back to the safety of your fathers. I wondered how the hell this was happening to both of us, when it looked like the only thing we had in common was a birthday.

But I remembered how desperate I'd been to put space between me and Benilda the moment I had a chance to escape.

And I remembered how you'd fought alongside me.

And our harmonizing notes still rang in my ears, the most spellbinding song I'd ever heard ...

"Come on, then!" I said, grabbing your arm. You squawked in surprise and tried to keep up with my long legs as I broke into a run. "I know a place."

35
Now

Age 30

I got my first apartment in Kelptown because it was one of the
only places left on the Slats where a person could afford to live
alone on a salter's pay. And as far as affordable neighborhoods
went, it was cute enough. The buildings leaned on each other
like drunks at the end of the night, to be sure. But there was
something welcoming about those tight-grained birch streets
below, and the faded green rooftops overhead. If I was going
to start over on my own, I decided, here was where I'd start.

When I first put down my deposit on the place, I didn't
figure on a runaway crashing on my cheap sofa for the next
ten years.

But then, I didn't figure on a lot of things.

I remember the first day I came through its threshold. It was
small and dusty and the last tenant hadn't taken great care of
the floors, if all the scratches and gouges were any sign. I could
already tell that the thin walls would be a problem in winter,
especially considering how expensive heat was. And while it
was supposed to have come furnished, the asshole before me

had decided to help themselves. They cleaned the place out so good, I felt lucky I still had a door.

I signed for it anyway. It wasn't a great place. Wasn't even a good one, honestly. It was small, at the ass end of the boatway line, and a seventh-story walk-up to boot. But it was something a whole lot more important than great, or good, or even bad:

Mine.

First, it was my home. Then, our home. Then, the secret headquarters of the notorious Thorn Orphans. Didn't matter, the seven flights of stairs we had to take every day to get to it. No place in Driftwood City ever sang to me as sweetly as those four walls.

I imagined all kinds of futures for us in that apartment, Cole. Ones where Binh moved in. Ones where I moved out. Ones where you and I stayed, fighting the good fight from our wobbly kitchen table until the very end. I thought it would be the site of every important moment in our friendship.

I never thought that would include the end of it.

After I hung up the phone, I could've teleported straight to you. And a big part of me *was* itching to get this done with already. But as I started to weave together the strands of the city that made up the phone booth and the ones of our old place, I caught myself. I took a deep breath, and then I let them all go.

I shouldn't rush this, I told myself. Once tonight's work was done, I'd have the rest of my life to live with the weight of it. These were gonna be my last hours unburdened. I might as well live them out.

Besides, the waiting would probably make you shit yourself.

So instead of drawing that thread tight, I decided to walk: unhurried, hands in my pockets, the city's ghostly song in my ears. My feet started to throb after the first couple of miles, the old diner soreness roaring back right when I needed it the least. But I walked on anyway. And with every step, I drank in my city the way I wanted to remember it: the golden lights overhead. The groaning of the Slats underfoot. And the good people of Driftwood City, throwing themselves out of my way when they saw me coming.

I ain't gonna lie: it stung, seeing that fear on the faces of the folk I'd fought and bled for. And it stung even more, hearing that fear in the ambient music the spirit piped to me as I passed them. But I had to look at this with clear eyes. No matter what I'd been fighting for, no matter what I thought I'd done for them, I hadn't done shit to show these people that they shouldn't be afraid of me. So instead of trying to change their tune, I walked in time with it. And a selfish part of me hoped that someday I'd find a way to play them my song instead.

All that said, no one gave me any grief as I made my way into Kelptown. Even the streetlights all changed to give me right of way the moment I approached them. Nothing slowed me down until I finally reached my destination: the seven-floor tenement house at the corner of Ash and Thuy. Roulette's department had slapped a fresh coat of yellow paint on the façade, but there was no fixing the way it leaned up against the building next to it, so that the door always stuck in the frame. The roof, I saw, they'd left untouched, its deep green turned shallow by sun and snow.

I smiled grimly at the sight. Home sweet home.

A police blockade had been set up at the end of the street. Uniformed officers stood at attention, and at my approach they reached for their weapons. I saw some of them were limping, or sporting bandages and casts. But the real thing that stood out to me was their faces. Even in the low light, it was obvious that you'd staffed your entire barricade with Biranese officers.

You do have a bastard's talent for twisting the knife, Cole.

"How much did he have to pay you assholes to stand here, neh?" I called loudly to them as I approached. I felt a ripple of fear pass through them, though they all stood their ground. "What kind of bonus did he give you all for the good optics?"

One of them stepped forward: a sergeant. "We were forbidden from officially defending our governor." His contempt was a hot iron, making all his words crisp and flat. "All of us are here on our own time, Red Rose." Behind him, the other badges fell in line with a discipline that would've made Jali proud.

I wasn't surprised when the city's song told me his answer was an honest one. I'd already seen the entire city rally to your side. Whatever the hell you really were, you still had it in you to make these folks love you.

"I'm going up there one way or another," I said. "I don't want to repeat what happened at the Plant. But if that's how you want this to go, your little honor guard ain't gonna be enough to stop me."

"We know we can't stop you," an officer piped up behind the sergeant. Behind her visor, I saw a young, angry face glaring back at me. And something else, just behind the anger: fear. "We're here to show the city that you don't speak for us."

"You ever hear me say I did?" I snapped.

"You know how this town works," said the sergeant. "No matter what we do, everyone else judges us by our worst. And right now, they're judging us by you."

The thrumming I felt from the assembled officers had a ring of agreement. The sheer unfairness of it was bitter in my mouth. But hadn't I heard the same shit from the priest just the other morning?

All of you had the gall to say you were helping our community. Parasites, every one of you.

442

"After yesterday, the people are calling you a monster," the sergeant went on. "But me, I know better, Red Rose. I know you're still just a person with a heart and a brain." His hand came to rest on the sidearm at his hip. "All it takes is one bullet."

I glared down at him as I fought to keep my temper in check. When someone wanted to be this much of a punk to me, I usually smacked them down on principle alone. But there was sincerity in his eyes, and in the music I heard when I stared into them. And I tell you what, Cole: I didn't have it in me to hit someone like that anymore. Not unless they made me.

With great effort, I forced the words out: "Stand aside."

Hatred poured from him like smoke from a gun's barrel. But he did.

I brushed past them all, listening to their disgust in stereo. I kept my back straight and my head up, and I told myself that what they thought of me didn't matter. After all, it wasn't them I was here to reckon with. But the longer I listened to the refrain, the more doubt crept into me.

I craned my neck skyward, all the way to the seventh floor. And sure enough, in that big round window, I saw a silhouette I would've recognized anywhere.

And as it turned away from the window, my grip tightened around Dawa's knife in my pocket.

Overhead, it began to rain.

There was a time I could've bounded up all seven flights of stairs in one go, taking them two at a time. But it turns out that when you turn the corner of thirty, your knees start to get other ideas. By the time I finally hauled myself on to the seventh-floor landing, I was halfway to choking. I leaned hard against the wall to catch my breath. I didn't want to kick off our final showdown gasping like a landed fish.

When I arrived at apartment 707, I saw the shadow of two

feet already standing behind its old, chipped door. I wondered which version of you stood there, waiting to greet me.

And then I didn't have to wonder. The door slid open, and you were looking up at me with mismatched eyes: one white, one blotched with blood. Your face, normally so symmetrical, was a patchwork of welts and bruises. You stood ramrod straight, but I could tell you were favoring one leg over the other. You looked, in short, like hell.

But at least the suit you'd chosen to die in was ironed and pressed.

You were close enough that I could've ended it then and there. I knew I was faster than you. One sweep of my knife hand across your throat, and that would be that. Blood spilled, scales balanced.

But no. This was going to be our last conversation.

And I wanted it to be a conversation, Cole.

We stood there for a long, tense moment.

And then you gave me a curt nod. "Thank you for being civil this time."

I shrugged. "The night could still go a lot of ways."

You eyed me, sharp and appraising. "Could it?"

"No," I admitted. "Not really."

You exhaled resignedly, and then stepped aside. "Please come i—"

I reached out to choke away your power again, but even as I tried I saw you'd been ready for me. You blocked my grasp, and just in time I managed to parry yours. The two of us stood there, our powers marshaled and ready. I could feel it in the spiritual energy around me, like a string stretched too tightly across a bridge.

"Do we really have to do this, Tenny?" you said eventually.

"You telling me I don't have a reason to?"

444

"I'm painfully aware that you do," you sighed. "But I was hoping you were here to reach an understanding."

"You let go first, and I'll do the same," I said.

"Can I trust you to uphold your end of the bargain?"

I gave your beat-up self a once-over with my eyes. "We both know which one of us really needs the spirit's help here."

You cocked your head to study me with your unbloodied eye. And after a few heartbeats, I felt the tension leave the air around me. Sure enough, I let the spirit slip out of my own grip. And then we were just two people again.

"It seems I spoke too soon about civility," you sniffed. "Now, come in before the kettle boils over."

You were a guy who always considered all the angles, so as I stepped in, I listened for any signs that you'd planned for my coming. But my footsteps didn't trigger a bomb under the floorboards. A bunch of assholes with guns didn't jump out as I came into our old front room. It really was just you, me, and the spirit of Driftwood City.

I wouldn't have wanted it any other way.

You preceded me into the apartment. At the familiar sound of your boots clicking on the wooden floor, my stomach tightened and my palms tingled. My breathing started to get staccato on me.

I was bleeding in a dark boathouse.

I was standing in a bright apartment.

I was bleeding in a dark—

The door slammed shut on its own ten feet behind me. You jolted at the sudden noise. Turned back to me. "Was that really necessary?" You said it with the kind of annoyance a well-bred guy like you never would've shown an enemy.

"Just pour the tea, asshole," I muttered as I stomped over to the table.

It was surprising enough you'd hung on to the old place.

It was even more surprising that instead of updating it with sleek, fancy furniture, you'd kept all the rickety shit we'd lived on through our twenties. The patchy couch that had been your bed. The mismatched chairs, both of them curbside finds. And the wobbly breakfast table in front of the huge window, leveled out by a warped chunk of birch I'd wedged under its bad foot.

I draped my longcoat over the chair. Underneath it, I'd worn a faded red dress for the occasion. It was the only red thing Pamin had owned. Not really my style—I like a loud, angry red, me—but I'd been determined to march in to my last battle wearing my own colors. I'd even taken the time to fold up a rose out of red paper for my coat lapel, but on that count I shouldn't have bothered. You'd put a vase in the center of the table, stuffed with the genuine article. Your color, and mine.

"I hope oolong is all right," you said, joining me at the table with two willow-patterned cups. As I inspected the leaves in the bottom of them, you went back to the kitchenette for the kettle. "I've lost my taste for most other leaves."

I stared flatly at you as you returned and poured. "In what world would you think I give a shit?"

Idly, you stirred your tea. I noted that your mug and mine were both full almost to the brim. "Do you recall the first time you brought me back here?" you said. "You didn't have enough water to split between us to get our mugs half-full. Now look. Not even a bucket out front."

I folded my arms over my chest.

You glanced out the window and watched the rain fall. "I just thought it was an interesting observation."

"Well, it ain't what I came here to talk to you about." I leaned forward on to my elbows, searching the familiar face opposite me for anything actually familiar. So close to you, I couldn't sit still. "I'm here to discuss an unresolved point of tension between us, stemming from that occasion upon which you elected to fuckin' kill me."

Your hand traced a lazy circle in the air to indicate me. "Clearly, I didn't."

"Killing someone ain't just about stopping their heart," I growled. "The whole time I was away from here, I was *nothing*, you understand that? I couldn't use the language I'd been born with. Couldn't go to all the places that meant something to me. Couldn't see any familiar faces. Couldn't sweat it all out in the ring. I couldn't hear the music anymore. Everything about me that made me Tenny, you took from me that day. I survived, Cole, but I sure as shit wasn't living."

I hadn't rehearsed those exact words, but in my head I'd given you plenty of speeches just like it. I was surprised that, finally given the chance, I hadn't roared it at you, or punctuated every sentence by slamming your head into the table. In fact, I was actually starting to like the feeling of calm I was carrying in me. My anger, my hatred, my hurt ... it was like water in my gut. No matter how I leaned, it stayed level.

"I suppose I can't deny that," you said stiffly. "And I similarly suppose there's no point in telling you that, given the situation four years ago, I felt I'd found myself without a choice?"

"I'm sure that's what you've told yourself," I said. "After all, you had to find some way to live with it."

You looked at me like a man trying to see through his opponent's pektong tiles. You'd clearly expected this conversation to go sideways fast. It gave me some satisfaction to know the longer I behaved myself, the more paranoid you'd get.

"It's not what I told myself; it's the truth." You sounded glassy-smooth, but the way you sat told me that there were already fractures. "A reputation is a story you tell the world. And what story did you tell the world, Tenny, with every action and word? 'Cross me and die.'"

I shifted in my seat.

"You were the Red Rose, always a machete and never a scalpel. There was no way we could have ever reached an understanding about the necessity of Binh's death. And once I knew his guilt had gotten the better of him, his death *did* become a necessity. Knowing your reaction would be invariably lethal . . . was my response really so surprising, Tenny?"

"You have no idea what I would have done if you'd come to me." I heard myself starting to talk a little faster, but that calm remained. I couldn't remember being this certain about anything I'd ever wanted to say. "Before killing me, before killing Binh. You have no clue what could have happened if you'd come to me with the truth and trusted that, even accounting for all that, our friendship meant something. You don't get to put this on the shoulders of what you think I would've done."

You shook your head. "Our friendship is why I chose to act as I did. No one knew you like I did. And I knew in my bones that as much as you loved me, you wouldn't choose me." An admirable attempt to keep yourself sounding level, but even you couldn't hide the bitterness. I heard it in the way your tongue hit your teeth, and I just about smelled it on the air around you. "Nobody ever does."

"So that's where you stand on it?" At last, I helped myself to some oolong. The spirit told me it was safe to drink, but I didn't need its help to know that. You weren't the poisoning type, even when you should've been. "You ain't sorry at all for what you did to those salters? To Binh? To me?"

"Are you sorry for what you did to our comrades, the late Thorn Orphans?" you shot back. "All of them, dead by your hand. Do you feel sorrow when you see that blood caked under your fingernails? Or do you simply regret that it was a necessary step to keep following the path of your destiny?"

I shook my head, amazed. You'd always believed that the

two of us were filled with glorious purpose. But without me around, you were talking like a totally different man. Specifically, like a man who'd forgotten that underneath everything else, he still was one.

"You told me once that you heard the screams of everyone your family had ever fucked over. Felt their pain. That was the spirit's birthday present for you. And you said you'd do anything and everything to make it stop. Tell me: you've had four years. Did it work?"

You swirled your tea.

"No," you admitted. "I hear more of them than ever. But I also realized that there was no point in running from that pain. I can't make it go away. I can't ever undo it. I've done what I've done, and I am what I am. But I can carry the memories of that pain forward. And I can honor them by keeping them close as I tend my rose garden." Your eyes searched mine for ... mercy? Understanding? Weakness? "Isn't that how you moved forward, Tenny? By keeping your pain close? By making it as much a part of yourself as your heartbeat?

"Because the truth is, I do regret what I did. I missed you every single day we were apart. The day after, I sent my fathers to their graves. With a snap of my fingers, I finally struck the decisive blow for every worker in Driftwood City. And all I could think was that the moment felt hollow without my other half to share it."

"That supposed to make me feel bad for you?" I kept myself even, but for the first time I felt that calm water inside me starting to bubble as I reassessed what kind of man I was sitting with. I'd come here with a specific mission in mind, but it was getting harder for me to keep to it when I heard you talking like this.

"I'm not trying to make you feel anything," you said. "I'm just trying to tell you the truth, as best I know it, whether you

449

want to hear it or not. And here's something I know you don't want to hear: this was the best thing that could have happened to us."

I had to fight not to spit out my mouthful of tea. I swallowed it carefully. "The hell you talking about?"

"The fire. What I did to you. They were both tragedies. But I've used them as foundations, and I've built incredible things on top of them. Social engines that churn out more than just profit. Things that actually help people. You've seen it for yourself, haven't you?" You indicated the big window beside us, and the city that lay beyond it. "Can't you sense how much happier people are? Don't you hear it in the songs the spirit sings you? Don't you see what you'll throw away if you go through with this?"

Another sip of tea to keep me calm. "That all sounds great for you, if I was to get behind that idea," I said. "But what's so good about what happened to me?"

You looked at me like I'd just forgotten my own name. "You became the shaman you needed to be to fight your way back to my side."

I didn't bother to hide my revulsion. I even leaned my chair back on its hind feet, just to get a few inches farther away from you. "You do know I fought my way here so I'd get a clean shot at your heart, right?"

"A significant difference, but not an insurmountable one."

"You really think that?"

"I do." You slid your now-empty teacup aside. I listened for any warnings from the spirit that it was some kind of signal, but I heard nothing. "The truth is, Tenny, I never believed you were dead. I knew you would survive, and I waited for you to make your return so we could find a way forward together."

I snorted: an ugly, derisive noise, but it was what you deserved.

450

"And when I noticed you were taking your sweet time in Malañong," you continued, "I decided to give you the push you needed to get back in the game."

My chair's front legs hit the floor with a heavy thud. I stared at you in disbelief as my mind worked to catch up with what my ears had just taken in. "You're telling me my run-in with Roulette wasn't just his bad luck?" My grip on the spirit started to tighten. Soon, I knew, I would have to act.

"I sent him on a business trip and told him to enjoy the local kare-kare," you replied. "I knew that you and fate would do the rest. I trusted that even after all these years, even after everything you'd been through, you would still be Tenny." You gestured to me. "And here you are."

"The Thorn Orphans all believed in you. Right to the very end." I made sure my voice dripped with disgust.

"Not Knife-Edge," you said mildly. "I always had to keep my eye on him."

"*And I was just another fire for you to chuck them in?*" I hissed.

You shrugged. "Again, something I regret. But the simple fact is this: the world didn't need the Thorn Orphans anymore. I gave them portions of my power, first to survive you and then to aid me in the task of running a city. But even the four of them together were never your equal. And that's to say nothing of what we achieved when in harmony." You smiled at me. "I'm sure you're angry at me, but that's just your temper talking. If you take a few minutes to calm yourself, I know you'll see the wisdom in forgiving me. And once we've put in the time to rebuild our trust, we can resume the good work we've always done together."

I met you with stony silence.

You sighed, resigned. "So there truly isn't anything I can say to change your mind, then? In that case—"

The floor rose up underneath us, flipping the table on to me. I sprang back just in time to avoid it from pinning me to the floor. I sensed you reaching for the door, trying to connect it to the one seven floors down where your goon squad was waiting. With a vicious spike of power, I snipped right through the knot you were tying.

"Don't even try it, Cole!" I shouted, as you staggered back clutching at your head. "This time it's just you and me!"

Fighting you alone in an apartment was actually harder than taking on the whole police department on the street. I knew perfectly well that there were innocent folks all around us, and one wrong move would be the end of them.

But as our fight wore on, I saw that you were the one being sloppy, not me. When I'd fought the Thorn Orphans—hell, when I'd fought you before—I'd been propelled by burning rage. Now, I was focused. Precise. Sunlight, perfectly captured in ice. So even as nails tore themselves out of the cabinets and hurled themselves at me, and wooden beams tried to grind me between them like molars, I was calm. I sidestepped, and spun, and danced out of harm's way. And the whole time, I listened for my cue.

And then I heard it: the lull in the music.

Time to play my solo.

I punched the air with my good hand, and our table skidded toward you like a runaway train. You threw yourself out of its way, landing on our old threadbare rug. You glanced down at your foot just in time to watch that rug snatch itself away from you.

And then you were up in the air.

And then you were hitting the floor hard.

And then I was curling my fingers over my upturned palm, and watching the floorboards curl up around you like vines.

I remembered how it had felt, listening to your approaching

footsteps as I'd lain there. I wondered if you felt the same terror, hearing mine. I didn't move in delicate clicks, like you did. My steps were a slow, thundering drumbeat.

As I came to stand over you, I drew Diwata's knife from my pocket. Held it up to make sure you could see it. "You lose, Cole."

You wrestled your mouth into a broken smile. "Did I?"

"You would've beaten anyone else. But no one knows you like I do." I grinned down at you. "They all would've missed that you were trying to die."

Real fear bled into the little show you were giving me. "What?"

I tossed the knife into the air and adeptly caught it by the hilt. You were so shocked, you didn't even flinch. "You like to tell the world that duty gets you out of bed in the morning. But I've seen you get out of bed too many times to count. I know what really puts your feet on the floor." I tossed the knife again.

"Guilt."

And caught it.

"Shame."

Another toss.

"The screams you can't escape."

Another catch.

"I've been seeing it all over the city since the moment I got back, only I didn't know what I was seeing at first," I went on, casually inspecting the knife's mirror-bright edge. "All the improvements, all the new developments … no mistaking it, it's all the work of a guilty heart. You didn't send Roulette after me. You didn't send any of the Thorn Orphans to die. You were just saying that to push me into finishing you off. And it would've fooled anyone who didn't know that this is what you do—pulling your little threads and making someone dance just how you want them."

You gazed up at me, wide-eyed. The fear on your face wasn't for your life. Clearly, yours wasn't precious to you anymore. No, I could tell: you were scared because I was seeing you.

"But here's the thing, Cole." I stared down at you over the top of my glasses, boring straight into your fearful amber eyes. "I didn't come here to kill you."

And then I let go of the floorboards that pinned you to the ground. They fell away and you sat up in a daze.

"W-what are you talking about?" you stammered.

"You like controlling other people to get what you want," I said. "The Brethren. The Thorn Orphans. Even me, when you wanted Benilda off the board for good. It's like you've never actually trusted another soul in your sad little life. And that right there? Trying to control me? Trying to make me take you out because you're too much of a coward to? That's how I figured you out. That's how you lost."

You gaped up at me. I'd never seen you more off balance. "But ... but the knife—"

"Pahingán," I said. "To us, it usually means revenge. But I've been thinking about it a while, and talking to a lot of smart people. And you know what I figured out, Cole?" I couldn't resist giving you another smirk. "Revenge is fucking stupid."

I started to pace in front of you. "Take the Thorn Orphans. We told ourselves we were doing good, but come on. You ever talk to the people who were just living their lives while we were doing our thing? We were just another crew of killers to them. Didn't matter that we had a cause. You and I had all the power in the world to make a difference here, and instead we picked revenge. I spent four years missing my power. Second I got it back, what did I use it for? Revenge. Had every tool

454

I needed to help the city again, and instead I just tore it up 'cause I was pissed. So I think I'm done with it."

You shook your head. "You can't be." And then again, much more forcefully. *"Tenny, you can't be!"*

I shrugged. "Watch me. You wanted to go to Hell knowing that as bad as you felt about what you did to me, deep down I was never any better than you. And now, every breath you get to take is proof that you were wrong. I can't think of a better way to end things between us. So, yeah. You lose."

Unsteadily, you climbed to your feet. "But the fire ... Binh ..."

"I tried to avenge Binh, and he turned out to not be worth the trouble," I said. "Tried to avenge the city, and it turned out the city didn't want me to. So I came here to settle things for myself tonight, and they feel good and settled to me."

You looked genuinely at a loss. It was something I'd never seen in you before. The Cole I'd known, the one who always knew what to say and always had a plan ... there was no sign of him now.

"I've lived all this time awaiting your judgment," you breathed. "I've lived knowing full well that I deserved it. And now you won't even give it to me?"

"No, Cole, I will not," I said. "I wanted to for a very long time, but slitting your throat ain't gonna fill the hole you punched through me. I only got the years I got, and I'm done filling them with more things I'll die regretting."

"But the other Thorn Orphans—!" you protested.

"I was angry. Afraid." I'd known it the whole time, Cole, but you were the first one to actually hear me say it, and there's power in giving ideas a voice. "When I let that guide me, it made me do shit I'll have to live with."

They flashed in front of me just then: Roulette. Anjali. Knife-Edge. The ... well, not the Monster. Only so much you could do when someone wasn't sorry. But I felt a weight on me as I thought about the Roulette, Knife-Edge, and Anjali-shaped holes I'd punched in the world. They'd had their regrets. They'd been honest with me, in their own ways. And even now ... even after all of this, Cole ...

"I should've been better than them," I said eventually. "But it ain't too late for me to be better than you."

I tried to think of what to say next. What could someone even say when they were letting go of such a big part of themselves? Nothing felt like it could actually encompass everything I was carrying inside me.

I tossed the knife down, and it stood straight up when it bit into the floor. "Be seeing you, Cole."

I'd gotten five steps away from you when you said, "I thought you might figure me out."

Don't do it, Tenny, I told myself. *Don't turn around. Not even for him.*

I turned around. You were on your feet, leaning against a torn-up wall for support.

And you were smiling.

"You were right. No one knows me better than you. If there was anyone who could see through me and divine my true intent, it would be you. In that regard, as in so many others, you're the worst enemy I could hope for." You used your shoulder to push yourself away from the wall so you could stand on your own two feet. I felt something change in the air around me as you pointed a finger at the floor. "But I'm not Roulette. I don't leave things to chance."

When you'd flipped over the table, it'd sent the kettle flying. Now, I saw that puddle of hot water on the floor starting to ripple. And then those ripples were becoming something else. A vision.

Your vision.

36

Three hours ago

Age 30

I am Mongkhul Pakuanjangnambharat.

I am the son of Suriwong Pakuanjangnambhar and Guan Ming Pakuanjangnambhar, the fifth-generation heads of House Pak. Heir to the Unified Utilities Plant. Even before the city anointed and chose me, I'd already been born highest of its citizens.

I am Cole: the White Rose, first among the Thorn Orphans. Protector. Governor. Shaman.

And right now, I'm standing outside a sheet metal house in the middle of a scrapyard, listening calmly to the sounds of a struggle from within.

"You don't have to be here for this, sir," says the officer at my side. Even though she sustained injuries in the showdown at the Plant yesterday, she's dutifully reported for her shift. I've already expressed my desire for her to rest, but I suppose I can't help the loyalty I've earned from my police department.

"I appreciate the sentiment, Lieutenant Chhorn," I tell her. "But in this particular case, I actually do have to bear witness."

457

She nods. Like everyone else, she assumes that whatever I'm doing is mystical in nature, and not for them to understand. Oftentimes, it is because I'm doing something shamanic. But it's also been a convenient smokescreen for the times I just want to be left alone.

I frown at the noises within the house. It sounds like she's really putting up a fight. My officers are under the strictest instructions to make sure she's taken alive, but I worry just the same. This won't work with a corpse. I ache to get in there and handle it myself, but I can't risk the harm a savvy person like my target might be able to inflict. Better to stay on the back lines. My task will come later, and it will be far more dangerous.

And then, the shouts grow nearer. Lieutenant Chhorn stirs as two officers appear in the doorway, dragging a half-conscious Diwata Lacanilao between them. She isn't bleeding, but she's clearly taken a hit to the head. It's the only way I would ever imagine her being so docile.

As the officers drag her closer to me, I find myself frowning as I wonder how Tenny concealed her from me all these years. Part of me supposes that she considered this family business. But I bristle at the notion that we weren't family then. We two were halves of the city's soul. How could we possibly be any closer?

One of the two arresting officers salutes me.

"We couldn't find the other occupant, sir."

I frown. I could use my powers to find them, I know, but zephyrs are as hard to grasp as their namesake. My powers let me tap into the currents of the city's past and present, and plumb them as deep as I dare, but even I never know who might owe a zephyr a favor.

I decide to let it pass for now. My top priority is Tenny. If I can persuade her to stand down, then nothing else need come

458

of this. I've never shied away from spilling blood before, but I'm not the sort of man who would reach for it as a first resort. I tell myself that would be the instinct of someone lesser, and I tell myself that the fact that the city chose me means that I am not lesser.

"Post officers nearby. If they should turn up, detain them. *Bloodlessly*," I add firmly. I know the officers are puzzled by my restraint, but they don't need the big picture.

They don't need to know what kind of fire I'm playing with right now.

Lieutenant Chhorn gives me an even stranger look when I insist on being left alone with the suspect for a moment in the back of the police wagon. But they know better than to question my powers. They leave me be, and I duck in through the back hatch and sit down on the bench opposite where she lies unconscious.

"I was going to be polite and ask if you remembered me," I say. "But I know better. Just like I know you're not asleep."

Her eyes snap open. Focus. And fix on me as she sits up.

"I've been pinched enough times to know my rights." She indicates the cold steel police van with a tilt of her head. "Guess you ain't even pretending to be the law anymore?"

It unsettles me, how much I see echoes of Tenny in her: her voice. Her vocabulary. Her posture. Even some of the expressions her face slides into. But I push that aside: a deed in which I'm well practiced.

"You're playing a game of pektong where you can see only your hand," I tell her. "I can see everyone's tiles. I alone understand what's at stake here. And while you don't believe it now, the day will come when you think of what I've done today and feel gratitude for where it led us."

Diwata looks at me with the hardened eyes of a career killer. I don't know what she's been up to since she went

459

underground, apart from associating with a zephyr. But when I study her, I see the woman she was: the most feared blade in the Lacanilao family ... if only because everyone underestimated Dalisa.

"We have something fairly significant in common, you know," I try. "We both care about Tenny very much. To both of us, she's family."

"Says the bastard who tried to kill her," she spits.

"Not a subject where you can profess innocence, Diwata." I fold my arms over my chest. My vocabulary is formidable, but suddenly I find myself unable to put together the right combination of words. I hastily compose a speech for her benefit, then trash it. The best thing I can be right now is direct.

"How ... did you do it?" I say quietly. "After all that transpired between you, how did you get her to forgive you?"

She sits back. In the spirit's song, I can hear the tremors of her surprise. That wasn't the question she expected from me at all. I tamp down a flutter of annoyance. Why do they always expect me to be some sneering serial villain? I've done everything for this city. Sacrificed everything that matters to me, all to balance the scales for the wrongs done by my family. Why does no one take a moment to look past my office and see that?

"Well," she says eventually, with another weary glance at the police van, "I sure as shit didn't do this."

Her words sting me. I open my mouth to defend myself, but the reminder hits me like a balm: I don't need to explain myself to her. I was misguided to think that I had to show her this much of myself, even.

She sees me seething and chuckles. "You and your little plans. You fucking know my sister. You really think she's just gonna go along with them?"

I decide to try a new countenance. When I answer now, my

460

voice is dangerous and controlled, like a blue gas flame. "Your very life depends on her doing so."

"Please. She already tried to let me die once. I ain't enough leverage to make her do what you want. She's only ever wanted to use me. It's why the two of you get along."

It would probably convince anyone else, I think. But even if I didn't have shamanic powers to help me divine the truth, her similarities to her sister render her transparent in my eyes.

"I disagree with that assessment, Diwata. You don't seem to understand that you're everything to her."

I rise and gesture for the door to open so I can leave. I've said all I need to say.

"Yeah?" she snarls at my back. "How do you figure that?"

The door opens, drenching the back of the van in white light. And I don't bother to look back as I reply, "Because she has nothing else left."

37
Now

Age 30

I surfaced from the vision and gulped down a fresh breath, like I'd been drowning in that puddle. I stood there, stunned.

And then in zero seconds flat I was right up on you, pinning you to the wall with my good hand. "*Where is she?*"

"Still alive," you rasped. "And she'll stay that way if you do what you need to."

My head spun. I'd been so certain that Diwata and Pamin would be safe. You hadn't clocked either of them before. I found myself heaping all kinds of curses on to my shoulders for not seeing it. That had always been your way: knowing just the right thread to pull, and pulling it just hard enough.

"I don't deserve to live anymore, Tenny," you went on. "You were right. I've built high, but on a hollow foundation. And in the absence of justice, that foundation will never sustain the weight of our city forever. I spent four years trying to run from that fact. But now, you can finally deliver that justice. Avenge my victims. Avenge yourself. And then," you breathed, "take your rightful place at the city's head."

"What if instead," I growled, "I say 'Fuck that,' and then beat the shit out of you until you tell me where my sister is?"

You shook your head. "She won't die unless absolutely necessary. But if you take too long, my officers will follow their orders. Surely then you'll have no choice. If you act now, though"—you paused to wince from the pain you were in, courtesy of my hand on your windpipe—"you can finish this and save her. Just let me help you these last few steps on your path."

I'd kept a pretty good grip on myself this whole time, but now desperation and disgust warred in me. I wished I could say I saw this coming, Cole. You've never been too high-minded to hit someone's pressure points. But somehow, I'd let myself be stupid enough to think that even after everything else you'd done, you'd still draw that line when it came to me.

"I could just toss you aside now," I said. "Go out there and find her myself. The spirit would tell me where to find her."

You shook your head. "You know how that would end. The moment you let me go, I could block your powers. Get there before you and finish her off. And even if you beat me there, there's no way to approach without them seeing you coming."

You were laying out a case for triumph, even though there was nothing triumphant about your face and voice. Instead, I only saw grim determination. The kind of mettle that might drive someone to provoke the death you wanted.

My jaw worked furiously. You were right: I had all the power in the world right now. But I felt like I was back on that boathouse floor, unable to so much as lift a finger. No matter what I did, you'd found a way to box me in. My brain raced down one path after another, but at the end of each one there was either your body or Diwata's. I refused to accept either.

But how could I escape your trap when you'd already thought of every way out?

463

"Please," I said, "call them off. She doesn't need to be part of this."

"I didn't want her to be." I had no reason to believe you, but somehow I did anyway. "You've once again left me without other options. Stop trying to pretend we're different. Take your revenge." That hardness in your eyes receded, and suddenly you looked so tired. "You've seen the same horrible machinery I have, that sits at the core of this city. It takes an exceptional person to stop it, and exceptional deeds to change the way its gears turn. You have a moral imperative, Tenny. *If you can do anything, do everything.*"

"*The world don't work that way, Cole!*" I roared in your face. "It's a pendulum! You can't make it swing at gunpoint! However hard you push it, it'll always. Push. Back."

You shook your head. "The world can change, and so can its people ... with help. Guidance. The city itself empowered you for this purpose. And as long as you have that power, I'm going to make sure you use it to do the right thing."

The machinery of my brain braked hard.

The way out. You had no idea, but you'd just given it to me.

I thought it through. Thought it through again. It would work. There was no guarantee I'd survive it, but it would work. Dread and sadness hit me, a one-two punch to the gut.

I didn't want to do this, Cole. I didn't want to lose this part of myself.

I fought those feelings back. This wasn't about me. It was about my city. My sister. About making sure you didn't get what you wanted. It was about doing anything and everything.

And I would have to do it fast.

It was difficult to split my focus between where I was and where I was looking for, but I couldn't betray to you what I was doing. You were a clever man. If I gave you even a single thread, you'd be able to reason out what sort of sweater it had come from.

But I had some things I could count on. You would never send her out of the city, for instance. Your power didn't extend past city limits, and there was no one in the world you trusted enough to take Diwata beyond your own reach. I knew wherever she was, it was somewhere you could get to her.

And if you could . . . so could I.

So as I sang out into the city for a sign of my sister, I made sure to meet your gaze. I relaxed my grip on your throat, and you breathed deep. "You really think this is gonna make up for what you've done, huh?" I said. "One life for all the ones you've taken?"

"And a Driftwood City left in the hands of a worthy heir," you said. "You couldn't ask for better justice."

I shook my head. "Ain't the job of the guilty to set their sentence."

You cocked your head, listening. "I can hear you trying to find her. Go ahead. It makes no difference now. There's only the choice you've been presented with. Now: make it." You stared imploringly into my eyes. "*Please.*"

Even as you called my shot, I heard it: a resonating flute sounded from deep in the Shoots. It was a shipyard, big and open: no doors nearby, so even if I teleported myself to the nearest one it'd be easy to spot my approach. You were right; there was no way I could sneak up on them.

But fortunately, I wouldn't have to.

The song in my ears took on mournful strings and a low, slow horn. It didn't feel like regret just yet, but it would in a moment. When the notes came together into an unasked question, my heart swelled damn near to breaking.

But I sang back, *Yes.*

I cried out and dropped you. You fell to the floor, and I collapsed right next to you, clutching my head.

"What are you doing?" You looked at me with fresh fear. "What's happening?"

And while you asked pointless questions, I screamed like I was being torn in half.

It was as if every single song I'd ever heard had burst to life between my ears. Hundreds of horns, thousands of strings, thundering drums, and endless clashing voices. It swirled around me, and the whole room spun. Your own shape twisted in my vision like you were trapped in a warped-out mirror. And then, that mirror shattered.

Shards of history blew past me: of this apartment. Of this building. Of us. In fleeting glimpses, I saw a thousand breakfasts at our table. A thousand late nights poring over blueprints and street maps. A thousand times when it was just you and me against the rest of the world, and the odds had been in our favor.

It was worse than that day in the boathouse, Cole. Worse than feeling the Monster snap my last splinter. Something at my core was tearing fiber by fiber, but I didn't feel it as mere pain. It was something stronger, the kind of thing that could poison a person long after their pain faded away. But I recognized it for the old friend it was, because I'd survived it before.

Grief. Powerful enough to dim the stars and chill the sun.

And the more I let go, the more grief flooded in to fill what was left.

The music in my ears was gaining tempo, gaining pitch, crescendoing, faster and higher and louder and faster and higher and louder and faster and higher and louder and—

—silence. Horrible, horrible silence.

I was kneeling on the floor. All around me, the room was

466

flatter, like it had gone from three dimensions to two. Your hair looked less like shining silver, and more like bleached white. In my ears, silence howled.

Your lip quivered. You hadn't seen the full picture yet, but there was no way you hadn't felt all that. "What ... did you just do?"

"What do you think?" I rose, a pained grin on my face. "You put me in a corner. I got out of it. And you know the best part, Cole? You're the one who taught me how."

"W-what do you mean?"

"I really thought you had me here," I went on. "You knew every pressure point to hit, and you hit them just hard enough to get me on my knees. You'd predicted what I would do. And you'd predicted what I wouldn't do. But you didn't predict what you've already done."

"*Will you stop talking in circles?*" you barked, pushing yourself back to your feet.

"I was just enjoying myself, but fine." I made myself smile, even as tears started to stream from my tired eyes. "You were only able to beat me because you gave away a bit of your power to the other Thorn Orphans. And look around. That gamble got you all the money in the pot. So I thought, why not try it myself?"

Your expression slid from anger to shock. And then, as your keen mind chewed and swallowed what I'd just served it: horror. "You ... You didn't."

Unsteadily, I climbed to my feet. "The spirit's gone from me, Cole. For good. And I think you can guess where I sent it."

"She ..." You staggered back from me, your voice numb with disbelief. "My officers will still be able to—"

"The spirit helps us learn how to use its gifts. You know that. With nothing but pure instinct, I was able to put out the biggest fire in the city with only my mind ... and you were

467

able to start it," I added venomously. "What do you think she'll be capable of, after all those years of watching us in action?"

"How much did you give her?" I didn't need my shaman ears to know what kind of harsh, minor music must've been playing in your head right now. "*How much?*"

It was deeply satisfying to know how much it probably hurt you to see me smiling right now. "Well, I didn't have time to divide it up into neat little toys for her," I said cheerfully. "So I just gave her all of it."

"*No!*" you shouted, like that was gonna make any kind of difference. "She's a thug! And you gave her the power she needs to remake our city forever! *What the* fuck *were you thinking?*"

Every muscle in my body tensed as I stared you down.

"I was thinking that she's my sister."

Behind me, I felt a dangerous tremor pass through the floor.

"That she's my friend."

In my pocket, my hand closed around Diwata's knife.

"And I was thinking that I trust her."

The floor rose up like a wooden tidal wave. I could've dodged it, but I was too tired, too beat up. And while before there might've been a song to tell me how to dance away from it, now there was only the silence.

The wood folded me right in two. I was lifted right off my feet, landed hard on my shoulder blades, and skidded across the floor—

—until another wall of wood rose up to stop me. I slammed against it with a grunt, and I was pretty sure I felt some shit break. I bent in on myself, twitching like a bug that a boot hadn't finished off just yet.

Click. Click. Click.

And there were the boots, right on cue.

It's a funny thing, the way life keeps bringing you back to a moment. Here I was, torn up to shit, lying on the floor, powerless to do anything but listen to my death's approaching footsteps.

But you wanna know something, Cole? I didn't feel the fear anymore. I felt peace.

I also felt like my ribcage had been crushed to splinters, but mostly it was peace.

You looked down at me with haunted eyes that were all out of tears to cry. I could see every one of the million questions you wanted to ask me, all of them practically tattooed on your face. But the only one you managed to get out was a broken "Why?"

I coughed and tasted blood. Not good. But there was a decent chance I'd just pushed you far enough that it wouldn't matter in a moment. "'Cause I'm the worst."

You shook your head ruefully. "No, you're not," you said. "You're the most incredible person I've ever met. I've wanted to be a lot of things on my own, but you're the only one who made me want to be better."

I coughed again. "Considering how," I said, "we've ended up ... I don't know if that means you did a bad job ... or I did."

You blinked back tears. I couldn't even bring myself to be mad at you for crying them. Letting go of the spirit had torn me apart like nothing else I'd ever done, but somehow everything about this moment felt right.

"Hey, Cole," I said. "Wanna hear something I've never told anyone?"

You breathed deep. Nodded.

"I wanted to die every day I was dead," I said. "Couldn't actually bring myself to do it. Hell, I wanted to die yesterday, and I couldn't do it again. Walking in here, I thought there

469

was a more than halfway chance all this would take me the rest of the way, too." I sighed, and my whole ribcage lit up like a pachinko machine. "But now that we're both here, I kinda want a tomorrow."

You smiled ruefully. "You could've had it."

And you clenched your fist.

I don't know if you burst a gas line, or made the wrong wires touch, or what. All I know is that at your command, flames rose all around the apartment. Sparks spat, and in moments the air was thick with stinking smoke. I had no choice but to breathe it in, and as the heat started to singe my cheeks I choked on our history.

You sank to your knees next to me, exhausted. Put a hand on my shoulder. Gripped it with a friendliness I welcomed.

"I lied earlier," you said. "I am sorry. For everything, Tenny. I wish I'd been a strong enough man to make it right." In your silver hair, the firelight danced.

I smiled weakly. "Wish you'd been that, too." I lay next to you and waited.

You frowned, in thought. "I welcome my overdue death, but you just told me you want to live on." All around, the fire marched toward us. "How can you be so at peace now?"

I let Diwata answer for me.

Your head jerked up as the roof groaned. And then, like the top of a sardine can, the whole thing ripped itself right off the building. You glanced around wildly as a downpour pelted on to your fires. They fought hard, but there was no denying the rain. All around you, those fires sputtered and went out. The heat dissipated, returning me to the sweet cold.

And two heavy boots hit the deck as Diwata landed hard on the floor. She strode toward us, an angry goddess in coveralls. *"Hands off my sister."*

You let your hand fall away from me. Took in the sputtering

470

ashes of your final plan. You bowed your head, presenting her with your bare neck. "Finish it."

Diwata raised her hand, then glanced at me.

And I shook my head.

You opened your eyes in surprise to see that you were still breathing as Diwata helped me to my feet. "You can't," you said as my sister started to carry me away. "You can't just leave me like this. Tenny, you owe me justice!"

I nudged Dawa's side so she'd stop. I glanced back at you over my shoulder, even though it was absolute murder on my neck. "I know I do," I said. "So why the hell would I give you exactly what you want?" I nodded to Diwata, and she helped me hobble to the door.

"I don't know what the fuck you did to me," she said. "But thanks. I think I'm gonna like being a wizard." Concern bled into her angular face. "Did it hurt?"

I winced. "You survived losing half your soul, right? Figure that means I can, too."

Pity flashed across my sister's face. And for once, I didn't hate her for it.

We were almost to the door when you shouted again to our retreating backs. "*But how?* How am I supposed to keep living with myself?"

"You sure I can't hit him just a little bit?" Diwata whispered to me. I shook my head.

"Don't rightly know, Cole," I called back. "But I hope you choose to."

And then we were through the door: not into the hallway, but exiting out of a telephone booth onto an empty street corner. A few blocks away, sirens wailed. I turned and managed to get one last glimpse of you, a dot of silver amid the black. And then Dawa waved her hand and the door slammed shut.

"I knew the White Rose was a bastard's bastard," said Dawa. "And I knew he was a tough opponent. But by the Bird, I had no idea the guy was such a whiner."

I shook my head. "He's just in pain."

She rolled her eyes. "Fuck him. We all are."

I grunted in agreement and wrapped an arm around my ribcage. "Speaking of ..."

As I slumped forward, my vision going black, I knew I wouldn't hit the wooden gutter.

I trusted my sister would catch me.

Part Eight

Anything and Everything!
The City of Roses Every Day

38

Twelve years ago

Age 18

We were at my dining table, counting stacks of money. You'd only been living with me for a week, so I still thought of it as *my* dining table. By the time the next week came, that would change: it would be *our* dining table. *Our* window. *Our* couch (which was also *your* bed). So soon, Cole, sooner than I could've dreamed, I'd be thinking of that apartment as *our* home.

But the cash on the table? That was definitely *our* stolen bootlegger money.

We'd boosted it from one of Benilda's trucks. The driver belonged to Loongon, the captain who was easily the weakest link in her organization. Guy was no criminal mastermind, and he wasn't even particularly fierce. He'd just been around for a while, and leaned on the weight of the Lacanilao name to make sure people didn't fuck with him.

It had made him the perfect target.

The truck had been easy enough to knock over. You'd stood right in its path, and willed the street to flip up like a spatula and spill the truck on to its side. When the driver tried to crawl their way out, I was already waiting for them. They put up a decent fight, but I could've beaten them easy on a bad day. With the power of Driftwood City's spirit behind me, I didn't even have to try.

"*H-hey ...*" they had said. I'd left them heaped in the gutter, as you made the street flip the truck back on to its tires. I'd been wearing a carpenter's mask and a flatcap, and we'd used the spirit to kill all the nearby lights, but I froze just the same. Had this driver somehow managed to catch sight of my face?

"*You ... don't know ... who you're messing with ...*" they wheezed.

I relaxed.

"Sure I do," I said. "It used to belong to Nanay Benilda. The same way this city used to belong to her. But we left you alive so you could let her know for us: the Slats are under new management. And soon enough, she ain't gonna have the water or the cash to enjoy ros—"

"Tenny."

I blinked hard and looked up to find you sitting across from me. Your cash was neatly stacked, while mine was in a mostly uncounted pile. Your teacup was empty, while mine was half-full and all cold.

You smiled. It was still a slightly uncomfortable expression on your face, like a shirt you hadn't quite grown into yet. But it was a good deal more relaxed than you'd been when we'd had our first conversation. "Welcome back," you said. "Reliving past glories? Say, from the last hour or so?"

"Hoy. You did cool shit, too. You seriously telling me you're not thinking about it?"

You put up your hands. Laughed softly. "No, I'm definitely having a hard time focusing." You toyed with the bottom button of your black waistcoat. "I suppose I'm nervous because I've never done this before."

"What?" I asked. "Magic shit? Targeted vigilantism? Staying out past nine?"

You mustered up a bittersweet smile. "Something that matters."

As I went back to my count, you stood up and walked over to admire the small stack of wooden crates we'd managed to bring upstairs. They were full of fresh water, straight from Benilda's underground stills. There were only eight crates here; the rest were all still in the truck, which we'd hidden in a garage near our place. The plan was to give it all away, but we'd have to go slow ... at least, until we found a place we could use to store and traffic the water we stole.

The take was small. The effect, just as small. Redistribution was gonna be a slow, careful game, and at any point someone could rat us out to Benilda.

But it was a start.

I set down my finished count and got up to join you. Together, we stood there and looked down on our meager take with pride.

You cleared your throat. "I don't wish to pry."

My turn to smile. Mine came to me a lot more naturally. Practice and all that. "Exactly the kind of thing a person says right before they jut a crowbar into you."

"When you gave that driver one last parting shot, you said something about Benilda. What was it?"

My glasses had slipped down my nose, and I rammed them back into place. "How could you even hear me?"

You looked oddly bashful for someone who'd just ripped off the biggest and scariest bootlegger in Driftwood City. "The wind carried it to me. The actual wind, not a zephyr, mind you. I still don't totally know how it works, myself."

"So if it did that, you know exactly what I said, little guy."

"Yes, I know you used the phrase 'roses every day,'" you

admitted. "I suppose what I was asking you was ... what does it mean, exactly?"

I weighed how much I wanted to tell you. We'd had a good week of living together, and you knew that I at least had some familiarity with the Lacanilaos. But to answer your question, I was gonna have to tell you more about me than I'd told anyone since I started working the line at the Plant.

"How much you know about Nanay Benilda?" I said eventually.

"Well." You ran your fingers through your silver hair. "I know she's a savvy businesswoman with talents that would have been appreciated on the Rock, if life worked differently."

I didn't laugh so much as grunt. The day a Biranese person got any respect from the parasites up on the Rock was a hell of a ways off.

"I know she has interests in water bootlegging, unregulated gambling, and sex work. I know that a lot of people have tried to have her killed, and none of them are still among the living. I know she throws an elaborate street festival in Birantown for the Feast of the First Flight, where she personally feeds every Biranese person in the streets. I know that she ... ah ..." You gave me a weak smile. "Likes ... hats?"

That time, I really did laugh.

"I don't know what you want from me here." Now you were the irritable one in our conversation. The tips of your ears were only a little red, but your hair made them stand out all the more. That was the moment I realized that my new friend was the kind of guy who didn't like not knowing an answer. A small moment, like so many to come after it, where I came closer to knowing you.

I wrestled for a moment longer with what I was going to say next. But I realized: it was stupid to hold back. You and I had fought a fire together. Stuck up a water truck together. And given how small my place was, it was only a matter of time before one of us was gonna catch the other shirtless.

"Don't feel too bad," I said. "I set you up there. It's a loaded question, asking a guy what he knows about a woman you know better than anyone."

You did an actual full-on double take, like something out of a motion picture. "What?" you said. "But how . . .?"

I shrugged as noncommittally as I could. "When your mom dies, a kid's gotta wind up somewhere, right?"

Your eyes went wide as spotlights. I was accustomed to seeing fear spread across someone's face when they realized who I was, but you came from a world where the people had nothing to fear from Benilda Lacanilao. She was nothing more than a thug to you people. To you, what she'd built barely amounted to more than an anthill, even if it was more than the rest of us would ever have.

But instead of judgment or disdain, you nodded for me to go on.

"In addition to hats," I said, "Benilda likes flowers. Has herself a whole greenhouse in the back of her estate. I ain't ever been up to the Rock, but I bet it'd measure up against anything you could find there."

You made a snooty little scoffing noise that I chose to ignore, 'cause I was a good friend.

"On top of that, she keeps roses in vases and pots all over the house. Almost every room's got at least one fresh rose in it at all times. Makes the whole place smell great, for one thing."

"I bet," you said distantly. I wondered if you were trying to conjure up the phantom scent of a rose yourself. Even talking about it, I could feel it creeping into my nose: sweet and grassy and kind of soapy, except in a good way. I remembered smelling it while helping Benilda mince garlic, or when I was sitting on the bed with her and Indawat, listening to them tell me a story. It was a smell that made me think of fresh brewed lapsang tea, and birthday lumpia, and sure fingers braiding my hair.

"But the thing about fresh roses is that they're pricey … both on their own, and in terms of the water they need to stay alive." Dalisa had run the numbers for me and Diwata once, just as a thought exercise. We were a house that never had to worry about where our next gulp of water was gonna come from, but I'd been floored all the same.

"So one day I flat-out asked Benilda, 'Why do you spend all this money on roses? Why not pay your soldiers more, or build more apartments in Birantown? Why throw money down a hole?' You know what she said?"

I noticed that I was borrowing my storytelling voice from you. I'd always been in the habit of coming at things straight on. All this buildup, all this introduction … that was something I'd learned from you. We'd barely known each other a week, and already you'd made a mark on me.

Gotta be honest, Cole: I didn't hate it.

"What?" you asked.

I smiled a storyteller's smile. It felt like the right thing to do here. "She said, 'I do it because roses make me happy.' That was all."

You recoiled, which in this case meant scooting your flat ass a few inches across our bare floor. "That's horrible," you whispered. "How can she be so callous? At least my family doesn't pretend to be some dignified class of public servant, and *why are you laughing at me?*"

"Because you're such a smart boy," I said. "And yet, if my point was the ground under your feet, you'd still find a way to miss it."

Near as I could tell a week in, the city wouldn't let us directly read each other the way we could other people. But I

480

didn't need my shaman powers to tell me you were annoyed. The flushed tips of your ears were all the hint I needed.

"Benilda was right, Cole," I said. "If you've got money, you should be allowed to spend it on the little things that make you happy, not just what you need. It's the difference between surviving and living. So now that you and I are here, that's what I'm using as the north on my compass. I wanna make a Driftwood City where ordinary folks can have enough water to make their own garden, if that's what makes them happy. Benilda shouldn't live like the rest of us. We should all live like Benilda."

Your annoyance had burned down to embers while I was talking. Now, as I reached my point, I saw something more reverent spark in your face.

"Roses every day," you whispered, more to yourself than to me. It was like you were tasting it.

I let you have the moment. Your brain made you intimidating as hell, even if I towered over you. It felt good to see that even someone like me could teach you something.

When you next looked at me, that spark in your eye had blossomed into a flame. "I want to use that," you said fervently. "Not just before we plunge into a job. I want that to be our calling, our symbol, our purpose. I want that to be our name."

I raised an eyebrow. "A name? Like we're a gang now?"

"Not a gang," you said. "But it does help for things to have names. Ideas are big and wild and they can grow into all kinds of unpredictable things. But to give an idea a name is to give it shape. When there's shape, there's order. And where there's order, there's understanding."

The words had a practiced texture to them, like a prayer that'd been drilled into you. If I had to guess, it was probably something one of your dads had brought you up to think. But while part of me automatically distrusted anything that came from the people who sat up atop the Rock, I begrudgingly guessed they couldn't be wrong about everything.

"All right," I said. "So a name. What're you thinking?"

You had your answer at the ready. "I think we're two people, born into different types of privilege, willingly turning our backs on our birthrights to pursue a higher call. And I think that your mantra—"

"Our mantra," I said, my voice suddenly firm.

Your smile was small but real. "*Our* mantra," you agreed, "has provided us with precisely the symbol we need. I think our name should be ..."

Even though we stood close to each other, I leaned in so I could hear you better.

"The Rose Soldiers."

The name didn't take flight, so much as just ... hang there.

"Well," I said with a laugh as you hung your head, "we can keep workshopping it."

39
Now

Age 30

Two days later, the front page of the *Meyongphirin Blue Star* ran a photograph: a white rose lying amid the wreckage of an apartment building. Its petals were crushed and stained with dark flecks. Didn't take a genius to figure out what they were.

And above it, a headline screamed:

GOVERNOR GHOULISHLY GUTTED

I dropped the paper on Pamin's table.

"Fucking Kueiyang."

"Was he even wearing a rose at your ... sit-down?" said the zephyr.

"You're supposed to be the know-it-all," I said. "What do you think?"

They smirked, then riffled through the dropped paper and pulled out the middle section. "I hope the comics are good today."

While they read the funny pages, I glanced through the

rest of the article. Surprisingly, it was a lot more respectful than its header. It talked about your childhood as Mongkhul Pakuanjangnambharat. Your adulthood as Cole. Your work as the city's first governor. It even elaborated on the miraculous and incredible powers you'd demonstrated, unlike anything Driftwood City had ever seen before. And of course, there was a single paragraph about the other work you'd done:

> Before creating and assuming his post, Cole was active as the ringleader of a vigilante outfit, the self-styled Thorn Orphans. Under the moniker of the White Rose, he masterminded a years-long campaign to support the nascent labor movement and undercut entrenched forces of organized crime. His dramatic unmasking coincided with his final act as the White Rose: the violent dethroning of his own family. As Governor, he was always candid about the act: "It was the first installment paid down in a long-standing debt to the people of Driftwood City."

I was pretty impressed at how well you'd been able to spin murdering your own family.

But then, you'd always known how to frame a story.

For the next week, the city mourned. I'd expected that: the memorials popping up on every street corner. The loving tributes broadcast on the radio and printed in even the smallest neighborhood circulars. The glasses lifted in your name at bars in every borough. But I hadn't expected it to be so much. I couldn't hear the song of the city anymore, but I could imagine it: stately and minor and inescapable.

I was there when your funeral march proceeded through the streets of Driftwood City. Everywhere I looked, I saw scarves and hats and coats and garlands and sashes, all in shades of white. Clutched in the hands of each and every person crowding the streets: a single white rose. It was even snowing. You couldn't have planned it better yourself. Hell, I wouldn't have been surprised to learn that you had somehow.

"You can't smell it anymore, can you?" said Dawa.

My sister cut a much more impressive figure than I did, standing on the rooftop. She wasn't wearing some kind of special shaman uniform or anything; just a long black dress and a short white coat. Her black hair was flecked with fallen snowflakes, and the chill put a flush on her cheeks and eartips. But even if I hadn't known what was up with her, my eye would've wandered to her naturally. Was this how the rest of the world had been treating me all this time?

"I was never so good on the smells," I said. "I always experienced it as music. You telling me you don't?"

She shook her head and tapped her nose.

There was an absence in me where my power had once lived, and now it throbbed like an old war wound. "What's it smell like?"

"With all those roses?" She took a deep sniff of the cold air, then barked a visible laugh. "Smells like her greenhouse."

I clenched my fist at my side. *You chose this*, I reminded myself. But funny enough, it didn't magically make the wrenching feeling in my chest go away.

Eventually, your funeral motorcade came around. I didn't see the cars first; I saw what came just ahead of them. Like a pearly wave, every mourner on the street raised their roses high, so that a field of flowers was waiting for you wherever you went.

Diwata and I both watched it drive past. In its wake, people stormed the barricades and flooded the street, so that you were being sent off by an informal parade of white flowers.

"Look at them, grieving over an empty car," I said bitterly.

485

Casually, Diwata produced a smoke and lit up. "You know it's empty, and they think it isn't. Which do you think really matters more?"

I shot her a look. "Just because you're a shaman doesn't give you a license to get cryptic on me, now."

She flashed me a grin. "Call it payback."

I glanced down at the mourners again. All those people, so devoted to you. They were bawling their fucking eyes out in the street over you. They'd gone all-out to give you the thing we'd always wanted: a rose for every citizen in Driftwood City. Not a single one of them knew who they mourned, and I hated them for it.

I was different. I knew who you were. And I knew they couldn't possibly come close to understanding what it meant to mourn you.

The wind stung particularly hard at the narrow trails my tears had carved down my cheeks. The snow at my feet was flecked with bald spots where they'd fallen. And the harder I tried to get myself back under control, the harder it got. I felt stupid; I knew I didn't need to be doing this. But after years of my life being one thing, I could feel it coming to a sudden end. And even if they'd been the worst years of my life, I couldn't stop myself from feeling the ache of letting go.

I stiffened as Diwata rested a gentle hand between my shoulder blades. I looked over at her, but she was staring straight ahead, eyes dry and a half-smoked cigarette dangling from her lips.

For the rest of that cigarette, we just stood there together.

"You wanna know something, Dawa?" I said eventually. "Something I never told anyone?"

She shrugged. "Bet you're gonna tell me anyway."

"Even when I hated the guy, even when I would've given anything to have him kneeling in front of me and a knife in

486

my hand ... I missed him." I looked out at the city as it grew whiter and whiter. "That mean I'm stupid or something?"

"'Course it doesn't." She dropped the spent smoke at her feet, where it melted all the snow it landed on.

"Ah, what the hell do you know about it?" My gruff tone was both a joke, and not.

She met my stare evenly. "Sometimes I missed you."

It hit me so suddenly, I nearly burst into tears again. But we didn't have time for that. We had to get going, and both of us knew it.

The streets of Birantown were snowy, just like the rooftop. It would probably be a few hours until the snowplows got to them. There were children playing in it: building forts, sliding on trash can lids, throwing clumps of it at each other's heads. We emerged from the doorway of a laundry, where the dryer steam had kept a five-foot halo of bare wood around the front stoop.

"You're doing good with that," I said as the door shut behind us. It was the same chill here that I'd felt up on the rooftop across town, but somehow it felt more familiar. Probably just a trick my head was playing on me, but it felt real enough. "You're gonna be a hell of a shaman."

Diwata accepted the compliment with a quick smile, then got serious. "I've been thinking."

I knew where this was going and sped up my walk. "I already told you no."

"You don't gotta punish yourself, Ten," she said. "You did what you did because it was the only way to win. And it ain't like I don't appreciate what you did. But this was ... part of you."

The thought made me trip over my own feet. The emptiness the spirit left behind screamed to be filled. It was right there, offering itself up, and my longing for it ran deep as marrow.

"Was," I agreed. Snow crunched underfoot as I sped up again.

"Even if the city does need a shaman ..." she tried. Her breath was growing short. "It ain't me."

I started walking faster. "You never gave up on Driftwood City, even when it gave you every reason in the world to. When *I* gave you every reason to. You stuck around. Stayed connected. Cared about the place. Made your own little corner better. Sounds like a good candidate for shaman to me."

"What," she puffed, "am I ... even ... supposed to ... do ...?"

I rounded on her. "For one thing, stop smoking." I jabbed a finger under her nose. "That shit killed Tatay Indawat, remember? Even if you weren't gonna be looking out for the people of Driftwood City, you should've quit. Now, you got responsibilities. You ain't gonna fulfill them if you're busy hacking up a lung every time you jump from one rooftop to the next."

Diwata was starting to look a bit wild-eyed in addition to breathless. "You know ... I could just ... crush you with my ... wizard powers ... right?"

"Maybe you could kick my ass now." I smirked. "But you'd get your own handed to you by a flight of stairs."

"But what am I supposed to do?" she said, after she'd caught her breath. "If you ain't gonna let me give it back to you, how am I supposed to use it?"

I shrugged. "Cole and I had to figure it out for ourselves."

She scowled at me.

"But we didn't have what you've got." I flashed her a grin. "Someone like me."

"Is it too late for me to go back to being his hostage, or ...?"

I shoved her in the shoulder. "You know what I've done. You know how I fucked up, so you know how you can do better. And when it's possible, we can talk, so you don't gotta be alone with this."

She absorbed this with a small, muted nod. "Then give me something to go on here. What am I supposed to do?"

The words hovered on the tip of my tongue, the answer I'd lived by for twelve whole years. Your answer.

Anything and everything.

"Your best," I said.

She stared at me. "The fuck's that supposed to mean?"

"It means you try to fix things, but you don't try to run them. You trust that the folks here are all trying their best. And when one of them tries their best to be the worst, you step in and do something about it. You do all you can to lift up the people on the edges until they can see eye to eye with the ones sitting pretty in the middle. When the middle tries to push, you step up and push back. The rest of the time, just help them all build something that'll last. Do better than we did."

Diwata cast an eye around the neighborhood. "You did just fine."

"Nah," I said. "This all looks nice, but you think any of it will hold together without me or Cole keeping it that way? Neither of us built something to last. Though at least he did better than me." Despite the chill around us, I caught myself thinking of warm, steamy Biranba, and how old everything there had been. "That kind of permanence, it can't come from just one person. Even if that person's a w—" I hesitated at the word.

"A what?" said Diwata, sensing the opportunity.

"You know what."

"Then say it."

"That's it, I've changed my mind. You can give the powers back now."

"*Say it.*" Only two syllables, but she made them take their sweet time, in that sing-song way every older sibling in history magically knows how to do.

I sighed. "A wizard."

She chewed on that for the rest of our walk. Neither of us had said a word about it, but I think both of us had known where we were headed.

The wreckage of the Lacanilao house had been tied up for the three years following its collapse. Nothing had been built there. Clearly, once I'd been taken out of the picture, you'd gotten to work on it. No trace of the old house remained. But in its place, I had to admit you'd built something not half-bad.

The park was full of families. They wore white roses and armbands, but I tried not to think about that. Instead, I focused on the parents. The kids were carefree because of course they were. They were kids. It was a nice snow out, and it hadn't been lying around long enough to turn nasty colors. But the parents were the real indicator. When I looked at them, I didn't see worry. They weren't taking the chance to whisper to each other about how they were going to make rent or put food on the table. They were just there at a park with their kids, enjoying a moment.

"You know," I said, "I never went back to my old house. Thought I wouldn't be able to handle the visions I'd get of my mom. And I reckon I was probably right. But I think you'll probably be fine if you hang out here, Dawa. Just know that you might see Sasa every now and then."

She just nodded. "I already do."

I slipped my hands into my pockets and turned to go.

"Hang on," Diwata said. "You said you'd build something, too, if you succeeded. You gonna keep that promise? Or am I gonna have to dust off my knife?"

I nodded, and some unmelted snowflakes fell off the brim

490

of my cap. "I'm gonna start small, though. Work my way up from there."

I could tell she was listening to see if I was lying. At last, she nodded. "You do what you gotta, Tenny. But I'm serious. This city needs you, too."

I smiled at them both: my sister and my city.

"I know," I told them. "But it ain't the only one who does."

You see a city from the sky, Cole, and you see all of it. But when you see a city from the street, you see all of what it is. You glimpse into windows, and you see lives being led. You hear ferries sloshing through the boatway canals as their passengers huddle together and swap stories about where they were when the Governor died. You smell the sweetness of fresh mango, deep out of season, as the newspaper vendor slides a knife through its neon-orange flesh. You note the way streets intersect, and remember that it's because the founders of the city had three different companies working off different maps to build this whole place.

And when you open your ears wide enough, Cole, it's impossible not to hear the music.

Pleasant, chilly numbness crept up my toes and feet as I made my way through the Slats, block by block. By the time I reached the front step of the three-story triplex, I could barely feel my feet anymore. It was a feeling I'd missed.

Phuong answered the door after only one knock. It was like she'd known who would be waiting on her doorstep. Without a word, she let me in to a home that was cozy, and warm, and empty.

The living room was still a caved-in disaster, so she led me to the kitchen where a tray of warm rice balls and a pot of smoky lapsang tea waited.

I took off my new glasses and used the hem of my shirt to wipe away the fog on them. "You expecting someone?"

"I always put out full tea in case someone comes home," Phuong said, taking her seat opposite me. Primly, she slid the tray of rice balls my way. When I took a bite into one, I got the sweet-sour of chopped pickled plums, the kind that came in jars from Honton overseas. She waited until I ate the whole thing before she said, "I imagine we both have things we regret."

I sipped my tea. Waited until I put my chipped cup down to nod in agreement.

"So," she said. "Was it you?"

I nodded again. Didn't need to ask to know what she was talking about.

She accepted the news quietly. "Thank you." She seemed to think that gave her permission to finally eat, herself. She reached for a rice ball.

I swallowed. "There's something else."

She froze. "What do you mean?"

"I . . . learned something," I said. Even thinking about it, it took all my effort to wrestle my anger back down so I could meet Phuong with a neutral face. "I could tell you what that something is."

"You should," Phuong said.

I held up a hand to stop her. "Listen. I want you to think about this. Because if you say yes, I will tell you, and I promise I'll be honest. And once I do, there'll be no unlearning it. It'll be something you have to live with for the rest of your life."

She regarded me warily. "Or?"

"Or . . ." I swallowed, more to buy myself a few more seconds than anything else. "You could say no. I won't tell you. I'll never bring it up again. You can live the rest of your life without having to think about it. And I ain't ever gonna think worse of you for it." I leaned back in my chair. Studied her face. Watched the way the light hit that familiar nose, or the slow, thoughtful frown of hers that I recognized from elsewhere. "Whatever you choose, I'll respect it, Phuong. But you've gotta choose now. So, what is it?"

For long minutes, she and I just sat there in silence.

And when she finally broke it, it was to give me her answer.

The gaudy Meyongphirin International Airport was quiet that day. City Hall had made it an official day of mourning, so there was only a skeleton crew working, and no waiting travelers at all. Walking in, I basically had the whole place to myself.

Well, almost.

My footsteps echoed loud as I strode through the empty airport. From the tinny speakers overhead, I could hear the city's anthem piping along, interrupted by the occasional six-language welcome to Driftwood City. I caught myself falling into rhythm with it as I approached the lone traveler waiting for his flight.

I didn't realize how much my image of you was stuck in the surface. You'd always been clean tailored lines and sleek silver hair. The slender little man sitting with his newspaper, on the other hand, wore loose, patchy trousers and scuffed boots. And what was more, he was bald as an egg. Hate to admit it, Cole, but if I hadn't been looking for you, my eyes might've skipped right over you.

You didn't look up from your paper. "You cut your hair."

I fingered my short locks, jagged from the knife I'd borrowed to saw through them. "And you salted the earth yours grew from."

You folded your newspaper and laid it in your lap. You looked up at me with just enough fear to make me feel respected. "I can sense you now," you said. "I've known you

493 ·

were coming for the past twenty minutes. And all that time, I've sat and wondered: what's about to happen here, Tenny?"

I nodded to the empty spot beside you. You swallowed warily, but nodded just the same. I sat.

"I'd hoped that you might come, actually," you said. "I wanted to see you one last time before I left."

My mouth thinned. "Still don't think you should leave. The city could use you, Cole."

In your pained smile, I saw a Cole I could recognize: a mouth shaped the right way, eyes that caught the light all wrong. "The city could use a good man. That has never been me."

I held back a sigh. "You *do* know a person's more than their worst moments, right?"

"Yours is an optimism I've always admired." You glanced down at the newspaper in your lap. "How was my funeral?"

"You're more missed than you know. Any person would be lucky to be mourned that way."

"I'm sorry you weren't." You frowned. "I'm sorry I made sure of that."

Overhead, the recording of the city anthem skipped as it reset. After a few seconds of silence, the horns started up afresh.

"So what, then?" I said. "Go out, see the world, find yourself, come back?"

"Yes to the first three." You studied your hand. "Maybe one day I'll believe myself worthy of the fourth."

Again, I held back a sigh. I didn't like you when you were mopey. But more than usual, I guessed you had a reason to mope. And besides, moping definitely beat you trying to kill me.

"How long you think you'll be gone?" I asked you.

"Who's to say?" You shrugged. "Could be years before I breathe Driftwood City air again."

494

I slouched down in my seat and got comfortable. "I've done years before. We'll survive."

You, on the other hand, somehow found a way to sit up even straighter. There are some things about a person that life just can't beat out of them, and yours was your patrician posture. "You can't," you said urgently.

I glanced over at you sidelong. "You always, *always* say that to me. You ever had much luck telling me what I could and couldn't do?"

You shook your head. "After everything I've done to you, you're the last person who should have to deal with me. I could travel for the rest of my life and never atone for what I did to my own best friend."

"Yeah, maybe." I slid my hands into my pockets and watched the snow fall outside. "You know the last thing the Black Rose said to me? About how we were different?" When you shook your head, I went on: "Guy said that we were different because I didn't build, and you did." I indulged in a sour little frown. "Don't you hate it when the biggest prick you know makes a really good point?"

"Then stay here!" The echo made you realize you'd raised your voice. You glanced around, saw an empty airport, and then lowered your voice anyway. "Don't throw your life away for me, Tenny. I'm not worth it."

"You ask me, the Rock wasn't worth it when those sailors crashed into it, either. They built anyway. So did your folks. Hell, even Benilda built. My whole life, what've I ever done except knock shit down?" I sucked in a breath. "I knocked you down."

"I des—"

"*I know you deserved it,*" I cut across you. "And I ain't sorry I did it. But now that you're off your feet, I reckon someone should help you get back on them." I know you think words

495

matter, Cole, so I was careful with the ones I chose for this next part. "And I want that someone to be me."

You got up. For just a sec, I thought you might actually run straight out the door. But instead, you began to pace agitatedly. Sitting there calm and composed, I smirked to myself. Pacing was supposed to be my job.

"How can you possibly forgive me?" you asked eventually.

I shrugged. "Honestly? I haven't yet."

I saw just a little hurt flicker across your face. You'd known that was more likely, but you'd hoped against hope anyway.

Yours is an optimism I've always admired, Cole.

"But I want to give you the chance to earn it," I continued. "I remember who you are. Not who you are right now, not who you were then. And I think that guy deserves a chance ... and help with taking it."

"What happens if I make another mistake?"

I could sense it: you were prodding me, looking for any sign that my offer wasn't on the level. But I wasn't about to let you confirm all your own little theories here. So I shrugged again. "Depends on the mistake. We ain't perfect, so I'll try to be understanding. I know I could use some work on that, myself." I made sure to meet your eyes. "But my understanding ain't infinite."

You nodded slowly. "Understood."

"Thought you would. You're a smart guy, much as it hurts to tell you to your face." I indicated the seat next to me, with your abandoned newspaper. "Now, you mind sitting down? You're giving me a fucking headache just looking at you."

"Just trying to avenge all the ones you've given me over the years." But you sat anyway. And while I can't say I was completely at ease, Cole, I can say that for a few minutes, I actually enjoyed the silence.

Ultimately, it was you that broke it. "How does it sound to your ears now?" you said. "The city."

I considered my answer.

"Quieter," I admitted. "Not in a way I like. You spend half your life drinking sweet, fresh water, and then suddenly all of it's stale and brackish. But," I added, "you get used to the taste."

You nodded, absorbing this. "I've never heard the silence," you said. "Not since the day of the fire." You closed your eyes and took a deep breath. "I hope I can handle it."

"At first, you think you never will," I said. "But after a few weeks, it starts to ..."

I sat up even straighter than you.

There was music in my ears.

As I turned to you, you fell off the bench and on to your knees. I wanted to help you, but I couldn't move. I was too consumed by the warmth spreading from my ears, down my neck, down into my fingers and toes before it turned inward and burrowed straight to my heart.

On second thought, it was more than just warmth, Cole. It was regrowing an arm. And when I reached out with that arm, I felt my city clasp it tight and hold it close. And I knew for these last few minutes we had together, it wouldn't let go.

But I couldn't embrace it back. Not like this. All-or-nothing had always been the wrong way to do this.

The music ebbed from me as I turned your gift back on you.

"W-what are you doing ...?"

I didn't answer. I needed to concentrate. But unlike the first two times I'd encountered this feeling, this time I faced it without fear.

And then, the moment had passed. The music played on: quieter and sparser, but steady nonetheless. And I knew that right now, you were hearing the exact same thing.

497

Your look of disbelief would've been worth a photograph. "*Why did you—?*"

"*You can't move forward if you're chained at the ankles, you idiot!*" I said. "*You need to be free, even if that means you're free to step back!*"

Neat thing about the way you built your airport, Cole. All its slick and hard surfaces mean that when you raise your voice enough, talking with someone else can so easily turn into talking with yourself.

You knelt there, rocking and clutching yourself, your face screwed up with pain. "All the gods in all the temples ... this is only half of what I did to you?" You looked like you were about to be sick.

I nodded. I didn't need to say anything else. I let the quiet be my voice.

"Then it appears I haven't even begun to truly apologize."

"Oh, you've begun, all right," I allowed. "You're just a few sentences into a real long book, is all." I studied you a long moment, trying to see into that head of yours. "This judgment of mine, Cole ... does it strike you fair?"

You thought it over, as my echo asked you the question a second time.

"I don't know," you admitted. "But in the very least, Tenny, I know that I trust you."

You reached for my hand.

And I helped you up.

498

Acknowledgements

At one point during the writing of this book, I came very close to taking my own life.

My thanks in their entirety are humbly offered to my family, friends, and especially my partner. Your love and support carried me when my own strength failed.

Credits

Paul Krueger and Gollancz would like to thank everyone at Orion who worked on the publication of *Driftwood Orphans* in the UK.

Editorial
Gillian Redfearn
Brendan Durkin

Copy editor
Steve O'Gorman

Proofreader
Gabriella Nemeth

Audio
Paul Stark

Contracts
Anne Goddard
Paul Bulos
Jake Alderson

Design
Lucie Stericker
Joanna Ridley
Nick May

Editorial Management
Charlie Panayiotou
Jane Hughes
Alice Davis

Finance
Jennifer Muchan
Jasdip Nandra
Afeera Ahmed
Elizabeth Beaumont
Sue Baker

Marketing
Lucy Cameron

Production
Paul Hussey

Publicity
Will O'Mullane

Sales
Jen Wilson
Esther Waters

Victoria Laws
Rachael Hum
Ellie Kyrke-Smith
Frances Doyle
Georgina Cutler

Operations
Jo Jacobs
Sharon Willis
Lisa Pryde
Lucy Brem